A
RHONDDA
ROMANCE

or

THE GREAT WELSH AUNTIE NOVEL

John Geraint

Published by
Llyfrau Cambria Books, Wales, United Kingdom.
*Cambria Books and Cambria Stories are imprints of
Cambria Publishing Ltd.*
Discover our other books at: www.cambriabooks.co.uk

…come kiss me, sweet and twenty.
Youth's a stuff will not endure.
William Shakespeare, 'Twelfth Night'

Mae marc y cwm fel nod ar ddafad arnaf. Acen. Atgofion. Cred.
Rhydwen Williams, 'Y Ffynhonnau'

…the boy I was not and the man I am not
met, hesitated, left double footsteps, then walked on.
Dannie Abse, 'Return To Cardiff'

...One is not quite sure
Whether it is fiction or not.
Harri Webb, 'Synopsis of the Great Welsh Novel'

For Ed and Greg.
And all the others.

A RHONDDA ROMANCE

or THE GREAT WELSH AUNTIE NOVEL

Editor's Note

A Rhondda Romance is published under this title – simple, straightforward, sellable – for the first time at my suggestion (though the author has stubbornly insisted on retaining *The Great Welsh Auntie Novel* as a sub-title).

It's an oddity of a novel – more of an anti-novel perhaps, which is what the original title hints at, I suppose, though many people unfamiliar with the Valleys accent (and, indeed, a fair number of those who do speak with it) expressed their puzzlement at the awful pun on 'Auntie' and 'anti'.

The novel still tries our patience with its length, my best efforts notwithstanding, but *A Rhondda Romance* should at least help readers to focus on what is at the heart of the 'story', such as it is.

Author's Note

Think of this as *A Rhondda Romance* if you like. (It is. Sort of. But…)

For me, it will always be *The Great Welsh Auntie Novel*. Though it wasn't really me who came up with that title: it was…

Well, you'll see.

The First Branch

SPRING

1

Tonypandy Square is the best place to begin.

Pandy Square. The Hub of the Universe. The Still Point in the Turning World.

Because everybody knows this is where Winston Churchill personally commandeered an army sub-machine gun and sprayed metal death into a crowd of defenceless Rhondda miners.

That's how Jac's Auntie always told him the story anyway.

Blue murder. Bodies in the street. Plebiscite.

Plebicide, she meant. Massacring the masses. Putting down the People's Uprising of 1910. Or Riots, as the Tories insisted on calling them. Tonypandemonium it was, according to them.

But it was them who caused it. The Tories. And Winston bloody Churchill.

Churchill. There was blood on his hands alright. Even if, when Jac looked into it properly for that History essay he'd done, it turned out it wasn't Churchill who'd done the actual shooting. That there may not have been much shooting. Or any at all.

But Churchill did send the troops here, that's a dead cert. There are photos that prove it. Actual photographic evidence. In black-and-white.

It was true. Ranks of soldiers, bayonets fixed. The Lancashire Fusiliers and the 18th Hussars. They'd stayed all winter long. Broken the strike. Butchered the dreams of 12,000 mid-Rhondda miners. Starved them back to work, their families Hungry as L, as their banners proclaimed.

Killing the kids to force their fathers back to the coalface. You couldn't deny that.

Though of course the Tories did. And were still denying it, all these years later.

Well, it all comes down to what you believe in the end, if you want to ask me, Jac reckoned. Arguing about the past – that wasn't something he'd picked up from a term-and-a-half in the Sixth Form with History's Most Eccentric History Teacher (*he* was actually a Dictator. A Great Dictator, as we'll see, but a Dictator nonetheless). The impulse, the necessity, the *fact* that you *had to* argue about history was something Jac had learned through seventeen years of being brought up in this Valley. Rhondda people had a duty to dispute the past. And it went without saying that if conventional wisdom was *pro* any given historical interpretation, then his Auntie, being his Auntie, would be *anti*.

Yes, thought Jac proudly, he'd always known this.

And always known that Tonypandy Square was the nub of it all.

In the gloom of the evening, his eyes were fixed on the corner by the chemist's. A façade that looked just the same now, in 1974, as it had in 1910. *Nothing lasts except permanence*, as his Auntie would say. Beyond it, silhouetted by the lights of the Pandy Inn, stood a gang of Greasers. A modern-day riotous assembly. One of them, Jac thought, looked like James Taylor. James Taylor from Penmaesglas. *Not* the peace-loving American folk-rocker, famous for *Sweet Baby James*. No, this was the James Taylor who'd taunted and bullied Jac ever since they'd been in Hendrecafn Junior School together. Though come to think of it, Jac's classmate, with his shoulder-length black hair parted in the centre, bore a highly misleading resemblance by now to his transatlantic namesake. The Rhondda version was no hippie, though, no peacenik, no Cowboy Jesus – more Penygraig Pinochet. Or Tonypandy Torquemada. No, that wasn't quite right, either. Jac would have to find the phrase, the *apposite* phrase. And store it up to share with Martyn.

Now that he really looked at them, Jac recognised some of the others on the threshold of the Pandy Inn, by reputation and nickname, if not personal acquaintance. MauMau, Parrot, Rat, Dodo… A couple of years older than him and James Taylor; proper men – drop-outs or labourers. More like Hell's Angels than Greasers, thought Jac. Though he wasn't totally sure of the difference. Was it just the motorbikes? Either way, two years ago – six months, if he was honest – they'd have terrified him. He'd

4

have been cowed by their leather jackets and tattoos, by the fug of woodbines (and reefers?) that hung around them, the crackle of untapped violence. And by his own history of humiliation in the face of physical aggression. Now, though, he knew better: he understood them as products of the counter-culture. Their anger just needed to be focused on a more *organised* way of breaking the straitjacket of The System. They were his Brothers.

Even so, Jac was relieved that, thirty yards away, they were safely beyond the range of eye contact.

To the left of them, on a far corner of the Square, diagonally opposite the Picturedrome, a side road curved upwards, squeezing past the ramparts of the Naval Club. From there, hemmed in on both sides by terraced houses, it began its implausible ascent to the plateau of Blaenclydach, before somehow hauling itself up, at angles challenging the perpendicular again, to Clydach Vale beyond. Jac couldn't actually see any of this from where he stood at the bus stop on the main Valley thoroughfare. But his *inward eye* pictured the precise degree of every slope and scarp. Like everyone here, he had a natural aptitude for Geometry. History was just a bonus.

Up that hill, up Court Street hill, lived honey-haired Lydia Peake.

Any moment now, she and Petra Griffiths would come sashaying round the corner by the chemist's, just in time to catch the bus to Treorchy with him. They'd have tottered down Court Street, winter-coated against the wind, all dolled up underneath in their party frocks. This might be Election Day, but nothing – not the ghost of Winston Churchill, not the Three-Day Week, not even a revolutionary watershed in history – *nothing* could stop a Rhondda eighteenth birthday party.

Lydia and Petra. An odd pairing. Lydia, a whole school year ahead of Petra and Jac, measured, even-tempered, a serious student who'd *read a lot*; and Petra, one of the self-styled Bad Girls of the B Form, who'd only got her act together through acting. But they'd have spent the day with each other, talking. Talking, talking, talking. What *did* girls talk about? It was a mystery. The *need* to talk. As though nothing had ever really happened unless it was talked about afterwards. Then, prompted by Petra, they'd have spent the last hour picking out *exactly* what to wear. Nothing too showy, outfits that were *just right*, of the moment. Both of them, nevertheless, dressed to impress. Done up to the nines. They'd have the boys at sixes and sevens. Especially by the time *they'd* had one over the eight…

Twpsyn, Jac scolded himself. *Stop it.* This word play, this child's play, had to be … not *extirpated*, but reined in. Jac could hear his father's voice admonishing him: *When I was a child, I spake as a child…*

No wonder he'd got called names, from his earliest years in grammar school. The Catchphrase Kid (he had an endless stock of them). The WordMadWelshMadManiac (unlike Martyn, unlike almost everyone, he'd dropped French and chosen Cymraeg in Form Three). The Prince of Repetition (the same 'joke' or inane pun, recycled over and over, just occasionally given a slight, new twist). The Prince of Repetition (the same 'joke'… *no, no, you've just done that one*).

But it was 1974 now and he was in the Sixth Form. O levels to A levels – the biggest jump of all, Dad had warned him. Comparatively, moving on to university was *pappish*. Not that Dad had actually gone to university (Caerleon was a college, a Teacher Training College back then, just after the War, the one that Churchill got his glory from. Dad had avoided National Service too – he was a conchie, a conscientious objector, but on religious, not political grounds). From what Jac had experienced so far, his father was right: for the first time, schoolwork was a stretch. A struggle. But struggle was good. It would help him attain the higher plane of seriousness, the *gravitas* he associated with Martyn. Help him, even if he couldn't accept his father's faith, to abide by the wisdom of the Biblical exhortation his father was always impressing on him: *when I became a man, I put away childish things.*

And Tonypandy Square was the best place to begin. Here. Now, on this last day of February. Polling Day, Election Day.

With the weight of history pressing all around. And the prospect of a new chapter in the long march of progress starting before another day dawned.

Jac didn't want to miss the frisson of Petra and Lydia's arrival, that first glimpse of them rounding the corner (and Catherine – Catherine might be with them too, despite… *Forget that, she won't be*). But he sensed the larger weight of the moment. He knew he ought to fix it, this time, this place, this whole scene in his mind. Its historic significance.

He turned away from the Greasers (or Hell's Angels?) to look back down De Winton Street, down the Valley, beyond the Public Library, down the main road's gently sloping tarmac. *Libury* and *Tar-mark* were the sounds in his head. An 'r' missing from one, added to the other. That was how he'd always said them, like most people here: it wasn't long since he'd realised that not everyone in the world did.

In the distance, opposite the derelict Theatre Royal, framed by the corroded black railway bridge that crossed high above the street much closer to him, a young woman was hurrying up the hill. That bridge, perched on stone pillars at a crazy slant, carried the disused Cambrian Colliery branch-line up from the Valley floor and onto the Pwll-yr-Hebog Incline. *13 in 1* it was, the Pwll-yr-Hebog, according to his Auntie, who habitually got such ratios the wrong way round. Though sometimes, climbing up it, you suspected she might be right.

The woman emerged from under the bridge. Early twenties, red-haired, tall. No-one Jac knew. Smart-looking, though, a Burberry wrapped tightly around her. A photographer might make a striking image of it, another piece of black-and-white evidence: a cross-hatch of tilted lines running across the frame and away from the lens. The woman's figure picked out in shadow and streetlight, a cold sheen on the tarmac of the carriageway. *Tar-mark*. Click, click, click. Give the print a name, and it would sell in one of those trendy galleries down Cardiff: 'Election Night'; or 'After the Coal Rush', perhaps, but that was already such a *cliché*.

Jac turned back towards the Square. For all his sense of destiny unfolding, Jac had to admit some disappointment. He'd expected more. More than the red posters on show in windows everywhere. He wanted noisy crowds occupying public spaces. Torches aflame. Revolution in the air. He could quote – that History essay again – a London newspaper account from 1910: the 'oppressive atmosphere' up and down these mid-Rhondda streets was 'like something experienced in Odessa and Sevastopol during the unrest in Russia.' Jac was primed for the anger of the people to be revealed, for a *manifestation* like that (decent pun, he thought, bilingual – Martyn, on track for a stellar result in A level French, would approve). But perhaps it was just *too* cold tonight. Cold? Bitter. I don't mind if I do. Clang. *Grow up, Jac, you silly boy.*

Shivering, he leant forward, fingering the icy metal stanchions. Bus-stop barriers, buckled with age, erected decades ago by Rhondda Transport to corral its impatient passengers. Unruly lot, Valleys people, left to their own devices. Given to Uprisings. But there was no queue on this wintry evening. He was waiting alone. At least until Lydia and Petra got there. Yet he couldn't help feeling agitated. Now was the hour. The Party. The Girls. The Vote. All of it coming together. And tomorrow, March 1st, St. David's Day. The start of a Glorious Welsh Spring.

But the world was slow to turn. Still no bus, no girls. Though, now, directly across the road, out of Melardi's café, came half-a-dozen men who could only be miners. They spilled onto the pavement just as the Redhead in the Burberry reached the same spot. She veered into the roadway to avoid them.

"Take care, lovely girl!" That was one of the miners, his hair parted roughly to one side, trying his luck. "Fancy a coffee, *cariad*?" The woman didn't break her stride. "Next time, then!" shrugged the collier.

Jac thought he saw the ghost of a smile play across her lips. Was it as easy as that? Could you ask someone out, as casually, as crudely as that? With no special coaching? And no worries about the outcome, no shame in being rebuffed?

Jac studied the colliers in wonder. They stood there, having a whiff before heading on – where?

If they hadn't been on strike, they'd have been waiting there outside the Bracchi's, the Italian café, with their tommy-boxes, for the night-shift bus down to Coedely or Lewis Merthyr. Survivors of the Cambrian. Or transferees from a dozen other Rhondda pits, all shut now. But tonight: tonight, they were free to go and drink wherever they pleased. At least as far and as much as their pockets would stretch to. No... *tonight*, they'd be heading off to the Strike Committee Meeting. The Lodge Chairman would stir them up with a little speech. About making sacrifices and making history. About the iniquity of the army being used against them once more – to shift coal stocks, to man the power stations. Yes, they'd called in the troops again, just like November 1910.

Something had moved back then, something had shifted. At precisely that moment.

Human nature had changed, here, on Tonypandy Square.

And something was moving now. That struggle was coming to its culmination, sixty-four years later, on these same Rhondda streets.

How extraordinary that they'd foreseen all this – those perfectly ordinary men who'd written that pamphlet in the sour aftermath of 1910. *The Miners' Next Step*. Jac had looked it up. In the *Li-bury*. It predicted *precisely* the nature of the confrontation that had rocked Britain in these last few months.

Well, Jac made a prediction of his own: in fifty years' time again, the WJEC would be setting exam questions about it. "Compare and contrast 7th November 1910 and 28th February 1974 as moments of pivotal change in the creation of a socialist Wales, and explain what links these dates."

The WJEC. The Welsh Joint Education Committee.

Soon, much sooner than half-a-century, its exams would determine the futures of Jac and all his friends. Mind you, his Auntie had always been under the impression that it was a Cannabis Awareness Programme.

Jac looked around. At the missing crowds. He stamped his feet against the cold. And the slowness of waiting. If Catherine had been coming too, he wouldn't have minded. *Catherine, Catherine, Catherine…*

He tried to distract himself by picturing the scene from above, the way he dreamt about it sometimes. A camera swooping over the pavements and the Picturedrome, the roofs of the shops and the cafés and the pubs… and there he would be, Jac himself, in the middle of it all, a painfully thin and restless seventeen-year-old standing alone, closer to the Colliers than the Greasers, yet knowing that he was part of neither gang, and never would be. But now – *Praise Ye the Lord!* as his Father would say – he did have something to belong to, a group who'd come together so quickly, with such intensity, that they'd already formed a bond that would never be broken. Never. Never ever. *Never ever, Trevor Evans…*

Clang. Another of his catchphrases. Jac made a conscious effort to stop the burble of words that kept springing unbidden to his mind. To look out, not in.

Even at this last gasp of winter, the early evening hour was dark. Their faces were in shadow, those colliers across the road: half-turned away, talking intently. Snatches of argument drifted across the gloom, difficult to catch, easy to reconstruct all the same. Something about winning the strike? Dominating the battle, getting on top? In the way they stood together, Jac saw the determination that would bring down Heath's Government. He could picture them as the leaders of those earlier, epic campaigns. 1910. 1921. 1926.

Yes, there they were, with him now today, born again in 1974! Jac suddenly recognised them as the heroes his Auntie had told him about. William Mainwaring, Arthur Horner, A. J. Cook and… Vernon Hartshorn, was it? Stalwarts of the South Wales Miners' Federation from decades past. The very leaders who'd argued that you couldn't trust leaders, who'd written that 'no man was ever good enough, brave enough, or strong enough, to have such power at his disposal, as real leadership implies.'

10

And the collier facing him, Jac realised, the one who'd accosted the Redhead, a questioning scowl on his face now, he must be Noah Ablett, the true Prophet-Author of *The Miners' Next Step*. Well, Noah, boy, this time your prophecy *will* come to pass. The Hard Rain will fall. The Flood will rise. Tonight, this February night – Jac felt it in his bones, shivering there on the bus stop – the Mighty would fall. It would be through the ballot box, fair enough: the Tories ousted, Wilson in. But it would be a Revolution all the same. And it would be those miners across the road who'd done it, those miners trying to decide on *their* next step. By tomorrow, they'd have brought down the British Government, and nothing would ever be the same again.

Eat your heart out, Winston Churchill.

So there and then, on that cold bus stop – why not? why not here? why not now? – he resolved to make a commitment, one fitting of the moment. A solemn vow, a promise to himself, to Jac Morgan, but sworn before a great cloud of witnesses, before all those who'd passed this way, all those who'd traversed Pandy Square, who'd been part of the struggle here, from 1910 on. He all but raised his right hand and spoke the words out loud. In the end, he settled for laying his palm against the bus-stop barrier-rail – the arctic chill reassured him that this was for real.

Then, silently, he took his vow.

To grow up.

And to ask Catherine out.

Just then, Noah Ablett stepped away from the lights of the Bracchi's to shoot a rhetorical flourish over his shoulder towards the rest of the Unofficial Reform Committee: "Call himself a left-winger?" Ablett hawked noisily from the depths of his chest, and spat, before barking out a final damning judgement: "The bugger couldn't side-step a pit prop!"

He marched away, leaving a thick gobbet of yellow phlegm sitting proud in the shining gutter.

2

"Petra!" cried Jac, "A rose-red beauty..."

It was just Petra and Lydia. No Catherine. As the two girls strode up to within proper talking distance, Lydia pulled a face. "Not again, Jac! Not that old chestnut again. Stop right there. Please."

Petra went ahead anyway, mimicking perfectly, from somewhere deep down in her boots, Jac delivering his well-worn parody of one of nineteenth-century literature's most quoted lines: "A rose-red beauty, half as old as I'm."

The Prince of Repetition laughed. At the accuracy of Petra's take-off of him, yes. But mainly at his own joke. His word-play would bear repeating many times yet.

Lydia took a different view: "You mangle that poem *every* time Petra wears her scarlet coat, and I still can't work out why you think she's half your age. It's pretty obvious which one of you is less mature."

In their hurry to make the bus, Lydia's glasses had steamed up. She swiped the brown frames off her face with a wave of her hand and polished the thick lenses in her scarf. Honey-haired Lydia Peake. No nonsense from her. Jac might have read *some* poetry; she'd read *a lot*. Her latest enthusiasm was for Wales' own Dannie Abse, newly raised to the canon of the Sixth Form syllabus: so reasonable, so precise. Of course, she *had* to rate him, given the odd coincidence of her name being a near-homophone of Lydia Pike, the fictional object of Abse's teenage obsessions. She'd even lent Jac a book by Abse, a coming-of-age novel. Autobiographical. *Ash On A Young Man's Sleeve.*

"Thank you, Miss Peake," Jac said. "Good evening and welcome to you, too."

Lydia Peake. Lydia Pike. It *was* an odd coincidence. How many A level candidates get to study a literary character of practically the same name? But this was the Rhondda. And there, over Lydia's left shoulder, Jac could still see James Taylor, in his

12

Welsh guise, so reminiscent of the American one. Strange conjunctions abounding: a charged synchronicity swirled around Pandy Square tonight. Well, it was the core of it all. The Node. The Epicentre.

A charged synchronicity? I like it, thought Jac. I must try it out on Martyn.

You'd better crack that Tonypandy Torquemada line first.

Synchronicity didn't seem to operate in favour of 'Petra'. The name was a rarity locally. In a way, she'd got off lightly. Her parents had decided to call her Cora Petula, which would have been insanely exotic for the Rhondda; but her father had stopped for a pint on his way to register the birth. He ended up not only getting the names in the wrong order but also squashing them together. *Pet-ra*. Petra from Pentre. Mind you, merged the other way round, she'd have been 'Coula', like a fridge compartment. What fun Jac would have had with that! All the same, it was a burden, being the namesake of a television dog. How many times had The Prince Of Repetition teased her about what she was up to on *Blue Peter* that week? Or wondered aloud whether ancient Jordan had boasted an enchantress called 'Pentre from Petra'?

A rose-red beauty…

This Rhondda Petra *was* a beauty. Dark-haired and dark-eyed, tall, slim. Not *Jac's* beauty, but Martyn's. They'd been seeing each other ever since they'd taken leading roles in the dramatised reading of *Under Milk Wood* which had been put on in the autumn to mark the Boys' and Girls' Grammars merging, in preparation for going Comprehensive. Martyn and Petra. A match made in Llareggub. First Voice and Rosie Probert. Like Burton and Taylor in the film version. *A passion fuelled by allure and alcohol.* Stars of the show. And about to shine again, next term, in a fully staged Shakespearean comedy.

Jac considered again the telling off he'd got from Lydia. So much for the solemn vow he'd just made. He couldn't rein in the punning for five minutes. Lydia was right, it was a form of showing off, of trying to prove how well-read he was, how cultured, almost like Martyn. Though Martyn was never childish, even at his most petulant…

Suddenly, the Blaencwm bus was at the stop. How had Jac managed to screen out the approach of a bright red twelve-ton double-decker? *His mind's on other things*, as his Auntie would say, whilst he sat in the corner reading, family life going on all around him.

They boarded, settled themselves on the maroon double-seats upstairs. A film of condensation fogged the windows. Jac reached across with his forefinger to spell out something witty on it. Then he remembered his vow, and used his whole hand to wipe an arc of the glass clear instead, just in time to glimpse the furniture shop on the corner opposite as the bus pulled away. 'Mr Burton's Wardrobe by Times Furnishings, Pandy Square'. He must use that some time. Or some variation on it. *Or maybe not. Grow up!* Then on, past The Record Shop, past Jerusalem. *O Jerusalem, Jerusalem….* How many places of worship did one town need? Here was another, Zion. The Methodists. The bus jerked, then picked up speed, as Llwynypia Road straightened into the distance.

This was sacred ground. Not the Promised Land prophesied in those chapels, but the roadway where thousands of miners had pushed forward on that November night in 1910, challenging the cordon of Metropolitan Police, newly arrived to guard the gates of the Scotch Colliery. Jac could feel himself moving with them, moving with the tide of history, ready and willing to break himself on the mole of that police line, to sink under the blows of their batons. To sink, only to rise again.

Something had moved then, something had shifted.

That was true now too. Not just politically, but personally. Amongst his friends. Looking at Petra, Jac knew it. Something in her relationship with Martyn had… *metastasised*, was that too strong? *Mutated?* Something that had always been there had stirred. *Is about to come spewing out.* No, not tonight, not again… but, yes, maybe that too. There was only so much vodka that even Martyn could swallow. Though he didn't seem to know it when he got in one of his moods. His *depressions*. Jac always tried to

14

attune himself early to shifts of emotion amongst his friends. The only one of them who never took a drink, he was continually on the look-out for trouble, seeking to head it off, to play the peacemaker or the comforter. That was how he saw himself, at any rate. He understood, or at least he thought he did, that the way Martyn drank was *different*. Other friends would begin in good heart, downing two or three drinks. Only then, when they took that one too many, would they get maudlin. Or sick. Or both. It could happen quickly, but it always seemed unintentional, accidental rather than purposeful. With Martyn, the downstroke was there from the beginning, designed into the process. He just kept sinking, lower and lower. It could be frightening. But in the last few days, something else had altered, something deeper again. Jac felt it, caught it, in the smallest of Martyn's responses, in the way he'd talked about plans for the party that night. Or not even that, just a look in his eyes. An avoidance of some reckoning to come.

Petra must sense it too, would have been the first to sense it, even if she couldn't fathom what it was. Something… sinister? Yet completely part of who he was, this man-boy she'd let herself fall in love with and wanted to love better.

D'you reckon that's how girls think? Really?

Jac had no way of knowing, no experience of true love, no romance of any description in his past, beyond a few short dates at the Picturedrome and the Plaza.

One short date at the Picturedrome, in point of fact.

Despite that, he allowed his conjectures to race onwards. Petra wanted to make Martyn right, to make him whole. To plumb his darknesses, to feel that from the bottom of her own heart she could speak to him and his needs and, yes, even his depressions. But always feeling adrift, out of her depth. Needing something, someone to anchor her, to anchor them.

Maybe that something was the crew, the gang, The Society of Friends. It was Petra herself who'd christened them that, one home-time after Jac had picked out those words from the sign outside Maes-yr-Haf, as the school-bus passed the Quaker

15

settlement on Brithweunydd Road. Reading aloud signs and notices that everybody could plainly see for themselves – that was another habit Jac was trying to teach himself to curb. But this time it had had a happy outcome: their *clique* was well named. The Society of Friends. There *was* something of a sect about them, the cast who'd come together for *Under Milk Wood*. For Jac, they represented an escape from the narrowness of his Chapel upbringing. But there was something spiritual in their commitment to each other all the same, something pure and demanding. Already, they'd spent so much precious time together, they were so much part of each other's hopes and dreams, so bound up in each other, that Jac *knew* that nothing could come between them. Petra and Martyn. Lydia, Penry, Nerys. Jac. And Catherine. All of them so different. But with so much in common. So intimate that it could hurt.

Now that bond would be reinforced, in the weeks of rehearsals that lay ahead for *Twelfth Night*. They could be fools, right enough – not just Penry who, with his fine, commanding baritone, would surely be cast as Feste, the singing jester – but all of them, pretty much, apart from Lydia. Idiots. But somehow, Jac sensed, *collectively* in their nonsenses, and occasional good sense, they held the key to whatever was locked up inside Martyn. Just as they needed her, Petra needed them to help her make it right with Martyn. Lydia with her calmness, her sureness of judgement. Penry with his music, his odd, intuitive notions, his quirky charm. Jac himself, who was 'wise enough to play the fool' when everyone got too serious about themselves and how they felt about each other. And yet scratch him and he too was a hopeless romantic, obsessed with history and place. That was how Petra must regard him, anyway. If his father was a miner rather than a teacher-cum-lay-preacher, she'd be thinking, he'd see things more like they really are. But even Jac might be savvy enough to… Or was this all too convoluted, just fevered imaginings?

'O Time, thou must untangle this, not I;
It is too hard a knot for me t' untie!'

16

Jac leaned forward. Petra and Lydia were talking about Catherine. There'd been a tragedy in her family, a real tragedy, not a piece of illusory teenage angst. Daniel, her step-brother – a couple of years older, but thin-skinned, volatile; a young man who seemed to depend on her – he had been found dead, hanged. He was away in his first year at Swansea University. There was talk that he'd got a fellow student pregnant. A scandal, perhaps. But who knew that shame could be that lethal? This was 1974, not the nineteenth century. The weekend before it had happened, Catherine told them that she was going down to Swansea, to help him sort it all out. There was a whisper that she herself had discovered the body. How terrible, if true. But in whatever way it had come to light, she would be deep in shock.

"I can't see her coming back to school," Petra was saying. "Not until after the funeral, at the very least."

"She won't be there tonight, then?" Jac asked, just to keep the subject open.

"Definitely not. She could hardly bring herself to speak to me on the phone. It's going to take a while, Jac… a long while, for her to get over this."

For Jac, Catherine was the one who made The Society of Friends *work*. And that was despite the fact – *because of* the fact – that she'd be the one outsiders would say was least likely to 'make it' (whatever that meant). Her ordinariness made her special for Jac. Since the autumn, they'd spent hours together, talking, listening to music – they shared the same taste, the same sense of humour, a fondness for the absurd. Catherine liked to hear Jac reciting poetry, at least he was pretty sure she did. He'd begun to make a point of memorising verses he thought would appeal to her.

But she wasn't going to be there tonight.

He forced his mind elsewhere. They'd reached the junction by Glyncornel Lake. 'Lake'? Pond, more like. But there was magic in those waters, and peril, or so his Auntie used to tell him. *Fearsome Celtic gods dwell beneath its surface, appeased by ancient tribal offerings of weapons and jewellery, but ready to rise again if provoked…*

The bus ignored them, carrying straight on. Away to the left, the New Road took the more direct route up the valley, through the Nant-y-Gwyddon woods, on to Gelli where Penry would be waiting to join them. *The New Road*. Built by the unemployed as long ago as the Depression of the 1930s. It had been in Jac's thoughts for another reason. In his head, he'd been writing The Great Rhondda Rock Song. Or trying to. It celebrated this road, with its long, flat straights, the only highway on the whole Valley floor that wasn't squeezed between houses and shops, an open invitation to teenage speedsters, on four wheels or two. The chorus of Jac's masterpiece-in-progress toasted the escapism it represented, the adrenalin rush of velocity.

Tonypandy Ton-Up,
Gonna take a run up
the New Road faster than light…

"Calm down, Jac," That was Lydia, alarmed by the vibrations rumbling through her seat. "We're not dancing yet."

Without being conscious of it, he must have been beating out the song's rhythm on the seat-back in front of him. He thrust his hands into his pockets. But the lyrics played on in his mind.

Flying in the car down to 'Pandy, smashed up like a bottle of coke,
Driving on a bottle of brandy is someone's idea of a joke.

Several ironies were wrapped up in this nascent attempt at a classic hit. One was that as a teetotal non-driver, Jac had no idea what a drunken racer might be feeling, careering at one-hundred-miles-an-hour through Tonypandy or anywhere else.

Just made the bend by the Plaza, can't see the shade on the Lights,
Feeling like Samson in Gaza, it's a Tonypandy Ton-Up tonight.

It was also true that he couldn't play an instrument, hold a tune or even keep a rock-steady rhythm. His chances of becoming The World's Top Teenage Rock'n'Roll Star were remote. He was the only person he'd ever heard of who'd failed the Grade I Piano exam. "I've realised you're not actually tone deaf," Penry had told him once, overhearing him struggle with some solo *acapella* Bowie. "You're just a vocal cripple." So, now that he'd promised himself to grow up, shouldn't he renounce

18

these musical fantasies?

But… he'd already worked out a name for his band, and a look: raw and gawky, polar opposite to the puppyish charm of the Osmonds and David Cassidy. Himself on vocals/rhythm guitar, three recruits who looked just as gangly and underfed on lead, bass and drums. *Jac and the Beanstalks.* Their string of hits would be one in the eye for James Taylor and everyone else back in Junior School who'd mocked his ignorance of pop music. *Well, a boy has to have a dream, or how would he ever get through the day?*

Jac realised he *had* been daydreaming. Again. A giant figure was towering over him, like a god risen from the waters of Glyncornel. Demanding to know what he wanted. It was the conductor.

"Single to the top of the charts, please, mister." Jac hoped his quip might get a cheap laugh. Or a cheap ticket. The conductor curled his lip and punched out a return to Treorchy, on the basis that that's what the two girls this joker was with had asked for. Jac examined it: he'd been given a child's half-fare. He blushed, coughed up the cash and went back to his music.

Tonypandy Ton-Up… it sounded good: it was *cynghanedd* – that resonant consonantal chime of Welsh bardic tradition – colliding playfully with the thrills of speed and Kerouac's American roadsters. All *so very Jac.* And authenticity was everything. So what if he couldn't sing? He'd recruit Beanstalks who weren't musical either. Their incompetence would *be* their appeal. It would put them on a level with their fans. Why should stardom be the domain of the naturally gifted? One day, maybe soon, Jac thought, music will be *democratised*, and virtuosity won't count for so much.

3

The trouble with what I've written so far is that it reads too much like a novel. It is a novel, I know that, and you know that. But for the next couple of hundred pages — if I ever get that far — we have to pretend that it isn't. That it's not a tale of some invented characters in a fictionalised version of the Valleys in the 1970s; not that, but instead a window on the real world, a direct, truthful rendering of the lives and struggles of some real people — what they really thought, what they really did, what they really felt.

That's the strange compact we've made with this novel, as we do with every novel; me as a writer, you as a reader. We know that it's a constructed narrative: artificial, fabricated, a well-designed escape from the world we live in. But we have to pretend to forget that, so that it feels natural, flowing in random, unresolved directions like our everyday experience. I mean, when did you last notice the plot *of real life? And the problem is that if this reads like a standard work of fiction — which, if I may break a confidence, is entirely the way my editor is trying to push it — then it's just* wrong.

Look, this is an autobiographical coming-of-age novel: the story of a gang of intense, bright teenagers, burning with idealism, learning to come to terms with realism. How they lose a whole world and gain their own souls (or will it be the other way round?). How for one brief season, they were in the right place at the right time, and sensed in those fleeting days... well, if not a way of living, nor quite a set of values that was close to what humanity has always been searching for, then at least the ghost of an idea that it wasn't futile to hope for such a thing, or that the pattern for it might not once have been laid down here, in the very place where their stories were beginning.

But if this fiction is at all successful in persuading you that it actually happened this way; if, by the effort I'm expending to drag events up from the dim-and-distant past, to find and shape a beginning, middle and end, a satisfying narrative structure; if, by any or all of that, it becomes convincing... *then it's just peddling a falsehood, deceiving you into believing it was as neat, as contained, as clear-cut as that.*

Because the truth is, the coming-of-age is taking a lifetime. The change, growth, character development that's necessary for any story (or so my editor insists) never happened as quickly, as unambiguously, or in anything like the way I'm being asked to set it down here. It hasn't really happened even now, as I'm writing it all up, half-a-century later. This story of a sensitive young boy growing up is, in fact, written by an over-sensitive boy who never grew up, who still needs reminding that isn't all about him, who stubbornly clings in defiance of all the evidence to a view of the Rhondda that's hopelessly starry-eyed, a bigging-up of his little world as it never was, and certainly isn't now, Oes Aur a fu, na fu erioed, *a Golden Age that never really happened. So the more successful it is as a piece of writing, the more it reads like one of those perfectly ordinary, perfectly structured romances where everything's resolved just before the end of the penultimate chapter, the less it will have to say that's useful about the real history it purports to describe, and the more profound will be its failure as an act of truth-telling.*

That's the big picture. Getting the writing to work at a granular level also involves deceptions. Compromises. Omissions. Making it readable involves discarding so much about what these characters have experienced, a myriad of seemingly-inconsequential details that nevertheless colours their way of thinking. Take those phrases from the chapter you've just read, where 'Jac' imagines himself 'moving with the tide of history, ready and willing to break himself on the mole of that police line…'. *It's slightly overwritten anyway, but that maritime metaphor leaping to the mind of a boy from the Coalfield may have struck you as slightly odd. Would he actually have known and used the word 'mole' to mean a sea-wall? But what if I told you that a hundred yards from the old Scotch Colliery on Llwynypia Road is the headquarters of the Rhondda Sea Cadets? Sea Cadets? In the Rhondda? Improbable, but true (we'll come to the Improbability Principle later; probably). And that in* The Onedin Line, *Series 3, Episode 13, which 'Jac' would have seen on BBC1 just a month before, 'mole' is used in this exact sense no less than seven times. More goes into writing a novel than you might think, and a lot more is left out. There are no great writers, just great editors (or so my editor says).*

There's another pitfall inherent in writing about the past. Less important, but perhaps more annoying: the temptation to credit my protagonist with unnatural foresight, with the gift of prophecy. Consider again the way that last chapter ended… 'Why should stardom be the domain of the naturally gifted? One day, maybe soon, music will be democratised, and virtuosity won't count for so much.' *Such a precise and prescient description of punk, and the way it turned the world upside down. Really? Did anyone in the Rhondda in 1974 see Johnny Rotten and his Pistols coming? Not me. Nor any of my friends. So it's a pretty cheap trick to suggest that 'Jac' did. Sorry. Now you're forewarned, you'll be on the look-out for such ruses from now on: don't trust me, any more than you would trust an ad that pops up on your Facebook timeline. It might be worth reminding yourself, though, before you get too het up, that as far 'Jac' and his friends are concerned,* you *are blessed – or cursed – with an astonishing degree of unnatural foresight. You know precisely how their world is going to turn out. Not in the small details of their lives, but certainly in what really matters: in the kind of politics and society that will emerge in the decades they've yet to see unfold, in what will happen to the hopes and dreams they cherish in their youthful idealism. You know about Thatcherism and Aids, the Miners' Strike of 1984-5, the Fall of the Wall and the Gulf Wars, Personal Computers, the Internet, Smartphones, Climate Change, Brexit, Covid, Putin. So, please, cut my characters – and me – some slack: in their naïve eyes, you're possessed of God-like foreknowledge.*

And, if my editor will let me lighten up for a moment before we go on, I'll mention one last difficulty I have in writing this novel: it's so wet. *Buckets and stair-rods, cats and dogs, cloudbursts, torrents, deluges: Rhondda's rain is* biblical. *It's a wonder there aren't* more *people here christened Noah. Tipping down, teeming down, pelting down, pissing down – you could write a book about it. If you could stay dry long enough. And that's what this book is, I suppose: the wettest novel on record. Makes* Wuthering Heights *read like one of those Mediterranean beach romances that 'Jac' imagined that his 'Auntie' must be engrossed in, all those times she went quiet on him. Now, in all things but her reading habits, this 'Auntie' – who you haven't really met yet – was one remarkable woman (or rather, as we shall see,* fifty-one *remarkable women. And one man). But her role in this coming-of-age story, to the extent that it is a coming-of-age story, was never anything like what I'll shortly suggest it was. I'm not kidding you about the rainfall though...*

4

It had come to rain, a barrage of opal droplets pounding the windows as the bus moved on, athwart the wind, spurning the New Road, sticking to the older route up the Valley. *Athwart?* Across from side to side. Not quite the apposite word, Jac realised. He'd just encountered it in a poem Martyn had told him about: 'What softer voice is hushed over the dead? Athwart what brow is that dark mantle thrown?' Shelley's Elegy on the Death of Keats.

Jac had a gift for memorising poetry. It was useful come exam time. And for impressing Catherine. *Catherine, Catherine, Catherine.* Her step-brother. Her *dead* step-brother. Beyond the reach of words now. *Silence is the only message.* Who'd said that? It wasn't Shelley. His Auntie perhaps. Or maybe she would say it, one day. It sounded like her.

The bus was passing the Ivor Hael. Jac approved of the pub name, a rare nod to South Wales' pre-Industrial past. Ifor Hael, Patron of Bards. Ivor the Generous, rather than Ivor the Engine, though the pub was right next to Llwynypia railway station. Ifor ap Llywelyn ab Ifor ap Bledri ap Cadifor Fawr. It had amused Jac to learn by heart this full chain of ancestry. He could rattle it off like a proper Welsh-speaker and annoy practically all his friends. He was tempted to do so now. But he could imagine Petra and Lydia's response.

Truth was, though he prided himself on his affinity with the language, Jac's grasp of Welsh was still rudimentary. For A level, they'd begun to study the *Mabinogion*. Reading Charlotte Guest's famous translation, he'd been enchanted by an incident in the First Branch. There was a kind of false start to the whole saga: the King of *Annwn*, the Underworld, changes places with Pwyll, the Prince of Dyfed, so that he can beget, in some original telling of the myth, a Wonder Child on an earthly mother, or so the introduction in Jac's textbook claimed. But in the version that

23

survives, that never happens. Instead, Pwyll returns to Dyfed and falls in love with a beauty, Rhiannon, who he sees, day after day, riding on a shining white stallion. She trots by at a stately pace, but every time Pwyll gallops harder and faster to try to catch up with her, the further from him Rhiannon gets.

Jac had become smitten with this marvel of elusive love, the more unreachable the more she's desired. It turned out that all Pwyll had to do to get her to stop was to ask her. But the first time Jac read it, it left him thinking *When is this bloody story going to start?*

"Pardon, beaut'?" That was Petra.

"When is this bloody story..." Jac stopped. He'd spoken his thoughts aloud. How stupid. *Gauche*, Martyn would have said... but there was *something* in that tale from the *Mabinogion*, something to do with his repeated failure to ask Catherine to go out with him, something he *did* want to explore with Petra and Lydia.

"I was just thinking... When we're older, much older, we'll look back on our lives and see that there's been a story to them, right? But when does that story begin?"

The girls exchanged a glance. Another of Jac's musings. He went on, regardless.

"We're born. We spend years and years with our parents, we depend on them, and they 'bring us up'. But that's not really our story: it's their story. *They're* making the choices, deciding what we do, how we dress, where we go... even what we believe..."

Unless they have a stubborn beggar of a child like you, Jac could hear his Auntie saying in response to that. But on he went again...

"Our parents decide what's important, showing us, telling us what to do, no matter what we think. We're stuck in their way of living, because that's all that we know, all we can see. We have no choice, no real freedom, no power, no..."

"No agency." It was Lydia who'd found the word. The *apposite* word.

"Yes, that's right, Lydia. No agency. So when does that begin? When do you start being... an agent?"

24

It was a strange phrase. Maybe Lydia's wasn't the right word after all. Jac decided to press on. "When do you start being the author of your own life? That's what I was trying to say. About a story."

He wasn't getting much of a response. But he felt committed now. "For you and Martyn, Petra, you have begun your story: you've made a choice about each other. But for me..."

Was it alright to say that about Martyn and Petra? Despite what he'd sensed about Martyn's mood?

Well, he'd said it now. Then, he remembered, just in time, that Lydia didn't have a boyfriend...

"...for me, and maybe you're different, Lydia... and I think you are, you're more... grown up already, more comfortable with yourself and your place in the world... but for someone like me, who's confused about a lot of things, and trying to puzzle them out, all I've got is... all I've got is what's going on inside my head."

"You've got us," said Petra, kindly. "The Friends."

"That's true. And I wasn't forgetting that. It's what keeps me sane. To the extent I am..."

He could feel himself losing his nerve, losing confidence in whether he was making sense, falling into his habitual trap of self-deprecation.

"What I'm trying to say is... things happen to me. Fair enough, they do to everyone. At school. In the house. With you lot. When I... when I go to chapel with my parents. But none of it hangs together. It doesn't add up to anything, it doesn't go anywhere: there's no story, just a jumble of incidents. Take tonight: we got on this bus in 'Pandy, now we're in Llwynypia, and at some point, unless we sink, which is quite likely by the looks of it, we'll arrive in Treorchy. There's a *progression*, a linear progression. But in my life, it feels like we might have got as far as this, but next moment the bus will be back down on Pandy Square again."

In fact, it was worse than that. It was as though he'd jump on a bus to Treorchy only to find he was halfway to Ponty on a train… But he sensed that Petra was about to ask him what it was that his Mam put in those marmite sandwiches he lived on, that made him think in such weird ways.

The bus had stopped at Partridge Square, opposite the Hospital entrance. A boarding passenger came and sat right opposite Jac. The newcomer was no Rhiannon: a solitary pensioner, a faded scarf knotted under her chin, returning home from Visiting Hour or off to Bingo. Why had she chosen *that* seat? Plenty of others were free. Perhaps she needed company. Whatever, her presence put a stop to the conversation. Jac was frustrated. But relieved too… What *was* it he'd been trying to say about his 'story'?

Unbidden, a new song began playing on the jukebox of his mind. A melody that old woman would know, *Tipperary*; but with words that had been sung on this road, right here, on the only protest march he'd ever been on, for all his radical pretensions. It was impressive enough, mind: thousands demonstrating against the closure of the Rhondda's only Casualty Unit here at Llwynypia, and the centralising of emergency services miles away at East Glamorgan Hospital, beyond Pontypridd. They'd paraded down to Pandy Square, and on to a public meeting in Judge's Hall: nurses and miners carrying banners, doctors and housewives, schoolchildren like himself.

It was two years ago, the first time he'd set eyes on Catherine. He knew nothing about her then, didn't know that she was another of the Bad Girls of the B Form. He was just struck by her *presence*. She seemed older than her years, much older than him. She was there, he learned later, because her mother had died waiting for an ambulance.

With other teenagers, they'd linked arms and joined in with the chanting and singing.

It's a long way to East Glamorgan, it's a long way to go.
It's a long way to East Glamorgan, and the roads are awful slow.
Goodbye Llwynypia, farewell Partridge Square,
It's a long, long way to East Glamorgan –
You're dead 'fore you're there.

It must have been hard for Catherine to sing those words, but at the time it was the cleverness of the parody that struck Jac. He wondered who'd thought it up, and how all those marchers had got to learn it.

It was a glorious cause. And a total failure. All that was left at Llwynypia now were the bookends of life – the geriatric wing, and the maternity unit where Jac himself had been born, seventeen years ago. *They'll put your plaque on the wall one day*, his Auntie was always telling him ("a plaque, not *my* plaque" – but he'd given up correcting her).

Jac wasn't one to dwell on the circumstances of his birth. Who did? One day, in a drawer at home, he'd come across a black-and-white photo taken on the maternity ward – three nurses in starched aprons holding up three bonny new-borns for the camera. But Jac wasn't even sure which one of them was him. His birth certificate was there too – Jacob Rhys, he'd been christened… well, strictly speaking, not christened, just registered: his parents were Baptists, and the whole point about Baptists was that they believed in *Adult* Baptism. You weren't baptised as an infant; you were admitted into church membership only after you'd made a solemn declaration of faith. *After* that conscious choice, you'd undergo a ritual of total immersion in a full-size baptistry. Baptisms were highlights of the Chapel calendar, given more weight than Christmas or Easter because – it struck Jac for the first time now, sitting there on the bus (he'd better hope his Auntie didn't find out, she'd give him grief for being so slow) – they guaranteed the future of the fellowship. Yes, that was why emotions would be wound up to breaking point with the impassioned four-part harmony of *Praise Ye the Lord*, as the white-robed candidates climbed the stairs at one side of the pulpit. One-by-one, they stepped down into the tank of chilly water (heating was an unnecessary indulgence of the flesh) which had been uncovered like a tiny swimming pool beneath the false floor. Quivering hands were grasped by the minister, who whispered sacred, comforting words to the nervous soul in the circle of his arm. Then, suddenly, he tilted

27

them forcefully backwards, so that they plunged fully under the water, symbolising their death to the sinful ways of the world, before being lifted upright again, and pushed to the stairs on the other side of the pool, gasping with the first breaths of their New Life in Christ. As they emerged, dripping, they were met by elders and wrapped in towels, but not before the congregation glimpsed the saturated gowns clinging to the contours of their bodies. The pubescent Sunday School boys who'd been allowed to watch from the gallery above – and, gazing down now, from the upper floor of that Rhondda bus, at the pavements of his Valley getting baptised yet again, immersed in icy rain, Jac forced himself to confess to himself that he'd been no better than any of them – those wicked, innocent boys would study solemnly the progress of every teenage girl, every shapely young woman amongst the candidates, praying for an extended glimpse of bra and panties under the sodden white overclothes. They were rarely disappointed. *Praise Ye the Lord*, indeed!

Stubborn Jac had never put himself up as a candidate for baptism, never made a 'Decision' for the Lord, never answered the earnest calls for those convicted by the Holy Spirit to come forward and declare that they'd 'accepted the Lord Jesus Christ as their own personal Saviour' (the only valid form of words that ensured Salvation). So he'd never been saved, never been baptised, and of course, as the son of Baptists, never christened as a baby. But he had a name all the same. Two given names in fact. Jacob Rhys. 'Rhys' – proclaiming his birth-right in the Land of his Fathers – spoken with a patriotic flourish on its 'rh'. 'Jacob' – after the Biblical trickster who stole his brother's birth-right – pronounced with a pure 'a' sound in the Welsh way his grandparents had been taught when they'd been in Sunday School: *Jack-ob*, not *Jay-cob*. And, even before he could say it properly himself, shortened by everyone to plain 'Jac'.

"Jac?"

Petra, it seemed, had asked a question, but he'd been too wrapped up in his ruminations about being born (but not born again) to grasp that his opinion had been sought.

28

"He's miles away," said Lydia, uncharacteristically stating the obvious.

"*My mind's on other things*," confirmed Jac, his Auntie's forgiving phrase springing far too readily to his lips.

"Well," sighed Petra, "far be it for us to intrude on his fantasies, Lydia," her rejoinder performed with a degree of archness sufficient to let him know she wasn't really annoyed. "As he always says, a boy has to have a dream, or how would he ever get through the day?" (What? Had he actually been using that phrase with his friends?) "I was going to ask him something about Catherine, but..."

Just then, the bus swung left, throwing them sideways in their seats. The moment, which suddenly seemed pregnant with significance, was lost. Rain streamed off the roof, falling in rivulets down the windows. They'd reached Carter's Corner. Mid-Rhondda was far behind now, but it was the best part of four miles still to Treorchy. The three Friends were alone again. The solitary pensioner must have got off somewhere during Jac's reverie.

The girls turned back towards each other. Jac tried to find something, anything to say, anything to continue the discussion, to find out what Petra wanted to ask. About Catherine.

"It's a long way to go..." he muttered unconvincingly, the protest song adaptation of *Tipperary* still rumbling on in his head. "And the roads are awful slow."

"Nobody's disputing that," said Lydia, in the kind of tone that Jac recognised as a signal for him to explain himself or shut up.

"My point is..." What was his point? The girls stared expectantly. He thought again about those baptismal services. Year after year, his refusal to commit. All that time saying 'no' to the biggest question of all, defining himself by what he was *not*, by what he refused to become.

"My point is that I feel *stuck*. I mean, do I have to wait until I go to university, assuming I do, to make my own... *Decisions*? To get up when I want, go to bed when I want, to eat, to *drink* what I want... And stuff that's far more important than that. Stuff that really matters. Because... I know I always go on about the Rhondda, its history, what it stands for, what it means to me... but it *has* formed me, shaped me, made me what I am..."

"You mean like your parents have shaped you? The Rhondda's prevented you from starting your own story, is that what you're saying?"

"No, I didn't mean that, quite the opposite... though it's a good point, Lydia. But there's a difference with the Valley: it's bigger than a family. It's a community, yes... but it's varied, there are people who aren't like me here, it's more..."

Diverse was the word he was searching for, but his mind was grappling with how to get his broader point across; indeed, still trying to get a grip on what exactly his point was.

He tried again.

"The Valley's got its own distinctive character, right enough, but if I was free to, I could choose my Rhondda. I could go to *that* chapel or *that* pub. Get involved in rugby or drama or politics or whatever. Or all of them. Or none. Decide which bits of it were important to me. And to me, they *would be* important. My own choices. So, what I'm getting at, is that I don't want to wait until I'm away from here for that begin. I don't want to start becoming who I really am in some godforsaken university town. Amongst strangers. Who won't understand where I'm coming from. I want *this* place to be the place where I find myself."

Jac stopped. He'd said his piece. It was down to Petra and Lydia now.

"We were just talking about Daniel, Catherine's step-brother..."

"Poor dab."

"...and Lydia was wondering what it was like for him to go away. To Swansea. Meeting new people there, from all over. It can throw you. Then this girl comes along... and I don't envy her, being pregnant at that age, and I hope to God I never am, but..."

Petra faltered. Lydia took up the account of their conversation.

"Maybe that's how it went wrong for him. Being away from home. He seems to have relied a lot on Catherine, even though he's older. Not having her there and… others who cared about him, people he cared about, not having them around, just as he was starting his story, as you put it."

Jac felt glad to be understood. Affirmed.

"Thanks. Both of you. I know I get all cryptic, sometimes. And complicated. Sometimes I think I must be a bit of a nutter…"

He nearly told them then. Told them his secret. The crazy secret he'd shared with nobody, not even his parents. The secret he'd kept for the best part of a decade. The secret, it struck him now, that was nearly *half as old as I'm*.

But something held him back.

"I suppose… I'm just impatient. For my story to begin. My Auntie's always telling me that I'm like a big kid, wanting everything to start *right now*."

They fell into silence. Out of the window, houses, streetlights, another chapel, a club. Jac knew this place, he loved it. He realised he hadn't got his question straight: it wasn't *when* would his story begin, but *where*. In his mind, he retraced the journey they were making, that *progression*: Pandy Square, the bus heading north, a line on a map, the main road up the narrow valley. Tonypandy flowing seamlessly into Llwynypia, Llwynypia into Tyntyla, Tyntyla to Ystrad and now Ystrad to Gelli. Unless you were a native, you'd never know where one place ended, and another began. Rhondda was an urban ribbon, spun out yard-by-yard, house by terraced house, township by township.

"This is a City," he suddenly declared, loudly. "A Linear City. And we are its Citizens!"

Yes, a Linear City. He could visualise every twist and turn they'd take from here on, through Gelli, Ton Pentre and Pentre, all the way to Treorchy – even though it was still *a long way to go*. He knew the name of every bus stop by heart. And every whipstitch of the route would be threaded through a metropolitan sprawl like this, every available square foot built on,

31

colonised by industrious, voracious, swaggering humanity. On and on it went, a dozen miles end-to-end. Eight more again, the Rhondda Fach, forking east from Porth up to Maerdy, that stronghold of communism, 'Little Moscow' (he tried not to dwell on the fact that his Auntie seemed to believe it was called that *because it's always so cold up there*).

But if the girls were intrigued by this latest outburst, they didn't show it. Perhaps they weren't up to unpacking another of Jac's *non-sequiturs*.

"Cheer up, beaut'," said Petra, eventually. She seemed cheered up herself. "Maybe tonight's the night. The night your story starts. The once-upon-a-time night."

5

So that was the Rhondda in the 1970s, was it? Full of lefties, evangelicals and teenagers who revelled in their industrial history and *knew their Pwyll Pendefig Dyfeds from their Ifor Haels?*

I hear howls of protest from nearly everyone I grew up with. Their *Valley was never so political, never so chapel-dominated, never so fixated on its own past. Never so* Welsh, *come to that.*

How can I disagree? I've already admitted being what my editor calls an unreliable narrator. Put plainly, I'm making some of this up. It's what novelists do. (Confession: in Chapter 3, explaining where 'Jac' got the word 'mole' for a sea-wall from, I invented that bit about The Onedin Line *script; although the series* was *on, and it features, in passing, later in this story. For the avoidance of doubt, the Rhondda Sea Cadets do exist and really are headquartered on Llwynypia Road).*

Many of my classmates, far from loving the Rhondda so much that they wanted their 'stories' to go on being rooted here, couldn't wait to get away. Those who stayed were hardly as sentimental about their birthplace as 'Jac'. Why would they be? Black spoil heaps on every horizon. A river black with coal-dust, still, despite the worked-out seams of the Black Diamond. Rotten housing stock. Empty, rotting places of worship. Dereliction all over the shop. All over the shops. Unemployment. Delinquency. Drugs.

As for working-class solidarity, many 'tidy' people – those who scrimped and saved to make ends meet; chapel people too – tended to blame those worse *off than themselves, rather than those who had more. 'Scroungers' and 'wasters' got fingers pointed at them far more often than fat cats and absentee landlords. When things got a little easier, we turned as rapaciously consumerist as any other part of Britain. Rhondda people loved treats and style and the fine things of life when they could afford them (and even if they couldn't). And who'll begrudge them that? Nothing's too good for the working class, as Nye Bevan is said to have said. But the working-class culture which had created the miners' welfare halls and libraries, the co-ops, the self-governing non-conformist chapels – that culture had run out of steam, if it hadn't collapsed completely. My friends' parents were watching Dick Emery and doing the Football Pools. Nothing distinctively Welsh or 'woke' about that. The radical struggle of the Depression was the struggle of a bygone era: an unimaginably long time ago when the world was unimaginably different. 1910 and* The Miners' Next Step *was more distant again. A few of us did have the privilege of doing A level with a teacher who recognised that History is more than a list of (English) kings and queens. But, even then, our own history was an option taught for a term or two, not fundamental to our education. So how could we have formulated a coherent analysis of it, let alone an Anarcho-Syndicalist one?*

Rhondda's 'Red' past did cast its shadow into the 1970s, it's true. When I first voted as an idealistic 18-year-old, it was for the veteran Communist Annie Powell – and she topped the poll in Penygraig, becoming Mayor of Rhondda. (The first draft of this novel had a lovely section about 'Jac' and his friendship with Mrs Powell, complete with tales of her teaching Hen Wlad Fy Nhadau *to Nikita Khrushchev on a visit to Moscow. My editor insisted I cut it: it was* research, *apparently,* not *narrative.* 'Research'! *As though I'd had to* research *something I'd lived.) But, by 1974, Rhondda voters overwhelmingly backed Labour not the Communists; their socialism, to quote one of Rhondda's most prominent – and now most discredited – parliamentarians, owed more to Methodism than to Marx. Instinctively, like George Thomas, Viscount Tonypandy, former Speaker of the House of Commons, they sought change through parliamentary democracy, however left-wing their convictions. Evolution not revolution.*

So I'll have to concede that 'Jac' is far from representative. His experience of evangelism is extreme (more of that later). His interest in the Welsh language and Welsh history marks him out as an oddball in that time and place. And as for his flirtations with revolutionary politics – his Auntie would have told him not to be so twp, *so* di-doreth. *She was one of those (or rather, as we shall see, fifty-two of those) who sided with Rhondda's preference for* constitutional *reform, as distinct from militancy intended to overthrow the system. She would have explained it to him with a gnomic juxtaposition, one of her nonsensical Rhondda sayings that may just be more profound than they seem. "In a collision... well, there you are," she'd have declaimed, pausing dramatically with a resigned, open-handed flourish. "In an explosion... where are you?"*

But if, as well as being hopelessly naïve, 'Jac' seems far too knowing *for his age (and my editor says he does), there's a couple of reasons for that.*

34

The first is to do with that Auntie, who gives him access to a vast repository of experience. Trust me on this (no, really): there's more about it to come. The second is down to me. I don't want to separate 'Jac' and his understandings – even if I was a good enough writer to do it – from lessons I've learned long after my schooldays. Things about belief, about doubt, about history. Things I'm still learning, about myself, about life. Things, crucially, I'm only bottoming out as I write this now. Defining, expanding, embracing that learning is what this novel is about. Pinning it all on a teenager may be awkward, absurd, cruel even, unrealistic, I'll give you that – but I can't paint a useful picture of what the Rhondda was then, what it meant to me, what it might mean to us still, unless I burden 'Jac' with at least a little of what I know now. Poor dab. Stuck on a bus, carrying the weight of the world, and aching for all that learning to begin. And for Catherine too. Sorry, kid.

6

'When is this bloody story going to start?'

Years had gone by, the whole of Jac's upbringing in Chapel, since they'd passed the Ivor Hael and Jac had re-imagined Pwyll galloping after Rhiannon; but they still hadn't reached the middle of Gelli. How could any bus travel so slowly?

Patience, Jac! The Life of Ivan Denisovich wasn't written in a day.

Jac weighed up the irritation in his question again. Maybe he was right to feel frustrated: if someone's story began only when they achieved a meaningful degree of independence, then certainly his opening chapter wasn't written yet. But the heart of any story was character, not narrative. And surely character began to be formed the first time a person asserted their own will, the first time they acted contrary to their parents' wishes, the first time they experienced love for something other than those parents or themselves.

What came to mind now, on the top deck of the bus, was his steering wheel. His lovely sky-blue steering wheel. He'd never adored anything with the purity of emotion he'd felt for that toy – not Mam, nor Dad, nor his Auntie. Certainly not the first crushes of his teens in their wet baptismal gowns. Not Bowie nor *The Great Gatsby*. Not the Romantic Poets he could quote so *appositely*. Not Catherine Evans…

Oh, that's interesting: so she's on the list now too?

It *was* interesting, Catherine appearing unbidden in a list of attachments, fundamental attachments. Attachments that would stay with him. It was the first time it had struck him that way, how much of a fixture she was. He couldn't deny how close he felt to her. But as a friend, as one of The Society of Friends, not as…

Really? Jac, be honest: how much you fancy her…

He parked the question, not for the first time, significant as it was. He'd ages to ponder it before he'd see her again.

But his steering wheel. He'd have been three or four when he was given it, he supposed. He kept it for years, long after classmates had grown out of whatever amused them as toddlers. Why would he get rid of it? It could take him anywhere. And he never went anywhere without it. The sky-blue wheel had a white gearstick attached, and a squishy red disc at its centre, a disc you could push to sound a squeaky horn (until the air-bag inside got tragically punctured somehow).

Best of all was the vertical column that the hub of the wheel sat on, a column with a black rubber suction-pad at its base. Using that pad, you could sit on the front seat on top of a double-decker like the one he was on now, fasten the steering wheel to the body of the vehicle and *drive the bus all the way to the Depot!* And not just there: to Blaencwm or Blaenrhondda, over to Maerdy, up Clydach, any route at all on the whole Rhondda Transport network.

His parents didn't have a car – his father had suffered blackouts, and was debarred from driving, even if they could have afforded one – so the bus featured large in life. Every time he boarded one, that steering wheel was fast in his grip. Jac memorised the routes, the locations and names of every stop.

Once, Uncle Stan had driven him and his Mam to Cardiff by car. Jac's puzzled yet caustic reaction to his uncle's serial failure to follow the meandering bus route into Talbot Green, Pontyclun and then Miskin become part of family lore.

"How come you can't stick to the proper route, Uncle Stan?" he'd asked, unable to hold back any longer as they by-passed the third successive village centre. "You do go an awful funny way to Cardiff."

The story was repeated *ad nauseam* by the adults. 'You do go an awful funny way' became the first of an endless succession of catchphrases coined by Jac.

Once he was old enough to use pen-and-pencil, he'd draw up detailed timetables of his own, sitting on the floor with his marvellous toy by his side, imagining routes to Charlie's sweet-shop, to School, to Chapel – routes down the side-streets, lanes and *gwlis* of mid-Rhondda, short-cuts inaccessible to double-deckers, but massively convenient to himself and his family, where his magic steering wheel would come into its own.

Eventually, inevitably, came the day when he told his parents soberly that he was too old for a steering wheel, that he wanted them to give it away. A week later, he was missing it so badly that he had to beg for its return. Whether his Dad had wisely kept the original hidden away, or his Mam had indulgently bought an identical new one – well, Jac was so familiar with his beloved toy that he must have known, but by now he'd forgotten which. The important thing was that he had it in his hands again. But from then on, it was a covert pleasure, one he never talked about playing out the back lane or up in Hughes Street beyond. With children his own age, the last thing he needed was to be shown up as childish.

He knew it was the right thing, the normal thing, to go out and play. Every child, no matter how tiny, played outside, in the muddy *gwlis*, on the spoil tips and derelict colliery workings. It was natural. Healthy. Except that his family had a reticence about it. They always questioned where he was going, when he'd be back; always warned him, sternly, to *take care*. Permission was provisional.

There was an incident that might have been the root of that. When Jac was still very small, he'd been given a fantastic birthday present: a racing car he could sit in and pedal. A beast of a thing, fashioned in metal, shiny and red, a big white number 1 painted on the bonnet. One afternoon, he was being looked after by his maternal grandparents, who shared the house on Tylacelyn Road with Jac and his Mam and Dad. His Grampa let him play 'out the front' beside the sunny doorstep. Somehow, Jac managed to launch himself and his car down the vertiginous garden path. *He was racing!...* to his death. The speeding car hit the kerb at the bottom of the concrete path, turned turtle, spun over the top of the garden railings... and smashed onto the *tar-mac* of the busy main road a dozen feet below. Miraculously, Jac had been thrown clear as the car overturned, landing awkwardly against the railings, still within the confines of the garden, alive but… Had he suffered a bang on the head? Was he concussed? Was there a scar on his brain, a line of weakness that caused the strange condition that he was careful to keep secret in later years? The doctor was called. He pronounced the boy perfectly well. Jac was left with just a hazy memory of nausea as the world had somersaulted. But the recriminations amongst the grown-ups must have been titanic. From then on, he would be, he must be sheltered from danger.

He'd always been the apple of his family's eye, an only child, born late in a marriage, praised for every small achievement. His grandmothers idolised him. 'My buttercup', they'd call him. 'He's worth all the tea in China'. Jac imagined butter and tea in china cups. It sounded messy. He knew it was supposed to mean that he was *priceless*, but he couldn't work out the logic behind the words. Or indeed why *priceless* meant the opposite of *worthless*. Grown-ups spoke a foreign language.

Recently, when Jac had told Catherine about all this, she'd asked straight out if he ever thought he might have been loved *too much*; if there wasn't something overprotective, neurotic, in the way he'd been cossetted. Jac didn't get it. How could you be loved too much?

But his homelife as an only child didn't commend him to other children. He was used only to the company of adults, to a pace set by those in the last decade of their lives, not the first: a Chapel boy, clever with schoolwork but not quick-witted or canny; ill-suited to the rough-and-tumble of street games, to Strong Horses and Bolter, to foot-races and wrestling matches. And there were things he knew that no other child did, things that Nan and Grampa talked about. Things like rheumatism and life assurance and adultery (which, surprisingly, was something only adults who weren't properly grown-up seemed to do). He wasn't entirely sure of these grown-up matters, and he knew it was wrong to show that he knew too much about them, because in the world of grown-ups there were things that it was *a sin* to know, like in the story of the Fruit of the Tree of Knowledge. So he hid things he knew from the adults, and he was always hiding things he knew from other children, hiding them like the yellowing vests his mother made him wear beneath his shirts. His haircut, his clothes, his whole house, gloomy with varnished sideboards, coal scuttles and bible-black Bibles – all this was *old-fashioned*, stuck in the past. It had no part in the world of electric fires and the *Daily Mirror* and formica tabletops, the world *normal* children lived in; the bright, flashy world that was changing and up-to-date and happening right now. So he lost both ways. His knowledge was shameful, and his ignorance of that modern world was shameful. He was *twp*. And too clever by half.

As an only child, Jac had little idea how to *negotiate* with other children. On the rare occasions he didn't get his own way at home, he had a tactic. Not so much a tactic, because he didn't feel in control of it. In fact, he felt overwhelmed by it, overwhelmed with anger and sadness directed at himself as much as anyone. He would *pout*. Sulking was a recognised ploy. His grandparents had a special Welsh word for it: *pwdu*. Cutting off his nose to spite his face was what his father called it: he disapproved mightily. Though with the rest of the family, and Mam in particular, it worked. But if he *pwdu*-ed with a playmate, they'd simply pick up their ball, literally or metaphorically, and head home to their brothers and sisters. Jac would be left alone, bereft, with nothing to do but go on pouting.

In a group, pouting was even more disastrous. He would be taunted and teased, mercilessly. And his attachment to telling the truth made it worse. In Sunday School, he'd been taught that God demands honesty from His children. It was a standard Jac's father adhered to at all times. 'The truth shall make you free'. But the truth could trap you too.

One Friday evening, a gang of them had been up the tumps, a patch of rough, grassy knolls at the end of Hughes Street. It looked down on the Incline, the derelict tramway that – when the Naval Colliery had been working – took the spoil from underground to be dumped as a massive pyramid, the Black Tip, which still loomed over mid-Rhondda from the mountain above.

They'd been talking about toys. Heading home, Belinda Owen made them all promise to bring their favourite toy out to play, first thing next day. The boys planned to bring Daleks, robots, binoculars; the girls roller skates, skipping elastics, Chatty Cathy. James Taylor had a tank that fired real shells. Belinda, tough as any boy, would turn up with her Action Man. She asked Jac what he'd bring. It was several months since he'd got his steering wheel back; no one there knew about it. He could have impressed them all by naming his Corgi gold-coloured James Bond Aston Martin, complete with working ejector seat. But he couldn't tell a lie. His favourite was the toy he'd told them he'd grown out of. They scoffed when he confessed he'd got it back. And worse – much worse – when they met at the tumps next morning, his steering wheel was the *only* toy in sight. But everyone had promised! As Jac began to remonstrate, James Taylor snatched the steering wheel from his grasp and wouldn't give it back. Not until Jac had paid a *forfeit*. Belinda said he had to name ten pop groups. Why she picked on that, goodness knows.

"Go on, Jac, just name ten. Name five. Then you can have your precious toy back," jeered James. "Why would I want to keep it?"

"Let him name three," someone suggested. "Everybody knows three pop groups."

They were right: it was the 1960s after all. But pop music didn't feature in Jac's house. There was no record player. No transistors. They didn't even have one of those Rediffusion boxes that piped in a couple of radio stations together with a relay of TV signals that you couldn't pick up otherwise because of the mountains. Their *wireless* was tuned to the Home Service. Hymns were the only music Jac was familiar with. He wasn't even sure what counted as pop music. He tried to brazen it out.

"Just three? That's *pappish*," he said.

"Come on then, Jac, name three," mocked Belinda. 'Everyone in the world can name three. Ena Sharples could name three..."

Who was Ena Sharples? She must go to another school.

"…my goldfish could name three!"

Perhaps Ena Sharples was Belinda's goldfish. But there was no way out now. He had to begin.

The Beatles. A good start. But that was all. Nothing else came. The laughter began.

"We'll give you a clue, Jac."

"We'll give you more than a clue. We'll give you one for free – the Dave Clark Five."

Was that a trick, a way of making him look even more stupid? Was Dave Clark a friend of Ena Sharples?

"*Glad All Over*, Jac?"

But Jac wasn't. No bit of him was glad. In fact, he was nearly crying. He gave up, and told James Taylor, as forcefully as he dared, to give the steering wheel back anyway. It was his. His *property*. Taylor poked his tongue out, said the wheel was now *forfeit* and threw it to Belinda. When Jac approached her, she tossed it back to Taylor. Jac became piggy-in-the-middle, trying – failing – to catch his beloved toy as it whizzed past him from one tormentor to the other.

"I'm fed up of this now," he warned them, red-faced.

Nonchalantly, Belinda yawned to let him know that she'd had enough too. Then, she simply turned and hurled the toy away with all her strength. Which was considerable. And the wheel was surprisingly aerodynamic. It soared across the tumps, a sky-blue whirr, up and over the edge of the banking, hovering there, before plunging way, way down towards the rusted metal cables of the Incline, disappearing as it landed short of the tramway, in the middle of the biggest patch of stingies in the whole of mid-Rhondda.

Jac spent the next half-hour in there, fruitlessly searching. The others cat-called down as he stumbled blindly about. By the time he pulled himself out, empty-handed, the red nettle-rash, hot on his skin, had covered every inch of his legs below his shorts and both his forearms up to the sleeves of his tee-shirt. Feeling more than sorry for himself, he tried to reason Belinda into an apology.

42

Without hesitation or warning, she walked straight up to him and punched him right in the guts. He doubled up in agony, and staggered home.

That night under his blankets, after Mam had dabbed calamine lotion over the stings for a second time, Jac played out the scene in his head yet again, tears pricking his eyes once more. If only they'd asked him something else, some other catalogue of names, it *would* have been 'pappish'. No bother at all. Chapels perhaps. Or better, streets – even in his distress, he realised it would be shameful to betray that he knew the names of ten chapels. Streets would have been alright; he could have done *twenty*. Tylacelyn, Hughes Street, Hill Street, Nantgwyn, Hendrecafn, Penmaesglas: those he knew well enough. Beyond that, what? Greenfield Street and Field Street – or were they one and the same, like you could shorten Tonypandy Square to Pandy Square though it was just the one place? He might get tripped up on that. Was there a Balaclava Row up towards Craig-yr-Eos? There couldn't be! Who'd name a street after a hat? Gilfach Road, that was easy; you could have it twice, an allowable doubler, one in Penygraig, one in Tonypandy, both heading directly up the mountain towards Gilfach, not that any bus could drive up them to get there. Llwynypia Road, on the other hand, certainly led to Llwynypia. But Trealaw Road was already in Trealaw, surely? It was all so confusing. Where was the Pymmer? Was it a street? How did you even spell it?

Small as he was, Jac understood something there in bed: *why* he'd embarked on this listing of streets. His skin was itchy and sore. He'd been humiliated by his ignorance of modern music. He'd lost a fight to a girl, something no boy he knew had ever, ever done. Worst of all, his precious steering wheel was gone forever. But he was *distracting* himself. And then he realised that that's what he was doing, and the pain came back.

"I could do with some help here," Jac found himself admitting, finally. "I could really do with some help." And perhaps there is a God after all. Perhaps He does answer prayer. Or maybe it's just that a seemingly cold, uncaring universe looks after its children in some beneficent way we're not equipped to understand. Or it could have been mere coincidence. Whatever the explanation, and although it didn't happen straightaway, Jac came in retrospect to credit his desperate plea that dark night for the fact that, eventually, in a way that nobody could have anticipated, and few would believe, someone did come to help him.

7

It was Tom Jones's fault. The Valleys Elvis belted out hit after hit in the mid-Sixties. *It's Not Unusual. What's New Pussycat? Thunderball.* And, of course, the Christmas Number One of 1966, *Green, Green Grass of Home.* Knicker-throwing matrons got hot and bothered by Tom's every move. His impact on Jac's life was just as crazy. But the truth about that was known only to Jac; and Jac was careful to keep it that way.

It was Jac's final year in Junior School. He was a big boy now. He walked to school all on his own, up to Hendrecafn, up through the tumps, past the Incline where his beloved steering wheel lay under an acre of nettles. He could still be awkward and unsure, bullied and fearful of bullying. But the anticipation, the dread was becoming worse than the reality. He'd begun – though he wouldn't have been capable of thinking of it like that – to develop *strategies* for coping. Resorting to a kind of zany humour was one. "Jac's a nutter," classmates would say, dismissively; but the dismissal might excuse him from a pummelling.

There were dark times, still. The previous winter, Jac's Nan had fallen sick, and taken to her bed upstairs. The house was silent, gloomy. The doctor was called and came. A nurse too. One evening, they sent for Uncle Stan. After a brief visit to his mother's bedroom, Stan sat in the middle-room clutching a cup of tea, but not drinking it. Talking quietly with Jac's Dad. Jac was on the sofa opposite, unsure whether to go or stay. His father spoke slowly to his uncle: "There's no coming from this, you know."

In that instant, Jac understood two things. First, what his father had said, what it meant for Nan. And secondly, but simultaneously, that his father had said it in that way, had chosen those careful words, so that Jac *wouldn't* understand. And so even as Jac's heart was flooding with grief, he struggled – and, somehow, he managed – to betray no hint of it on his face.

They buried her, not many days later, after a service of hymns and prayers and readings at home. Jac wasn't allowed to accompany her to her last resting place – *no women or children at the graveside* – but when spring came and the headstone had been replaced, he was taken over to Llethrddu to see it.

The dead of Trealaw Cemetery enjoyed the sunniest spot in the whole valley. Jac's parents approached the family grave reverently. Uncle Stan had come too, but he seemed more interested in showing Jac a more impressive memorial a few feet away. A carved white angel stood between four black marble pillars which supported a cut-stone roof topped by a cross.

"Tommy Farr had that put there. For his mam and dad. Tommy Farr, the Tonypandy Terror. He fought Joe Louis for World Heavyweight Championship. Yankee Stadium, 1937."

Jac knew all about Farr's heroics. It was one of the stories Nan herself had told him. How they'd got up in the middle of the night to hear the commentary on the wireless via the transatlantic cable. How Farr had so nearly upset the odds, taking the Brown Bomber the full fifteen rounds. Jac realised Uncle Stan wanted him to feel awed by the fact that his grandmother's grave was right next to the family tomb of a Rhondda titan. But he couldn't help feeling sorry for Stan. He knew – after the way he himself had focused on those street names the night after his steering wheel had been taken from him – that his uncle was *distracting* himself, that he couldn't bear to face up squarely to his loss.

Loss was no stranger to the coalfield. One Dinner Time, Jac had come home from school as usual (his delicate stomach couldn't stand school meals: he had to have his Mam's cooking; or just her marmite sandwiches). Kicking a ball around the backyard, he heard a low boom coming from the Incline or from further into Tonypandy. It didn't sound like much, but it struck him as significant. Just then his Mam called him in to eat.

"What was that noise? Now just?"

Lightly, his mother passed it off.

"Just a car back-firing, I expect."

Did she know? Had she heard it too? Did she realise…?

Probably. She was a woman of the Rhondda, after all. By the time Jac had come home again from Hendrecafn that afternoon, the news was out. Thirty-one men killed. Underground in an explosion at the Cambrian Colliery. Thirty-one souls gone. In that instant. As he'd been playing ball a mile away.

Days later, he stood with hundreds, thousands of others, lining Dunraven Street, as the dead miners' comrades processed behind the hearses, an endless line of funeral suits and black ties. The tramp of heels the only sound. Policemen saluted. Women wept silently. And the hearses took their bodies, united in death as they had been at work, to Llethrddu.

Just a year later, Aberfan. Two valleys distant, but too close, far too close. Those dead children, 116 of them, were of an age with Jac. That fateful October morning, their Junior School had stood like Jac's, directly below a massive colliery spoil tip. Saturated by underground springs that the authorities knew about but ignored, the Aberfan tip collapsed, catastrophically. The one above Hendrecafn remained. The Black Tip. A monumental reminder to Jac as he walked to school every morning, to the whole of mid-Rhondda, of the price of coal.

No, loss was never far away. Not far enough from Jac himself, despite all his family did to shield him. He never knew until he was an adult himself, but his mother, already in her forties, suffered a miscarriage shortly after his grandmother died: losing the sister that Jac always felt the lack of, always felt he was searching for somehow. And his father – well, his father died over breakfast one morning, slumping forward in his chair, his nose coming to a stop inches above his bowl of cornflakes…

It was a faint, though, not a fatality. And not the first he'd suffered. But Jac had never seen anyone pass out. It terrified him. His mother too. In her panic, she directed him with an uncharacteristic curtness: "Look at the clock, Jac! Look at the clock!" She began to slap his father's cheeks. Ever obedient, Jac twisted his head to fix his gaze on the timepiece on the mantelshelf. His body was still squarely facing the table. He was aware of his neck muscles stiffening. By the time his father came to, he'd nearly lost consciousness himself. His mother asked him, then, how long his Dad's blackout had lasted. She needed to know to tell the doctor. Jac wasn't able to help. He'd been told to look at the *clock*, not the *time*. He'd stared at it blankly, taking nothing in, assuming he had to avert his eyes because a child was not permitted to look upon a stricken father.

His father survived, unlike others'; though Jac never liked the idea that his Dad had a weakness. He buried the knowledge deep within himself. The young have a gift for doing that. *In the midst of death, they are in life.* Aberfan's schoolyard was silent; Hendrecafn's still echoed each playtime with the sounds of serious play. Titches of six and seven tackling the big boys of Standard Four. Ten-year-old girls doing jumpsies in the middle of the pitch. And then, one never-to-be-forgotten Dinner Time, play was suddenly abandoned, as the rumour flashed around the yard: *Tom Jones Is Down In Nantgwyn!*

It was Jac who'd started the rumour. Jac, who a short while before, famously hadn't been able to name more than a single pop group. He'd learned by now. He'd made sure to. He knew who Tom Jones was. He knew – like everyone – that Tom came from Pontypridd. He knew the words of Tom's biggest hit. And, crucially, he even knew – somehow, because not everybody did know this – that his manager, a man called Gordon Mills, had a home in Nantgwyn, the street immediately below Hendrecafn school. Dawdling on his way back to school after dinner, Jac noticed a big posh car – a *lim-o-sine!* – parked opposite the terraced houses. Jac was top of the class in mental arithmetic, and he wasn't slow to put two and two together. Tom himself must be inside, meeting his manager, planning his next assault on the charts.

Jac ran up to the schoolyard as fast as he could. He blurted out to Robbie Preece what he'd seen; Robbie told James Taylor; and he told Belinda. Suddenly *everyone* knew. They crowded the school gate, trying to peek down the hill, round the corner, desperate for a glimpse of the biggest pop star ever to come out of the Valleys.

No-one could actually spy anything from inside the yard. But the push-and-shove at the big open double-gates got so heavy that half-a-dozen titches toppled out onto the pavement: forbidden ground for anyone who stayed in school for Dinner. Before Jac knew it, before he could do anything to stop it, they were *all* outside, Jac too, the whole schoolful of them pelting down the hill, careering round the bench at the bottom, coming to a breathless stop right outside Mr Mills's.

And there they stood, stock-still. A big silent semi-circle, gawping at the front door. Waiting for something to happen. Though precisely what, none of them could imagine. Certainly, no one was brave enough to go and knock at the door. Time passed. No one moved. The distant school bell sounded the end of Dinner Time. There was no sign of Tom. Perhaps he had his dinner later than they did.

"Perhaps his... man-anager won't let him come out to play," said one of the titches.

Still no one moved. Everyone knew they should be back in the yard lining up for afternoon lessons before the teachers came out to count them in. Jac, for one, could see how much trouble they were in, how much trouble *he* was in. But everybody was rooted to the spot. A minute went by. An age. Eventually, Jac came to his senses, or panicked, he wasn't sure which. He scarpered back to the school, sprinting through the gate... running smack bang into Mr Coakes. The headmaster's face was red. He had his cane in his hand. "Jac Morgan! Where is everyone?" he bawled. For the second time, Jac blurted out his fateful news: "With Tom Jones! He's down in Nantgwyn!"

They were rounded up and marched back up the hill. Made to stand in the Hall, stony silent, in perfect lines, class-by-class. All resigned to dreadful punishment. Mass flouting of the rules had *never* happened before. And Jac knew that, for him, a whack on the knuckles with that cane would be far from the end of it. *He*'d started the rumour. *He*'d got everyone wound up and caused the stampede to Nantgwyn. *He*'d broken away, headed back to school, split on them all. Once school was over, that afternoon and every day for the rest of the week, his classmates would take it out on him. He'd be beaten up, many times, by boys his age, and younger. Maybe even by some girls. And he'd deserve it, that was the worst of it. How stupid he'd been! How desperate he was now. Coakes was about to pronounce judgement. The whole school held its breath.

And this was the moment, the life-changing moment, when Jac became aware of a voice, a voice inside his own head. To Jac, it was no less real for that. He knew that no-one else could hear it. But it wasn't simply his imagination. It certainly wasn't under his conscious control. It was clear and compelling, weirdly domineering and comforting at one and the same time. A voice he'd never heard before, but perfectly familiar all the same. As though, somehow or other, he'd tuned at last bang on to the wavelength of a radio station that had been an indecipherable buzz in the back of his mind. A voice that would return to him time after time from then on, at moments of stress or indecision. A voice he trusted immediately and could recognise and put a label on. A woman's voice, middle-aged, pleasant, recognisably Rhondda in accent. It was his auntie. Or rather his Auntie. His Auntie. Just that. No given name was necessary. The voice was a composite, a perfect fusion of the voices of all the aunties he'd ever known. Not a specific aunt, but an amalgam of them all. And, as for any Rhondda child, what counted as an aunt for Jac wasn't confined to his parents' siblings and their spouses. Jac had many, many aunties. Friends of his parents, friends of his grandparents, neighbours, practically any well-disposed woman who had any contact with his extended family. Sometime later, when Jac made a list, as he was wont to do, *fifty-one* such aunties came readily to mind. And, as it happened, one uncle (out of all his uncles) too – because there was something else in that perfectly-blended voice, one bottom-note, a hint of manliness amidst the dominant feminine.

It took him a long time to realise all of this, and longer still to come to terms with it. But the benefits were instantaneous. In a direct and miraculous way, he had access to this collective

50

intelligence. To all this wisdom and experience (to mass foolishness and naivety, too, as soon became evident). Because right now, this voice, this Auntie, was responding in real time to the predicament Jac found himself in. And he was *in the pickies*, no doubt of that. But she was telling him, calmly and decisively, what to do. And precisely what to say.

"Sir, sir, sir!" he began, in the words supplied by this inner voice, "Sir, sir, sir!", louder, more confident each time. "Sir, sir, sir!"

"Who's sir-sir-sirring me?" bellowed Mr Coakes.

"Me, me, me, sir, sir, sir!"

"Jac Morgan? *Jac Morgan?* Step forward. This had better be important."

"Yes, it is, sir. Important."

Jac realised he must try to sound confident, and indeed he *was* confident, trusting in the words he was being urged to say; but all the same! This bold-faced cheek was being triggered and phrased by a voice in his head. Was he crazy? Had he gone mad, realising the consequences of what he'd done? Had he suffered *a stroke* or something? Was it that bang he'd had when his racing car overturned all those years ago?

But now that he'd started this brazen intervention, there was no choice but to plough on.

Something important, something puzzling, prompted the voice, his Auntie's voice.

"Something important, sir, that's been puzzling me," said Jac out loud, in his own voice. There was a deathly silence throughout the Hall. The whole School had never heard anything like it. Neither had Jac, other than inside his own head a few seconds before.

"Is that so, Master Morgan?" Coakes didn't trouble himself to disguise the sarcasm. Jac might be one of his star pupils, and normally impeccably behaved, but this newfound impudence was beyond the limits of any headteacher's tolerance.

"Please share your puzzlement with us, since it's clearly so *important* at this very moment."

This wasn't going to end well. But Jac's trust in that guiding voice had become strangely, instantly complete. All he had to do was repeat what she said, repeat it with exactly the same intonation and timing. Timing was everything.

"It's just this, sir," he said, parroting the words he heard his Auntie saying. "I thought that Tom Jones was from Ponty…'

Good, Jac. Pause there.

"He is, boy! He's from Pontypridd," shouted Mr Coakes, his annoyance rising now. "What of it?"

"*Well…*" Jac's Auntie's prompt was crystal clear.

"Well, if Tom Jones *is* from Ponty, how come the last line of that song of his goes, *Neath* the…"

Wait just a beat.

"…Green, Green Grass Of Home?"

Jac understood the wordplay, though it wasn't something he'd ever have come up with himself. It took a few moments for his schoolmates to get it. Many of the younger ones didn't understand at all, had probably never heard of the distant town of Neath, never shortened 'underneath' to the more poetic monosyllable which fitted the metre of the song and enabled Jac – or rather his Auntie – to make this mildly amusing pun. But they sensed, all the same, that some kind of joke was being attempted, and at the expense of the headmaster, just when severe punishment was about to descend on them. The terrible tension which had gripped everyone was punctured. A fit of the *ha-ha*s broke out. The whole school started to giggle. "Jac Morgan, what a star!" Laughter is infectious. "A real headcase!" It became unstoppable. Even the teachers chuckled quietly. Old Coakes himself couldn't entirely stifle a smirk.

Of course, Jac didn't get off scot-free. Order was restored. The headmaster administered to him, and to him alone, not just a single stroke of the cane, but six of the best. It hurt, badly. Jac cried. But once it was over, and for the rest of the term, he was a hero to his classmates, a legend to the rest of the school. No-one bullied him now, not even James Taylor. He'd been punished for the sins of the many, and the many wanted now to bask in the friendship of the boy who'd saved them all, the famous boy who'd told a silly joke, and made the headmaster smile, when he was about to cane the whole School.

Though no-one ever discovered whether Tom Jones had actually been in Nantgwyn Street that day, Jac was *popular*. It took some getting used to. But it didn't turn his head. He knew – as no-one else did – the secret of who'd really got them all out of that jam. It wasn't him. It was his Auntie. Though the better he got to know her, the more he wondered if what she'd told him to say to the headmaster that day hadn't been intended as a joke at all, but, coming from her, was nothing but a genuine question.

It was hard to judge that – and lots of other things she said. She spoke confidently, plainly and fluently, though she had surprising gaps in her knowledge. And there was no knowing which aspects of her multi-persona might come to the fore in any particular circumstance. She wasn't there constantly – Jac didn't wake up to her every morning, nor fall asleep with her in his ears at night. Days could go by with complete radio silence, as it were. He couldn't summon her up by an act of will, if she wasn't willing. No, his Auntie only ever spoke when she wanted to, though usually it was when she reckoned that Jac needed her, when he was stressed or puzzled. But when she did speak, she was hard to ignore. He'd find himself repeating out loud what she told him, *almost* like an automaton, word-for-word, scarcely a gap between her voice and his, with precious little control (or even understanding sometimes) over what he was saying – as had happened with the Tom Jones incident. Her interventions could be as blunt and ham-fisted as that first one. Surprisingly, as then, they often worked out well in the end. Though not always…

8

Jac's Auntie. The voice in his head. It's weird. But… it's not unusual (thanks, Tom!). Literature is peopled with sufferers of auditory hallucinations. Real life, too. Saints and mystics. Schizophrenics. 'Normal' people. Researchers claim that as many as 10% of us have 'heard voices'. That seems a little high to me. Though Napoleon Bonaparte has just told me that it's not. I'm joking. It was Cleopatra.

No, sorry, I really am joking. Forgive me. I shouldn't: it's no laughing matter. At one extreme, we have clear cases of psychosis: murderers, serial killers even, who believe they're being directed by God or by mere mortals. But not everyone who hears a voice has a severe mental health problem. And though his friends sometimes call him a real headcase, *Jac isn't, really. Naïve he may be, but in everything else he behaves fairly normally for a bright boy of his age, class and background. He's capable (for the most part) of making rational decisions of his own. For him, this voice is real, and hard to ignore, but not all-powerful. He's no puppet: he's not possessed by a demon or any kind of spirit, good or bad. If he does have a brain injury, caused by that runaway racing car, it doesn't seem to affect him otherwise. He has a* relationship *with his Auntie, some perspective on the wisdom and advice she dispenses.*

So what's going on here? I'm hardly expert enough to turn this novel into a dissertation on contemporary fiction (neither is my editor, for all that she pretends), so I'll just point you in the direction of Magical Realism. It's a genre that – amongst much else – takes on the elites, the rich, powerful and privileged, from perspectives outside the dominant ones, from the fringes. But don't bother reading the whole of Márquez and Borges, Allende and Murakami, Günter Grass and Toni Morrison (I haven't). What you're looking for are enigmatic guiding voices in the head. Google (if you haven't read the book) Salman Rushdie *and his* Midnight's Children, *an army of youngsters with supernatural powers who chatter to each other via trans-subcontinental telepathy, and become a threat to the corrupt regime of Indira Gandhi. It's clear what they represent, how subversive they are.*

So what about Jac's Auntie? What does she signify? What's special about her? If she's true to the spirit of Magical Realism, what criticism, implicit or explicit, of the status quo *does she offer?*

The most striking thing about her is that hers is a collective *voice. Fifty-two individuals, easily enough to be a representative cross-section of a society like the Rhondda, as surprisingly* diverse *as it was in its homogeneity; but she's fifty-two individuals speaking as one. She's a counterblast to the atomisation of experience, to the selfishness and individualism of contemporary life. She asserts the truth that there* is *such a thing as society, that we are stronger together.*

Why an Auntie, asks my editor? Why not! The Anglo-Saxons believed that the bond between a man and his sister's son was special, so perhaps Celts operate on the basis of the female equivalent. Despite the sliver of masculinity that Jac recognises in her, it's important that what he's hearing is a woman's voice. Like other hotbeds of heavy industry, the Valleys Jac grew up in could be oppressively male-dominated. His Auntie is not *his feminine side in any airy-fairy, 'right on' way;* not *his inner woman expressing herself. But she does articulate the experience and the insight of women. And she forces Jac (and so, you, the reader) to consider those things too. She's funny with it.*

She's not a soft option though. Just like many devices in Magical Realist fiction, she's not there to distract. *Her function is not to shield you from the hard facts of history — of telling it like it is, like it was. So let's be clear: the South Wales Coalfield really did play a significant part in powering the late stages of the Industrial Revolution; its men* and *women did have the wealth they created plundered, their health destroyed, their environment trashed, their best hopes crushed, and — yes — their voices, collective and individual, ignored. And then, when it was all over, when the coal began to run out and Thatcher and her monetarist bovver boys piled in, they were simply abandoned.*

Jac's Auntie is not *there to make us forget that raw deal. The poverty, the sickness, the suffering. Far from it. She knew, as well as any miner, that our Annwn, our Hades, was choked with firedamp and its deadly cousins. Blackdamp, whitedamp, stinkdamp, afterdamp. A gassy underworld primed, at any moment, to explode onto the surface of our lives, exactly as it did at the Cambrian Colliery. As tragic (and I remember the man I've called here History's Most Eccentric History Teacher using that very phrase to us in class) were the roof-falls and tramway accidents that widowed one woman at a time. Jac's Auntie and women like her were the ones who held it all together after each small tragedy, as well as after Cambrian and Aberfan and all of the scores of other places in the terrible, terrible roll-call of Welsh mine disasters. She could list them for you. The catalogue would fill page after page after page of this novel. Allow her to mention now just three of them, a Triad from 'the Golden Age of King Coal':*

272 killed at the Prince of Wales Colliery, Abercarn on September 11th, 1878.

290 killed at the Albion Colliery, Cilfynydd on June 25th, 1894.

439 killed at the Universal Colliery, Senghenydd on October 14th, 1913.

Is that enough carnage for you? It's far too much for me. But all those aunties, those mothers, those daughters – they had to look death in the face, over and again, and keep going.

Let's leave it there.

Because there's another side to the Rhondda. And the Great Welsh Auntie in Jac's head, she's the distillation, the expression of that other side. The bizarre, the absurd, the colourful. Everything that lifts life here out of the drab and the grey, the things that sociologists and doctrinaire politicians so often miss. We've begun to see it with her and Tom Jones. There's much more. The carnival of Valleys life. The surreal black comedy of the whole shooting match. Of strong women, as well as Strong Men. Of sopranos and leading ladies, streaky snooker players and dead-eye darters. Of brass bands and jazz bands, drinking songs and harp recitals. Of jokers and dreamers, painters and popstars, budgie breeders and champion-leek growers. Of holy wells and pop factories, steamy Chinese laundries and icy open-air public baths. All of this, and much more, was what life in the Rhondda was made of. Forget any of it, and you diminish it all.

When his Auntie prompts Jac to say ridiculous, inappropriate things or clever-because-they're-silly, diversionary things, she's speaking for a valley that's refused to be cowed by everything that's been done to it. You've heard that she's given to suggesting that the only thing that lasts is permanence, or that Maerdy was called Little Moscow because it's so cold there; but don't dismiss her as stupid. She may be playing with us, teasing, testing us, as she sometimes does with Jac (though she takes his part pretty seriously too). She won't always say what she means, about the Rhondda or anything else. But she knows that the people of her valley are more than mere victims, that they have agency. *She understands, first-hand, that their lives are fuller, more nuanced and layered and rounded than the* clichés *peddled by a right-wing press. But neither, she says, can their stories, their* story, *be summed up by the truisms of some partisan pamphlet left trampled in the mud by the onward march of capitalism. She's a Magical Rhondda-ist. I hope you'll like her for that. I suspect Annie Powell would have. I know I do.*

9

'Jac, behave yourself!'

It was Lydia. *Not* his Auntie. Lydia's voice, out there in the real world, not the one inside his head.

When Jac realised that, he snapped to. He found himself facing forward on the front seat of the top deck of the bus. He must have moved there after they rounded Carter's Corner. But why? Had he been 'driving' the bus? Making *brrwmm brrwmm* noises, imitating the engine and its gear changes? His hands were held out in front of him as though gripping an imaginary steering wheel. Embarrassing.

Deciding you were going *to grow up*, it began to dawn on him, wasn't the same as actually doing it. Still, he'd probably given Petra a laugh. Something to *distract* her from worrying about Martyn. But was distraction always a good thing?

The bus squished to a halt. The downpour hadn't eased. The Gelli passengers waded aboard. One final late-coming young couple leapt onto the lower deck, disappearing towards the back. From the distorted glimpse Jac caught in the conductor's mirror over the stairs, the boy looked like James Taylor. The one from Penmaesglas. But it couldn't be. When the bus had left Pandy Square, Taylor still been loafing outside the Pandy Inn with those Greasers, MauMau and Parrot, Rat and Dodo. Hadn't he?

The Devil moves in mysterious ways, whispered Jac's Auntie darkly.

But how? Had one of the Hell's Angels sped Taylor directly to Gelli on the back of his motorcycle whilst the bus had laboured from stop to stop on the old route up the valley? Had he taken *a run up the New Road faster than light*? A *Tonypandy Ton-Up* would have been far quicker than this interminable time-loop of a journey Jac was trapped in. But why was Taylor boarding the bus here? If he was getting a lift to the party, he could have got the biker to go straight to Treorchy.

Unless he had to pick his date up in Gelli on the way.

So who *was* his mystery companion? The only girl Jac could think of who lived in Gelli was…

Juliette Llewellyn.

It couldn't be her, could it?

Jac's speculation was ended by the exuberance of another newcomer's entry.

"The legendary Penry Cadogan!" shouted Petra in delight, as he danced his way up the stairs, belting out a song for the whole bus to hear.

"When that I was and a little tiny boy," he crooned.

"With hey, ho, the wind and the rain…"

Penry – having assumed, even before the auditions, that the role of Feste was *made* for no-one but himself – had been mastering the songs from *Twelfth Night*. As ever, with an audience to play to, he was acting the showman. He'd sung Eli Jenkins' Prayer the same way when they'd 'read' *Under Milk Wood*, whether so much *gusto* was truly appropriate in that context or not. It certainly wasn't the way Wales' Smallest English Mistress had directed him to do it. But Penry got away with a lot of things with her, ribbing her openly about her name, which in a piece of not-really-very-charged synchronicity was Donna Osmond. Just the one letter different from the teenyboppers' idol. Awkward. If Porth County Grammar was full of pubescent girls who had a crush on her (which was quite likely, now that Jac thought about it) they didn't have *her* name inked inside their satchels. Not quite anyway. But she had charisma all the same. And a talent for finding talent in the most unlikely pupils. She had a wicked temper, too, so Penry's attitude – though she clearly admired him as a performer – was brave if not foolhardy.

And now here he was, serenading a Rhondda bus with a Shakespearean ballad. A shameless show-off, that was Penry. His delivery was always so big, had so much attack in it, that it made you forget he was well under five foot: Wales' Smallest English Mistress's Smallest Pupil (that's why, Jac used to tell him, they always saw eye-to-eye, *ha! ha!*). His flamboyant behaviour was at odds, too, with his dress sense. His clothes made him seem old before his time. Tonight, an ill-cut three-piece suit in an indistinct taupe check. Together with his whiskery sideburns, it made him look Dickensian. He was often mistaken for someone aged and wizened, someone in his thirties – "twice as old as he's", it occurred to Jac now, on the model of "half as old as I'm". That didn't work so well.

The original wasn't particularly witty either, his Auntie told him bluntly.

Penry styled himself a Gelli Nationalist, championing his own patch above all other parts of the Rhondda, indeed the whole world. He was too warm-hearted to be belligerent about it, but something in his attitude (or just his surname?) always put Jac in mind of Cadwgan ap Meurig whose motto was *hog dy fwyell*, 'whet your battleaxe'. Penry lived below the bare hill, Moel Cadwgan, named after the ancient chief, and was given to hinting that those who dwelt beneath it were possessed of sorcery deriving from the Otherworld.

On occasion, Jac wondered if there might not be something in it, the way Penry carried on. He could enchant a full house – on public transport or in a proper performance space, where his grand gestures seemed totally natural. Yet, off-stage, as it were, he made little allowance for what was appropriate to the circumstances and the scale of things. Jac himself could be embarrassing in public – he'd just proved that, it seemed, with his imaginary bus-driving – but there was something... well, *otherworldly* about Penry, as though he really might be away with the fairies.

But here he was, large/small as life, full of the joys of a wet Thursday night; and much to Lydia's discomfort, throwing himself onto her lap as he serenaded her:

"For the rain it raineth every day."

The choice of song surprised Jac: rain was a psychological no-no for Penry. He was obsessed with the annual rainfall figure for Gelli. He'd read somewhere that it was 61 inches. Standing well shorter than this, he was always in fear that one year it might pour down all at once. And maybe tonight was the night!

The Three Tragic Inundations:
Thirdly, Noah's Flood.
Secondly, the Drowning of Capel Celyn.
Above All, the Great Gelli Deluge of 1974.

Pathetic, Jac realised, even as he was thinking it up. Feeble. Unworthy of adding to their collection of New Triads of the Isle of Britain. It was Penry who'd first applied this Ancient Celtic device – mnemonic listings of heroes, significant places and events – to the inconsequentiality of their everyday lives. He'd found in Jac a willing collaborator: it appealed to the Catchphrase Kid. They'd given it a twist by ranking their invented Triads in reverse order, adding an element of dramatic tension to the humdrum. But surely it was time to stop wasting time on them. To tell Penry he'd outgrown them. Though if Jac put it that way, it would only be taken as a snide reference to how short Penry was.

"Jac's been driving the bus for us," Lydia informed Penry, shoving him firmly back onto his feet, with the implication she'd be obliged if they talked rather than sang for the rest of the journey, and at a decent distance. The vehicle moved forward again, without Jac's guidance, towards Ton Pentre. Penry took a proper seat, and Lydia struck up what she clearly hoped would be a *quiet* conversation about the plans for the evening ahead. The Society of Friends was gathering. Nerys would meet them at the party. Martyn too. Since the schools had a day off for the Election, he'd have spent it in his uncle's Bracchi café, polishing up his Italian. Once he joined them at The Beach, the gang would be complete, Catherine aside.

Catherine, Catherine, Catherine.

Jac had still to consider her unexpected appearance in that list of attachments.

Whether...

Now wasn't the time. Too much was going on. Penry's song for one thing. He'd started up again.

"When that I was and a little tiny boy,
A foolish thing was but a toy..."

61

A toy. Had Jac *actually* been pretending to drive the bus? That steering wheel, it was part of him still, Belinda Owen and James Taylor hadn't got rid of it after all. And *was* that Taylor who had just got on the bus? If it was, *who* was the girl? *Was it* Juliette Llewellyn?

Jac's first-ever, only-ever date had been with Juliette. At the Picturedrome, the previous summer. Like most boys of his age, he found the prospect of asking a girl out *excruciating.* It might have been the same whichever girl he'd had on his eye on. But *Juliette Llewellyn*? He knew her too well. They'd grown up together in Sunday School. In fact, he could never remember *not* knowing her. But the night she was baptised – she was barely sixteen – he saw her in a different way.

Every Sunday, all through their early teens, Jac had sat next to Juliette in Bethel, as the evening hymns swelled up from the pews all around them. Jac didn't mind hymn-singing: the natural four-part harmonies and the minor-key tunes themselves were the true folk-music of Wales, he reckoned. But when the preacher rose to deliver the sermon, he knew he had to steel himself. His soul, his dearest essence would be interrogated, battered: he *must* surrender to the Almighty, confess his unrighteousness, and throw himself, all unworthy, on His Mercy at the foot of the Cross. Then, bathed in the blood of Jesus, he would be changed, utterly, in the twinkling of an eye. God would burst into the tabernacle of his soul, the curtain that shielded his innermost longings would be *rent in twain* from top to bottom, the altars of his idolatry overthrown. Nothing would ever be the same again.

The closest he'd come to yielding to this repeated proselytising was when he was much, much younger, no more than eight or nine. Bethel had been hosting a 'Mission', a week of intense gospel services led by a visiting evangelist. After one meeting, Jac's father – himself a lay preacher of some renown up and down the Valley – was counselling fresh converts in the Chapel's clammy under-vestry. Jac had gone down there to wait for him, so that they could walk home together. Several other deacons were paired with penitents who'd 'come forward'; they sat, heads bent together, in fervent prayer. Jac stood patiently alone. And Ernie the Cripple saw his chance. Ernie the Cripple – called that, routinely, even to his face, with no sense of inappropriateness, by everyone. He wore a calliper: childhood polio, or so they said. His head rested at a twisted angle to his body, and he grinned constantly in a strange, toothy manner. But he was full of such zeal for the Lord that he lacked the social restraint that even the most ardent fundamentalists observed. Now, he mistook Jac for a would-be convert anxious to be conducted to the Throne of Grace. It wasn't common for a child so young to be convicted by the Holy Ghost, but it wasn't unknown: anyone who'd reached the age of reason could make a 'Decision'. So before Jac knew it, Ernie had pinned him to a chair, instructing, forcing him to repeat, word for word, a boilerplate prayer in which he surrendered his heart, his whole life, to the Lord.

When they'd finished, Jac saw Ernie open his eyes in rapture. It must have been the first conversion he'd ever effected. Jac was distraught. He'd meant none of it, but he was simply too polite, too much the good, biddable child, to tell Ernie to back off. He walked home with his father, managing to hold himself together. But the moment they reached the house, his heart burst as he told the story. He was terrified that his Dad would declare him 'saved', no matter what. He had spoken the sacred words: nothing could be done about it. Instead, Davy Morgan looked at him tenderly, wisely; and spoke to him as though he was a grown-up: "Remember that story I told you about John Wesley and the Inward Witness? How true Christians *know* the presence of God? God sees into your innermost being, Jac. He's heard your prayer, heard everything you said with Ernie and He knows whether you truly meant it. If His Holy Spirit has come to dwell within you, you will have that assurance. But I have faith that whatever happens, my son, the Lord is at work in your life. His love is seeking to shape you, like the potter working his clay."

Jac went to his bed, imagining his soul as a heavy, soggy mass and the hands of God, the thumbs of God, ready to press down upon him in the night, the instant he fell asleep, eager to mould him, to fashion him into something that he was not. The image, the potential reality, horrified him. He fought against it, obstinate in his wrestling with the angels of the Lord. But fall asleep he did. And the next morning, he woke as himself, shaken but unchanged. The Inward Witness remained silent.

And yet there was no end to it. Every Sunday, through the long years of adolescence, he was confronted with the same binary choice – embrace that *Love Divine, all loves excelling* or else surrender to the lusts of the flesh, to those dripping baptismal-robed bodies who visited his night-time fantasies. But it wasn't simply a reluctance to renounce his natural desires that made him turn his face from the Lord. He remained aghast at the idea of the Living God *entering* him, coming to dwell inside him, rushing into his soul like a mighty wind, beaming His Holy Light into every dark corner. Jac's father would use as an 'Illustration' (as such folksy metaphors in sermons were called in evangelical circles) the cockroach and its love of darkness, its shying away from the light. Such was the sinful nature of humanity, having fallen short of the glory of God. The cockroach. Jac pondered this and was forced to acknowledge its truth. He was 'a good boy', obedient, conscientious; but he knew that he harboured thoughts he'd be mortally ashamed to lay bare before the rest of the congregation. But if that *was* his nature, so be it, he would be faithful to himself. And he cherished even his most ordinary, innocent notions. How could he follow his dreams, his convictions, how could he be who he really was, if suddenly, irrevocably, all of that was wrenched from him, and his very spirit bent to conform with the iron laws of the Almighty?

It was no small stand that he was making. Despite knowing that his father longed for, prayed for his Salvation, Jac persisted in his dogged refusal to submit. And yet, come the next Sunday, he'd have to face it all again. It was a long war. To survive it, he needed to shut God out every time he was forced to that fateful moment of choice. The All-Powerful had only to breach his defences the once. For Jac, the price of damnation was eternal vigilance. But it was some comfort that Juliette, too, remained impervious to the Gospel Call. They never talked about it, but her defiance strengthened his. They sat together, Sabbath after Sabbath, as the cost of their intransigence was spelt out in terrifying detail by preachers less measured than Jac's father. They would be separated forever from their parents. They would burn in the Fires of Hell. And there were *degrees of punishment*: for unrepentant sinners brought up as they'd been in Christian households, sinners who'd had ample, recurrent opportunities to come to the Lord, for them were reserved the most excruciating perpetual agonies of all.

Then, one awful Sunday night, Juliette 'came forward'. She was saved. And, a few weeks later, baptised. Jac got to see her in those dripping white robes, not in his imagination now, but *in the flesh*. She was no longer the friend he'd known since infancy. She was much, much more. Amongst his male friends, in those days of mini-skirts and hot pants, she'd long been known as The Girl With The Best Legs In Sunday School. Jac had been too close to her to think of her like that. Now, the distance she'd put between them by turning to the Lord had, paradoxically, allowed him to see her as lustfully they did. But how did she think of him…?

As a newly baptised Christian, she'd be far more likely to agree to go out with him if he was saved too. 'Be ye not unequally yoked together with unbelievers: for what fellowship hath righteousness with unrighteousness? and what communion hath light with darkness?' Jac, despite his own unbelief, knew the verse by heart. II Corinthians 6: 14. If he gave in to God, he might get the girl. It was tempting… but no, it would be *perverse*. Yet common sense told him he stood little chance on his own merits. By now, though, Jac had something other than common sense to counsel him. He had his Auntie.

That voice inside his head had become useful to him in many ways since he'd first heard it. His Auntie could be wise; she could be foolish. Often, she'd contrive to be both at the same time. She could be shrewd. She could be crude (which, frankly, shocked Jac, who wasn't given to innuendo and profanity). She might be as warm and comforting as a coal fire, sweet as a Welsh cake; she could be a bit of a dragon. She might completely misunderstand the simplest of things. Or cut through to the nub of an issue he was finding difficult to grasp. If Jac was struggling, she might prompt him with answers to questions in class. And throughout his first years in Grammar School, Jac's academic performance went from strength to strength. 'Shows strong aptitude for Arts subjects,' read his Reports. 'However, Mathematics and Chemistry need more attention.' Yes, his Auntie certainly had her blind spots.

And, yes, it was his Auntie who coached him in how to approach Juliette Llewellyn for a date. She gave him the words he needed, when he'd deliberately fallen into step with Juliette after chapel the Sunday following her Baptism – though his mouth went dry and his mind screamed that he should back away and forget the whole thing. Thanks to his Auntie, he'd persisted. There was a secret to these things, it turned out: to pretend, even as you put the question, that the answer didn't matter. And that it wasn't your idea anyway.

Someone asked me the other day if I'd ever thought about asking you out…

So Juliette said yes. And he got to take her to the pictures that Wednesday. To hold hands, put his arm around her, even to kiss her, briefly, at the end of her street as he walked her home. It became known at school that he'd been out with *The Girl With….* For the rest of the week, despite his Auntie's strictures *not* to let it go to his head, he walked a few inches taller. But then – and it was his Auntie who was responsible – it blew apart, spectacularly. So spectacularly that one that no-one present ever spoke about it again.

It happened at the Young People's Fellowship, which met on Friday evenings in that damp Vestry where Ernie the Cripple had ambushed Jac years before. The atmosphere was more relaxed than a Sunday service, but serious nevertheless. There were quizzes – Bible quizzes – and singalong 'choruses', rather than hymns. The centrepiece was Bible Study, discussion of a few verses to which regulars were expected to contribute. Juliette and Jac had been attending for a year or so; now here they were together after their first date. Jac planned to ask her that night for another.

But someone else came to Bethel that night, a newcomer so unexpected that Jac couldn't believe his eyes when he walked in. James Taylor. At school, Taylor had turned into a teacher-pleaser, but the dark side of his personality hadn't gone away. Between lessons, he became a thug, bullying weaker boys with a degree of sophisticated brutality unrivalled in the whole school. So he'd acquired a nickname: *Swotzi*. As in half *swot*, half *Nazi*. Here in the Vestry, though, he was welcomed warmly, as all potential converts were. But James Taylor, a repentant sinner? Jac wasn't fooled. This was no Lost Sheep returning to the fold. Wolf In Sheep's Clothing, more like. Jac suspected he'd come along because he'd heard who Juliette was going out with. He'd made up his mind that a girl like her could do better. He was going to step in and pluck her from Jac's grasp.

Indeed, as the Young People broke into groups to discuss that week's text, Swotzi rushed to sit himself next to Juliette. But Jac got there first, sliding in next to her. His rival had no choice but to take the chair next to him. So then it started. Under the table, Swotzi began a surreptitious but vicious assault on Jac's leg. Prodding. Pinching. Punching. He picked up a biro and pushed the hard plastic forcefully into Jac's thigh, until Jac could feel his bruised flesh tearing under his trousers. Jac knew that all he had to do to make it stop was to admit defeat, to give up and get up, and let his adversary move next to Juliette. He flinched. He felt hot and sick. But he was determined not to yield. No-one in charge – a handful of young-ish Christian adults and two older Deacons – seemed to notice. They were focused on Higher Things. But, here below, there was no let-up. Jac felt himself getting angry, and angrier. It didn't help that the verses for study were about turning the other cheek.

"Then came Peter to him," Juliette was reading out loud, from her small black King James Version, "and said, Lord, how oft shall my brother sin against me, and I forgive him? till seven times?"

His temples throbbing, Jac could scarcely hear her read on. But he knew his Bible well enough to remember Jesus's response: 'I say not unto thee, until seven times: but, until seventy times seven'.

Beneath the table, out of sight, the stabbing continued. After each thrust, Jac thought he might endure the next by counting it off against a running tally. Could he get to seventy times seven? But now Jac was aware of a different voice. His Auntie's voice. His focus shifted from the pain James Taylor was inflicting to the message from within.

Jac, you shouldn't let anyone bully you like that.

For once, it was the male element, the one uncle amongst those fifty-one aunts, that was to the fore…

Why don't you just tell Swotzi to fuck off?

Jac knew the F-word. He'd spoken it himself; but no more than three or four times in his entire life. Certainly never in circumstances like these. Now, though, he turned boldly to Taylor, fixing him with what he hoped was a gimlet stare.

"James…" Jac began, loud enough for everyone in the Vestry to hear, and with an edge born of years of hurt, of all the humiliations that Taylor had ever visited upon him, as much as of the physical pain of the last five minutes: "…FUCK OFF."

There was a sudden silence, all over the Vestry. A silence that began instantly and rolled on into Eternity. Juliette blushed furiously. It went without saying that *that* word had never been uttered in Bethel before. The House of the Lord had been desecrated, besmirched with the most foul language. And He was a Righteous God, a God whose sinless perfection could not abide profanity. Punishment would be swift. And just. Surely, the perpetrator would be struck down. If not by God Himself, then by the Deacons. They would be righteously angry. The sinner who'd voiced this vile word would be cast out. That it was the son of Davy Morgan the Scripture Teacher, made it much, much worse: seventy times seven worse.

It was so monstrously egregious, so appallingly wicked, that those grown-ups with authority who'd heard it, those upright servants of the Lord – and half-a-dozen of them could have cast the first stone at Jac from where they sat – all came instantly to a common mind, without having to confer by any audible means. There was but one way in which this outrage could be dealt with. That way was final, complete and irreversible. *They would ignore it.*

It had never happened. It was simply too offensive, too outrageous a fall from grace to be acknowledged. So the silence persisted for another beat or two, long enough for Jac to exhale. And then everyone expunged from their minds the evidence of their own ears, and the respectful mumble of Bible-focused conversation started up again.

James Taylor was so completely taken aback that he could do nothing. Was this how Chapel went? He remained frozen where he sat, until attention had shifted back to the discussion they'd been engaged in. Then, as quietly, as casually as he could, picking up his coat in one hand, he tiptoed away, as though answering a call of nature, slipping out through the Vestry door never to darken it again.

As for Jac's Auntie, that would be the last time she'd urge him to swear. Once was enough. Enough to get James Taylor off his back for a good while. Enough, too, to destroy any prospect of a second date with Juliette Llewellyn. That was the end of that. Jac was sad. Though not devastated, as he thought he might be. It was always unlikely that the first girl he dated would be the last. He wasn't even *that* annoyed with his Auntie. As she reminded him, in her vulgar way, but in the smooth blend of fifty-one-women's-voices-and-a-single-man's, it was all down to her that he'd got to walk out – if only once – with The Best Legs In Sunday School.

10

Fifty-one aunties? Is that plausible? So many?

You can tell by my editor's questions that she wasn't reared in the Rhondda, or anywhere like it (I'm told Mumbai is just like Tonypandy; in terms of aunties, at least).

I can assure her that fifty-one was nothing out of the ordinary. Of course, like 'Jac', I'm not using the strict definition of an aunt. I'm talking about women I called *'Auntie…'*

In my generation, such 'aunties' featured large in Rhondda life – minding us children, treating us, praising us, putting us in our place sometimes. Spoiling or scolding, they had influence, *much more so than our uncles. But – whilst they came broadly from the same generation and class – they were* diverse *in character and attitude. So, to give you – and my editor – a better idea of the complexities that might underlie that singular voice in Jac's head, it's occurred to me that I could compile pen-pictures of some of my own aunties. "Go ahead," says my editor. "Go right ahead. List fifty-one of them if you want. It's not like you've got any sort of narrative progression to interrupt."*

Is she serious?

Fifty-one?

I could name a dozen more. It would be pappish.

But I'll stick to her suggestion. Fifty-one. Like Jac. Read into that whatever you like. I'm hinting at nothing. Jac is a fictional character. I most certainly am not.

Anyway, here goes…

Auntie Marion was my one true aunt by blood: my father's only sister, two years younger than him, nothing like as religious, just as shrewd. As befits the primacy of our relationship, she was always my favourite auntie. She was married to Uncle Rees, a Penygraig man she'd met when he was home on leave from the Navy, and she was not yet quite sixteen. In the middle of the VE night celebrations, out of the thousands of revellers thronging Tonypandy Square (where else?), it was their eyes that locked – and, scandalously, *she didn't come home until three in the morning. They wed soon after, moving in with my paternal grandparents in Holborn*

Terrace, a stone's throw from the house where I grew up (almost literally a stone's throw – many a time, we Penygraig boys sent projectiles hurtling towards our adversaries from 'Pandy across the Incline that divided us). My grandmother – Marion's mother – spoiled me rotten (yes, "my buttercup", "worth all the tea in China" etc). Auntie Marion never took it to that pitch, but I always knew she was on my side.

Auntie Bet was technically a great-aunt, my paternal grandfather's sister, so Auntie Marion's auntie. She wore a wig, and seemed ancient, though she wasn't yet sixty when I was a boy. She lived on Court Street, the hill up to Clydach, with her husband, Uncle Niff (properly 'Nephi', a good old-fashioned Biblical name) who'd lost three fingers in a runaway accident on the 'spake', the underground train that brought miners to the coal-face. Bet and Niff had a quarrelsome relationship. They'd go weeks without speaking to each other, withdrawing to separate rooms, communicating only via their budgie. Honestly. If they really needed to let their spouse know something, they told the budgie, loudly.

Then there was Auntie Pam who lived in Balaclava. Not the site of the battle in the Crimean War, but the ramshackle terrace of houses in Penygraig which were no grander than slums. She was something like a 'second cousin, once removed' to me. Anyway, in short order, she removed herself and her family from the Rhondda, emigrating to Australia. She sent back a photo of her gorgeous new house with picket fence and garden bathed in sunshine, her children paddling in a pool outside. Balaclava Row was condemned and knocked down shortly afterwards, coincidentally no doubt.

But look, I'll have to be more succinct, because I've named just three aunties so far, and my editor will be changing her mind or telling me she was just being sarcastic and getting me to cut this whole chapter unless I'm careful.

Uncle Rees's sisters, Auntie Vi and Auntie Winnie, were smokers who drank in clubs (imagine!). I saw little of them, though they always gave me selection boxes at Christmas. Auntie Joyce was a bosom-friend of Auntie Marion and had been since they were nine. Auntie Caryl was, like me, a regular at Sunday tea in Holborn Terrace, though what she was doing there and how she fitted into the family, I never really grasped. She was by far the youngest auntie of all, barely out of her teens and done up like a 1960s dyed-blonde dolly bird, false eyelashes, mini-skirt and all. She would have been of the moment in Soho, but was well ahead of her time in Tonypandy; though

71

that can't have been the reason that she'd graduated at so tender an age to the status of auntie. Who knows! Maybe it was to discourage me from having licentious ideas about her. As if.

That's seven aunties. On my mother's side of the family, Auntie Cassie and Auntie Ceinwen played a large part in my upbringing, though they were dead. Aunts of my grandfather, their stiff photographic portraits hung above the mantelpiece, next to a large white plate commemorating the Christian witness of Dr Spurgeon. Long deceased, the great-great-aunts gazed down in puritanical judgement on us sinners. To this day, I fear that they'll suddenly appear in the flesh to chastise me for the slightest impure thought or self-indulgence.

Auntie Tillie, married to Mam's brother Robert, was very different. Quite sophisticated for our family. She smoked long cigarettes, and dressed in elegant style, certainly compared with my mother. Auntie Tillie's sisters, Auntie Gladys and Auntie Nancy worked in Marks and Spencer's in Pontypridd, which, come to think of it, was probably where Auntie Tillie got her fancy clothes from. Twelve aunties so far.

My mother's other brother, Len, wasn't married, so no aunties there. I mention him because if there's a model for the single male contributor to the voice in Jac's head, alongside those fifty-one aunties, Len was the Uncle who'd have told 'Swotzi' where to go so emphatically. One of the most contrary, cantankerous, cussed customers you could meet, Len loved arguing. Rugby, politics, religion, the weight of the moon – the subject didn't matter. Once he'd started an argument, his only aim was to keep it going. Just as the steam was going out of the dispute, he'd change his opinion, adopting the reverse of the position he'd begun with, which confused and frustrated everyone involved, and started the whole thing off again.

Mam and Len and Robert had Welsh-speaking relatives in Treorchy, Auntie Lizzie and her daughters, Auntie Non and Auntie Lillian. (There's a great Welsh word for Auntie: 'Bopa'. To me it suggests weight and clout. It was used widely in the Valleys. But in my family, even if they spoke Welsh, Aunties were just called 'Auntie' – though Lizzie signed her Christmas cards with the phonetic Welsh spelling: 'Anti'.)

Closer to home, Auntie Sis and Auntie Bess lived with Uncle Emlyn in the most spartan of houses on Hill Street, the steepest slope in Penygraig. Every week I had to struggle up it to deliver a dozen eggs to them. Emlyn *was a gentle giant who shuffled along arthritically, his large bald head disfigured by a form of elephantiasis. I was never sure which of the two aunties he was married to, and whose sister the other woman was – his or his wife's. No money changed hands for the eggs, and though my aunties took a kindly interest in me, there was never even a thrupenny bit to spare me for sweets.*

Auntie Annie, auntie number 18, was a Cardi who served the people of Tonyrefail for decades as a district nurse, sharing her house with her brother and his wife, Auntie Margaret. Her sister, Auntie Megan still lived near Cardigan; and her cousin, Auntie Siriol kept a smallholding above St Dogmaels. I was sent there for summer holidays, a magical idyll for a boy from urban Rhondda, though Auntie Siriol spent most of the time talking in Welsh with two visiting relatives, Auntie Non and Auntie Ann, Pencwm. Auntie Siriol had three children. A year older than me, golden-haired Heulwen was the sunshine of my life when I was 10. If heaven was real, and you were allowed to design your own, and The Society of Friends weren't available, mine would be on Llwyndafydd Farm. I'd fall asleep every night with Heulwen, Joy and David, under the roof of Auntie Siriol's barn, up on top of the hay bales, wrapped in Welsh blankets, after a hot summer's day spent swimming at Poppit Sands.

Twenty-three aunts so far.

My maternal grandfather had three nieces by marriage. Auntie Winnie had gone into 'service', doing domestic chores for a pittance in posh people's houses in London. She settled there, so she and her daughters, Auntie Grace and Auntie Gwen seemed quite posh themselves to me. Not as posh as Auntie Gertie, who'd married a businessman and moved to Penarth! The third niece, Auntie Flossie, wasn't posh at all. A delightful dwt *of a woman, like a little bird, she lived in a tiny house in Penrhiwfer and worked in a clothes shop for 'the mature lady' on Hannah Street, Porth owned by Auntie Doris; and* her *sister Auntie Amy was (who knows how or why!) the Archivist at the Brontë Parsonage in Haworth. She showed me and my parents around the museum when we visited Yorkshire just before my A levels.* Wuthering Heights *was a set text: it was a shame I didn't have Auntie Amy's voice in* my *head come exam time.*

I'm up to 30 aunties.

Auntie Marian – with an 'a' not an 'o' – worked in Shirley's cake-shop on Dunraven Street in 'Pandy; and what were aunties for, if not for slipping sly treats to growing boys? Her sister, Auntie Florrie, from Trealaw, had a son with long hair and a Gold Flash motorbike (enough said – until later).

Auntie Edie and Auntie Beattie, numbers 33 and 34, kept a boarding house in Weston-super-Mare, where we went for holidays at Whitsun, when Whitsun was still a thing. Edie was stick-thin, dark in complexion; Beattie white-skinned, talcum-powdered and plump. On arrival, I'd be expected to give them a small-boy's kiss. I could just about bring myself to embrace Auntie Edie, but ach-y-fi, *Beattie's corpulence was too much, even though these aunties reminded me of two fancy biscuits – a dark-chocolate finger, and a round one covered in white chocolate.*

Auntie Katie, Auntie Kath, and Auntie Charlotte taught us in Sunday School, all about Noah and his Ark, and David and Goliath, and Jesus who wanted me for a Sunbeam, so I had to shine out, sh-sh-sh-shine for Him. That's 37 aunties. Also in chapel, Mam's Sisterhood friends: Auntie Mair, and three *more Auntie Margarets (my mother was a Margaret too: why was the name so popular in the 1920s?). Amongst the Deacons' wives, Auntie Nansi, Auntie Gwladys and Auntie Phyllis – numbers 42 to 44 – all wore hats, but so did Mrs Edmunds and Mrs Lewis, who were never called Auntie, for some unknown reason.*

A similar impenetrable logic applied to our neighbours on Tylacelyn Road. Next door down lived Mrs Morgan, *but next-door-but-one was* Auntie Elsie. And up the street were Auntie Barbara *and* Auntie Muriel; *but right next door was* Mrs Fry.

Four aunties to go! The last house in the terrace, next to the gwli, *belonged to Auntie Polly, who was housebound and 'needed company', so I'd be sent to visit her. She was scarily witch-like, a dark shawl wrapped around her head, a web of long white hairs sprouting from her chin. The house stank of damp and old age. In my dim memories, a cage hung high over the fireplace in her back-kitchen; a cage occupied by a terrifying, squawking parrot which gave off a whiff all of its own. But perhaps I'm getting confused by Auntie Polly's name.*

So finally, a Triad of unmarried aunties who lived in Brithweunydd Road in a kind of under-house which fascinated a small boy like me. Auntie Flo used to come to Tylacelyn Road to 'do' for my mother, who sometimes found domestic chores too much. Flo spoke with a West Country burr, and drank coffee, *though that was the only sign of urbanity about her. On Sunday mornings, she'd march up Tylacelyn in full quasi-military uniform, bonnet and all, towards the Salvation Army Hall. She lived with her sisters, Auntie Ada, and a third sister, my fifty-first auntie; but after all these years – though, as I told my editor, I could name plenty more –* her *name stubbornly refuses to come to mind. It's a pity, because as far as I know, the sisters have no living relatives now; perhaps it's only me in the whole wide world who remembers them. So I lay a wreath, now, figuratively, at her grave, to honour all such women who've passed from memory. At the tomb, as it were, of The Unknown Auntie.*

11

At long last, some narrative progression. The bus was arriving in Treorchy. It was behind schedule, Jac noted disapprovingly (those rainy roads, more like canals, *were* 'awful slow'). They'd passed St Peter's clock-tower in Pentre eleven minutes late, on the stroke of eight.

'Who,' asked the chimes, 'made the mine owner?' Jac couldn't help hearing them through the filter of Idris Davies's *Bells of Rhymney*. His Auntie couldn't help herself either. She reminded Jac that the poem had been turned into a hit by *Peter Seeger and his Birds*. Ever since the Tom Jones incident, she'd delighted in bigging up the Welsh contribution to popular music.

The party-goers stepped off the bus, scurrying along Treorchy's High Street two-by-two.

Like animals washed up on the heights of Ararat. You've survived the Flood, and now...

That's enough, Auntie!

Twenty yards ahead, Jac spotted James Taylor. So it *was* Swotzi who'd boarded the bus in Gelli. By his side, a girl. Jac tried hard not to identify her by any particular part of her body, but there was no doubt who it was. The randy Romeo had finally got his Juliette. After all that Jac had gone through, to try to keep them apart. But Jac realised now that he wasn't jealous, though he was disappointed in *her*. Dating a reprobate like him was contrary to God's Law. II Corinthians 6: 14 again. But maybe Juliette had only agreed so she could evangelise him. Taylor's hopes of getting to know her in the Biblical sense might end only in him getting a dose of Scripture. *Amen* to that.

The teenage crocodile turned left, heading for The Beach. The dilapidated party venue had an official name, the Treorchy and District Workingmen's Social Labour Constitutional Club & Institute (or some permutation of those words). But Jac had only ever heard it called The Beach. It stood at the end of this terraced side-street, right next to a body of water: the River Rhondda. After tonight's rain, the river was a seething, raging torrent; but this close to its source at the head of the *cwm*, a torrent less than five yards wide. The Beach. Typical Valleys snark in that nickname. The Copacabana it was not.

Petra shook the rain off her *rose-red* coat. They made their way inside. An attempt had been made to make the lounge look festive. Revolving coloured beams of disco lights illuminated a gaudy banner extending eighteenth birthday wishes to 'Ninelives' Bowen. Hung skewwhiff from the ceiling, it looked drunk already. A scuffed row of tables, with a paper tablecloth that stretched *most* of the way along them, displayed a classic Rhondda party buffet: sausage rolls, pasties, cheddar-and-pineapple skewers, pickled onions, hula-hoops. Little of it would be eaten. The focus, for everyone apart from teetotaller Jac, would be firmly on the bar.

Swotzi was introducing Juliette – she went to school in Pentre, not with them in Porth – to a group of classmates already well into their first drinks. Jac saw Martyn in the far corner, talking to Nerys. An odd contrast: Martyn Rees, fashionably groomed, always aware of the impact his appearance made; Nerys Lewis-Morris shapeless and scruffy in a beige trouser-suit even here at a party, and seeming not to care. She had a big round face, her left cheek marked by a large mole. A skin-blemish, not a sea-wall. The triple rhyme of her name – her mother had married a Mr Lewis-Morris second time around – was by far the most exotic thing about her. Jac sometimes wondered, when he saw her and Martyn together, what they had in common. Nerys was a fine singer, and she could be sharp and quite political, but she never struck Jac as having the kind of questioning, speculative mind that would hold Martyn's interest for long.

Martyn stood to greet them. He wore his straight, glossy, jet-black hair down to his collar. The dim lighting emphasised how naturally olive-skinned he was. You'd have guessed that his uncle kept a Bracchi's. But then that was nonsense, Jac reminded himself: Martyn had no Italian blood. It was his auntie, his mother's sister Eve, who'd married into the café culture of the immigrants from Bardi. The Rees DNA was pure Welsh. Martyn might even admit it, if pushed. Once the Italian connection had come to mind, though, it all seemed of a piece: Martyn's love of opera and wine, his clothes, the way he brandished his cigarettes. The *costume* he was wearing now – Jac thought of it with precisely that word – paid homage to Italian refinement, albeit via America. The flared pinstripe suit was bang on trend for 1974, but like his two-tone brogues, it was channelling the Prohibition Era mafia chic of Scott Fitzgerald's novels. No wonder Jac called him *The Great Martsby*.

Martyn was a self-made man, like Jay Gatsby. Nothing in his family background pushed him towards High Culture and High Style. He put Jac in mind of another great: Richard Burton. Even in that modest reading of *Under Milk Wood* they'd staged before Christmas, there were echoes in Martyn's performance of Burton's triumphant radio version. Burton's father, like Martyn's, was a scraggy collier with little education and no hint of leading-man good looks. Burton had catapulted himself from a struggling family of thirteen in a Welsh mining village to global stardom and the arms of the world's most desired woman. Martyn's trajectory might be every bit as stellar. He could be charmingly attentive to his friends, sensitive to their sensibilities, but it didn't take much imagination to see him soaring far beyond their orbit. He spoke with a slight softening of his 'r's, but his voice, his good looks, his *presence*, would grace the Stratford stage or the West End. Possessing *the gift* came at a price, though. Jac sensed that Martyn was always *self*-dramatising – not just on stage but every moment of his life. And it was different from Penry's play-acting, which was all bluster. Martyn played 'Martyn' subtly, with depth and complexity.

As he crossed the dancefloor towards him, Jac remembered the first proper conversation they'd ever had, after one of the rehearsals for the Dylan Thomas reading. There'd been a wildcat strike at the Porth Depot, so the two of them set off to walk the length of Trealaw together hoping that Martyn would find the buses home to Treorchy running from Tonypandy Square. Plenty of time to talk, then. Jac had just seen the film version of *Under Milk Wood*, the one with Burton and Taylor, and every Welsh actor under the sun (and the rain). He was patriotically positive about it.

Martyn thought it was execrable.

"I know Captain Cat *is* blind, but boy, is he blind in that film! The makeup's way over the top. It adds nothing. And the performances are no better. *Milk Wood* is *A Play for Voices*, Jac. It just doesn't work as cinema. The pictures will always be better in radio."

"But it's *ours*, Martyn. Welsh talent on the big screen for once, saying something about Wales? It's who we are."

"It's not who I am, Jac. And whoever you are, you've got to be able to criticise your own culture."

Jac resented being characterised as a narrow-minded Welsh Nat. He started to enthuse about other movies, British and American, middle-brow Peter Sellars comedies, *Dr Strangelove, I'm Alright Jack, What's New Pussycat?* Good popular entertainment, he said, proud that his tastes were humble. He was chancing his arm. Cinema had always been regarded at home as The Devil's Work, along with gambling, alcohol and Sunday newspapers. The movies Jac got to see were subject to strict puritanical censorship. Martyn had seen a hell of a lot more, and not just the Hollywood classics. Without patronising him (almost), he gave Jac a teach-in as they walked on – about the *Nouvelle Vague*, Godard and Truffaut.

By the time they got to Maes-yr-Haf, they both needed a change of subject. Jac expressed admiration for the social work the Quakers did there during the Depression. But that only set them arguing about the Rhondda now. For Jac, its trade union traditions remained potent. That's why they were having to make this journey on foot! Circumstances might have changed, but Rhondda people's convictions hadn't. Martyn told him that that was the problem. *His* Rhondda had been left behind by *avant garde* cinema, by existentialism, by the rise of material wealth.

79

"No one looks to us now for a lead in any kind of struggle, Jac. Open your eyes – it's all around you: a culture that's ossified. I'm not saying I blame people here. God knows poverty and neglect takes its toll. But they've put up the barricades and retreated behind them. This place pioneered radical working-class thinking? Well, it's too scared to think now. Scared of the new, scared of the truly nonconformist. Intolerant of deviance. A mean place, full of neuroses. I see it in my own father. Impotent people, *worrying the carcase of an old song*. Look…"

They had turned a corner. Martyn pointed up at Judge's Hall. They both knew its history: opened just before the Riots, it was a place of entertainment, yes; but it had always been a forum, too, for politics, for oratory, for eloquence. *The Miners Next Step* had been debated there. Now, it was adorned with a neon sign consisting of five capital letters: BINGO.

"That's your Valley for you now, Jac: playing *housey housey* whilst the world turns. And hugging its bad luck to itself tighter and tighter. Before long, it'll choke itself to death on its own despair. God knows, I wish my old man would."

The personal *animus* shocked Jac. But he too had skin in the game. His cherishing of the Rhondda came from down in the depths of his being. The Valley, he insisted, was still fighting for justice. He was thinking of the rally he'd witnessed at Judge's, after that protest march from Llwynypia hospital: though it seemed too flimsy an example to specify.

They parted that day on bad terms. But rehearsals threw them back into each other's company, like it or not. Jac saw that he'd earned some respect in Martyn's eyes, even if it was mixed with pity for how *gauche* he was. He'd stuck to his guns. Martyn had the better arguments, and more evidence to bring to them, but even he had to admit that he'd gone too far. There was merit on both sides of the case. In the end – Jac's History lessons' lesson – it all comes down to what you believe.

So the quarrel gave them a bridge into friendship, though it was hardly a rapport of equals. Martyn educated Jac's taste in rock music (as he seemed to have done with Petra), though opera and classical remained a step too far. Even when they shared enthusiasms, Jac's judgements always seemed shallower, more conservative. Jac was affronted that Bowie had killed off Ziggy Stardust; Martyn delighted in the star's willingness to reinvent himself. And whilst both of them could quote chunks of 'Tintern Abbey', Jac was drawn to Wordsworth's salute to *little, nameless, unremembered acts Of kindness and of love*. It was Martyn who exalted in *a sense sublime Of something far more deeply interfused*.

Jac found safer ground in their scorn for the school's Rugby Boys. The entire team, Ninelives Bowen apart, were 'Scientists', inheritors of the Boys' School tradition of sporting thuggery coupled with outstanding results in Maths, Physics, Chem and Biol – but, according to Martyn, that was only because these were subjects where you could score 100% in an exam, where you were either right or wrong, where you just memorised stuff, where creativity, judgement and critical thinking weren't needed. "There's more culture in one of their Petri dishes than in the whole lot of them," he said. Though not to their faces.

Jac had nothing against rugby *per se*. He didn't, of course, play himself, but he delighted in the 'Golden Era' that Wales were enjoying. He tried to draw Martyn into the aesthetics of the game. Penygraig had a new outside-half – barely out of school and rejoicing in the name Meurig Montague – who had the balance and elegance of a young Barry John, and his cute looks too, apparently. Martyn got *mildly* interested at that point (it must have been Meurig's name that intrigued him, because Martyn didn't seem to know who Barry John was, or what made him special). So Jac found himself telling Martyn about the time he'd overheard Ninelives Bowen discussing Welsh team selection with the school rugby captain Blindside Pugh (woe betide any opponent fixed by *his* murderous stare, the Black Spot).

"I'll tell you who they should 'ave. That Swansea flanker. Trevor Evans."

"Never. Trevor Evans?"

"Trevor Evans."

"Trevor Evans? Never. Never ever. Trevor Evans?"

81

"Trevor Evans! Aye. Why not? Who would you 'ave then?"

"I dunno, do I? But... Never ever Trevor Evans."

Never ever Trevor Evans. It was a slender thing, not even a pun, just a double-triple rhyme (and a half). But somehow it became important: an in-joke, shorthand for inane punditry and pointless speculation. Something Martyn and Jac jumped in to recite every time the words 'ever' or 'never' crept up in conversation. The Prince of Repetition loved the routine, never – *never ever* – missing a chance to use it. Martyn played up to it, too, deliberately exaggerating his lisp, saying something like *Newuh ewuh Twewuh Ewans.* The self-mockery was endearing. For Jac, it cemented the bond between them.

And now, here at the Beach, as Martyn hugged him in greeting, Jac responded with a warmth of genuine admiration, as well as a sliver of envy. For Martyn turned immediately to Petra, slid an arm around her back, ushered her into a graceful *pirouette* – showing off to everyone her crimson dress – drew her in, kissed her forehead, and guided her with a flourish to the seat next to him. It was utterly outrageous *and* impeccably well-judged. No-one but Martyn could have pulled it off. If personality, as Scott Fitzgerald insisted, was an unbroken series of perfect gestures, then Martyn, like Gatsby, had something gorgeous about him.

But as everyone sat down, Jac sensed that Martyn's theatrical welcome for Petra was just that – an act. Underneath the grand performance, something dark *was* going on. Jac had been right to fear it earlier, right to intuit that Petra feared it too. Was it an overspill from whatever Martyn had been talking to Nerys about? Or a deeper-seated *malaise*?

Martyn – Jac realised now – had been drinking before they'd all arrived. Was it going to be one of *those* nights? Jac hated Martyn's depressions. The expansive possibilities he'd harboured for the evening shrank.

Penry had already abandoned them to play up to some Fifth Form girls across the room. Jac saw him head over to the DJ and put in a request. No doubt that would raise a laugh when it came on later – Penry was always asking for spoof dedications – but Jac wasn't in the mood anymore. Suddenly, though, Martyn was all cheer again.

"Whose round is it?" he asked, pointedly in Jac's direction.

"Mine again," agreed Jac, glad to get away to the bar.

He took their orders – another vodka for Martyn, a double; brandy-and-babycham for Petra and Lydia; a pint of Allbright for Nerys. Loosehead Jones and Tighthead Jones, the school team's props, were *um...* propping up the bar. Their hooker Blinginate Jenkins, who'd come close to a schoolboy cap for Wales, but had turned up at the Final Trial drunk, was already sloshed. Blinginate (as in 'I blinking hate...' compressed in the strongest Rhondda Fach accent) only ever spoke to express his dislike of whatever was under discussion: *Blinginate 'omework, Blinginate pouffters, Blinginate sobriety.* Drink had silenced completely him now though, – unlike Ninelives Bowen, who bawled "Jac! The WelshMadWordMadManiac!" straight into Jac's face.

Ninelives? He had a shock of red hair and a temper on the field of play to match the *cliché.* By the time he was fifteen, he'd been banned *sine die* by the Welsh Schools Rugby Union, the Rhondda Boys' Clubs Football League, Glamorgan Youth Basketball, the Welsh Athletics Association and the South Wales Chess Union. Somehow, he was still taking an active part in everything apart from chess. So he was on his second lives in four sports, and had lost a less-than-promising chess career too. Count 'em up: '*Ninelives*'.

Strangely, despite his near-homicidal sporting tendencies, he was characteristically amiable off the pitch; though no-one with any sense would entirely trust his moods.

"Come to get the round in, almost like a real man, eh Jac? What's it to be, one of those head-banging coca-colas? One day, you'll grow up."

Had he intuited something about Jac's vow? Jac decided that was out of the question.

"Yeah, perhaps I will someday, Ninelives. But you – you'll *always* be thick."

83

It could have gone either way. But Ninelives broke into a goofy smile.

"Jac the Lad," he said, clapping him on the back. "Always good for a laugh. The Catchphrase King."

The Catchphrase *Kid*, and the *Prince* of Repetition; but it wasn't the moment to berate Ninelives for getting his regalities in a twist. Jac had pushed his luck far enough already.

No one was dancing yet. The DJ, getting anxious, switched from the Heavy Psych of local band Ancient Grease to the other end of the spectrum. *You've Got A Friend*. The James Taylor version. His namesake was still showing off Juliette to his friends.

Back at the table, Jac found Martyn on own. The girls had left for the toilets. *En masse*. Jac thought about saying so. He rehearsed the phrase quickly in his mind: "The girls have gone to the toilet, then. *En masse*." Although he'd dropped French early on, Jac had a *penchant* for working little phrases *en Français* into his sentences. Martyn, who – like Gatsby (again) – was an Oxford man, or soon would be, with a scholarship in Modern Languages to take up after A levels that summer, hardly ever dignified Jac's efforts with a reaction. And since Martyn had been sitting right there when they'd got up and left, telling him that the girls were gone was a little *too* self-evident, even for Jac, whose stock-in-trade was retailing the obvious. Instead, he decided to talk about his *bon mot* at the bar.

"I came up with this *bon mot* at the bar."

Jac wasn't totally sure how to pronounce *bon mot*, but Martyn didn't seem to jib, so Jac carried on with his anecdote. The *One day you'll grow up/You'll always be thick* thing worked well, Jac thought, even the second time around.

"That could have gone either way with Ninelives," said Martyn. "And you, of all people – you should be ashamed."

"Ashamed?"

"Yes, mightily ashamed. You stole that gag off your *bête noire*."

It was clear that Jac was failing to follow – on at least two counts. Martyn decided to help him out.

"Churchill."

"I stole the gag off Winston Churchill?"

"Correct. The epithets were 'sober' and 'ugly' the way he told it, but the same difference."

Martyn's explanation meant nothing to Jac. He cast around for something to say. James Taylor – the American one – was still crooning pledges of *amitié*.

"Ah, well... there's a *charged synchronicity* about the place tonight."

And now Martyn did roll his eyes.

But Jac didn't pay much attention to that.

Because just then, at the doorway, quite simply, was Catherine.

12

Catherine Evans. Always 'Catherine', never Cathy, Cat, Katie or any other cute diminutive. She wasn't that kind of girl, Catherine Evans from Gilfach Goch.

She shouldn't have been at their school at all. Her parents had moved over the mountain from the Rhondda proper, out of its catchment area, the year after she'd passed the Eleven Plus. They'd left the 'Concretes' in Dinas, Rhondda's oldest houses, which were being demolished as slums, for a council house in Gilfach. Was that going up in the world? It wasn't anything special, for sure; but Jac sometimes reckoned *that* was what made it special, what made her special.

They hadn't long moved – Catherine was thirteen – when her mother died. The following year, her father re-married. That was how Daniel, her step-brother, had come into her life. Probably because of her mother's death, she'd been allowed to keep her place at school, or Jac and she would never have met. Though in that Alternative Universe, his Dad would have taught her in Tonyrefail Grammar. *But anyway…*

Catherine's reputation as one of the Bad Girls of the B Form was cemented the night she finished with Gerwyn Evans, a handsome, shiny-haired, slightly posh boy from a slightly posh bit of Porth. Two years ahead of them in school, he'd been 'courting' Catherine for a whole term: Evans & Evans were an item. Gerwyn rated himself as a ladies' man: he just didn't see his comeuppance coming up. Or falling down, in fact. Spurning a date with Catherine one night, he'd gone drinking in the Naval on Pandy Square with a girl his own age. Catherine got to hear of it and rushed there to have it out with him. The steward, spotting trouble, refused to let her in on the grounds that she wasn't even sixteen (she wasn't, then, but when had that ever been a problem?). So she climbed in through a window which gave onto the basement cloakroom. Squeezing through the opening, she lost her grip and tumbled inside. Her fall was broken by the coat-rack below – the belt of her coat got tangled up in the pegs. She hung there, upside down, a yard off the ground, screaming. Her voice carried to the bar. The steward rushed down to discover the cause of the disturbance. Gerwyn and his drinking partner, recognising her voice, were hot on his heels. Catherine made it crystal clear to them all that she'd broken in solely to speak her mind to her *ex*-boyfriend, and that she never wanted to see him again. *Never ever, Gerwyn Evans.*

Stories like that made Jac certain that Catherine was way out of his league. She could have the pick of the boys in his year, or the year above come to that. Why would she bother with him? The Rugby Boys affirmed – Jac had heard them say it more crudely – that you couldn't fault her appearance. Good-looking, certainly; but was she beautiful, the way he figured Petra was? They were both tall for girls, roughly the same height. In the dim light of a dance at Judge's Hall, they might get mistaken for each other. Petra had the sultrier look, Catherine the more pleasing, more open face. Nature or artifice – Jac couldn't say which – had made Catherine's eyebrows so fine that they looked like they'd been drawn with a single pencil line. Her eyes were ice-blue, noticeably lovely. Her hair, though, was regulation mousy brown, lighter than Petra's, long and straight and parted off centre, *à la mode.* Jac had heard that, back in her Bad Girls period, Catherine used to head-bang at Judge's, bent over and shaking this mane madly from side-to-side. Even off the dancefloor, there was nervous energy to her movements, lots of hand-waving emphasising what she was saying. When she was on form, everyone's attention would be on her. But, like Jac, if she was down, she was really down. She was thin (*too thin?*), and when tired her complexion was so china-white it could have been an inspiration for Procol Harum. Was she a little bloodless in spirit, too, now she'd left her B Form days behind? Well, she still had that wicked smile and a dirty laugh (though it was heard less often), and she never said no to a rum-and-black. Her voice, normally mezzo-soprano, would go all smoky and deep when she'd caught a cold or had a drink. Jac considered himself a vocal connoisseur, and Catherine's huskiness was something to savour.

By her own account, Catherine had struggled in her early years in Grammar School. She still wondered, sometimes, if she belonged there. She was no match for the all-round genius that was Martyn; but then, who was? Might she be a little *too* ordinary? A teacher more conventional than Donna Osmond would have missed her talent for acting – and Petra's too. But no-one who'd passed the Eleven Plus was anything but bright, even if they'd ended up in the B Form (what a stupid system!). Jac respected Catherine's judgement and her taste. Though she rarely spoke up in class, if she did, it was never less than good sense well expressed. Slowly, he'd begun to find more and more in Catherine Evans, to find she occupied more and more of his thinking-time. And slowly, he'd begun to allow himself to hope, to think, to dream that she might be falling into his orbit, as he was into hers.

The more time they spent together – never alone, always in The Society of Friends – the easier they were with each other, the more natural the fit. Martyn and Petra, Jac and Catherine: it began to seem like an obvious foursome. Sometimes he and Catherine did 'pair off', even in company, finding the corner of a room to share some gossip. Was he drawn to her as the sister whose loss he had somehow intuited? They were great friends; but almost without realising it, he'd started to plot a way towards a day when they might become more than that. He'd leap upon some foible of hers, tease her gently and yet, of course, repeatedly about it. On occasion – on *occasions* – he went too far, and she'd pretend to take offence (at least, he assumed she was pretending). So then, if he was feeling bold, he'd mention one of his father's sayings, that teasing was a sign of affection. In any case, she never had any problem – unlike him – about getting over a tiff. But the more Jac imagined himself inching towards her, coming closer, and closer again, until it felt like some invisible force was willing something to happen between them, the more he seemed to focus not on the distance they'd travelled, but on the impossible final step, the unbridged chasm that remained. For once, his Auntie stayed silent, offering no assistance. Without her counsel, Jac found himself becalmed, unwilling to put at jeopardy this precious friendship, and all its intimacies, by making a false move, by declaring his heart's truth, even to himself. Worse, he realised the bind he was putting himself into, even as it was happening, which tied him up in yet another knot. 'Do I dare?' he asked himself again and again. All those Double English lessons, all that poring over Prufrock together, only added to his confusion. What, indeed, if she should say *That is not what I meant at all?*

So it had gone on, all autumn, into winter. At Christmas, when the Friends agreed that, although nobody had cash to spare, they'd swap small presents, Jac and Catherine had splashed out on LPs for each other. He'd given her Carole King's *Tapestry*. On Christmas morning, after the well-meant, ill-judged family presents (what, after all, does a real auntie buy for a boy who's going on 17?), he'd found himself unwrapping Don McLean's *American Pie* from her. As an exchange of tokens, the subtext couldn't have been clearer. In the Rhondda in 1973, proposals of marriage had been made less obviously. But the *impasse* remained, into the New Year. They were still no more than *just good friends*. January came and went, and now all but a few hours of February. And she'd be absent from school for *ages* yet, mourning her step-brother. The harder Jac visualised himself galloping towards her, like that Prince from the *Mabinogion*, the more steadily she rode away from his reach.

But… here she was, contrary to all expectations, despite the tragedy that had befallen her family down in Swansea. Catherine Evans. And Jac Morgan. All dressed up, at a disco-dance. Fancy-free. And so fond of each other. Sure as hell, tonight *was* going to be the once-upon-a-time night. Pun-doubtedly (*grow up, Jac!*), the night his story finally, finally would begin.

13

The Three Super-Sexy Smoochie Songs Of The Seventies.

At Number Three... Gladys Knight & the Pips: *Help Me Make It Through The Night* (Kris Kristofferson).

Number Two.... The Moody Blues: *Nights In White Satin* (Justin Hayward).

It's Number One, it's Top of the Pops... Harry Nilsson: *Without You* (Pete Ham/Tom Evans).

A Modern Welsh Triad? Well... it was Modern, and it did (as we'll see) have a Welsh dimension, but this was scarcely a proper Triad. You couldn't say that these three smoochies outclassed a bunch of others. Santana's *Samba Pa Ti*. Fleetwood Mac's *Albatross* (though strictly speaking, like *Je T'Aime*, that belonged to the 1960s). Roberta Flack's *The First Time Ever I Saw Your Face*. Even Belinda Owen's goldfish could have named enough alternatives to fill a double-album. It all comes down in the end, to adapt Jac's History lessons' lesson, to who you were dancing with.

What was certain was that Catherine's presence at a party would *normally* have presented Jac with the perfect chance to ask her for a smooch; and a smooch might lead, at last, to something more. But would it be right *in these circumstances*? The shock of her step-brother's death was so recent... Yet here she was, all of her own accord. Someone with less strength of character would never have been up to a night out. Though when she'd arrived, she signalled, wordlessly – a shake of her head, hands held up, palms open, facing them – that she didn't want to talk about Daniel. She still had the funeral to go through.

She needs a break from it all, Jac reasoned. Needs support, needs her Friends, but needs them simply to be themselves, to carry on as normal. But maybe she was seeking – even if she didn't know it – a special friend, someone closer than a brother, to help her through all this. How could Jac tell? What should he do?

He'd have to decide quickly. It wouldn't be long before the upbeat numbers turned to something slower. Catherine's presence was a wonder, but so unexpected that it was both a blessing and a curse. Jac hadn't had to spend days agonising about finally making his move. On the other hand, he hadn't rehearsed what he would say. He was quick to offer – *so gallantly!* – to go back to the bar for her. He fetched her rum-and-black, and sat down again, feigning interest in the chit-chat. The Friends were walking on eggshells, keeping it light, avoiding anything that might remind Catherine of bereavement. Lydia leaned over and whispered in Jac's ear. There was an Elton John song she was worried about, one usually played at some point in Sixth Form parties. Elton sang of scars that won't heal, of his older 'brother', whose eyes had died, who was now a star in the face of the sky. The brother's name? *Daniel.* Cruelly close to home. Jac understood. The words were just too *apposite*. Lydia was right to ask him to go and make sure that it *didn't* feature that evening. It was an odd request, a request *not* to play something, but the DJ finally got it.

Gladys Knight heralded the start of the smooches. When it came to it, Jac couldn't have said how it was that he and Catherine found themselves up there, on the dancefloor, amongst the established couples, by the time the second slow number began. But there they were, swaying gently in each other's arms, to the heavy reverb of the Moody Blues. There was nothing more to say, about bereavement or anything else. *Silence is the only message.* Who had said that? His Auntie? Catherine's head was so close to his, the sides of their temples touching now and then. Something more profound came to him then, those lines of Shelley's: *Athwart what brow is that dark mantle thrown?* And still they held tight to each other. *Nights In White Satin* began its long-drawn-out coda.

Jac knew that there was a delicate manoeuvre he should be making now, drawing back so that he could look into Catherine's lovely blue eyes; deciding in that instant whether to whisper some sweet nothing, or to read, in her look back at him, an invitation to go straight in for their first kiss. Whatever it was, if this wasn't to end now, if he wanted to be sure of another smooch, that she wouldn't slip from his clutch back to her seat, he knew he had to do or say something to keep her there. But this was the moment insecurity, uncertainty kicked back in. Was this the *right* moment? Wasn't he taking advantage of her emotional state? Was it what *he* really wanted, was it Catherine herself he desired? Or was it simply to be more deeply connected than ever, if that were possible, to the whole group? Was she more like a sister to him? What if she said 'no'? What would that do to him and her, to the friendship he valued, to the companionship they'd found? What might it do to The Society of Friends?

Months of deferred gratification – and now here he was, helpless, frightened to risk anything, anything at all.

But just then the DJ came to his rescue, segueing without losing a beat into the opening piano notes of *Without You*. Catherine was still there, and they began to sway again, in time with Harry Nilsson now.

Jac's heartbeat slowed. He tucked himself against her, luxuriating in the warmth of her body.

But soon – too soon – he realised that nothing had been resolved. The crux of the matter had merely been postponed. When this track came to an end, he would face the same dilemma: either grasp this chance, this golden chance he'd waited so long for; or be left, like Nilsson himself, living with regret, dying with remorse at the end of the night. Knowing that he had her there and then he let her go.

Which is it to be, Jac?

His Auntie! Never had Jac been so grateful to hear her voice. Now he knew that the words he had to say would come to him, would be given to him, when the time arrived, when the song finished. He closed his eyes, surrendering to the gentle motion for a few more blissful lines. He sensed that Catherine was with him in this, that he would find acceptance, that it would end well. Here was the final chorus. *Without You*. Nilsson couldn't li-i-i-ive, if living was…

With a sudden panic, Jac realised that the song might be about suicide. But its last notes were already subsiding. And his Auntie spoke.

Her tone, as ever, was warm and sure of herself.

"Did you know, Catherine…?" he whispered, repeating word-for-word his Auntie's prompt as it came to him, though his confidence drained away as he realised where this sentence was headed, this death sentence for his hopes, "…it's a strange thing, but the bloke who wrote *Without You*…" – one final, vanishingly-brief look of sweet accord passed between them – "…*he* lives in Swansea."

Appalled, she tore herself away from his embrace. A huge burden, a grief, repossessed her, the evening's short respite shattered. She stared at Jac. No words came. Tears flooded her eyes, and she turned and fled towards the toilets. Lydia and Petra chased after her. Their eyes had never left the dancefloor, in case it should end like this. A buzz of excitement pinballed around the room. Though it had been *almost* too quick for anyone to notice, *something had happened*. Jac Morgan had done or said something awful to Catherine Evans, who was in such a delicate state anyway. Something everyone could speculate about for the rest of the night. And bitch about at school tomorrow.

Jac's Auntie, Jac himself, whoever it was that came up with that fateful piece of trivia, had got it almost right. Fun fact: though he may have moved to London, Pete Ham, lead vocalist with Badfinger, co-writer of *Without You*, was a Swansea boy, through-and-through. It was the kind of thing that *would* appeal to his Auntie's parochial pride, her weakness for quoting scraps of Welsh-related pop history. But that was no excuse, no reason… Of all the possible ways that Catherine could have been wooed at that moment, to name the very place where Daniel had died!

Jac turned in a slow circle at the edge of the dancefloor, as though he still had a partner with him. Martyn caught his eye and smiled faintly, pitifully; conveying silently something Nilsson-ish, like he supposed that was just the way the story went… Then the smile disappeared suddenly, and the colour drained from Martyn's face. Off *he* rushed to the toilets. To throw up.

Lydia was the first to return, alone.

"Of all the stupid things to say…."

"I know. Believe me, Lydia, I know. This is the worst night of my life."

"Not everything's about you, Jac."

The DJ was cheerily announcing a special request. "This one's for Martyn and Petra. I'm told they're very, very close to each other." As it happened, the loved-up couple were both in the bog. Separately. One of them comforting her distraught friend. The other, vomiting copiously. "And also for Jac 'The Prince of Repetition' Morgan…" It would have been Penry who'd put him up to this, "…let's hope tonight's not a repeat of all the other nights he's tried to get off with someone!" The DJ's voice was replaced by Roger Daltrey's. *Giving It All Away.* Jac cringed.

The evening was ruined. Jac wanted to protest that he wasn't to blame. But how he could he possibly explain to anyone? Who would believe his weird tale about a voice in his head?

There was no stopping Daltrey. Jac was just a boy. He didn't know how to play.

The boy plotted, as though on some ancient, faded chart, the route back to his seat. As he toiled across the dancefloor, James Taylor, who'd been entwined with Juliette in the corner all evening, rushed up and made a performance of grabbing his arm and shaking his hand. More material for the watching gossips.

"Sorry about all this, Jac. No hard feelings, eh?"

Jac didn't have a clue what he was talking about. Days later – he was still replaying the whole *débâcle* over and over in his head – he worked out that Taylor was apologising, insincerely, for stealing the girl he still thought of as being Jac's. Jac *didn't care* who Juliette was seeing. That was all behind him. But there and then, he was mortified that Taylor was acting this out so publicly, milking it. Another piece of psychodrama to add to the night's theatrics. Why did everything have to be so emotional, so over the top? Why was everyone behaving like there'd been a bloody car crash? They were all at it. Him. Swotzi. Martyn… At least his Auntie had gone quiet. But what was he doing thinking about *her*? Madness. Everyone would go mad at this rate, if they weren't mad already. Catherine. Petra. Even honey-haired Lydia Peake. Despite her steadiness and her judgement and the fact that she'd read a lot, she'd end up going crazy. Doing something stupid. Marrying a biker or something. Yes, a biker. From Trealaw.

Jac realised that he'd become over-wrought. Taking a deep breath, he shrugged Taylor off and went out into the hallway. Petra stood waiting by the cloakroom. Her face matched her scarlet coat. She *was* mad. With him.

"Catherine's still in the toilet, if you want to know."

This was bad, very bad. Or was it? What Jac had said to Catherine was thoughtless. Insensitive. But it wasn't cruel. He hadn't *meant* to hurt her. She'd find it in her heart to forgive him, wouldn't she? That was the kind of girl she was.

"I'm taking her home with me, Jac. I don't want her going all the way back to Gilfach tonight in this state. You wait here for Martyn. Make sure *he* gets home safe. He's in a bad way, too."

Suddenly, she looked more vulnerable than angry. "I don't know what's going on with him, I really don't. It's not just the drink. He's more… *fragile* than you might think. More fragile than I've realised. More than I've understood, anyway. So do one thing right tonight and get him home without any more tears."

She turned on her heel back towards the toilet.

"Petra…" Jac pleaded.

Her swivel back towards him only served to remind Jac of the *pirouette* that Martyn had made her do when they'd arrived, when everything was still unbroken.

"…tell Catherine I'm sorry, will you?"

"I hope you are, Jac. But that's something you'll have to tell her yourself sometime. Not now. It's too soon, too raw. Can't you see that?"

"Of course. I can. Do that. Say sorry. Really sorry. Say I am. When the time comes."

He was burbling. In truncated sentences.

95

"She should never have come here tonight. But you, of all people, Jac, you should have seen that, instead of trying to force things with her, when she's going through all this heartache."

Jac's own heart sank. Petra walked away. He stayed there awkwardly by the door of the Members' Bar, waiting for Martyn to emerge from the gents. Once he'd finished throwing up. The TV in the bar was relaying the Election Results. Psephologists and pundits and pointless speculation. The polls must be closed, Jac realised. Down the road, in Ystrad Leisure Centre, they'd be weighing the Labour votes, as the local joke went. But mid-Rhondda wouldn't decide the Election – Middle England would. It was going to be a close-run thing, but they were forecasting that Harold Wilson was on course to form a minority government. The promised Labour Victory. But hardly the start of a Glorious Revolution. A false start. Just like that romance in the *Mabinogion*. Just like him and Catherine.

The politics didn't seem important now. Martyn emerged. He didn't look Italian anymore: his face sallow, sweat on his brow and sick on his brogues. Jac hoped there wouldn't be another bout before he got him home. It was only just across the main road, but right then it seemed as distant as Scott Fitzgerald's New York.

The rain, at least, had stopped. It was slow going, Jac half-supporting his friend when he was allowed to. Once or twice Martyn halted and began to retch, but each time the moment passed. When they got to the Cardiff Arms, Martyn refused point blank to turn into Cemetery Road. He couldn't face his father in this state. He might say or do something he'd regret. No, he couldn't go home until he'd sobered up. That would take all night, Jac reckoned. They limped on up the main road. There was a chapel there, Gosen, fronting the pavement. *Methodistiaid Calfinaidd* carved in stone above the entrance. Calvinists. Welsh-speaking. Martyn was neither. Surprisingly, as though he was reading Jac's mind, he pulled himself upright like a preacher in a pulpit, and with sudden fluency, pronounced himself *doubly damned*.

"Behold, it is predestined, preordained. I, Martyn Rees, am on the path to perdition. I can't speak a word of Welsh, and I'm…"

He tailed off.

"You're on the way home, Martyn, not the road to Hell."

"This is Hell, nor am I out of it."

He could hardly stand, but quoting Elizabethan drama wasn't a problem.

Immediately, though, his whole body began to tremble. Jac manoeuvred him towards the chapel railings. Martyn leaned against them, grasping a metal upright in each fist, shaking with an uncontrolled rhythm.

There were no passers-by, thank goodness. It was *quiet*. Jac imagined he heard, from down the Valley, the bells of St. Peter's striking midnight. The first of March. It didn't feel like Spring. He too began to shiver.

Martyn wouldn't let go of the railings. He bent towards them, head down, as though praying, prostrating himself before the House of the Lord. Jac wondered if he was going to be sick again. But instead, he began a kind of tearless sobbing, moaning almost as violently as he'd been shaking, with the same involuntary rhythm.

Finally, he summoned up enough control to speak.

"Petra will finish with me, Jac. I know she will."

"Don't be silly, Martyn. She's crazy about you. She wouldn't do that just because you've had too much to drink tonight. Believe me, it'll all be forgotten in the morning."

Jac almost believed it himself. At least as far as Martyn's memory was concerned.

"It's not that, Jac. Not the drink. It's… When she finds out, she won't be able to cope with it. I know she won't. She'll finish with me."

"Don't talk wet, Martyn. You're pissed, and upset, that's all."

"No, Jac, you don't understand. Someone's going to tell her. That's what I found out tonight. That's what I'm sure of now. That's why I drank… and drank… Someone is going to tell her. And then it'll all be over. All be all over."

"Martyn, you're not making any sense. Tell her what? I have no idea what you're on about. You've just had too much. Come on, let's get you home."

But he wouldn't be shifted. The shaking started again. His monochrome shoes were still splattered with technicolour. Martyn sensed that Jac had clocked it.

"Sick. Sums up the whole night," he said, abruptly seeming sober again.

And then: "Jac, if I tell you, you'll never speak to me again."

"Don't be daft, Martyn. You can tell me anything. Anything at all. We're best butties. Always will be. The Society of Friends? Remember?"

The ghost of a smile rose on Martyn's face, the possibility of acceptance; but then the torture he was going through wiped it away again.

"I know you'll try to understand. I know *she* will try to understand. But she won't. She can't. It's not in her nature. I've heard her say things. And other people will stick their oars in. Petra will do her best to be kind, but she'll feel that she has to finish with me. I know she will. Once it gets out. When that bloody... *so-and-so* splits on me."

It was clear that he meant something a lot stronger than *so-and-so*.

"And will *you* understand, Jac? Will you?"

Jac was still at a loss. But then, suddenly, Martyn found the courage to say it.

"See, the thing is, Jac, before I met Petra... I was queer."

Shock.

It was a shock. Not something that Jac had come close to suspecting. Why would he? Martyn was with Petra. Not far off being engaged to her. Queer?

Jac tried to get a new focus on his friend, who'd started retching again. Martyn, queer? Was he serious?

But Jac knew immediately the answer to that: this was no joke. And now that it was said, it already made sense; made sense of things that hadn't been making sense.

It *was* shocking, though. And would be for others, if they knew. The kind of shock that would upset the whole architecture of the friendships they'd built. Petra had been right: *tonight's the night*. The *bloody story* had started.

"I was queer, Jac, and I still am. Queer. That's who I am. A queer. Despite everything that I feel for Petra. I'm not faking that. You know that, don't you? I'm just a queer who's… a bit perverted. A queer who's in love with a girl just now."

Could that be right? It was way beyond Jac's experience. But he understood one thing: it made the depths of Martyn's despair ring true. Unlike the histrionics that had been sweeping over them all back at The Beach. Unlike Swotzi and his over-dramatised handshake, whatever it was for. Unlike Jac himself and his pathetic indecisiveness about Catherine. Unlike the moodiness Martyn projected so often. Martyn's emotions now were genuine, authentic. They stood in proper proportion to the magnitude of what he was going through. His *suffering*. Jac could see that. They'd hit bedrock here. Something solid. Solid, and potentially lethal, something that would take incredible sensitivity and skill to negotiate. And then some. This went far deeper than the backwash of teenage crushes.

The mind works quickly at such moments, and at many different planes all at once. Feelings, insights, beliefs. Attitudes, doubts, principles. Prejudices, intuitions, certainties. Multiple lines of thought seemed to race away from Jac, no longer under his control, disappearing in every direction. But something more profound – his very essence, the kernel of who he was – was still here, calm and grounded, as though in the eye of a storm, seeing unclouded to the core of the matter.

He'd known, from the moment Martyn had spoken, with no shadow of ambiguity, that at the most fundamental level of all, this made no difference. Jac himself wasn't gay, that he knew for sure. If this had been a test of Jac's own orientation, if anyone else had been there, and had overheard Martyn coming out to him, and imagined that it was the prelude to the possibility of a relationship between them, well, that was never, ever going to happen. *Never ever, Trevor Evans.* But neither, Jac knew, would it be the end of their closeness, the rapport, the *camaraderie* that he already valued so highly though it had scarcely begun. That sense of coming from the same place, and, despite all their differences, of facing in the same direction. Jac was crystal clear about that. He wouldn't walk away. He didn't feel disgusted, he didn't feel repelled. He just knew that it wasn't for him. And, of course, he understood that wasn't the main thing, wasn't anything like the main thing. For once, he saw without being told that this wasn't about him. It was about Martyn and everything he must have gone through before meeting Petra, everything he'd gone through since, everything he'd still have to face. The Rhondda might be all that Jac claimed it was, but it was a cruel place to be gay, even in 1974. And Martyn and Petra? How *did* this leave them? How *would* she react if she knew?

Just now, Jac didn't even know what *his* reaction should be: what was the right thing to do, the right thing to say? He knew he should say something. And for once, the only thing he could do and say came to him without prompting from his Auntie. Probably just as well, given her recent track record.

He reached out and put his arm warmly around his friend's shoulders.

"It's alright, Martyn. It's alright. Alright. It's alright, alright?"

Martyn raised his head, suddenly amused by something. Amused *and* bitter, if it was possible to be both at once. Jac was puzzled how to read it. He seemed to need reassurance himself now.

"You *are* alright, aren't you, Martyn? Deep down, I mean, not when you're drunk like tonight."

"Yeah," came the answer at last, with that same weak smile he'd smiled at the Beach. "I'm alright, Jac."

The Second Branch

SUMMER

14

Tonypandy Square is the best place to begin (again).

Pandy Square. The best place. The only place.

Because where else would the Prince of Repetition begin again, other than where he'd already begun. The Prince of Repetition. The Catchphrase Kid. The Curator Of New Welsh Triads. The Boy Who Swore He'd Grow Up.

It was the last day of August, six months on from the solemn vow Jac had made on Pandy Square, six months exactly from that fateful Night at the Beach, his abortive smooch with Catherine, and Martyn's inebriated confession.

For Jac, this day of new beginnings would also become a day of endings. The end of summer. The end of innocence. And for the Triple Crown, the end of never having tasted a drop of alcohol. But it would go down in history (or at least his story) as the august August Day of a different Triad: *The Three Glorious Traverses of Tonypandy Square.*

Thirdly, The Traverse When TheWordMadManiac Invented A World-Conquering Musical Genre (really speaking, his Auntie should get at least half the credit).

Secondly, The Traverse After The Society of Friends Lost The Whole World But Regained Their Own Soul.

Above All, The Traverse That Was Worth Waiting For.

To discover what it was that made that ultimate, chart-topping traverse Worth Waiting For, we'll have to wait (it's worth waiting for). Because the day hasn't yet begun. So…

To begin again (again) at the beginning: it was the early hours of Saturday 31st August, 1974. Jac was in his bed. Alone. Again. Dreaming. Of Tonypandy Square.

It was a dream he'd had before. Many times. He was the Prince of Repetitive Dreams: his id, as much as his conscious will, craved recurring patterns. In the dream, he was flying. Swooping above the Square, observing the scene below with a sense of *déjà vu*. He zoomed over the pavements, over the

Picturedrome, over the roofs of the shops and the cafés and the pubs… Suddenly, there he himself was, as he knew he would be, down at the centre of it all, a painfully thin and restless seventeen-year-old, not at the bus stop, but standing alone, seeking admittance to the Pandy Inn, rapping at the shut door with bare knuckles. The dream cut to a close-up: his bare knuckles rapping.

Knock, knock!

Who's there? An angry response from inside. Jac couldn't see who'd answered so belligerently. But he knew who it was. A boxer – a bare-knuckle fighter. Now he was confronted, in another tight shot, with the boxer's bare knuckles. They were bigger than his own, much bigger. They belonged to James Taylor (the local one, not the Cowboy Jesus); but also, simultaneously, to Tommy Farr, the Tonypandy Terror.

Knockout, knockout!

There must have been a knocking, a real one, on the roof above Jac's bedroom, or on somewhere Tylacelyn Road outside, because the noise, this real noise, began to wake Jac from his dream. A joke floated up to the surface of his mind, a *knock-knock* 'joke' his Auntie had told him based on his nickname. It was a 'joke' he'd repeated so often that it had become a 'joke' about a joke. The humour was in the recurrence. Except that it might never have been funny in the first place. (But it was *better* if it wasn't funny, because the humour was then in the repetition, not in the joke itself).

Knock, knock!

Who's there?

The Prince of Repetition.

The Prince of Repetition who?

The Prince of Repetition.

His slowly-waking mind struggled to focus. The details of his troubling dream began to dissolve into tiny fragments. Once again, he'd failed to get through the door of the Pandy Inn, failed to put himself to some test he dreaded, toe-to-toe with his bare-knuckled nemesis.

It was pitch black. Hours yet to dawn. The rapping, whatever it was, had stopped. Jac rolled over in the narrow bed, and, with a mild effort, farted. There was something deeply satisfying about a good fart, at least there was when there was no chance of being embarrassed by it. Satisfying. Gratifying. Jac liked to feel satisfied.

Feeling satisfied gives you a lot of satisfaction, doesn't it Jac?

His Auntie was always making semi-witticisms like that. This one was certainly feeble. But that might not stop him using it sometime. Many times. The Prince of Repetition.

The question was – and, for once, here in the dark, private silence of his bedroom, prompted by his Auntie, he forced himself to face it – was he *self*-satisfied? In the six months since that Party at the Beach, he'd experienced so much, learnt so much – or had the chance to learn, at least, and in so many unexpected ways. And yet…

Yes, Jac, so many chances. The chance to learn from the Stranger Who Came To Town. To learn from Martyn – of all people – about Puritanism. To learn from Petra's Advice with a capital A. From that Deadly Fight you had with Catherine. From Penry's assault on Miss Osmond. From Lydia's midnight walk, and its otherworldly reflection. From Nerys who…

Alright, Auntie, he admitted, he'd been given lessons, chances to learn.

But you've failed in your first avowed intent.

To grow up.

You're a pilgrim whose progress to maturity is always being put off until another day.

She was right. Time and again, he'd made excuses, let himself off lightly, promised he'd try harder in future.

He tried hard now, tried harder than ever, to see himself as his Auntie did, as others might. As his more tough-minded friends did, Martyn or Nerys. Here in the darkness, where there was nowhere to hide from his Auntie, or from his better self.

The thing is Jac, you're not lazy or stupid. But you lack rigour.

Rigour? What sort of rigour?

The sort that Martyn and your father have.

Martyn and Dad? They're so different! In every possible way. *Think about it, Jac.*

Jac thought. Hard. The only thing they had in common was... *Yes?*

...the capacity to measure themselves against some ultimate standard, against perfection itself.

Yes.

Jac's father's faith was founded on the rock of his conviction that all have sinned and fallen short of the Glory of God. He practised a confessional life which reinforced in him, every day, the necessity of acknowledging in his own soul the stain of original sin; to admit before the Throne of Grace that he, Davy Morgan – although, in the eyes of all who knew him, he stood as a beacon of unblemished Christian virtue – yes, Lord, he too belonged to fallen humanity. He too depended on Christ's sacrifice for his Salvation. Christ's sacrifice, which alone was enough to pay the price of Atonement; which alone could reconcile man with God.

For Martyn, it was his soaring ambition that led him to hold his own feet to the fire. To discover and master the highest forms and expressions of human culture, to test himself against some supreme, unattainable measure of artistic accomplishment. To satisfy himself with nothing less. The difference was that as he acknowledged his failure to live out perfection, Martyn had no merciful God to forgive his sins, no Sacrificial Lamb to take upon Himself the price of his falling short. There remained the unbridged gap, the chasm Jac had seen Martyn fall into, on that night of the Party as he clung to the chapel railings. Since then, too. A black pit from which there was no escape. For Martyn, there was no Atonement. He crucified himself, over and over: but the sacrifice was insufficient to redeem his soul. No Easter Morning, no Rising Again, only Calvary. Even if he sought deliverance in alcohol – and he always did – the darkness closed around him. The darkness of Good Friday, of unimaginable suffering, of torn flesh and piercing nails, of abandonment without hope.

Jac wrenched his body violently across the bed. That image – of his crucified, abandoned friend – was too lurid, too exaggerated. His Auntie had pushed him too far. Martyn was no Christ. Jac gagged, sickened by the train of thoughts that had led him there.

And yet there's a part of you that sees the truth in it.

Yes, he saw it alright. Judged by the standards that his father and Martyn lived by, Jac was shallow…

There, you've named it. But if you want to give yourself an excuse…

Jac was all too ready, even now, to give himself any sort of excuse.

I blame all that childhood affirmation.

All those mornings he'd been greeted as 'my buttercup', all those nights he'd been soothed to sleep assured he was 'worth all the tea in China'.

The result: you like yourself.

There's nothing wrong with that, he told himself. If you didn't like yourself, how could you truly like other people? His endeavours to grow up might not have succeeded, but judged by most people's standards…

"I've done my best," he could hear himself saying, "And that's the best that you can do."

And that, he supposed now, remained the best, the only comfort he could give himself. That he would go on doing his best. It wasn't much. And he knew it wasn't enough, if he was going to take his Auntie seriously. If he was going to take *himself* seriously. It certainly wasn't the same as pushing yourself beyond what you felt capable of, of measuring yourself against the ultimate, the transcendent, the sublime.

Just then, he heard that *Knock, knock!* Again. It *was* coming from across the road. He got up and went to the small window. Under the glow of its sodium lights, the street was deserted, the Shell petrol station directly opposite empty, shut up. Jac looked up the *cwm*, away from Penygraig, towards Penrhys. The sky was just as dark as the massive bulk of the mountain underneath. No line between the two, no way to tell where one ended and the other began. Closer to home, the provenance of the sound remained hidden too. All was hushed again.

Silence is the only message, said his Auntie.

She could be like that. Switching from the profound to the pretentious.

I was just thinking...

"So was I," he snapped irritably.

...the lights look like a lasso in the sky.

Typical. Another nonsensical non-sequitur, just when she'd stung him into some serious self-criticism.

"What? What on earth...?"

At night, the lights look like a lasso in the sky.

Incensed, he looked away again, up the Valley. The dark mountainside merged with the black sky. Nothing to see. But then he realised that there was one feature, so familiar he'd discounted it, standing out against the primeval blackness: the streetlights lining the road from Ystrad up to Penrhys and ringing the hilltop estate itself. The orange dots, a steeply rising diagonal across the mountain, crowned by the circle of lights around the streets on the summit: they *did* suggest the shape of giant cowboy's lariat rising up hundreds of feet above the valley, an enormous length of rope frozen with its open noose poised to snare a steer.

Why this unlikely comparison might be relevant right now was another matter. Sometimes there was *some* wisdom hidden in the incoherence of his Auntie's rambles and tangents. Was she pointing him, if he truly wanted to be a pilgrim, in the direction of Holy Well at Penrhys, the destination in Rhondda's forgotten mediaeval past for seekers of healing and wholeness? Was she trying to tell him that God was about to lasso his soul, to capture and pen and tame at last his wayward spirit? Or was it a call to political action, to solidarity with the residents of the beleaguered modern-day housing estate, barely half-a-decade old but already a byword for fecklessness and depravity? Jac was about to ask, when the *Knock, knock!* that had woken him sounded again, cutting his line of thinking.

And there, obvious now that he'd spotted it, perched atop the sign at the front of the filling station, was an insomniac bird. A woodpecker? Were there woodpeckers in the Rhondda? One of the letters on the logo had fallen off weeks ago, and they still hadn't replaced it, so for the moment it proclaimed HELL. The bird flew down and poked vigorously at the H with its beak.

Knock, knock!

Jac wondered if it that was how the S had fallen off, whether it was *this* bird which was responsible. If so, the woodpecker or whatever it was seemed to have lost the knack. Or the H was more durable.

"He's not giving up with that rapping, though," thought Jac, somewhat in admiration.

He's pecking at the wrong bark, pronounced his Auntie.

And with that, as though offended by her bizarrely phrased judgement, the bird flew off into the dark sky towards Pandy Square. Soon, it would be swooping over the pavements, over the Picturedrome, over the roofs of the shops and the cafés and the pubs...

Jac's thoughts, sleeping and waking, in this disturbing Nocturnal Intermission had come full circle. He left the window and fell back into bed.

Better a Nocturnal Intermission than a nocturnal emission.

"Thank you for that, Auntie," said Jac.

Sweet dreams, she replied, drily.

He assumed he'd be kept tossing and turning for ages by the troubling reflections he'd had about the nature of his own complacency. By his deep thoughts about his shallowness. Or by trying to puzzle out the meaning of his Auntie's enigmatic phrase about the night-time lasso above Penrhys. But, somehow, with scarcely an effort, and after just one more fart, he fell heavily back to sleep. And he dreamt that he and Catherine and Petra were flying, swooping over the pavements, over the Picturedrome, over...

15

Tonypandy Square.

Jac was writing about Pandy Square. *Not* in a dream, but in real life. *Not* in his bedroom, but in school, in the Sixth Form *Library*. And *not* at the end of August 1974, not on the night when he would have that strange Nocturnal Intermission and his Auntie would point out a lasso in the sky; but *almost six months before that*, back in the March of that year. (It's confusing, obviously, to have to wind back the clock again like this, just after we've jumped forward half a year; but as he himself has come to realise, Jac's story *refuses* to progress in a neat, linear, chronological fashion).

So, anyway… it was Monday morning, March 11th, 1974: less than a fortnight after the disastrous Party at the Beach, the Party when he'd upset Catherine and taken a drunken Martyn home instead of her. For the first time since that Party, Jac was happy. The rest of March, the coming Spring, the whole Summer lay ahead of him. But more importantly, he'd just discovered his True Purpose in life. In his head – and in his school Rough Book – he'd begun to write the first sentence of a novel.

"Tonypandy Square – it was the best of places, it was the worst of places …"

It would be a special sort of novel. An anti-novel. An anti-novel called *The Great Welsh Auntie Novel*. The autobiography of a sensitive 17-year-old boy who never grows up. A tragicomic fantasy about a bookish weirdo who sometimes gets out of trouble, and sometimes plunges into it, because of an inexplicable voice inside his head. A Rhondda Romance… (*Is that the equivalent of a Glasgow Kiss?* mused the voice inside Jac's head) …celebrating a gang of friends who care so much about each other that they tear each other to pieces. A coming-of-age saga, satirising half-a-dozen bright young working-class idealists who gain the whole world but lose their own souls. An agit-prop tract championing the Miners who brought the Tory government crashing down. A street-by-street psycho-geography of the Valley, a picture *so* complete that if this Linear City suddenly disappeared from the earth, it could be reconstructed out of his book. No, it would be…

"…a Transformational Grammar!", announced Penry, waltzing into the Library at the very moment Jac was trying to work out exactly what his novel was about. *A Transformational Grammar?* Penry was brandishing a copy of a beginner's guide to the linguistics of Noam Chomsky with this very title, a textbook he'd just found on a shelf in the English Department. "That's what it is. This whole school. You may have been conned into thinking that it's now a Comprehensive, but in fact it's a Transformational Grammar."

A kind of half-cheer, half-chortle came from his fellow pupils hunched over the long table in the middle of the room. To gain entrance to the school, they'd had to face the terrors of the Eleven Plus (still fresh in the memory, though it was six long years ago now); they were fed up with all the propaganda there'd been in the past year about it reforming itself as an egalitarian institution open to everyone.

In the corner, at a table on his own, Jac kept his head down, shielding his Rough Book with his arm. The last thing he wanted was to be drawn into one of Penry's 'performances', to have the extrovert Gelli Nationalist come over, snatch his book and start *declaiming* the text he was in the arduous process of crafting. Jac turned back to his opening sentence. He knew it was essential for it to be an *arresting* opening.

"Tonypandy Square – it was the best of places, it was the worst of places, it was the Hub of the Universe, it was the Back of Beyond…"

Great! Though now that he read over it, rather… *derivative*. He crossed it out and started again.

"Tonypandy Square is the best place to begin because, viewed in three dimensions, it is actually Tonypandy Cubed."

That was *really* feeble. Jac scored heavily across it with his fountain pen, until the blue ink puddled, rendering it totally illegible. The truth was, Jac didn't know what his novel would be about. But he was convinced that, if only he could get beyond this first sentence, its true nature and subject-matter would reveal itself. But that opening sentence! It couldn't be *that* difficult – every story began somewhere, every book had one. And he already had the crucial first two words: 'Tonypandy Square…'. It was the third that was causing difficulty. And the ones beyond that.

He brought to mind the openings of other novels he'd studied. Was there inspiration there?

"Tonypandy Square is a foreign country – they do things differently there."

Churchill certainly had. But it wouldn't do.

"Tonypandy Square – it was a dark, wet night in November, and the clocks were striking 1910."

Cross that one out too.

"Last night I dreamt I went to Tonypandy Square again."

Definitely not. You had to read *seven whole words* before you got to 'Tonypandy Square'. If he knew one thing about novels, he knew that it was vital to hook the reader from *the very start*.

The problem was that each successive draft of his opening was even less convincing than the last. The 'wit' got worse. And the thought behind it, such as it was, got further and further away from what he wanted to say. But what did he want to say?

"Tonypandy Square was what they called him, because for a 17-year-old Rhondda boy, his attitudes, behaviours and clothes were all so pathetically unhip."

There was something in that. Possibly.

Jac had found himself, for reasons that will become clear, embarking on this pathetically-unhip literary endeavour in early Spring – long, long before that August day which would begin with an early-hours conversation with his Auntie sparked by a bird that might have been woodpecker; long before *The Three Glorious Traverses of Tonypandy Square*. But he already knew, then, back in March, that Pandy Square was *the* place. The epicentre. The eye of the storm.

Nothing dramatic had happened in the week or so that had gone by since the night Martyn had confided in him that he was – or had been – queer, the night Jac's smooch with Catherine had ended in his (or rather *his Auntie*'s) unforgivable tactlessness. In those ten wet Spring days after the Party at the Beach, Jac's world had revolved so slowly that it seemed stuck. Everything was on stop, and Jac couldn't see how it might start again. The warmth, the intimacy which had grown so naturally, so quickly between The Society of Friends, all that seemed now to be frozen. At school, Martyn kept a wary distance: not surprising given the nature of what had been revealed that night. Martyn's coolness was a relief to Jac – it spared him an embarrassing conversation he had no idea how to approach. But it disappointed him too. He was eager to support his friend, from good intentions – *and* less worthy ones. After all, what could be more impressive, more glamorous than being seen to be Martyn's special confidant?

How could Martyn bear alone the secret of the way he was? A secret that Jac's own father, as merciful in his judgement as any evangelical could be to a lost sinner, would have condemned as an utterly iniquitous sickness. A secret that exposed any Rhondda youth who divulged it, in any way whatsoever, whether acted upon or not, to the material risk of brutal violence. Then there were the ambiguities of Martyn's feelings for Petra, which must have hit him almost like a betrayal of his true nature, a nature he'd still be learning to come to terms with. Because Jac never doubted that Martyn's feelings for Petra were real, whatever Martyn's past might have been. And how touching, that Martyn had chosen Jac to be the one to hear his admission, drunk as he was. But no wonder that, now he was sober again, and had had time to reflect, he was keeping Jac at arm's length.

Then again, maybe Jac was exaggerating the distance Martyn seemed to be putting between them. At school, their paths didn't naturally cross very often. Martyn was in the year ahead of Jac. Their timetables seldom gave them free periods together in the *Li-bury*. So Jac couldn't be sure whether a deliberate attempt to

113

avoid him was being made. Was he reading too much into nothing at all?

With Petra, who did English and History with Jac, the aftermath of the Party was less easy to ignore. Jac simply felt awkward. He was possessed of a fact, a significant fact, something deep and difficult about Martyn, which she, his girlfriend, didn't know. Jac was clear that wasn't his place to tell her anything about what Martyn had said that night; that he must, above all else, honour Martyn's confidence, keep his secret safe. So Jac had a real fear of any conversation with Petra about what had happened after they'd gone their separate ways from the Beach. However guarded he might be, she had a knack of hearing the unsaid. Could he bury the truth so deep that she wouldn't divine it? On top of that, there was the upset he'd caused Catherine at the Party, the stupid, insensitive way he'd hurt Petra's soul-sister. The channel of trust between him and Petra must surely be fractured. He hoped the damage wasn't beyond repair. In those first lessons back at school, they took their usual desks next to each other, but avoided meaningful contact by concentrating far too studiously on whatever History's Most Eccentric History Teacher or Wales' Smallest English Mistress was trying to impart. Of course, the classes were full of people – Ninelives Bowen, Nerys, Penry, others – who'd seen Catherine flee the dancefloor. No doubt there were whispers about what had happened, but Jac was so painfully focused on those immediately involved that what the rest of the school thought didn't bother him. He dreaded a clear-the-air conversation with Lydia, who'd be frank and reasonable in her views: 'frank and reasonable' would be devastating. Fortunately, like Martyn, Lydia was a year above Jac, kept out of his way by the school timetable. Daniel's funeral had taken place, but Catherine herself was still absent, grieving.

Beyond school, things seemed stuck too. Jac followed, in the papers and on television, the deadlock in Westminster. As he'd gleaned on that fateful Thursday night of the Election, the new Labour Government was short of an overall majority. The miners, promised the pay rise which had been at the heart of the strike, returned to work claiming victory, but it hardly seemed the Great Socialist Dawn Jac had sensed coming on Pandy Square.

First thing that Monday morning, as the pit wheels started spinning again, Jac too was hard at it. Double English. The topic was The Anti-Novel. The traditional novel, Wales' Smallest English Mistress explained, had certain conventions. Rational structure. Character development. Narrative coherence. An attempt at realism.

"Conventional novels are about change, about characters in conflict with themselves or others or the world, *protagonists* motivated by the desire for change. When those desires are blocked, the struggle to overcome those difficulties results in the protagonists themselves changing and growing."

In the front row, James Taylor was making copious notes.

"None of these rules applies to the anti-novel. It deliberately draws attention to the fact that it's just a piece of fiction, reminding readers constantly that they're reading a novel."

"Like a play 'breaking the fourth wall', Miss? Like Brecht?". That was Swotzi. God, what a creep he could be. As though he knew anything about drama.

The anti-novel, Osmond emphasised, forces the reader to try to construct any coherence the story may have from a narrative that's splintered and disordered, often playfully so. She chalked up on the blackboard a quote: 'the characters buzz about sluggishly like winter flies.'

Paradoxically, Jac sat up when he saw what she'd written. That was exactly how he felt, how he'd been feeling ever since the night of the Party. Sluggish. Like a winter fly. But now, he began to wake up as Wales' Smallest English Mistress described the typical anti-hero of the typical anti-novel. Listless. Insecure. Lost. That could be Jac himself! There was a *malaise* in his soul. He didn't know what he wanted. He wasn't even sure of his feelings for Catherine, but if he didn't want her, he wasn't sure that he wanted anything. On the most mundane of levels, he didn't know any longer which role he wanted in *Twelfth Night*, didn't know if he wanted to take part in the school play at all, dreaded going through the audition that Osmond had announced for later that same day: wouldn't it just be embarrassing to try to act alongside Martyn and Petra and Catherine?

Jac remembered the conversation he'd had with Lydia and Petra on the way to the Party. About there being no *linear progression* in his life. Since then, he'd been simply trying to get through each day, to deal with his insecurities, his need for affirmation and reassurance. But every time he felt he'd made some progress, he'd immediately find himself right back at the beginning again, adrift as ever. As though there really was no secure chronology he could rely on, no dependable basis for growth, as though his life was devoid of conventional narrative development. Just like the anti-novel!

"So what's the point?" Osmond asked the class. The killer question.

Silence.

None of the class ventured to put their hands up. Jac himself had no answer, but he was on tenterhooks to discover what Osmond's would be.

"Well, think about it, Form Six! That's what you're here to do. It's writing designed to jolt us out of the warm bath that we sink into when we read those cosy novels we've all been brought up on, those Mediterranean beach romances that top the best-seller charts. The anti-novel makes it plain that the text is only a *representation* of reality, not reality itself. And yet, you could say that it's much more like real life than the conventional novel. Real life doesn't have a neat storyline, a structure, a beginning, a middle and an end. So both these things – the anti-novel's flouting of realism, and its likeness to real life – push us back into the world around us, challenging us to respond by taking *action*. Instead of literature being a diversion, a lullaby designed to send our consciences and our wills off to sleep, this is a wake-up call. A sounding of the Revolutionary Trumpet, a ringing of the Cosmic Alarm Clock!"

If Wales' Smallest English Mistress had been seeking to provoke her Sixth Form into rising up out of their desks and storming the staffroom, or any other nearby citadel of power, she must have been sorely disappointed. Few of them raised so much as an eyebrow, let alone the Red Flag. Ninelives Bowen seemed actually to be asleep. Was he *still* getting over his birthday celebrations?

Osmond was seldom so directly opinionated with her pupils, and perhaps this was why. But for Jac, her sermon hit home. Hit home in a way that the hundreds of Chapel sermons he'd sat through had never succeeded in doing. He was convicted by its power. He was ready to stand up, to come forward, to commit himself to the cause. He'd been saved! Saved from *ennui*, from the apathy and nihilism that, ironically, were central to the anti-novel itself. It was evident to him, now, what the Universe was calling him to do. He must give up his far-fetched attempts to become a rock star. He must abandon comic Triads. Instead, he must dedicate himself wholeheartedly to a new crusade. He must write an anti-novel. Indeed, he must write The Anti-Novel. The Great Welsh Anti-Novel.

The Great Welsh Auntie Novel! exclaimed his Auntie suddenly, in delight. She rarely paid attention in class these days. She would sit at the back, moping, barely awake, as though nursing a hangover. Just like Ninelives, in fact. But now she was awake, itching to make a start.

Let's do it, Jac. Let's write this novel. This Great Welsh Auntie Novel.

'Anti' and 'Auntie'. Perfect homophones in her accent, their accent. A *Great* pun, or at any rate that's what she seemed to think. And so, in the double free-period that followed, Jac found himself in a corner of the Sixth Form *Li-bury*, where he could be sure that he wouldn't be overlooked, to begin, at last, his life's work.

From the depths of his satchel, he pulled out an A4-sized Office Diary which Uncle Stan had given him at Christmas. On the first page he'd written in block capitals JAC MORGAN'S EXTREMELY ROUGH BOOK. The daily pages that followed

117

were filled not with diary entries, but with drafts of essays, lists of topics for English, Welsh and History, exercises in rhetoric, translation and the evaluation of historical evidence.

The sheer volume of material he was expected to master was daunting. His father had been right about that jump up from O level to A level. Here was the proof, set out page after page in Jac's large, upright, horribly ugly handwriting.

Flicking through the diary to find the first available blank space, he caught brief glimpses of his term's work. A catalogue of Welsh idioms: 'o ben bwy'i gilydd = from end to end' (but what was the Welsh for *athwart?*). A disaggregation of the Jesuits' role in the Counter Reformation: 'confessors, educationalists, preachers, missionaries...' (was Jac's father a Jesuit then? He ticked all the boxes!). Phrases highlighted with asterisks: 'the longing for a rural idyll'; 'the legitimacy of the Tudor claim'; 'multifoliate rose'.

So much detail, so much *stuff.* No wonder his thoughts often flipped into fantasy.

The academic graft was interspersed with favourite quotes, not from great literature but odd sayings from classmates or teachers, raw material for catchphrases – like the time that Bull, the fearsome Deputy Head (and former Girls' School Headmistress), had put her head around the Library door and bawled, "Pick up that chocolate or you'll have rats!".

Jac had simply treated the diary as an exercise book, filling it sequentially page-by-page irrespective of the date heading. So on Friday May 3, an overly-confident character-appraisal of *Wuthering Heights'* Catherine Earnshaw sat next to a note that Catherine the Great had sent emissaries to discover how Wales' pioneering Sunday Schools had made it most literate nation on earth. On Tuesday August 6, there was an appraisal of an essay by the Welsh academic Goronwy Rees. A Cambridge contemporary of Burgess and Maclean, and – allegedly – himself a Soviet spy, Rees posed the question *'Have the Welsh a future?'* His answer (pulled apart by Jac) was this: though they'd been fixated for decades on stale controversies about blood, religion, morals and language, they *might* just have a future, if only they could get over their 'obsession with *hiraeth*' and remake themselves as far more akin to the English. *Hmmn.*

Jac turned quickly overleaf. The first of the unused pages fell on August 31st. As he sat there in the *Li-bury* back in early spring, Jac had no way of knowing that this was another strange instance of *charged synchronicity*: that the last Saturday in August would turn out to be *The Day Of The Three Glorious Traverses*. His mind was focused not on the date, but on what he would now write beneath it. The title of his magnum opus. *The Great Welsh Auntie Novel*. Just as his Auntie had demanded. Down it went, big and bold, heading the page. But what next? He hesitated. Contemplated. Thought again. Finally, he began to write that great Opening Sentence...

"Tonypandy Square – it was the best of places, it was the worst of places…"

Then, as we've heard, he crossed it out, and reconsidered, repeating the pattern – think, write, erase – five more times, until there were half-a-dozen solid blocks of blue ink obscuring his efforts. As he obliterated his sixth attempt, he realised that he'd hit a problem experienced by many famous authors. *Writer's block*. It was hard work, being a novelist. Undeterred, he embarked on a new tack. Instead of focusing so hard, so head-on, on his arresting Opening, he began to consider the Big Picture of his novel. The themes. The plot and subplots. The characters. The narrative twists and turns. The *inciting incident* (another thing he'd read about). But did an *anti*-novel have to have any of these elements? That was the question, and it was a real poser. His fountain pen was in his hand, ready for inspiration, poised above the white page; but it seemed more fruitful just to *think*. So that's what he did, retreating into his imagination (as writers must), losing track of what was going on around him. *His mind was on other things*. What a fascinating process it was, this writing. He was half-conscious that, from time to time, his hand, his pen might be moving to jot something down, bullet-points, headings, one-word ideas based on his cogitations, perhaps, as they occurred to him; but, actually, his mind was romping like the mind of God, ranging over the broad canvas of his novel, his masterpiece, his ground-breaking contribution to literature. Time passed. He felt he might be making progress, though not necessarily in a linear fashion. His thoughts circled and circled in a most interesting way. Suddenly, he was rudely brought back to his senses by a poke in the back.

"What's this you're writing that's so important, that you don't even clock one of your Friends walking into the Library?"

It was Catherine. *Catherine*. He wasn't daydreaming. For once. It *was* Catherine, standing above him, staring down at his Rough Book. She looked different, was Jac's first thought. Slowly, he realised that instead of a grey skirt and v-neck school jumper, she was wearing everyday clothes, bell-bottomed jeans and a teal smock-top. The colours made her complexion look even more ashen than usual. *A Whiter Shade Of Pale*. She'd been grieving, Jac reminded himself. And angry. With him. Rightly so. But now she was smiling. And talking to him. Ready to forgive him? Perhaps. Ready to move on? He couldn't be certain. She'd only said one thing. It was a slim body of evidence. Scarcely enough for the kind of authoritative judgement he'd made about Goronwy Rees. But she'd come up with an arresting Opening Sentence. It certainly grabbed his attention. And there she was, looking down at him, nothing but amusement on her face. Her lovely face.

"Lost your tongue, Jac? Come on, what's all this scribbling about?"

Jac never talked about anything he wrote, never showed it even to his closest Friends, but he was so taken aback by Catherine's unheralded appearance that he didn't have the nous to speak anything but the truth.

"It's a novel," he blurted out. "An anti-novel. *The Great Welsh Auntie Novel*."

"So I see," she replied, but with no edge to her voice. Her deep, lush voice.

Jac turned back to look at what she was reading, at the double page open in front of him. Under the title and following the six attempts at *his* Opening Sentence (which were all scored out), Jac was astonished to see that that he'd written a single word over and over again. A name. A girl's name. *Catherine*.

On and on it went, filling both pages. *Catherine, Catherine, Catherine...*

Just her name, again and again. Four-hundred-and-twenty-one times (Jac counted them later, when he got home, before ripping the pages out of the book and tearing them to pieces in embarrassment at coming across like a lovestruck teenybopper).

Catherine, Catherine, Catherine...

"You're mad, you are, Jac Morgan."

Jac slumped, open-mouthed. What could he say? What possible explanation could he give?

Nothing came, nothing at all.

He listened, desperate, for his Auntie's prompt. *She* was responsible for his plight, she'd started this anti-novel business, she should get him out of it. She remained shtum.

Catherine, Catherine, Catherine. Jac was appalled. But the real, flesh-and-blood Catherine kept smiling.

"*Wuthering Heights*," he offered weakly, at last, evidently unconvinced himself. "It turned into the first draft of an essay on *Wuthering Heights*."

Just then, thank goodness, he was saved by the bell. Three times it rang, silencing their conversation, marking the end of the first lesson of his double free period.

Across the *Li-bury*, others stirred, gathered up their books: more of a commotion than usual between lessons. Catherine began to move away, too.

"Aren't you coming, Jac?"

His blank look told Catherine he needed reminding.

"Donna. Donna Osmond. She's auditioning us now. For the play. Over the lunch break? In the Hall? *Twelfth Night*? I've come in specially for it..."

So not just one, but *both* of Jac's free periods had slipped by whilst he was in his reverie. The audition had long gone from his mind.

He snapped his Rough Book shut – *Catherine, Catherine, Catherine* – thrusting the incriminating evidence deep into his satchel and following her down the corridor. Some tiny part of his brain clung to the hopeless hope that she'd forget the whole thing, *The Great Welsh Auntie Novel*, the stupid title and what he'd written under it. (And to her enormous credit, in all that happened afterwards, she never mentioned it again. *Never ever, Trevor Evans.* At least not until they were much, much older, and the circumstances very different. But we'll come to that. In the end.)

16

"You've all had the chance to read the text by now. Some of you seem to have been studying it right up until the last moment – and have found it difficult to tear yourselves away from it, perhaps."

Miss Osmond directed this towards Jac and Catherine as they hurried into the Hall, the last to arrive. Already Martyn and Petra, Lydia, Penry and Nerys, and a couple of other hopefuls, had pulled their chairs up in a horseshoe facing Wales' Smallest English Mistress. Fiery-eyed, but slim, as well as short, still boyish though approaching fifty, she shared a house with the School's French Mistress – and a bed, too, if the salacious schoolyard rumours were true. But it was also said that, when she was sweet and twenty, she'd been engaged to a man who'd become a famous TV personality.

Who knew, really?

Jac *had* read the play she'd elected to stage. Several times. Planning and preparation rarely let him down. Being an idiot, often. Failing to organise himself? Once in a blue moon.

"It has a famous opening line," continued Osmond.

Jac's attempts at his own first sentence flashed up in his mind. He tried not catch Catherine's eye. But then he remembered that he'd crossed out all those efforts before she'd arrived. It was just her name that she'd read. *Catherine, Catherine, Catherine.*

"If *music* be the food of love, play on!" That was Penry, all but singing the words: ever the showman, even more certain as decision time approached that he'd be cast as Feste, the singer and Fool.

"Yes, thank you, Penry – we'll come to the music later. *Twelfth Night...*"

"Or *What You Will*," insisted Penry.

He was right, of course. Shakespeare was having it both ways; his version of *it all comes down to what you believe in the end.*

Osmond ignored him this time.

"As the title suggests, it's a festive piece. Full of holiday Misrule. So, we're going to have fun, *revels*..."

It was evident that she was going to begin with a straight-faced lecture.

"For one night only, Elizabethan society allowed the established order of things to be turned upside down – a bit like this new conjoined Comprehensive of ours, you may be thinking."

That was sharper than usual. Was something up? Some resentment amongst the former Girls' School staff at the way the Headmaster was running things?

"Twelfth Night, when this play was first performed, is the very last night of Christmas, but it's still a holiday. There's licence for mischief. There may be trouble ahead, but a kind of benign comic spirit keeps this world from spinning out of control. It's Shakespeare's 'Night Before The Morning After'. His characters carouse merrily into the small hours, and yet there's no damage done in the end. But Shakespeare is forewarning his audience that it's they who're in danger of waking up with a terrible hangover. Because he knows that in *their* world, Puritanism is on the rise. The Puritans will seize control, and they *will* be 'revenged on the whole pack' of them, as Malvolio, the play's Puritan, swears that he will be."

Jac nodded, sagely. He felt he had experience in the matter. Four centuries later, he was being brought up by living, breathing Puritans. According to his Auntie, he was a bit of an old Puritan himself, though he didn't like to admit it.

Ever since Osmond had told them they'd be doing *Twelfth Night*, he'd been trying to work out who'd be cast as who. He knew it was immature, not the best way to give the best of himself to this collective enterprise – but he'd been calculating which role he should target so that he'd end up with Catherine in his arms, whichever character she was playing. (And he'd realised now, just now, since she'd surprised him in the *Li-bury*, that he really *did* want Catherine in his arms). Duke Orsino and Lady Olivia were the play's high-status characters. Martyn and

124

Petra – the troupe's established lead actors – were the obvious choices to play them. But if that happened, the only way Catherine and Jac could finish up together was if they played Maria, the crafty servant, and Sir Toby Belch. That would be an unlikely casting against type: Belch was a big-bellied glutton and sot; Jac, painfully stick-thin, was teetotal. He tried to stop his calculations – he was always thinking things out in advance, *over-thinking* things. But once he'd started…

The play's real heroine was Viola, the resourceful twin shipwrecked in a foreign country who disguises herself as a young man to seek refuge in the Duke's court. So, what if Petra was Viola? She'd end up marrying Martyn as Orsino. That could work. Catherine would be Lady Olivia and Jac could get his wish and marry her… if he was cast as Sebastian, Viola's twin brother. Yes, that was the part Jac should aim for. Sebastian.

"Before we finalise things," said Osmond, "I'd like to hear some different combinations – casting isn't just about the individual, it's also about who they're playing opposite. Drama comes from dialogue, not soliloquy."

For the first read-through, Osmond chose Martyn as Orsino, and Petra as Viola. Jac had been right in his guessing game, second time around anyway. And Catherine, yes, she would read Lady Olivia. So now, if Jac was Sebastian, it would be perfect…

"Jac, please read…" Dramatic pause. Osmond was a bit of an actor herself. "… Malvolio."

Malvolio? Jac didn't see that coming. Though he'd just been reminding himself that he knew what Puritans were like. He could give it a go. He'd get to act out an infatuation with Lady Olivia – *Catherine!* It might not be a total disaster. It would certainly give him a bigger profile in the production than he'd expected.

Osmond directed them to a scene late in the play. Maria and Sir Toby have convinced Malvolio that Lady Olivia has sent him an extravagant love-letter. He's unhinged by the trickery, and mistakes Olivia's concern – that he's gone mad and needs to rest and recuperate – as a sign that she really has fallen for him.

OLIVIA/CATHERINE: "Wilt thou go to bed, Malvolio?"

This was Jac's big moment. He gazed into Catherine's eyes and took a deep breath...

MALVOLIO/JAC: "To bed! ay, sweet-heart, and I'll come to thee."

And so Malvolio quotes the famous maxim that he believes Lady Olivia has used in her letter to encourage him, a mere servant, to propose to her: *some are born great, some achieve greatness, and some have greatness thrust upon them.*

It didn't go well for Jac. It wasn't so much Catherine's line inviting him to go to bed: that was too direct, too on-the-nose to take seriously. But *acting* an obsession for her was beyond him. He was unhinged, off-kilter, but not in a Malvolio-like way. *Greatness* had been thrust some distance beyond him.

They took a break. When they reconvened, Osmond shuffled the pack. Jac, unsurprisingly, was no longer Malvolio. There *were* some surprising choices, though – Penry as Sir Toby Belch (really?), and Nerys, not Penry, as Feste. Nerys had a splendid voice, and – as Osmond said – if the laws of his day forced Shakespeare to cast male actors in female roles, why couldn't she experiment with girls in boys' parts?

Most surprising of all, to Jac at any rate, was the new Malvolio. It was Martyn!

He was brilliant, of course, taking to the role as though born to it. Even in this first reading with a script in his hand, you could sense how he would command the stage. Jac remembered a conversation they'd had about *The Lord of the Rings*. Jac had read Tolkien's saga *twice* and was, of course, smitten with Arwen Evenstar. In his dreams he was Aragorn, her noble, fearless lover. In reality, he knew he was more of a Sam Gamgee, a stout-hearted, faithful sidekick. But when he asked Martyn which character *he* identified with, the surprise answer was Gollum. *Gollum?* The misshapen villain, eaten up with lust for the Ring he'd lost? "He's the only one with any internal life," Martyn explained. "The only one with any sort of moral dilemma going on inside him. Everyone else is simply either good or evil."

Yes, Jac could see it now. Martyn would bring that sense of complexity, of inner struggle to Malvolio: an obnoxious social climber – yes – but also a victim, the butt of others' japes. Even at his worst, Malvolio was more than a simple baddie. In the end, the audience would have to have some sympathy for him, not just be revelling in his downfall. Martyn would play him with just the right balance of ambition, overweening pride, self-regard and needy vulnerability. Casting him as Malvolio would put the comedy into relief and make the whole play work.

So now – it seemed – casting was settled. Martyn as Malvolio, Lydia as Maria, Penry as Sir Toby, Nerys as Feste.

But Osmond was still experimenting. She asked Petra and Catherine to exchange roles. Catherine was now Viola, Petra was Lady Olivia.

It was all very confusing. The only major role left to fill was… Orsino. If Jac was the Duke, and Catherine stayed as Viola, he'd spend most of the play half in love with her, and get to marry her in the end. Bingo!

"Ah, Jac," said Osmond, "I'd like you to have a go at reading the part of…"

But before she could finish, a deafening *rat-tat-tat* came from the windows which gave a view into the Hall from the corridor outside. A second later, the doors were flung open with terrific force. In marched the Deputy Headmistress, Bull herself, snorting with rage.

"Jac Morgan! So *this* is where you've secreted yourself!"

A stifled titter rose in the mouths of Jac's friends. He might be indeed secreting himself, right now, but not in the way Bull meant.

"Beg pardon, Miss Osmond, but the presence of this… *boy* is required in my office. Now!"

It was the worst possible moment, but Jac was powerless to object. The others stared at him with a mixture of horror, sympathy and amusement. What had he done? He scurried out of the double-doors, the Deputy Headmistress breathing hotly down his neck. His Auntie stirred in the back of his mind.

Exit pursued by Bull, she observed, with a wit more erudite than usual.

All the way down the corridor, Jac searched for a clue, any clue, as to what his misdemeanour might have been. Surely, writing a novel (even an Anti-Novel!) during a free period was no crime. Bull pushed past him into her office. Jac followed, warily. He prayed that his Auntie wouldn't cause problems, though he sensed her preparing to speak her mind, as usual when he was under stress.

In the inner sanctum, he was surprised, and relieved, to see that Bull was not alone. Sitting upright in a chair facing Bull's huge desk, was a lad of Jac's own age. The most noticeable thing about him was a shock of very, very blond hair. From under it, he smiled weakly at Jac.

"This is a new member of the Sixth Form."

Bull acknowledged the newcomer with a tilt of her head. Her *deputy head*, whispered his Auntie, back to her usual standard of pun.

Jac managed to stop himself repeating it aloud.

"He's just moved to the Rhondda."

Aha! said his Auntie, *'a stranger comes to town'. One of only two ways all Great Literature begins. Said someone famous.*

She must have been paying more attention in class than Jac realised. But whose quote was that? And… what was the other way?

Maybe this is where you should start your story.

Jac didn't want to be thinking about his anti-novel now.

Your Auntie Novel, his Auntie corrected him.

"His mother," continued Bull, "has brought him here from Belfast. As you know there are some… difficulties over there."

Troubles, said his Auntie. *They're known as The Troubles.*

"Troubles, Miss," said Jac, failing to stop himself this time. Thankfully, Bull ignored him.

"His name is Ciaran McGuire. Ciaran. Spelt C-I-A-R-A-N. With… I'm not sure, some sort of accent apparently, but I've asked him to drop that to make things easy for us."

Some sort of accent? said Jac's Auntie, in disgust. *It's bound to be a Belfast one. Like Ian Paisley's.*

Jac didn't bother trying to educate *her*. Ciaran, meanwhile, had said nothing. A wise head and a quick learner, then, keeping his counsel in front of Bull. Jac followed his lead, letting Bull do the talking.

"Ciaran's father is a Belfast man, but he's… gone away for a while. Ciaran's mother has decided, prudently in the circumstances, to move back to the Rhondda. She grew up in Treorchy and came to this institution when it was a proper Girls' Grammar. One of my schoolfriends, in actual fact."

Jac grasped for the first time that Bull had once been young enough to attend school.

And she had friends! said his Auntie. But Jac sensed that now it was obvious he wasn't in trouble – now that Bull was becoming discursive, confidential even – his Auntie was losing interest.

"Ciaran's mother reckons that he'll be safer finishing his A levels here in Wales. You, Morgan, are to take him under your wing. The ways of this school will be strange to him, as they are becoming to me."

So it was true: she hated the transition to co-education and all-ability intakes. But was bitter, all the same, about not getting the top job in the new Comp. You can glean so much, Jac realised again – he'd experienced it with Catherine not so long before – from a few short words. The wounded Bull, if that was what she was, stood to dismiss them.

"You can start with whatever Miss Osmond is doing in the Hall. Ciaran has a liking for drama. A prize-winning elocutionist, I'm told."

The boys set off together back down the corridor. Jac's Auntie went back to reading that Mediterranean beach romance or whatever it was she did when she felt that her nephew didn't need her. As his head cleared, Jac remembered who it was who'd claimed there are only two ways that Great Literature begins. Leo Tolstoy. *A stranger comes to town* was one, and… the other was… *a man goes on a journey*. Yes, that was it. In something they were supposed to read for homework. The other week. He'd rushed through it just before he'd set off... on a journey. To the Party at the Beach. That strange bus trip. From Tonypandy Square.

Jac realised his trivial cogitations about Great Literature were making him forget his manners. He'd said nothing to Ciaran since they'd left Bull's office. And Ciaran had said nothing since they'd been introduced. So what kind of accent *did* he have? Unlike his Auntie, Jac wasn't expecting a harsh loyalist rasp – he'd guessed that someone with an Irish name like Ciaran must be Catholic. Jac asked him which subjects he'd be taking. The response came with an intonation softer than Paisley's, and an underlay of his mother's Rhondda lilt; but it was unmistakeably *not* from Treorchy all the same. The vowels seemed to have shifted around. History came out as *Hus-tiry*. And English, he'd be doing *Anglush*: he liked Literature, he said. *Lut-rit-cherr.*

They'd arrived back at the Hall. There'd been another round of musical chairs in the casting. Petra was Viola again. Penry was no longer Sir Toby Belch. He'd got his wish and was playing Feste. So Nerys was now Maria, and Lydia had become Lady Olivia. Jac was just trying to work out what the knock-on effect of *that* was, when the scene they'd been reading ended. Jac took his cue to present their new classmate.

"Everyone, this is Ciaran. From Belfast. He's joining Form Six. An actor himself, by all accounts."

"Is that right?" said Osmond. "Very timely."

"It's grand to be here, Miss". The vowels could be diphthongs, too, it seemed. *Graund. Hee-yerr.*

"Well, we're just firming up the casting for our School Play. *Twelfth Night.* Perhaps you know it? Anyway, you're welcome and... sorry to spring this on you, but I wonder if you'd like to give us a flavour of something yourself. By way of introduction. No obligation. Only if you'd feel comfortable..."

To everyone's surprise, the newcomer walked to the centre of the semi-circle, bowed, shook his blond hair from his face and stood tall again. Then, purely from memory, he delivered the opening lines of their play.

"If music be the food of love, play on;
Give me excess of it, that, surfeiting,
The appetite may sicken, and so die..."

The voice and the accent had changed. Forget the Falls Road, or the Ardoyne, or wherever it was Churchill's successor as Home Secretary had sent troops to shoot the locals this time. Ciaran sounded like he'd be perfectly at home in the RSC. The right cadences. The right emotions. The right rhythm. Even the pauses seemed to sing.

If it wasn't perfect – and it *wasn't*, quite – Jac wouldn't have been able to say there and then how it could be improved. It was hard to credit that it was happening. When Ciaran finished the whole speech, everyone, Osmond included, simply applauded. The new boy blushed.

"Youse are all very kind," he said, back in his own accent, and seemingly abashed by his own audacity. "It happens to be a set piece we had to learn last year for O level Drama. It's on the syllabus over there – back home. The luck of the Irish, eh?"

Another round of applause. The modesty was beguiling (though disingenuous, as Ciaran admitted to them, a few weeks later: Bull had told his mother about Osmond's plans for the School Play, and he'd taken the trouble to "refresh his memory" about the speech the night before). There was no doubting, though, the quality of his performance.

"Ladies and gentlemen," announced Osmond, "I believe we've found our Duke Orsino."

A third round of applause. Penry would probably make a Triad of them.

And then, quickly, because Dinner Hour was nearly over, Wales' Smallest English Mistress delivered two more surprises. The first to Jac.

"I'd like you to play Sir Toby Belch."

"Hurrah!" shouted Penry, clapping Jac on the back. "The thinnest, soberest fat drunk in the whole history of Shakespearean theatre! We'll slip a pillow up his tunic. And a vodka in his coke".

131

Penry, playing the Fool, thought Jac. Even in shock, the WordMadManiac couldn't stop the wordplay. But Toby Belch?

You'll get the most famous line of all, whispered his Auntie encouragingly. *'Toby or not Toby, that is the...'*

Jac ignored her. There was nothing to done about it. Sir Toby he was.

After all the shifting round and swapping of parts, that left... Catherine. *Catherine, Catherine, Catherine.* That was Osmond's final surprise.

"It's unorthodox. But Shakespeare would approve, I'm sure. Petra is cast as Viola. Only one person here is a credible match for her in size and stature and looks, only one who's anything like her twin. And I'm sure *she*'ll play the part to perfection, even though it's a male character... with a little practice. Well, with a *lot* of practice. But you'll all need that. Rehearsals start at Dinner Time tomorrow. Catherine, you're our Sebastian."

If it was possible for the colour to drain any further from Catherine's face, it did right then. But she nodded in silent acceptance of the role.

Jac, too, was shocked. *Did* Catherine look like Petra?

He used to think of them as twins, he supposed, Terrible Twins, the Bad Girls of The B Form. But once you got to know them...

The audition was done. Osmond hurried away. Jac's mind was whirling. He'd gone from the slough of despond that morning, to discovering his True Calling as an anti-novelist, to being surprised by Catherine, to taking care of a Stranger, to finding that he was a fat drunk, as Penry put it. He needed time to drink it all in, as it were *(puns again!)*.

He turned to leave, but Catherine took his arm in a sisterly fashion. It was one of those unforced moments where they seemed to find each other alone, even in a crowd. There was an intimacy, a natural intimacy, like a cloak around them.

"Well, that didn't work out as you expected, Jac. If Penry can't find a pillow, we'll have to feed you up."

"Yeah, feed me up. Suppose so. Why not?"

132

As he spoke, he realised how ungracious his reply was. The tone betrayed something – to himself if not to her: that he was still working through the damage he'd done to their relationship. That he wasn't ready to be joshed into high spirits, even by Catherine herself. But then he remembered, or tried to, that it wasn't all about him.

"It'll be strange for you, playing a man. You're pleased, though, are you? With Sebastian?"

"Pleased to be in the Play at all, Jac. Pleased just to be here."

Pleased just to be here. Of course. Suddenly, Jac realised that, amidst all the twists-and-turns, he hadn't found the moment to do what he'd promised himself – and Petra – that he would do. *Get your priorities right, Jac.* Some things were more important than play-acting.

"Catherine, I meant to say: I'm sorry... so sorry... about Daniel..."

They exchanged a look. It lasted barely a second but spoke volumes. And he understood that it wasn't necessary to say more. But there was still an apology to make.

"... and I'm sorry for my thoughtlessness – at the Beach. I have this..."

Could he tell her? *Could she possibly understand?* About his Auntie? If anyone might, it would be Catherine. But, no, no, no, he would just sound mad.

"...sometimes, I just panic and say the first thing that comes into my mind."

"We'll put it behind us, Jac. A fresh start."

Jac had no poker face. His face betrayed his emotions – his disappointment in himself for lacking the courage to confess his secret. Catherine must have mistaken it for doubt, doubt that her reassurance had been enough. She pinched his arm lightly.

"If you still feel bad, you can make it up to me by showing me how to act like a real man. I'm going to need a model."

It was tease, Jac realised. They'd swapped roles. *She* was teasing *him*. Catherine had just been cast as Sebastian, the character he was aiming for, and here she was, 'off-stage', taking the part that he normally played with her. The Teaser. So now he had to convince himself of something he'd often told her: that teasing was a sign of affection. Despite the mess he'd made of things. But then…

"So where did you find a *blond* Irishman, Jac? I thought they were supposed to be ginger. But that poise! That voice! It's a rare bit of talent you've brought us there."

Rare bit. Rarebit. *Catherine, Catherine, Catherine, rarebits are supposed to be Welsh, not Irish.* Jac swallowed hard. She was teasing still. Despite that, he felt the first pangs of jealousy welling up inside.

17

What kind of a single-sex/co-ed Grammar-Comprehensive was this? Full of RADA-candidates or rugby boors? Thespians or thugs? My editor says the reader will be confused. The precinct needs to be more consistent. *I need to* explicate the background more clearly.

I'm surprised and not surprised.

Surprised she's asked for an explanation – because it seems like a classic matter of research *which she insists I avoid.*

But I'm not surprised by her confusion. In that precise nick of time, the school 'Jac' attended, where there'd always been a messy mix of cramming and chaos, was undergoing a series of complex transitions. So since she's asked…

Education had long been prized in the Rhondda. It was The Way Out – the means of escape from the drudgery of the pits or of going into 'service'. Miners put pennies aside, built schools for their sons and daughters, and when universal secondary education became a right, the Rhondda Borough Council invested heavily in it. Not just one, but two levels of grammar school – local grammars up and down both valleys (like the one that 'Juliette' went to in Pentre), and for those passing their Eleven Plus with the highest marks of all, there was the Rhondda County Grammar School at Porth. Porth County.

The Boys' School's reputation was well-established by the time a driven but unconventional young man became headmaster in 1961. Sporting a fine Zapata moustache, he was known to everyone as 'Santos'. The legends about him were legion. He courted his wife, apparently, by galloping on horseback up to her terraced house in Blaenclydach. Conventional school discipline wasn't his thing (the maverick in him sought a degree of anarchy) but he modernised the school's technology, pioneering the use of a Language Lab, and commandeering a whole classroom to install a mainframe computer. At the time, pupils boasted, with schoolboy exaggeration, there were only three such computers in the whole world – in the Kremlin, the Pentagon… and Porth County.

'Santos' was determined that his school was going places. But there were places its pupils weren't *going. Oxford and Cambridge Admissions Tutors*

wouldn't admit that any good thing could come out of a Welsh mining valley. Year after year, exceptional candidates with exceptional results were rejected out of hand. But Santos was mightily persistent. He stopped short of saddling up and tilting at the Dreaming Spires, but he refused to admit defeat. Once the first acceptance came, more followed. Soon a stream, then a torrent of Rhondda talent flowed towards Oxbridge every autumn. Santos fostered a special link with one of the top Oxford colleges. I'm told that when that college researched its own past to mark its 500th anniversary recently, it discovered that, in all that time, over any ten-year period, no other headmaster had secured more admissions. Winchester and Eton, Harrow and Charterhouse – all the elite, historic fee-paying public schools of Olde England – Porth County gave your boys one hell of a beating!

But, like 'Santos', the school had a split personality. During *lessons, it was heads down: masters dictated, pupils filled their notebooks with the formulae and theorems that would secure outstanding grades from the WJEC.* Between *lessons it was bedlam. The first three forms were housed in a wooden structure put up as a temporary measure during the Second World War, known as The Ranch. The Wild West had nothing on it. Once the teachers retreated to the Staff Room, outlaws – bullies like 'Swotzi' – roamed the corridors and burst into classrooms. There were snacks to snaffle, dinner money to be extorted, pain to be inflicted simply for the pleasure of it.*

The school's academic strengths were in the Sciences. It produced phenomenal Physicists, champion Chemists, brilliant Biologists, maestros of Mathematics. Many of them excelled, too, on the rugby pitch. But in the Arts – some Latin scholars aside – there was less to shout about. This was no citadel of culture. There were occasional, token attempts to suggest that a rounded education went beyond the demands of the curriculum. Once a year, a trio of stiff classical instrumentalists were summoned up from Cardiff on a mission to bathe the unwashed in the delights of Mozart and Beethoven. The whole school was assembled and forced to listen, with no context, to music their instincts told them was desperately boring and fuddy-duddy. The results were predictable. Catcalls and sniggers. Card schools got underway on the back benches. Wrestling matches broke out. Makeshift projectiles were launched. 'Santos' might make a show of chastising the boys with a swish of his cane. One year, it all got so bad that he had to intervene just as the trio were getting into their stride mid-Movement. Their playing ground to a halt.

136

"This behaviour must stop," 'Santos' shouted. "If not, be warned…" We waited for the terrible threat. "…I Will Make Them Play The Whole Concert All Over Again. From. The. Very. Beginning." The poor musicians, clutching their instruments like shields, sat with fixed grins, their vocation to bring music to the masses reduced to a penance.

Drama fared better, but only just. Unlike the Girls' School, there was no Shakespearean tradition, no big annual School Play. So, for boys like me, it was a relief to merge with the Girls' Grammar, in preparation for going Comprehensive. A Boys' School, dominated by sporty scientists and macho mayhem, meeting a Girls' School – which was much more disciplined and more like a liberal arts college – on the way to wising up or dumbing down (it all depends on what you believe) as a co-ed 'Comp' for one and all. 'Penry' was right to call it 'a Transformational Grammar'. It was a sea-change to be in an institution that valued the Arts, that rated tackling Chomsky and Brecht as highly as delivering quick ball from a ruck. And, of course, having both sexes taught together made it a more rounded, more fully human place to learn. Even if 'Santos' gave free rein to 'Bull' – his deputy – to enforce discipline amidst the turmoil.

The coming Comprehensive ethos was transformative too – opening the School to different kinds of achievement, different measures of success. And rightly so: a preparation for life should be more than academic hothousing. But, in practice, something was lost in the transition: the ambition to give every child not just schooling, which focuses the mind, but education, which broadens it. A true education, as those early pioneers of schools in the Rhondda knew, makes the best in human learning and experience accessible to all.

To be clear – I'm a sucker for nostalgia, but this novel isn't a prospectus for a return to the 'good old days of Grammar Schools'. Porth's Oxbridge tradition withered and died when it went 'Comp'. But more was gained, for more pupils, by treating everyone as though they had the right to the best that school could offer, by refusing to make anyone think they'd be second best for life just because they hadn't excelled in a certain sort of test when they were 11. All I'm saying is that I was, as we used to put it, 'jammy'. Jammy to be born in the Rhondda where education was valued. Jammy to pass the Eleven Plus. Jammy to come under the sway of teachers who had ambitions. Jammy to be gifted an education which was the match – and more, as I've explained! – of any that money could buy. Jammy that our time was the *time when Boys began to meet Girls in class as well outside school.*

For me, that last piece of luck was the best of all: because I fell under the spell of someone who would never have taught me otherwise, one of the Girls' School staff: an inspirational English teacher who knew how to conjure life out of words on a page, how to spark magic on stage, how to work the alchemy that brings poetry alive in young minds. Even if she wasn't very tall.

And after all that, my editor says a long-form explanation wasn't what she had in mind at all. These interstitial chapters are in danger of destroying the novel's narrative coherence, *seemingly. I've asked her to read the bit about the anti-novel again. But I have promised to be more succinct next time.*

18

"Catherine, your ears are beautiful…"

It was Jac who was trying this corny romantic line on Catherine. But he was allowed to. Indeed, obliged to. They were *in rehearsal*.

The cast was together for the first time. Osmond had explained her approach: stay faithful to Shakespeare's story and words, but introduce an element of improvisation to the physical comedy. She told them about the *Commedia dell'Arte* tradition, how they'd have to learn to put great trust in each other on stage, even more than actors customarily do.

They'd begun with a basic Physical Trust Exercise – choose a partner, get them to stand behind you and fall back into their arms without looking. Jac was delighted when Catherine made a beeline for him. He collapsed, she caught him, and *vice versa*: the first time they'd held each other since the infamous smooch, but in circumstances so different, so safe – it felt like they really had closed that awkward chapter.

Soon, they were told to find new partners. And again. When Jac stood and caught Petra, he realised how close she was in height, weight and body-shape to Catherine. Osmond's casting had been canny. The Terrible Twins. A bothersome thought occurred. If they were so alike, did that mean he must be attracted to Petra too?

Next, they were told to sit in groups of three or four. Building a team also required emotional trust. Opening up to others, making yourself vulnerable. So Osmond explained the rules of the Blank Game. Each player had to compliment another, phrasing the compliment in a very precise form: "(Name), your (blank) is beautiful, because…" You could choose what the blank was, but it had to be a physical feature. It was a risky game for excitable teenagers (and a *risqué* game if you weren't playing in front of a teacher). Jac understood from experience how sensitive people could be about their appearance, how much of an obstacle it was to being truly at ease with others. But Osmond must know what she was doing. This was a way of breaking down those barriers, boosting everyone's self-confidence *and* – in the specifics you chose – revealing a lot about your own predilections, exposing yourself in a very intimate way. Jac was up for it. Catherine looked panicked. The two of them were in a group with Lydia and Ciaran.

Jac took it upon himself to go first. *Softly, softly.* It would be too easy to be vulgar.

"Catherine, your ears are beautiful… because they're the portal to your mind."

"You crawler!" she mouthed silently back, evidently relieved he hadn't said anything coarser.

Lydia went next. Ciaran's feet were beautiful: straight and strong. And Lydia's beautiful hair reminded Ciaran of honey. True, but unoriginal, thought Jac. In fairness to Ciaran, he was playing this game with people who were still essentially strangers, whose backstories he didn't know, whose *clichés* and catchphrases he'd never heard.

Now it was Catherine's turn with Jac. He was hoping she would go for his back. She had a thing about backs. Bryan Ferry's back in particular. A slightly unusual… fetish, if that's what it was, but innocent enough as these things went.

"Jac, your…"

…a long hesitation, far too long for him. And then very slowly…

"…your *eyes* are beautiful…"

His eyes? *Well, well.*

"…because your irises have two colours in them… brown inside blue… like a round stone down in a deep pool."

Two-tone eyes? *What?* Stones in pools? Jac was speechless. *Where did that come from?* If he did have irises like that, no one had ever remarked on them before. And those words – *a round stone down in a deep pool* – were they Catherine's? Or from some pop song? A piece of poetry she'd read? It sounded like *cynghanedd.* Catherine herself looked every bit as shocked as he was by what she'd ended up saying. Her hand had shot up to her mouth the moment she'd finished speaking. She and Jac gazed at each other, dumb. Lydia came to their rescue.

"Your go, Ciaran. To Catherine."

"Catherine, your hands are beautiful because they're so pearly white."

He's playing softly, softly too. Clever boy.

So, finally, Catherine had to return Ciaran's compliment. To Jac's surprise, she didn't go for the obvious – Ciaran's blond locks. How much thought she put into it, Jac couldn't be sure, but this time round there was no pause.

"Ciaran, your back is beautiful because it's so broad and manly."

Ouch.

Evidently, it was Catherine's turn to send Jac rushing to the toilets in emotional turmoil. Because as soon as Osmond brought the session to a close, off he went. He stood there, staring at his reflection in the cracked mirror above the washbasins, trying to focus precisely enough to determine whether he really was blessed with couple-colour irises. Though why he was bothering he didn't know. *His eyes. Ciaran's back.* There was no competition.

Slowly, he realised someone was watching him. Martyn.

"What's up, Sir Toby? Checking those gorgeous peepers of yours? You'll go blind, you know!"

Jac didn't feel like being forced into matching Martyn's cheerfulness. He kept his focus straight ahead, on his own reflection. He saw that he was scowling. In a right *pwdu*. But Martyn wasn't to be rebuffed so easily. He waited his moment, then tried again.

"They say they're the best form of beauty, the irises. They never fade or wither with age… *Never ever Trevor Evans.* And yours are special, or so the word goes. Special but weird – part brown and part blue, isn't it? Mind you, it's hard to tell with those rose-tinted glasses you wear most of the time. Though clearly not just at the moment."

It was easy, well-judged; the first thing of substance or warmth he'd said to Jac since the Party at the Beach. An invitation to resume friendship. To put his drunken confession to one side and carry on with the business in hand. Or maybe… to acknowledge what had been revealed. Either way, it deserved a reply.

Jac turned from the mirror, summoning up an apology of a smile. But try as he might, he couldn't work out how to broach further discussion of what Martyn had confided in him without tumbling into deep waters again. Gay sensitivities and the whole gay scene were outside Jac's experience. No one he knew at school was openly queer. No one outside school for that matter. Who was it that Martyn was worried about, the *so-and-so* who would split on him and tell Petra? How had they discovered Martyn's secret? Jac had no idea. Though he realised it might be important to ask. But, as they stood there awkwardly, who should walk in on them but Ciaran.

"Am I interrupting something…?"

"No, no," chorused Jac and Martyn, too quickly.

"See, in Belfast, it's the *girls* who spend ages together in the toilets. Well, girls and…"

"Jac and I were just catching up on an old argument about the Rhondda."

"It's a quare ould place, right enough," replied Ciaran, disappearing into one of the cubicles.

Afterwards, Jac couldn't decide if 'quare' meant *queer*, or just strange. Was it a personal insinuation or a social point? What did the Rhondda look like from Ciaran's point of view, anyway? Someone moving in for the first time must see it like Martyn did: narrow, obsolescent. The Black Tips of Treorchy were no sunlit uplands. But Ciaran wouldn't be fussing himself about the Rhondda's place in the world. He had too much else on his plate: new country, new home, new school, whole new curriculum.

As rehearsals progressed, Jac began to get the measure of Ciaran the actor. His performance never dipped below that first speech, when he'd amazed them all at the audition. With every new scene, Ciaran's first pass was nearer the mark than anyone else's. But it never developed beyond that, never soared higher. As though he knew what he was capable of, was comfortable with that, felt no need to strive for more. Or feared that in doing so he might be exposed. Such a contrast with Martyn: *he* often struggled to find the right pitch, the place where his character fitted the text and action, but when he did, he could transform a scene, take it to another level altogether. Ciaran's Orsino was consistently good. Martyn's Malvolio might grow into something tremendous. But he might just fail spectacularly too.

Jac wondered what Ciaran made of the rest of the cast, of the artful delicacy that characterised the feedback they gave each other. *Ciaran* always spoke out just as he saw things: if straight-talk exposed mediocrity, or lazy thinking or acting, well… what was wrong with that? And he lampooned the way they habitually took their leave of each other – an endless round of *goodbye, ta-ta then, see you, all the best, take care, bye now, ta-ra* … "Why can't youse simply go?" he asked, his accent probably making it sound more aggressive than intended. "Are youse afraid you'll never see each other again? None of youse work down the pit, and it's not like the IRA are on active service in Porth, so youse are unlikely to be blown to smithereens between now and Dinner Time. Catch yourselves on!"

Catch yourselves on! – the Belfast idiom, so strange to the Rhondda ear, became another of Jac's catchphrases. But whether Ciaran's bluntness was a cultural thing – the Ulster in him – or whether it was personal, proclaiming true self-confidence, or masking some lack of the same, Jac couldn't judge.

In class, it was History that posed the biggest challenge for Ciaran. History's Most Eccentric History Teacher was one of the pioneers of the idea that Rhondda boys ought to study Rhondda history. He squeezed as much local history as possible onto a syllabus which, even under the *Welsh* Joint Education Committee was dominated by English Kings and European Wars. A pioneer, yes – but Dai Toads was a true oddball. He styled himself a Time Lord, claiming the clapped-out Morris Minor he drove was his

Tardis. A strict disciplinarian, he pulled errant pupils back into line with a vicious yanking of their hair: 'Side-head Tweaks', a sudden twist of the sideburns, for minor misdemeanours; 'Excruciatingly Painful Top-head Extractions' for anything more serious. If ever he had to admonish the entire class, he threatened angrily and apparently in all seriousness to *turn them into toads and tie them to his windscreen wipers.* Hence his nickname. No-one really believed him, though on the final day of the previous Summer Term, Penry had knotted a dozen plastic toy frogs to the wipers of the Morris Minor.

Every pupil walking past shivered with a moment's doubt: were Toads' supernatural powers real after all?

Dai Toads was a Dictator. Literally so. He spent 95% of every lesson reading out, at breakneck speed, whole chapters of his own research and theses, which the class had to take down word-for-word, page-after-page, directly into their exercise books. The boys were well-used to it by now, though it was daunting when they'd first encountered it, in Form Three of the old single-sex Grammar School. Stakhanovite scribbling at such pace was too much for thirteen-year-old wrists, even wrists accustomed as most of them were to vigorous exercise. It was a style of learning quite alien to the girls who'd joined them for A level, and to Ciaran as well, of course; one recommended in no theory of education Jac had heard of.

In the final Double Lesson before Easter, they were back onto Dai Toads' banker topic: the rise of entrepreneurship in the South Wales Coalfield.

"In 1828, Robert Thomas opened an exceptionally productive pit at Abercanaid, near Merthyr, but he died five years later…"

The dozen or so Sixth Formers were flagging, longing for the bell. Toads habitually left the room for a full ten minutes between the two halves of the double period, and they'd nearly reached that mid-point, but he powered on with his dictation:

"However, when Thomas's widow Lucy took over the business, she hit upon the idea of selling the coal…"

Toads had got precisely as far as that, and had taken the merest hint of a breath when Jac was astounded to hear Ciaran interject, as bold and loud as you like:

"*Jaysis!* Sounds to me like you Taffies were a bit slow to cotton on to the whole point of digging up this bloody mineral."

There was uproar from all corners of the classroom. Jeers. Belly-laughs. No pupil had dared to butt in on Dai Toads ever before. *Never ever, Trevor Evans.* It took a full minute for History's Most Eccentric History Teacher to restore order. By then, he was History's Most Apoplectic History Teacher. Several of those present swore he actually had steam coming out of his ears. But when the hullaballoo finally subsided, he rebuked Ciaran with pity, rather than anger.

"McGuire, you're new to this class, so you won't be aware of what I mean by a Distressingly Unbearable Nape-Of-The-Neck Wrench. But for the sake of your golden locks, I'd advise you to seek enlightenment whilst I'm out of the room. Next time, if there is a next time, and I trust there won't be, your singular misfortune would be to experience it for yourself. As for the rest of you, *Toads and Windscreen Wipers!*"

He proceeded to dictate the sentence which had been truncated with such exquisite timing by Ciaran. This time there was not even the sliver of a gap between any of the words.

"When his widow Lucy took over the business, she hit upon the idea of selling the coal further afield in the lucrative London market."

And with that, he turned on his heels, and was gone. The second he'd shut the door behind him, Ciaran was surrounded by a circle of admirers. Even those who'd jeered his jokey take-down of the Welsh delighted in Dai Toads' discomfiture. Petra and Catherine beamed at him. As part of the Cast, he was *their* boy. Only Jac stood apart. Of course, it had to be Swotzi who clocked his sour look.

"*Indeed to goodness!* The WelshMadManiac can't take a joke about Taffies. Well, *twll tin* to that, boyo – *we're* all Welsh, and we loved it."

"I'm not sure it was meant as a joke." Jac knew he sounded pompous, but he couldn't stop himself. "And it was perfectly obvious what the sentence was going to go on to say."

"It really wasn't, Jac," said Catherine, reasonably, "Anyway, that's not the point. Don't take it so seriously."

"What *is* the point, then? I can't see it."

"I was just trying to keep up with the dictation," explained Ciaran, unnecessarily as far as everyone but Jac was concerned, but perfectly pleasantly. "I know next to nothing about Welsh history – we had other things to study in Belfast – but when he came out with that line about the widow taking *five years* to come up with the notion of selling the coal… this mental picture just popped up. Like *How Green Was My Valley* or something. The pit gear, and a huge black pyramid of stuff towering over it, and no-one in Wales having the sense to see it could be *sold*."

That was when Jac lost it. Or rather his Auntie did. He heard her response loud and clear in his mind, and before he'd stopped to think, he was repeating it word-for-word straight out of his mouth.

It was an ugly speech.

"Look, Ciaran, we've all heard about your Troubles over in Ireland. The whole world has. And we're sorry, *very sorry*, about it. But we've suffered here too. And been exploited. For centuries. Precisely by means of the coal trade that seems to amuse you so much. And, actually, *huge black pyramids of stuff* towering over us aren't that funny to those of us brought up in this part of Wales."

Ciaran looked genuinely puzzled. And then he got it. He understood what Jac was referring to. *Aberfan*.

He studied Jac carefully, appalled. It was unforgivable. Jac knew that too. Unforgivable for Jac even to hint that Ciaran had had such a terrible, terrible tragedy in his mind, unforgivable to drag it into a silly schoolboy squabble. It was a crass and hypocritical betrayal of all that Jac claimed to hold dear, to use the suffering of those whose history he claimed to be defending – to make… what? A cheap rhetorical point.

146

Jac knew he didn't deserve forgiveness; and *he* wouldn't forgive either, wouldn't forgive the way the words had sprung into his mind, the way they were *put into his mouth,* wouldn't forgive his Auntie, which is to say that he wouldn't, couldn't forgive himself. Because who was she after all? Someone, some *thing,* that he'd allowed to take possession of part of his mind, and all to avoid taking responsibility for his own thoughts, his own actions, his own ineptitude and unkindness, his own culpability.

He sensed her then, cowering, silent; cowering because *she* wasn't going to take responsibility. He hated her in that moment. And hated himself for ever having allowed her to *dictate* to him, though he was so very young when he'd begun to do that. Hated himself for tolerating her for so long. For using her as a crutch, for taking the credit that accrued from her interventions himself and shifting any blame onto her. The blame for *his* failures, *his* faults; for his failure to live as wholeheartedly, as generously as he could despite those faults. His failure to stop clinging so stubbornly to his own selfishness, to give himself for others… to love his neighbour as himself, which he knew, in his heart of hearts, was the essence of what his father was asking him to do, was praying for him to do. His failure to measure himself against the sublime, the transcendent, which is what Martyn – in *his* best moments and for all *his* faults – was showing him was possible; the Golden Rule that was the Way, the Truth and the Life, the true way to live life in all its fullness, to find Paradise here on earth…

Despite these tangled, meandering notions (had he really thought all of that, there and then, with everyone hanging on his next words? *The mind works quickly at such moments, and at many different planes all at once* – but all the same…), in that moment, trapped in this pointless argument, ringed around by doubtful Friends and scornful classmates, he *still* couldn't bring himself to back down, couldn't bring himself to see that that's what he had to do, couldn't face the inevitability of losing face. He ploughed on, or tried to…

"So, if you please, Ciaran, don't come over here and belittle what we've been through, just because of what you've seen in Belfast…"

So jealousy was bound up in this, too? A perverse envy that Northern Ireland now had more suffering to parade than South Wales? He really had sunk low. Thankfully, Ciaran cut him off. Seemingly with kindly intentions.

"Come on, Jac, I never tried to make any comparison of your situation here and what's going on in Ulster."

"Well, maybe that's because you aren't in any position to. Perhaps you aren't aware – though apparently your mother's from around here originally – of our true history. This was England's first colony. Before Ireland ever was…"

Where was this vitriol, this bile coming from? He wasn't doing himself one iota of good, not in anyone's eyes. Ciaran had heard enough.

"Well, it hasn't stopped you colluding with the colonists."

"We *fought* the English. What would you know about us and colonialism?"

"I know that my Da – my totally innocent Da – has been banged up in Long Kesh for six months now. Six months with no charge, no trial, no release date, no privileges. I know that he was taken from us in the middle of the night by four squaddies who smashed down our front door. Four squaddies who dragged him away to their armoured car. Four squaddies with accents exactly like yours, Jac Morgan."

It was spoken quietly, with no huge rancour, and it was all the more devastating for that.

Jac was finished. But he wasn't finished with. From the corner of his eye, he saw Swotzi bearing down on him. He tried to get his apology in first.

"Fair enough, Ciaran. I'm sorry. I'm being an idiot. We're on the same side…"

But Swotzi wasn't going to let him off so lightly.

"So this is how you speak to someone who's sought refuge in our country? Not much of a *croeso*, is it, Jac? Not from a big internationalist like you. I'm sure I heard you say the other day that what the world needs is a revolution. You were wrong, Jac…"

Where was this going? Jac didn't know, but he knew it wasn't anywhere good.

"…it's not *the world* that needs a revolution. It's *you*."

With that, he came up alongside Jac, planted his own feet firmly, crossed one arm over the other as he raised them up and made a sudden grab for Jac's shoulders. With an iron grasp, Swotzi twisted and applied what must have been an immense amount of upward force. Up and over Jac went. He felt his feet leaving the ground, his legs describing an arc high in the air. His whole body flew over Swotzi's head, and he kept going, upside down, until gravity began to bring his legs down again as they circled onto the far side of his assailant. Without expending a single ounce of effort himself, he'd turned a cartwheel six feet above the floor. Or rather, as it seemed to him, he'd stood perfectly still whilst the walls and ceiling revolved, and the classroom went spinning upside down and righted itself again. It would have been a beautiful, balletic move – if it hadn't been executed with such brutal intent. In the split-second that his brain remained free to retrieve such things, there was a flash of memory: somersaulting in his toy racing-car in the Tylacelyn Road garden, that time he'd nearly died when he was a toddler.

The floor found its place under his feet again – or was it the other way round? He landed all in one piece, perfectly upright and static. It must have been a stunt that Swotzi had studied and practised, some manoeuvre he'd picked up from a martial art. But no one there had seen anything like it. Their shock was palpable. Jac himself had been taken completely by surprise, but instinctively his shoulders and neck had pushed back against the twisting, had tried to resist what his body was being compelled to do. The torque of the forces brought to bear on them must have been enormous. Swotzi released him, and Jac set off to walk back to his desk. But then he felt his knees buckle, and all the lights in his head went dark.

19

When the lights came back on, Jac was safely restored to his seat. "Here comes Dai Toads!" someone shouted. Jac's classmates scurried back to their desks for the second half of the Double Lesson. An ominous hush. The door opened. Heads went down, feigning preoccupation with exercise books. It wasn't difficult to guess what mood History's Most Eccentric History Teacher would be in. The pace of his dictation would be wound up to an *excruciatingly painful* pitch. *Absolutelynopausesbetweenwordsthistime.*

Jac readied himself, shaking the residual stiffness out of his wrist. He had a nasty twinge in his neck and shoulders, but he was up for the challenge. He bent over his desk, eyes down, face close to the blank page, fountain pen poised.

He was surprised, though, when the door shut behind the teacher, to hear Dai Toads' footsteps moving directly towards the blackboard – something he seldom made use of – and the scrape of chalk across the board itself.

Except that it wasn't Dai Toads.

It was Goronwy Rees. Jac had never seen a photograph of Goronwy Rees. But he knew the instant he looked up that that's who it was. The unmistakeable jowly look of Oxbridge academia and Cold War espionage. The very image of a mole. A spy, not a breakwater or a skin-blemish.

In the Staff Room, the Time Lord must have assumed a new physical form – one of those complicated regeneration things. Jac wondered if the other teachers had noticed. Rees turned back to the class, pointing over his shoulder at two sentences he'd chalked up: 'Wales has no future. That's what history teaches us.'

It was evident that, as well as a new body, the Time Lord had a new pedagogic method. He wasn't going to dictate to them. He offered the one-word invitation, familiar to anyone who's ever sat an exam: "Discuss."

No-one dared begin. They sat still, shocked and disturbed. Discuss? *Think for themselves?* What the devil was going on?

"Come on," urged Rees, "You won't get turned into toads. I want to hear your opinions. It all comes down to what you believe in the end."

A hand was raised gingerly.

"Yes, you at the front, boy."

"Well, if Wales has no future, it's got one hell of a past."

Swotzi. Always first in with a clever-sounding answer.

"*Twpsyn boio*! Give me thoughts, ideas, not slogans. If you can glory in our past, you've obviously got an unhealthy obsession with *hiraeth*."

All the bluster, all the air suddenly went out of Swotzi. He slowly deflated, collapsing into himself, exposed as the fraud he was. The line about *hiraeth* was the killer. If it got back to MauMau and Parrot that he was *sentimental*, he'd be done for. But now another pupil wanted to take up the argument. Brave, indeed, given the way Rees had slapped Swotzi down. The voice came from right behind Jac: he couldn't place it.

"What you've put on the board is partially true. But it's based on a falsely precise premise. The statement applies not just to Wales. It applies to all people. It's the common condition of humanity. We have no future. No future, unless and until we take control, direct control of the conditions under which we live and work. We have no *necessary* future: we have to make our own. *That's* what history teaches us…"

Wow. Who was this, so fluent in his reasoning, so willing to have a go?

Jac turned. At first, he didn't recognise the face, half-hidden under thick, black hair parted roughly to one side. It was the scowl that gave the clue. Jac had seen it before. On the Night of the Election. On Tonypandy Square. It was… *Noah Ablett*! Jac must have completely forgotten that the veteran miners' leader was taking A level History with them. It was very humble of Ablett, and probably quite unnecessary, but Jac supposed that he'd be bound to get a good grade.

"N-n-nothing's too good for those who work in class," said Aneurin Bevan, slightly misquoting himself. He was sitting next

151

to Jac. His presence seemed both startling and entirely to be expected.

"It's the Bollinger Bolshevik," confirmed Nerys, who preferred beer.

One of the other girls piped up just then. It was Lucy Thomas. From Abercanaid. The coal entrepreneur and businesswoman. "I've hit upon an idea, about the coal…"

Before she could explain, a serious-looking young man stood up. He wore a black beret, just like Che Guevara, but rather than the hammer-and-sickle it had a snazzy badge on the front: a multifoliate rose with petals of red and white. He seemed to know what Lucy Thomas was about to say.

"It's all very well *selling* things to the 'lucrative London market'," he told her. "But if you want to shape the future, you've got to go there and *take control*, take control like Ablett said. That's what I did. I stole their crown."

"Stealing is not big, and it's not clever," Goronwy Rees admonished him.

Suddenly, despite his beret, he looked lost, like a naughty little boy, and sat back down again.

"Who on earth was that?" asked Nerys.

"Henry Tudor," answered Petra. "Don't you remember? We did him in Form Four."

The boys sniggered. The Bad Girls of the B Form refused to blush. Neither did Charlotte Guest. She was sitting quietly, getting on with her Welsh Translation. It was cheeky of her to be working on another subject during History, and right in front of the teacher. But then Jac remembered that the staff were going easy on her. She'd been struggling recently. Rendering the *Mabinogion* into English was a big ask.

"The Tudors forgot about Wales once they got to London," opined Penry. "Forgot Gelli too."

"Did Gelli exist in 1485?" demanded Goronwy Rees, as unimpressed as a breakwater.

"Gelli has *always* existed," boasted Penry. "It's a state of mind."

152

"Well, at least the Tudors won their battles," argued Nerys, remembering her Form Four work now. "Unlike that Owain Glyndwr. Fantastic vision he had, fair enough – a Welsh Parliament, a Welsh University, a Welsh Church, proper independent country, foreign alliances, and all. Big. Bold. Ambitious. A Free Wales. Glorious cause. Total failure."

"Glyndwr wasn't interested in Wales," reasoned Penry. "He just fancied a bit of land that belonged to somebody who was vaguely English."

"He *fought* for the English, you know. Up in Scotland. Killed a fair few Scots." This was Ninelives Bowen, who took a great interest in violent conflict. "Should have been punished for being offside. Banned. *Sine die.*"

"No one knows *anything* about fighting," proclaimed Tommy Farr, "unless they've gone the full fifteen rounds with Joe Louis. Look, I'll show you."

The Tonypandy Terror began pounding his bare knuckles into Jac's temples, like waves whacking a mole. It *hurt*.

"*Sir! Sir! Sir!* Tommy Farr is hitting me."

"Fight back, Jac, fight back," Henry Tudor exhorted him. "He might be British Heavyweight Champion, but you can take his crown."

"Don't talk wet! You'll never beat him in a fair fight. Try guerrilla tactics instead. Get stuck in from behind."

This was from a big, big girl. Front row. On the far left. Dungarees instead of a school uniform. 'Chile Fights' badge. Shaved head.

She spells trouble, thought Jac. And, indeed, the scarlet tee-shirt stretched across her mountainous bosom was emblazoned with the letters T-R-O-U-B-L-E.

"That's Boadicea," explained Catherine, who was wearing a theatrical mask divided into two distinct halves. On one side she was Cathy from *Wuthering Heights*. On the other, Catherine the Great. "I've come to find out about literacy in Wales, about how it is that you can all read..." she announced, favouring her Russian Empress side.

153

"We. Build. Our. Words. Up," replied Tighthead Jones. "One. Letter. At. A. Time."

"Indeed," added Penry, "As Chomsky argues, we have an innate genius for language."

"... but there's something I want to ask Boadicea first," Catherine continued, ignoring them. "Do you fancy a game of rugby?"

"Boudica, if you don't mind!" came the terse correction. "But yes, I've always felt destined to play for Wales."

"You're not qualified," objected Blindside Pugh. "You're an Essex girl."

"Unlike Glyndwr. He was *ours*," Loosehead Jones bragged, "Our Son of Destiny."

"*Son of Destiny*, my arse," retorted Nerys. "*Son of Losing To The English* more like. Where is he now?"

"Owen Glendower has secreted himself somewhere in the Welsh Marches," roared Bull, who'd slipped in while Jac wasn't looking. Most unlike her. She began to head back towards the door, berating poor old Aneurin Bevan as she went: "Pick up that chocolate or you'll have rats!"

"S-s-s-so far as I am concerned, they are lower than vermin," stammered Nye, in some confusion, but quoting himself correctly this time.

"Blinginate chocolate," grunted Blinginate Jenkins. "Blinginate rats too. And as for Tories..."

"You should be dissecting them, Jenkins, up in the Biology Lab." That was Bull: it was unclear if she meant rodents or Conservatives. "Off you go! The rest of you Rugby Scientists too."

"She's *absobloominlutely* right," agreed Boadicea, clearly recognising a sister soul – in Nerys. "About Glyndwr, I mean. *That*'s where he is – *nowhere*. Instead of sounding the Revolutionary Trumpet, he's slunk off, disappeared from History, kipping in some dark cave, pretending he's waiting for the Cosmic Alarm Clock to wake him, so that he can ride out heroically with his trusty knights to redeem his people in their

Hour of Need. As if we'll ever see him when the Hour of Need actually comes."

"I thought that was King Arthur," posited Petra, puzzled.

"Don't you bring my husband into this," cooed a thin beauty with absurdly long hair who had draped herself languorously all over Ninelives Bowen, for once the only Rugby Boy who hadn't been sent off. She seemed not to care that her school skirt had ridden *way* up over her thighs. "Anyway, a *fat* lot of good you were, Boadicea…"

"*Boudica*! And it's all about my weight, now, is it? Call yourself a feminist, *Queen* Guinevere!? You think you're so bloody liberated, sleeping with half the Round Table, and all behind Arthur's back. Well, look who he's sleeping with now!"

Indeed, in the back row, snoring in perfect rhythm with Ciaran, their arms wrapped tenderly around each other, there was a suspiciously regal-looking youth. Our Once and Future King. If, indeed, we had a Future. Guinevere went back to nibbling Ninelives Bowen's ear.

"O, my Lancelot, ride out and unsheathe your mighty sword," she begged him, breathily.

"Hold your horses," snapped Ninelives. "This argument is just getting interesting. There's nothing like a bit of contested History."

"I'll contest your history for you. Just like I contested Elections. And won them. Henry Tudor's not the only Welshman who's battled his way into power in London, you know."

David Lloyd George! DLG had arrived. The Welsh Wizard. The Celtic Goat. Lloyd George. He knew Jac's father. Allegedly.

"Self-serving creep," pronounced Boadicea. "And the original Welsh windbag."

"C-c-careful," stuttered Nye Bevan.

"The original's still the greatest," intoned Bryan Ferry.

What was he doing there? In Welsh History?

"If that's the way you feel, Morgan, I'm off," pouted Ferry, turning his back on them. Catherine moaned. With pleasure. Jac

155

was pleased for her. It must be tough running a country the size of Russia from a wind-swept Yorkshire moor.

"There he goes," commented Nye, as Ferry left, "naked into the Staff Room."

Catherine moaned again. She'd gone all *Wuthering Heights*. "Throw me a line," she sang. She was sinking fast.

"Call that music?" sneered Tommy Farr, who had the voice of a classic crooner himself.

"I call it an emotional sp-sp-spasm," concluded Bevan unkindly, but quoting himself accurately again.

"The finest eloquence is that which gets things done," crowed Lloyd George, returning to the argument and not to be outdone in the citing oneself stakes. "Who introduced the Old Age Pension? Who created the Welfare State?"

"I th-th-thought that was me," protested Nye.

"… who won a World War?"

Jac tried to ignore this last boast of DLG's. He didn't want Winston Churchill shooting off about how *he* was the one who sorted the Huns out; *and* got Tonypandy squared.

"My achievements are beyond contest," contended DLG.

"I contest that," countered Tommy Farr.

"I'll take you the full fifteen rounds," vowed the fiery Celt from Criccieth.

The Contested History Championship of the World, thought Jac. You could write an essay about it. Then he remembered that that *was* their homework. He hadn't written a word. He'd be turned into a toad.

Helpfully, Nerys began listing DLG's failures: "The League of Nations. Ireland. Cosying up to Hitler. The womanising. The financial scandals…"

"*Knockout!*" declared Boadicea.

"Power inevitably leads to corruption," Ablett reminded them all. "All leaders become corrupt, in spite of their own good intentions."

"Yes, yes, we know. Blah-di-blah," Lloyd George muttered, tetchily. "*No man was ever good enough, brave enough* blah-di-blah *to have such power* blah-di-blah *as real leadership implies.* But where does that get us?"

"To true democracy," preached Ablett from his soapbox. "To workers' control. To syndicalism. To Tonypandy Square and *The Miners' Next Step.*"

"So how's all *that* going to work in practice? Are you going to mandate a vote of the rank-and-bloody-file every time someone wants to go the toilet?"

"Please, sir," interjected Jac, "can I go the toilet?"

"*Order! Order!* The Question is that Sir Toby Fart be allowed to proceed to the lavatory."

History's Most Eccentric History Teacher had regenerated again. He was now Rt Hon George Thomas, a sensitive boy from Trealaw who never grew up, but had somehow been elected Deputy Speaker of the House of Commons.

"As many as are of that opinion say aye."

Silence was the only message.

"Of the contrary, no."

Acclamation from all around. Waving of exam papers on the back benches.

The noise subsided. Jac let off a deafening bum-belch. A stench of decaying Welsh rarebit spread instantly over the whole classroom. It was *deeply* satisfying.

"I think the nose has it, the nose has it," sniffed the Deputy Speaker.

But just then, the Cosmic Alarm Clock went off, the Revolutionary Trumpet sounded, and Jac was waking up in the Sick Bay, with the smell of smelling salts in his nostrils and a whomping headache.

20

Contested history. You can't argue with that. Can you?

[Is that succinct enough?]

21

A Modern Welsh Triad: The Three Profound Lessons of A Dress Rehearsal...

Thirdly, that Taking Yourself Seriously is no joke.

Secondly, that Losing A Fight to A Girl is no shame.

Above all, that when a Deadly Weapon is present, you should Never Act The Fool (*never ever, Trevor Evans*).

It was the Saturday immediately before the week of the performances. A day of final rehearsals, costume fittings, lighting and make-up tests. The Cast arrived early, eager, with packed lunches to keep themselves going. Jac's Mam had given him his marmite sandwiches, and a big bottle of Corona pop, Dandelion and Burdock flavour, his favourite, which he'd never normally be allowed to bring to school. It would be a long day. The empty corridors, silent and gloomy, quietened their mood, spooked them a little. The parquet-floored Hall was chilly even on a summer morning, and they were glad to get into their warm-ups. An armourer had been called in, to oversee the final blocking out of the swordfights. He'd brought with him foils sharp enough to do damage if they weren't handled properly. Jac and Catherine, who had to skirmish as Sir Toby and Sebastian, eyed them with misgiving. They'd rehearsed the moves over and over, but only ever with toy swords. This was for real.

It felt as though they were all arriving somewhere after a long journey. Easter was a distant memory. Even the infamous History Lesson was fading into school legend, rather than being the subject of lively gossip. Swotzi had been suspended from school, but only for a week. Jac was fine the next day. Right as rain. But there was an ironic upshot. Swotzi had *saved* Jac. The bizarre, circus-like assault and the toll it took on Jac had shifted the sympathies of those who'd witnessed it. Jac was no longer the mean-spirited, stubborn hypocrite, the real-life Malvolio in the classroom. Like Malvolio, he'd been in the wrong, but he'd been punished overly harshly. He was a victim. And victims deserve sympathy, however badly they've behaved. Thankfully, the other principal involved, Ciaran, wasn't one to bear grudges. No doubt he realised that Jac had come off worse anyway.

From the start of the Summer Term, after-school rehearsals had been added to the Dinner Time sessions. The trust the Cast were establishing on stage was becoming real, not just an exercise now. As the performance dates loomed, there was less and less time and energy for the emotional tangles they were prone to otherwise. There were arguments when rehearsals went badly, delight when a scene began to gel; but they were arguments and delights about *the work*, not about their relationships, as pairs or as a group. So Jac's feelings for Catherine were put on hold again. The relationship didn't progress in the natural way it might have done after she'd come across her name inscribed so many times in his Rough Book. There was no awkwardness between them, but neither did she open the way for him to take things further. It was frustrating, but what could he do? He wasn't brave enough to make a move himself, to risk an emotional upset between them, which would be bound to have repercussions just as they were putting the play on. And if the truth were told, he became less certain about his feelings once more. He felt foolish for blowing hot then cold again (*again!*). But the chances were, after all, that this was just a crush, a Puppy Love soon to be forgotten. Why jeopardise all they were working for in these long weeks of rehearsal for that?

Something of the same caution made Jac shy away from Martyn. He knew that he ought to assure Martyn that his secret was safe with him, to ask him whether his fear that he'd be exposed was still gnawing away at his relationship with Petra, to see if he could help somehow. But how? Did Martyn even remember what he'd told Jac that night? He'd been so drunk, it might all have been simply wiped from his memory. Martyn and Petra seemed better together, calmer, as though they too were being careful to keep things on an even keel, which was *a good thing*, since the success of the whole play depended on their pivotal roles.

The Cast was being drilled constantly, taught how to modulate their performances, how to control the adolescent tendency to overact. "Less is more," Osmond reminded them time and again: "keep a grip on it". Something of that self-control spilled over into their time together outside of rehearsals. *Catch yourselves on!* they told each other, Jac having repeated Ciaran's phrase so often it became a kind of Cast Motto. There was no need, no tolerance, no excuse for self-indulgence. It surprised them all, and it thrilled Jac, how disciplined they could be, how respectful of each other's talents, how they began to know instinctively when to improvise and when to stick to the text; how kind and tender they could be off-stage, how rigorous and demanding when necessary.

The intensity was exhausting, and yet like some extended drug-fuelled trip (or so Jac imagined) the thing itself gave you the stamina to go on experiencing it, and to experience it so vividly in each and every moment. For those few weeks, they lived inside a metaphor, or rather they lived it out: a metaphor for an ideal society, where the *from each* and the *to each* is in perfect balance; a metaphor for life itself, in that you never wanted it to end, and yet you knew that it was only because there was an end that it had any meaning.

After one tough rehearsal, sweaty yet exhilarated, coming down slowly, Jac found himself at the end of the Hall, staring at the bust of William Evans that stood on one of the window alcoves. They all knew the history behind the memorial: the School Prizes for academic achievement had been endowed by this philanthropist who'd made his fortune from Corona pop. Evans, so the story went, had been in his grocery store in Hannah Street, Porth one day when a stranger walked in, claiming to be a Medicine Man who'd been run out of Dallas, Texas after a gunfight. It was outlandish, but just the sort of thing that *might* happen in the Rhondda back in 1910. The Valley was pioneer territory too.

The American, down on his luck, offered to teach the grocer, in exchange for a square meal, 'the secret of making mineral water the like of which your customers will never have tasted'. It was the genesis of one of the most successful brands Wales had ever seen.

"If William Evans could have bottled what we've got here," mused Penry, meaning what the Cast was experiencing together, "he'd have made millions of pounds more."

Jac hadn't noticed Penry come up alongside him and intuit what had been going through his mind. Martyn had joined them too, and he put it better.

"If you could bottle *this*, there'd be no need for millionaires ever again."

With Ciaran, the focus on the acting, not the actor, didn't apply. They all had to triangulate their relationships with him for the first time, to make him feel included, to ask the most basic things about family, interests, life in Belfast. The Troubles were so dominant in their picture of Ireland that they kept returning to questions they feared would seem naïve to him. What was a bomb scare like? Had he felt safe when he went shopping, and on his way to and from school? Did he hate 'the Brits'? Who *are* 'the Brits'? Were *the Friends themselves* 'Brits'? Why had his father been targeted?

They all felt an instinctive sympathy for the principle of a United Ireland, but it was scarcely possible for them to comprehend life in a place, in a society so riven, so divided. The Rhondda was at peace – with itself, and with the world at large, in the sense that it hadn't taken up guns and bombs to fight its corner, even if it too was engaged in a struggle. As they tried to get their head around these things, there were more outrages in the news. A Catholic pub in Belfast was bombed: six dead. There was a strike – led by something called the Ulster Workers' Council – but it seemed to be entirely on the wrong side of the argument. Loyalists exploded four bombs in the Republic, killing thirty-three, wounding 300 more. It was impossible to know what to say, given the scale of the atrocities. Jac felt increasingly foolish for having tried to lecture Ciaran about colonialism. Ciaran himself began to show signs of being burdened by their questions. He confessed that his mother was worried about his father. *He* was worried about his father. But he seemed glad to be away from Belfast, and rarely mentioned friends he'd left behind.

There were lighter moments. Ciaran's accent amused them still. Rehearsals gave them laughs, too. It was a *comedy* after all! They improvised routines with silly props. Not pure *Commedia dell'Arte*, but it gave them a sense of ownership over Shakespeare's plot, Shakespeare's words. Penry devised an ungainly dance for Feste and Sir Toby to do with the freestanding artificial trees they were supposed to be hiding behind to spy on Malvolio. Penry and Jac were in danger of ruining it by over-acting, but Martyn's comic timing made it work: he *almost* caught a glimpse of them each time they picked up the trees and did a 360-degree revolve. And then he finally *did* spot them, only to act out brilliantly a man refusing to believe the evidence of his own eyes. It was every bit as convincing as one of Bowie's mimes. Sir Toby, of course, had to learn how to *belch* at will – sucking in a mouthful of air, trapping it in his throat, and forcing it straight back out again, jaws wide open. It became Jac's party trick. *Dost thou think, because thou art virtuous...* BURP! *there shall be no more cakes and ale?*

So here they were, the final rehearsal. The next time they'd speak their lines would be in front of an audience. Martyn and Lydia were running through the scene where Malvolio appears with *ridiculous boldness* before the Lady Olivia. He's following to a T the instructions in the love-letter that he believes she's sent him. Dressed in lurid garters, he grins (*thy smiles become thee well*, hints the letter) and smirks and preens so oddly that Olivia will eventually allow Sir Toby and his accomplices to shut him up as a madman. Halfway up the Hall, Jac watched with Petra, keeping up a whispered commentary.

"Martyn's terrific in this scene, absolutely terrific. The way he builds those smiles up – natural at first, then more and more exaggerated, until they become grotesque. And then something beyond that again. It'll bring the house down. If I'd been doing it, I'd have started smiling as bizarrely as I could, and just stayed there."

"I know what you mean," whispered Petra. "He always gives himself somewhere to go in a scene, some headroom, another gear."

"*The Great Martsby.*"

"He *is* great in this, isn't he?"

And then the pay-off line came to both of them at exactly the same moment, so they chorused it together: *some are born great, some achieve greatness, and some have greatness thrust upon them.*

There was a loud *Sh-sh-shush!* Osmond swung round and *glared* at them. Shamed, they moved further from the stage. They watched in silence for a while, and then – *very, very quietly* – started talking again.

"Which is it, do you think… with Martyn? His greatness: in-born, achieved or thrust upon him?"

"His *greatness*? I didn't mean to put it that way, Jac. I'm biased, of course. But they say if you have a talent for acting, a real talent like Martyn's got, you must have been born with it."

"But that's not what Shakespeare's getting at, is it? By *born great* he means born into wealth and status."

Under her breath, Petra laughed.

"Well, then none of us here are blessed with *that* sort of greatness, are we? Martyn least of all. You'd never think that someone with the tastes he's got, his Italian operas and his French literature… that someone so *cultured* would have grown up in a home like his."

"Culture *is* ordinary, though," pronounced Jac. At Martyn's suggestion, he'd started reading Raymond Williams. Or trying to.

"What I mean, Jac, is… I'm from a perfectly ordinary background myself – father a miner and all of that – but the first time I went to Martyn's house I was shocked. How little they had. The basic mod cons, fair enough. But nothing to spare. Nothing but the necessities. No books at all. No pictures on the wall. So where did he get it all from, this love of words and art and beauty?"

"His father's been on the sick for years, hasn't he? Is that why things are tight?"

"Well, Martyn's aunt stumps up when they're desperate, I think – Eve, the one who's married to the Bracchi. But Martyn can be... well, he wouldn't like me saying this, but... *bitter* towards his father. As though he blames him for being disabled."

"He thinks his father's malingering?"

"He just thinks he's weak. And *despises* him for it. As though he's not man enough to face down his problems. Which is very unfair. The poor dab's practically paralysed."

Not man enough. They were getting into deep waters. Dangerous ones, given what Jac knew about Martyn, and – seemingly – Petra still didn't. Having to whisper lent an intimacy to the conversation that it wouldn't otherwise have had. Time to change tack.

"What about you, Petra? Or should I say, *Viola?* You seem born to that role. Very natural, you are. Anyone would think you really were falling in love with our Duke Orsino."

Petra laughed again, gently. She was untroubled, impervious by now to Jac's teasing.

"*Catch yourself on, Jac Morgan!* Ciaran's very balanced. Very cool. But quite vulnerable, I think, underneath it all. It's been good to get to know him better. *Grand*, as he would say. But falling in love with him? I assure you that's just the greatness of *my* acting."

She paused, just long enough to make sure Jac understood this wasn't a serious boast, simply a piece of self-mockery to make her point stick.

"I'll tell you what's been strange for me, though, Jac. And *educational.* Acting as a woman disguised as a man. Exploring the male psyche. Martyn likes it. Thinks it's done us good. Tells me I understand him better."

Deep waters again. Martyn's feelings about his girl play-acting a man. Jac didn't want to go there. Thankfully, Petra turned the question back to Jac.

"So how about you? What's Jac Morgan learnt from *Twelfth Night?*"

"Well... how to belch pretty well, I suppose."

He felt tempted to demonstrate. But even he knew it wasn't the time for a theatrical *BURP!* They'd annoyed Osmond once already.

Just as well he held back for once, because Petra wasn't amused.

"O, Jac... You should take yourself more seriously, you know."

Her directness surprised him, although she was only saying something his Auntie had been telling him for years. *Take yourself seriously.* In that moment, in that one small statement – though it was a big thing to hang on one statement – he knew that Petra *was* taking him seriously. She'd given him Advice. Advice with a capital A.

Her gaze was still fixed on him. It was uncomfortable. Some tender part of him was being probed. Instinctively, he didn't want this to go any further. He felt tempted to push her away, or to turn away himself. At the same time, he knew that this was what he was seeking, deep down; this was why he was here, with her, with Catherine, with Martyn, with The Society of Friends. To feel this closeness, to feel understood, to experience a connection that would take him out of himself. Yet it was easier, even now, to wall himself in with his own pain. To feel sorry for himself. He couldn't find the energy, the *unselfishness* – yes, that's what it was – to get over himself, to take what Petra was offering. To make himself big enough, brave enough, *man enough* to grasp this simple thing she'd said and use it as a springboard... to reach for his true potential, his own *greatness* even – if greatness was the word for what anyone could be, for what all of us are, when we're most fully ourselves.

His doubt, his confusion must have been written on his face.

"Has it ever occurred to you, Jac, that you take everything that happens to you far too seriously... but you yourself nothing like seriously enough?"

Petra's words. A gift. Jac struggled to summon up the grace to accept them. To do what those words, what her taking of him

166

seriously was prompting him to do. He glimpsed the path to his own Salvation: it was right there in front of him. But that first step…

No, it was easier to fall back into the prison of self-pity he'd made for himself.

"It's pretty hard to do that, to take yourself seriously, when you're playing the fat drunken idiot. I mean, I'm not exactly the leading man here, am I? It's not like I've been given a part with any depth or scope. But fair enough, because obviously that's all that I'm capable of."

It was pathetic, and Jac knew it. Petra was merciful, all the same.

"That's nonsense. There's *plenty* you can do with the part you've been given. Plenty that you are doing. But you could push yourself even further. You're one of the high-flyers here. Martyn's always saying that. He quite admires you, you know."

Well, now… that was a surprise. Martyn praising him. And there was something else in what Petra had said, an assumption she'd made, which struck Jac just as forcibly. There were *high-flyers* in the cast. Jac – despite his own insecurities – had always thought of them all as equals, Martyn aside, their talents and intelligence evenly-matched. As being on the same trajectory. If they were going to fly high, they'd fly high together. They'd always be there for each other, always bound up with each other. The idea that their paths in life might diverge, that some would soar and others not… that was a new and strange thought.

Just then, they were all summoned to make-up and wardrobe. Jac had his pillow – *yes, really* – stuffed inside his tunic. Gluing the false beard to his cheeks and chin took ages, but the boys were still ready and back in the Hall well before anyone emerged from the Girls' Dressing Room. The delay lent an element of dramatic tension to *their* entrance. It was the first time they'd all get to see each other in greasepaint and full costume.

Catherine and Petra came first, identical twins in matching doublet and hose, all russet and orange, with capes and knee-length boots. It was a stunning look. For a brief instant Jac couldn't tell which was which, mistaking Petra for Catherine. A disturbing feeling.

An apple, cleft in two, is not more twin
Than these two creatures.

Nerys made a presentable Maria – stage make-up softened the prominence of her mole and the period costume suited her, though she had no figure to speak of. Lydia certainly *did* have a figure. Her splendid aristocrat's gown did little to disguise it. But the reveal that made the boys gasp was when she drew back the black veil that was Lady Olivia's symbol of mourning. Her hair was pulled off her temples, piled high and handsome above. Her face glowed with a subtle tan. And the glasses she *always* wore were gone, her eyes accentuated by mascara instead, and large, fluttering false eyelashes. Penry gave a wolf whistle.

"Why, Miss Peake," he declaimed, milking the moment, "you're beautiful."

"*Take the fool away!*" she replied, using one of Olivia's lines to Feste.

But he was right. Animated, her features were even more striking. *The nonpareil of beauty*, indeed. Honey-haired Lydia Peake – her loveliness had always been there, but she never flaunted it, and in everyday life it played second-fiddle to how level-headed she was.

Now came the swordfight rehearsal, in full costume, with those blades that were sharp enough to make Jac and Catherine wary. They had to have a proper set-to, making it clear to the audience that Sebastian was – just – getting the better of Sir Toby. So it began. *Concentrate, Jac.* Leading leg pushed forward with knee bent, back footed planted at ninety degrees, free arm aloft for balance, body turned parallel to the action to make the target as narrow as possible, and… dart forward to attack, shuffle back to avoid the counterstroke, parry and… thrust forward again. It was an aggressive tango – not that Jac had ever danced a tango. And intimate, amazingly intimate. Even with the armourer watching like a hawk, and with everyone else in the Hall in rapt attention – there must have been thirty there

altogether, wardrobe assistants and lighting technicians and all –
he and Catherine were *alone*. They mirrored, in minute, precise
detail, each other's actions; responding, in split seconds, to every
motion, every feint of each other's bodies, to every tiny
rebalancing. It felt *real*, not like acting at all: a closeness, a
connection every bit as powerful and direct as the one he'd just
experienced talking to Petra, but this was *physical*, purely physical.
All he knew was *Catherine, Catherine, Catherine*. Thrust after thrust
after thrust. Her doublet and hose, the tights clinging to her
thighs. The shape of her, this girl revealed to him as a woman,
and yet a woman playing a man, strong and masterful. But he
himself was her equal, the control and the responsibility shared
between them. Though he followed the script faithfully,
willingly, letting her gain the upper hand in the fight, this was
something they were creating together, making anew there and
then, in those very moments, despite the jeopardy of those
flashing blades, with more poise and assurance than his awkward
body could ever remember. *This is it*, he told himself. *This is what
taking yourself seriously feels like*. The climax came. He acknowledged
her victory. *Touché*.

It was over. He was aware of cheering from the onlookers.
But as they stepped out of character, his eyes were only for
Catherine. Had she experienced it the way he had? She blew out
her cheeks as she recovered herself.

"That's the trick, Jac. Well done. It was special." She glanced
down at her sword, its steely edge catching a reflection of the
stage lights; and then back up at him. "And thank you. I wouldn't
have done that with anyone I couldn't trust."

And she hugged him. *Touché, encore*.

The day was nearly done. Everyone changed back into their
own clothes. All that remained was one final pep talk. Osmond
stood in the middle of the Hall, gathering her thoughts. Jac was
suddenly weary. He sat on the edge of the stage, elbows on knees,
palms up supporting his chin, looking – with no real focus –
towards Catherine and Martyn, who were leaning against the wall
bars, talking to each other. Nerys came to sit next to him.

169

"Got a crush on somebody, Jac?"

She glanced across the Hall to where Catherine and Martyn were still chatting.

"...You need to be careful, boy. There's more going on there than you might think."

What did she mean? Was she just winding him up? He felt an anger rise within him, but she lightened her tone again.

"Anyway, you're supposed to be marrying *me*. That's what it says in the script, you know," she said with a wink, pointing down at a rolled-up sheaf of papers that one of the lighting crew had dropped.

She shimmied away, leaving Jac unsure how to take her warning. Her jokiness at the end didn't convince him. Something precious inside himself had been fingered, interfered with.

It must have been that emotional jolt which woke his Auntie up. His Auntie, who'd been silent, hiding away from his wrath, ever since the *débâcle* with Ciaran in the History lesson. He'd almost forgotten how much he'd hated her that day for what she'd made him say. She'd been wise to lie low. But now she was back.

Do something, she urged him. *Don't let Nerys get the impression she's rattled you. Don't sit there in a* pwdu. *Show her how strong you are.*

It seemed to make sense, another way of saying *take yourself more seriously.* But should he forgive his Auntie? Should he – could he – trust her?

He stood up. He had no idea what he was going to do. Nerys had struck up a conversation with Catherine, and he didn't want a scene in front of *her.* Lydia, Petra and Martyn were chatting together. *Go and have a word with Penry then*, suggested his Auntie. *Have two words with him.* What words? *I don't know! Those French words: on guard. Pretend to start a swordfight with him. That'll show Nerys you're not pouting at least!* Yes, why not? Swordfights were his strong suit. He stooped to gather the rolled-up script, and rushed towards Penry, holding the tube of papers in his outstretched hand like a rapier.

"En garde!"

Penry laughed at the mock challenge. He needed a 'sword' of his own to respond. The nearest thing to hand sat next to him on the wooden floor. Jac's Corona pop bottle, left over from lunch. It was large – the size of a flagon. Even empty, the glass was heavy. Penry grabbed it one-handed near the tapered top. In one swift, ill-judged motion, he swung it forcefully in an arc up to shoulder level as a counter to Jac's weapon, completing the extravagant theatrical gesture with a flick of his wrist. With that final flourish, his grasp on the glass failed, and there it was, this beautiful bottle, bearing the Corona logo and the words *Dandelion and Burdock*, propelled like a guided missile at head height across the Hall. The shallow parabola of its track was disastrously on a direct collision course… with Osmond's forehead. She stood there unaware of her impending doom. She would be knocked unconscious. Worse.

All this happened in an instant. But Jac had just been processing the perilous thrusts of the swordfight in fractions of a second. He saw the bottle fly in slow motion. He even had time to decide whether to look away before the impact. He cringed. And heard an explosion.

Somehow, at the very last, the bottle had gathered a smidgeon of fresh momentum, taking it clear of Osmond's head by the merest inch. If she hadn't been Wales' Smallest English Mistress she'd have been virtually decapitated. Five yards beyond her, the bottle detonated on the hardwood floor into a hundred shards.

A terrible silence fell. Everyone was locked, speechless, in a *tableau* of dread. They'd seen Osmond's death, it was etched on their faces still, despite her miraculous escape. Penry was openly aghast, half-crouched, frozen with his arm outstretched, the guilty, empty hand on the end of it. An absence of noise filled the Hall. Jac felt sick: he'd all but committed manslaughter. Penry might get the blame, but it was Jac who'd brought the deadly weapon to school, Jac who'd initiated the horseplay. He stared at all that was left of the bottle: the torn label, its large Corona 'C'. It suddenly seemed appallingly symbolic. A product – like them all – of the Rhondda. Jac hoped, hoped in his heart, that it was no ill omen. For the production. For the closeness he'd just found with Catherine. For the whole Valley.

Osmond had still said nothing. Finally...

"PENRY CADOGAN!" she thundered.

And then: "How many times have I told you? *Keep a grip on it!*"

With that, she burst out laughing. Clearly, she'd calculated that the timing wasn't right to make a thing of it. Penry was left to offer an ashen-faced explanation – as much to himself as to Osmond, since he still couldn't credit how the bottle had shot out of his grasp:

"There was a drop of pop on the top."

22

PORTH COUNTY COMPREHENSIVE SCHOOL

presents

TWELFTH NIGHT

(or, It All Comes Down To What You Believe In The End)

by William Shakespeare

There was a drop of pop on the top. The inadvertent triple-rhyme of Penry's explanation lodged itself in the mind of the Catchphrase Kid. It became the expression Jac applied to any cack-handed accident or pratfall, even if its cause was completely unrelated to slippery moisture. His habit of repeating 'witticisms' hadn't been broken by Petra's Advice. To Penry's *chagrin*, he worked up a pun-ridden routine based on the Cadwgan motto, all about 'w(h)etting your battleaxe'.

But Jac's worry that incident might be a sinister portent proved unfounded, at least as far as the play was concerned. *Twelfth Night* was a triumph. The *Rhondda Leader*, no less, rushed out a five-star review. Martyn got the lion's share of praise for 'carrying off this Malvolio in garish yellow cross-garters with a masterful insouciance' and for 'such surprising and touching pathos at the end of this *Night*'. Petra's poise and diction, her assured command of the role, heralded the rising of a new Rhondda star. And 'the gamble of casting pretty Catherine Evans in the male role of Sebastian was richly rewarded'. There were honourable mentions for Lydia ('a delicate reading of a key character') and for a 'handsome' Duke Orsino. Penry's 'fine vocal embellishments' got a special commendation. Jac tried to hide his disappointment that though Sir Toby was noted in passing as the 'Lord of Misrule', nothing was said of his performance in the role; but, all in all, it was a fulsome appraisal, so unlike the paper's customary style that Nerys suggested that it was Osmond herself who deserved the by-line.

What struck the Cast most of all was the presence of an audience: packed, appreciative houses, a real sense of a communal event. The comedy, the drama, was something they were making together, cast and congregation; and the meaning of what was made depended on both. The Cast themselves were keenly aware of the blemishes – missed lines, wrong cues, technical glitches. On the final night, one of Lady Olivia's spectacular eyelashes detached itself, and began to slide slowly down her cheek. Lydia delivered the rest of her lines in that scene with her head cocked to one side in effort to prevent it from slipping further. Martyn could hardly stop himself from corpsing. The loudest laughs, though, came from the *groundlings* – the school's younger pupils (who'd been 'encouraged' to buy tickets for the show) – in response to Jac's humungous belches.

Then, too soon, after the weeks and months of preparation, it was all over.

All over bar the party. The cast had booked the Archery Club for a celebration on the Saturday after the shows. They called it *Thirteenth Night.*

The barn-like club, claiming the title 'Rhondda's Highest Licensed Premises', was accessed by a *tar-mark* track which left Jac's famous New Road near Glyncornel Lake, winding its way to the summit, hairpin after hairpin, up the steep slopes populated by Forestry Commission evergreens. The Rhondda Bowmen had a course of targets set out in the woods, but it was their clubhouse that attracted young drinkers.

The whole Sixth Form had been invited. Even the Rugby Boys came. Though as they arrived, Blinginate Jenkins was heard to mutter "Blinginate archery." There were a couple gate-crashers too. One of the Tonypandy Square Hell's Angels, Rat, turned up with a leather-jacketed biker friend in tow. Rat wasn't *quite* as scary as his butties, MauMau, Parrot and Dodo, and it turned out he was an Archery Club member, so there was no way they could refuse him entry. His long hair, full of dandruff and goodness knows what else, unwashed for months no doubt, a proper rat's nest (*so that's how he got his nickname!* – Jac's Auntie), looked out of place all the same. Sixth Form boys were allowed hair down to their shirt collars, no longer.

No matter. It was going to be some party. *Thirteenth Night?* Unlucky for some, but not for them. Especially not for Lydia, as it turned out. The DJ was all set up, and they'd arranged an extra mic so that Martyn could give a little speech of thanks. That didn't take long. Soon they were bopping to the Stones – *Brown Sugar, Satisfaction, Honky Tonk Women* – Petra and Catherine jiving with each other.

"Rhondda's Glimmer Twins!", shouted Jumpin' Jac Flash to them over the boom of the bass.

They did the Monster Mash. They did the Locomotion. With Roxy Music, they did the Strand (it was very *them*: their teenage revolution given a danceable solution, there and then).

"Bryan Ferry's back," stage-whispered Martyn into Catherine's ear. He knew about her fetish. They all did.

"He never went away," she giggled, and her own back shivered and shook, as though an icy thrill had passed down it.

The dancefloor was packed. In one corner, Nerys, in a bat-winged top and black jeans, was gyrating, wiggling her bum suggestively, surrounded by a circle of Rugby Boys who were clapping her in time to the music. "Good for her," thought Jac. "She might even get off with one of them."

Next, Jac was mouthing the words of *Rebel Rebel*, duetting with Bowie himself. Martyn, caught up in the exuberance, began to mime along too, boasting in synch with the track that, dancing being his thing, he looked divine. Not to be outdone, Jac started to leap around, arms aloft, chanting the lyrics, pointing down at Petra and Catherine with his forefingers. It was all about them. Bowie's allusions to cross-dressing, to girls mistaken for boys, were written specially for *this* Viola and *this* Sebastian. Bouncing up and down, Jac tried to make it obvious without making it obvious which hot tramp *he* was obsessed with. Then he went back to playing air guitar.

Finally, they headed back to their seats, dripping with sweat. Jac made it a grand exit by deliberately letting loose one of his famous Toby Belch BURPS across the dancefloor. Rat's friend came and commented on his antics to Lydia, who'd been sitting watching all of this. Obviously, he was impressed by Jac's lack of inhibitions.

"That boy must 'ave 'ad an absolute skinful," Jac overheard him say.

"He's teetotal, if you want to know." A tart response, sharper than Lydia usually was. "He says his body manufactures its own alcohol. Though it's none of your business, really."

"'e's a nutter," came the reply, from somewhere underneath the biker's thatch. "Fair play to 'im."

The biker was short, hardly taller than Penry. In fact, he seemed harmless close up. Unlike Rat, it looked like he'd actually washed his hair before coming out.

The DJ switched to quieter stuff. Jac had requested tracks from *Tapestry* and *American Pie*, hoping they'd spark something with Catherine. If he could get her to dance with him to one of their old favourites, it would be a sign that he *was* forgiven for the mess he'd made of that smooch, up in the Beach. When *Way Over Yonder* came on, he readied himself to make a move, even though it wasn't a number you could properly dance to, and nobody else was on the floor. As he hesitated, Penry rushed across the empty space and grabbed the spare mic. He started crooning over the top of Carole King's vocals, adapting her words on the fly to make them refer to Gelli. "Way up the Rhondda, is a place that I know, Where if it's not raining, it's turning to snow…" Everyone loved it. *Way Up The Rhondda* the song would always be from then on. But any romantic associations it had went out the window.

Next, *American Pie* – the whole Sixth Form belting out the choruses in unison. But now Catherine was talking to Ciaran, their heads bent close together so that they could hear each other. *Ciaran. Duke Orsino.* That *Rhondda Leader* review. Was he 'handsome'? Jac supposed so. More handsome than Jac? Not too much doubt about that either. Did that matter as far as Catherine was concerned? That was the question. Jac might have the *eyes*, but Ciaran had the *back*. Catherine was certainly giving him her undivided attention. Jac stared, willing their conversation to be over, willing Catherine to turn her head towards *him*. He tried to think of a way to attract her attention. Come on, Jac be nimble, he told himself, Jac be quick... But by the time he managed to catch her eye, the song was into last verse; and, then, as though prompted by McLean's words, she just smiled, right on cue, and turned away.

Jac felt his spirits sink. He was starting to feel sorry for himself. He'd longed for this night to be picture-perfect, longed to relive the feeling he'd found – that had found him – at the Dress Rehearsal, in the swordfight with Catherine; that grace, that sense of faultless flow, of *taking himself seriously*. But he'd tried too hard, and gone and spoiled it by over-acting on the dancefloor, lolloping like a drunken maniac. He sensed the sweat from his exertions drying in his armpits. He felt feverish all of a sudden. A line from the play came to mind, Olivia's judgement on Malvolio, that he was *sick of self-love*...

Was he making it all about himself again?

Jac turned his attention to their Malvolio. *His* mood had darkened too. Martyn had been left on his own – Petra and Catherine were dancing with Penry and Ciaran – holding a double vodka and a cigarette. He downed the drink in one, stubbed out the fag, and headed for the bar again, glaring at Nerys as he went. But she'd done nothing, except flirt with the Rugby Boys – she was sitting with two of them now, *on* two of them in fact, having a laugh. Sometimes Jac simply didn't get Martyn, where all that resentment came from.

There was no way back, Jac realised, no way to recapture the highs of those first few dances. He'd seen it before: there always came this tipping point. It was the reason he never touched a drop of alcohol himself. Plenty of fun, plenty of drink and everyone was happy, the good times rolled. But just one more, that *one* too many, and suddenly everything was ruined, darkness descended. He saw it happening all around him, once again. Only Lydia seemed exempt. Sane, level-headed Lydia. You could depend on her. Except that, when he looked for her, he spotted her on the dancefloor – *with The Biker Who'd Washed His Hair*!

"Have you seen *that!?*"

They all had.

"She must be pissed," was Catherine's judgement.

"I better go and check…" said Petra, as the unlikely couple left the dancefloor and sat down… *together.*

Petra sauntered over, acting casual. Even after a few, she was a fine actress. They saw her strike up – as though by chance – a conversation with Lydia on the Biker's blindside.

When she walked back to the others, her expression was unreadable.

"*Well…?*

"Lydia's fine. In fact, she says she's having an *epic* evening."

"*Epic?* That doesn't sound like her. Are you sure she's not had one or two too many?"

"Absolutely. She said she's learned something from you, though, Jac."

"From *me?*"

"Yeah – not to be quite so buttoned up, even if she's not merry."

Penry laughed. "Sounds like Biker Boy might be in for a bumpier ride than he bargained for."

Biker Boy he was from then on. It was more succinct than *The Biker Who'd Washed His Hair.* He'd already got Lydia up to dance again. Jac thought back to that night at the Beach, when he'd reckoned *everybody* was going mad and that even Lydia would end up with a biker. Even worse, he'd predicted, a biker *from Trealaw.* Well, there she was now, in a clinch with *Biker Boy.* Jac wondered whether he was a *Trealaw* Biker Boy.

Wherever he came from, he kept Lydia dancing until the lights came up.

Unlike Lydia, Martyn was quite, quite drunk by then. Incapable of getting up from his chair. Petra motioned to Jac. He went over to help her haul him to his feet. It was time to go. But Martyn didn't want help, from anyone.

Then, suddenly, he jumped up all by himself, spun round and accosted Ninelives Bowen, who was standing there, doing nothing, with a bunch of his fellow rugby forwards.

"I'll be revenged on the whole *pack* of you!" Martyn hissed at them, in a souped-up, drunken half-parody of his own delivery of Malvolio's final line. Jac had to admire his fearlessness. And the pun. If it was intended. The Rugby Boys seemed to have no idea what he was on about.

"*Such surprising and touching pathos at the end of the night,*" quoted Petra, drily, with perfect diction. She suddenly seemed sober again.

In the end, it took the whole gang of them to get Martyn underway. But outside, when the night air hit him, he started to stagger again. The forest canopy was all around, but there was still light in the sky, enough to show up this midsummer madness for what it was. Martyn threw his arm around Jac's shoulders. They set off down the long and winding road, the others soon a good few turns ahead. Heading downwards, the momentum kept them going, and they succeeded in negotiating two hairpins. But the New Road was still far below. Then, from the trees above the roadway, came a sudden, blood-curdling shriek. Jac and Martyn froze.

A moment later, a monstrous figure crashed through the curtain of branches and fell from the top of the embankment smack in front of their feet. Blinginate Jenkins. Tanked-up, his befuddled brain must have insisted it was a waste of time to use the zigzagging track, so he was plunging directly through the Forestry in a near vertical descent to the Valley floor. He was covered in pine needles. He shook himself, got up and stared at Martyn and Jac, as though *they* were the weirdos for taking the metalled track.

"Blinginate hairpins," he told them by way of explanation. Then, he clocked Martyn's arm around Jac's shoulders. "Blinginate homos too," he sneered.

With that he jumped off the track, down to the next level of the woods, and galumphed his way onwards, rumbling and

179

roaring downhill, straight through the trees. They heard him fulminating – "Blinginate Forestry!" – until his words were lost in the distance.

Martyn was slurring now, heavily. Blinginate's sudden appearance had unnerved him, but he was trying to say something, something important he *needed* to tell Jac.

"That Nerys, you want to watch her…"

Nerys? Why Nerys? What did she have to do with Blinginate Jenkins? Drunken nonsense, Jac decided, and he was about to try to pacify his friend, to say something innocuous like *there's no harm in her, you've all just had a bit too much* when Martyn found his next phrase.

"… that *bloody so-and-so*."

That's all he said, but it was enough for the penny to drop. It was the same phrase he'd used up against the railings of Gosen Chapel: "…when that *bloody so-and-so* splits on me".

So it was Nerys who knew the secret of Martyn's past. She was the *so-and-so* who was threatening him. Was blackmailing him, in effect.

"And there's another thing, Jacob boy…"

Nobody used the full version of his name. It surprised Jac that Martyn even knew it.

"… another thing that your old friend Martyn here has simply *got* to let you know."

"You're *smashed* Martyn, that's what I know."

Martyn brought himself to an abrupt halt. He was still using Jac to support his weight, and he all but pulled the two of them to the ground. He gasped suddenly, as though he hadn't noticed Jac there until then, did a drunken double-take, then fought to get his eyes back in focus.

"I'm *smashed* – that's what I've got to tell you."

Jac knew that wasn't what he'd wanted to say. There was something else, some other piece of the puzzle, something he needed to reveal.

"What is it, Martyn? What's the problem?"

Martyn turned and bellowed into the night.

"The problem is that *I am an angry passionate soul crying out in this tortuous mediocrity!*"

"What…?"

If that was a quote, Jac didn't recognise it. Martyn might just have made it up. But then, much more quietly, he spoke again.

"Jac, I think I fancy you."

Or it might have been "Jac, I think I've answered you."

His speech had become so incoherent that it was impossible to tell which one he'd actually said, or had meant to say.

Jac decided to act as though it was the second of the two possibilities. The first just threw up too many complications.

"Come on, Martyn, let's get back to the rest of them, and let's get you home."

At the bottom of the track, at the edge of the Lake, a hundred yards beyond them all, Jac spotted two figures, arm-in-arm. Lydia and the Biker Boy. There was just enough light to see another couple, strolling in synch with them: their reflections on the surface of the water. They kept perfect time, the four of them.

Jac realised that it was the start of something.

And something's coming to an end, too.

Lydia was moving beyond them.

If this was a novel, she'd be walking out of it now, walking right out of the book, into the first chapter of her own story.

The pair on the bank reached the far side of the Lake. As though in a fairy tale, they turned to kiss each other. But strangely, when Jac looked down at their reflection, it no longer matched the real world above. There was something in his Auntie's tales of ancient Celtic magic in the waters, after all. The lovers in the Lake were just holding hands, not kissing. And it wasn't Lydia and her biker down there.

The girl was Catherine. Or was it Petra? It was hard to tell. The two were so alike now in Jac's mind.

And the boy, slightly turned away: was that Martyn or Jac himself?

The couple in this watery Otherworld, this *Annwn* of theirs, seemed to hesitate. Would they too seal their love with a kiss?

181

Suddenly, a huge splash. And another.

Blinginate.

He must have thought it would be amusing to hurl rocks into the water.

The backwash sped to the shore, shattering the mirrored reflection. Another image came to Jac then: the Corona bottle, its shards lying scattered on the wooden floor of the School Hall.

23

It was Saturday 31st August. The morning after the Nocturnal Intermission. The morning after the night of the woodpecker in the petrol station. If woodpecker it was. The morning after Jac's Auntie had confronted him with some home truths. That he was too ready to make excuses for himself. That he never pushed himself to the ultimate. That he didn't take himself seriously. Still.

But it was a new dawn, a day of new beginnings. A(nother) Stranger would come to town. A sensitive boy who never grows up would set out on a journey. A Triad of journeys, in fact. *The Three Glorious Traverses of Tonypandy Square.*

As he woke, Jac knew little of what lay ahead. But it was the last weekend of the Summer Holidays. And The Society of Friends were getting back together. At last. It had been a long, long time. *Aeons* since the Archery Club, Blinginate leaping through Glyncornel Woods covered in pine needles, and whatever it was that Martyn had said.

Immediately after *Thirteenth Night*, the cast had gone into exam mode. Martyn and Lydia had A levels to sit. The rest of them, well behind with their classwork, faced year-end tests of their own. There was a feeling that everyone could do with a break from each other anyway. Then, suddenly, the holidays were upon them. Instead of being available to each other almost all the time, they were pulled apart by whatever their families had planned for that summer.

Ciaran's mother had packed him off to Ireland. Things in Belfast were grim, but his uncle had a place on the North Coast, so he was staying there, in a resort called Portrush. It looked like Porthcawl, funfair and all, judging by the postcard he sent Jac, but there wasn't much 'action', he said. Jac couldn't make out if he meant with girls or paramilitaries.

Jac's Mam and Dad took him to Yorkshire, to the Brontë Museum. Jac walked on Haworth Moor, and tried to write a poem about Catherine, the *Wuthering Heights* Catherine, though the ambiguity was deliberate.

When Jac *was* at home in the Rhondda, everyone else was away with *their* families. So now, here he was, on the last Saturday before he went back to school for his final year. Heading off, finally, to meet his friends.

"Don't be late tonight, there's a good boy," his Dad counselled him, as he was leaving the house. "Back to school on Monday, and you've got a big twelvemonth coming up. Always best to start as you mean to continue. You can't burn the candle at both ends." Jac was only mildly annoyed – his father meant well, and the string of unbiblical *clichés* constituted a piece of worldly counsel, not a Holy Commandment – but, all the same, was this how it was going to be all year long?

"Keep faith, my son." As always, his father's parting words. Jac *did* have beliefs, and hope in the future; but he didn't, couldn't share the creed that was the cornerstone of his father's life, that *was* his father's life. His father must know that too, though it was never openly acknowledged. Every time his father enjoined him to *keep faith*, Jac felt a shadow pass between them, as much as he loved his father in every other way that a son, an only son, should. The moment he was safely out onto the street, though, another of his Dad's unscriptural maxims came to mind, a much less freighted one: *let the dog see the rabbit!* He bounded with excitement to the bus stop beyond the Lights.

The arrangement was to meet in Petra's to celebrate Martyn and Lydia's A level results. They'd both got the grades they needed. University next: Oxford for Martyn, Lydia to Canterbury. Martyn was going to cook lunch for everyone. *Lunch*, not 'Dinner'. Very sophisticated. Naturally, it came to rain before the bus arrived, but Jac was determined not to let his spirits be dampened. "I'm not going to let my spirits be dampened," he said to himself, as he boarded. The platitude reminded him of his Auntie. It was then he remembered the conversation they'd had during the night, about the bird rapping on the petrol station sign, *pecking at the wrong bark*. And what else was it she came up with, that funny phrase about Penrhys?

The lights look like a lasso in the sky, said his Auntie, suddenly paying attention.

Yes, that was it. *At night, the lights look like a lasso in the sky.* The cowboy's lariat hanging high above the valley, the rope frozen with its noose open. Whacky stuff.

The bus had reached Tonypandy Square. Saturday shoppers boarded, bags in every hand. A skinhead took the seat in front of him, lit up a fag and paid the conductor for a single to The Star Hotel. Jac tried not get distracted by his Auntie's corny joke about Penrhys being the highest mountain in the world (*'because it's above The Star'*). He peered across the Valley to remind himself what the estate looked like during the day. Way, way above it, beyond the black clouds, there was a tiny patch of blue.

Why is the sky so high? asked his Auntie idly. Her inadvertent triple-rhyme harked back to Penry's "drop of pop on the top". Something sparked in Jac's imagination, and it all began to come together. He gathered up the phrases in his mind, and without thinking, completed his Auntie's question: *At night the lights look like a lasso in the sky and why is the sky so high… when I lie on my back?* What was this? A piece of inconsequential doggerel? Or – who could tell? – the start of the Great Rhondda Rock Song he still sometimes felt destined to write? To be honest, the cross-cutting rhythms and imperfect metre weren't promising. Impossible to accommodate in a conventional verse-chorus structure. But his Auntie urged him on. *You're on the right track,* she said. A notion took him then, a style of performance he'd never heard before, anywhere: rhyme and rhythm, strings of local idiom and history, not sung, but recited or chanted over a driving beat suggested by that 'woodpecker' and his knock-knock-knocking.

I don't know what you've got here, said his Auntie, more doubtful now. Neither did Jac, but it sounded like something that could be… different? Striking? Important? If he could *say* the lyrics, it wouldn't matter that he couldn't keep in tune. Jac and the Beanstalks might just be onto something. But his Auntie was right: there was so little to go on, it was hard to be sure.

"I know," he told her. "It's not a lot."

Somehow, though, the tumble of words kept coming, rhymes and half-rhymes, capturing memory and angst. Some voicing social comment, some suggesting macabre teenage horror. The Catchphrase Kid catching a kaleidoscope of phrases, phrases that chimed with ones he'd already stumbled into, conversing with his Auntie. A pattern. A story. Sort of.

At night, the lights look like a lasso in the sky, and why is the sky so high when I lie on my back? Then I don't know what I've got but I know it's not a lot and it's not very hot when you're living in a bedsit, that's it, everybody dreads it, whistles in the darkness but the fog will hide the starkness where the boys are getting ready for a rendezvous with Eddie on... Penrhys!

Yes, end on 'Penrhys'. That was good. You could just chant the place-name repeatedly instead of a chorus. *Penrhys, Penrhys, Penrhys.* Like *Knock, knock! Knock, knock! Knock, knock!* But who was Eddie? Did it matter? He sounded interesting. Maybe he was that skinhead smoking on the seat in front. Jac knew where the fog and the *whistles in the darkness* had come from. A witness statement from an infamous murder case. In an ill omen, the year estate was opened, even before the building work was complete, a twelve-year-old girl had been killed on Penrhys. She was exactly the same age as Jac. He'd been horrified *and* fascinated by the reports of the trial. Even now, there on the bus, the fog and the spooky whistling sent a shiver down his spine.

So he had a verse of his masterpiece already. If it was a masterpiece. If, indeed, it was a verse. It didn't hold together like a normal song. But that, he suddenly realised, was its power, its authenticity, that was why... *that was why it was what the world had been waiting for.* It might sound grandiose, put like that, but he felt immediately convinced. So did his Auntie. *Sounds crazy*, she said. Precisely! With this revolutionary approach, the Beanstalks would burst the boundaries of popular music, take it to a level where it could represent the fragmentary, absurd nature of modern experience with the same grit and energy as expressionist art, or Dadaism, or *Catch 22*. It was on a different plane to your conventional pop ditty. It was cubism in song.

Jac tried to bring other things about Penrhys to mind, things he could catalogue, like the Holy Spring dedicated to the Virgin Mary which had made it a destination for mediaeval pilgrimage. But every time the skinhead took a puff of his cigarette and exhaled, it was blowing back right into Jac's face. *Smoke gets in your eyes.* Bryan Ferry. No, not him. *Concentrate! Think!* The skinhead was reading the *Echo*, and fidgeting with what seemed to be a can of Bird's Custard Powder which he'd carefully placed on the seat beside him. What was that about? Other people's lives. They seldom made much sense. But they were so *rich*. You could write a whole novel about this one skinhead on a bus journey. An anti-novel probably. Now that Jac looked carefully at him again, though, he realised that this was no skinhead after all. It was Rat! *Rat the Hell's Angel*, but with all his hair shorn off. Why? What on earth would make a biker do that?

Unless he had to.

Unless someone had shaved him whether he liked or not…

Unless… he'd been in prison!

Well, well. *Well.* It sprang to Jac's mind then, the first verse of his *tour de force*, complete and whole in one chain of thought, one go, a stream of consciousness that would drown… no, *baptise* the listener in a torrent of beat and rhyme and allusion.

When the police get to Penrhys then they seize all the Greasers, shouting 'freeze!', cos they're living in a tent but they haven't paid their rent, and these coppers are all bent on doing them for intent, so they're sent to some reformatory in Swansea where they're never ever wrong, see, never ever Trevor Evans, cos they'll shave you and they'll fleece you, try to save you then release you, but the only thing they'll lease you is a rehab flat in Ystrad which is not exactly mustard, but you get a can of custard, and you've bussed it up the mountain and you spot St Mary's Fountain on… Penrhys!

It still needed a bit of work, some editing: but he'd get to that. The custard reference was cryptic, but Jac *wanted* it to be enigmatic, as incongruous as everyday life. Like this bus journey he was taking. The rent strike was happening right then: he'd read reports in the *Rhondda Leader*. Now that oil prices had rocketed, the only residents who could afford the estate's spanking new

187

communal heating system were those on benefits, those whose housing costs the State paid in full. Arrests had been made. Riots brewing. The *Rhondda Leader* predicted what would happen next. Those with jobs would leave. Those who stayed would be stigmatised as scroungers and wasters. The estate would get *a reputation*. No-one who had any choice would want to move there. A vicious spiral of decline.

Jac the Socialist was appalled by all that. But Jac the Composer was on a roll. Though still puzzled by the custard tin. Were Greasers into making trifles these days? But… it might not be custard powder inside. It might be… drugs! Cocaine… or something. Jac looked suspiciously at Rat. Was he high? He'd been gazing at the same page of that *Echo* for yonks. What was so interesting about Births, Deaths and Marriages? Maybe he'd killed someone! He was a member of the Archery Club, after all. Maybe… it was someone's ashes inside that can!

The bus had got to The Star, at the foot of Penrhys. Rat was so absorbed with his *Echo*, he nearly missed the stop. He leapt up, leaving the custard tin behind in his hurry.

"Oi…," Jac called after him, not knowing whether to address him as Rat, "…um, butty, you've forgotten your… um, *stash?*"

Rat turned, glared, snatched the can, stared at it as though he'd never seen it before, and scurried down the stairs. The other passengers tutted. Jac was left with nothing but their disapproval and the final stanza of his genre-busting work of genius…

Rat searches Hatches, Matches and Dispatches, twenty Embassy and a box of matches, he's forgotten where his stash is, or is it full of ashes? But the central heating system's not his own ideal of wisdom, though he's got his Rediffusion so he watches television, and the bloke on Panorama talks about his social drama, but the pills will make him calmer, they're a charmer for a good night, that's right, when he's feeling uptight then he pops out for a quick one, but the mix will make him sick soon, there's an empty cigarette pack and he knows it's time to get back to… Penrhys!

Penrhys! The title of the track was obvious, but this whole new style, this revolution in popular music, this democratisation of drum and bass and lyrics – this *genre* needed a name. Jac remembered its genesis: that first phrase last night, the *lasso in the sky*, after he'd been woken by the bird attacking the Shell logo. The logo that actually said 'Hell'. *Pecking at the wrong bark.* The little creature up against the evils of corporate capitalism, nature tapping out a warning about man's thirst for fossil fuel. What a symbol. What a sign. *Knock, knock!* Yes, it was the beating beak that had inspired the insistent rhythm that would typify this new form of music... Jac would call it *Peck* music. Give it a year or two, and they'd be Pecking All Over The World.

Sounds too… tinny, for what that bird was doing, his Auntie objected.

She was right. It had more punch than that.

You said it yourself, she insisted. *It was more of a rap than a peck. Rapping, that's what it was.*

Got it, thought Jac. That's what we'll call it. Rap music.

It'll never catch on, said his Auntie.

24

My editor is livid. She's not from Belfast, but she's actually used the phrase catch yourself on. *Claiming a premonition of punk as a cover for musical ineptitude is one thing, she warns me. But cultural appropriation of rap is quite another. It's practically racist.*

She has a point. Whilst the history of rap may be contested (it all comes down what you believe in the end), and its African roots go back centuries, it's undeniable that its modern expression originates in New York City. It was in the Big Apple, not the Rhondda Fawr, that black DJs began to sample percussion from funk, soul and disco tracks, looping the sounds to produce a repetitive beat over which they'd voice a cascade of syncopated, heavily rhymed speech. To claim that it was invented by a white guy on a Rhondda bus, well...!

Even as late as 1974, the Rhondda was an almost exclusively white community. The first wave of Asian doctors and their families had settled in – Nye Bevan's health service needed them in places like his native Valleys where it was increasingly hard to attract British medics to go into practice. Chinese takeaways were beginning to open just as the Chinese laundries were closing. But people of African descent were so rare that they enjoyed a kind of fame simply because of the colour of their skin. I could name one well-loved collier from Maerdy for whom that was literally true. There's a line in that 1940s film, Proud Valley *– though I've actually heard a black man use it in real life, as a generous extension of brotherhood – that because coal dust got everywhere,* everyone *underground was black. Even after the advent of pithead baths, you sometimes saw a black-faced miner on the streets, if he'd left his shift early to head home for some reason. As I type this, sitting on the shelf above my desk is a wonderful photo of my own grandfather, black with dust, posing outside the house in Holborn Terrace with two of my 'aunties', evacuees who still made occasional return visits to their hosts in Tonypandy decades after the War ended and they'd gone home to London. He looks like Dai Francis. Not the Miners' Leader, but the Black and White Minstrel.*

There was *an affinity between South Wales and the Deep South, as there is between downtrodden peoples the world over, I suppose. It was*

Rhondda coal, exported from Cardiff docks, that sparked the growth of one of Britain's earliest multi-racial communities, Tiger Bay; often, it was Rhondda women who married and settled down with the African and Caribbean sailors who put into port there. And, of course, there's Paul Robeson. After starring in Proud Valley, the black American singer-activist felt a lasting attachment to the people of the South Wales Coalfield. Years later, when the McCarthyites had banned him from travelling outside the States, Robeson famously sidestepped their embargo by singing via the transatlantic cable to the Miners' Eisteddfod in Porthcawl ("I just couldn't receive an invitation that could mean more to me"). When his passport was restored, he came to Wales to appear in person at both the Miners' and the National Eisteddfod.

All of this is true, but it can't justify claiming that one of the crowning glories of black culture – rap – began in the Valleys.

And yet… also in my possession, in a drawer which sits under that shelf with my 'black' grandfather's photo, is a cassette recording which comfortably pre-dates Rapper's Delight, the Sugarhill Gang's 1979 hit generally acknowledged to be the first commercial manifestation of rap. It's an amateur recording of a band, taped in the garage of one of my schoolfriends. Several witnesses can confirm the circumstances and date. One of the tracks is a kind of spoken poem, incorporating rhyme, rhythmic speech and street vernacular, chanted over a repeated, pulsing instrumental bed. As such, it conforms exactly to the commonly-accepted definition of rap. The lyrics feature Eddie, Rat and Trevor Evans, a tin of custard in Ystrad, Rediffusion and an ill-conceived central heating system. It's called Penrhys.

25

"Wales Forever Young Gifted and Black Magic Lantern Show me the way to go Home…"

This *wasn't* another reflection on Welshness and race. It *wasn't* Jac and his Auntie composing another track in their freshly minted, ground-breaking musical genre. And it *wasn't* one of Bowie's cut-ups, a technique he used to inspire *his* imagination to break new ground in popular music; though, as it happened, in the background, Petra's stereo was playing *Hunky Dory* (She had a great collection of albums, dating back years. In fact, Jac had begun to wonder if it wasn't Petra who'd educated Martyn's musical taste, rather than the other way round).

No, the Friends were playing the Word Association Football Game, a variation on radio's Tennis Elbow Foot Game they'd invented back in the autumn. Instead of simply responding with a word suggested by the previous one, players in their version had to repeat – without stumbling – the whole chain of phrases that they'd already come up with, before adding a new one of their own. So, Martyn had begun with *Wales*; Petra responded *Wales Forever*; Jac said *Wales Forever Young*; Catherine repeated the whole chain completing it with a phrase of her own – *Wales Forever Young Gifted and Black*; and so on. The fun was in the bizarre associations and the struggle to remember the links, especially when players had had a drink or two. But Penry and Martyn had got so good at repeating enormous strings of phrases that rounds could go on almost *ad infinitum*. So a new rule was introduced – *Finnegans Wake*: if a player added a word or phrase at the end of the chain which could *also* be placed legitimately *before* the very first word in the chain, thereby closing the chain back on itself to make an endless circle (like James Joyce's unreadable novel), then that player was declared the winner instantly, no matter how many others were still 'in' the round.

It was Martyn's turn. "Wales Forever Young, Gifted and Black Magic Lantern Show me the way to go Home… *Run*."

Petra followed, adding 'Rabbit' to 'Run'. Jac was next. He nearly stumbled halfway through, but he managed to get there: "Wales Forever Young, Gifted and Black Magic Lantern... Show me the way to go Home Run Rabbit... *Pie*."

Rabbit Pie? No-one challenged it, so now it was Catherine's go.

"Wales Forever Young, Gifted and Black Magic Lantern Show me the way to go Home Run Rabbit Pie... *in the Sky when you die*."

Just the four of them were playing. Jac had got off the bus, after what he'd already begun to think of as his Glorious Traverse of Tonypandy Square, with the words of *Penrhys* buzzing in his head. He was still distracted when he greeted them all. He'd almost forgotten that he hadn't seen them all summer long. Catherine had a *tan*! He was reminded how pale she normally looked.

And how much you fancy her, said his Auntie, bluntly.

It's not just that, Jac wanted to say. It was the bond they had, the bond they shared with the others, how much they *all* meant to each other. As though to prove it, in no time, it was as if the quartet had never been apart.

They had the run of the house. Petra's parents had gone on a coach trip to Symonds Yat and Tintern Abbey.

"Martyn met them on the doorstep as they were leaving," explained Petra. "He told them all about Wordsworth's visits there, his poetic thoughts about nature, and something about a profound sense of ..."

"*A sense sublime*," Martyn interrupted, "*Of something...*"

"That's the one. But Mam said they were just going because they'd heard there were some great pubs there. She had a flask of vodka in her bag as well, so goodness knows what state they'll be in by the time they get home."

Far more deeply interfused, I should think, quipped Jac's Auntie.

They'd been expecting Penry to join them, Lydia too, and possibly Nerys (Petra must have invited her without asking Martyn), but there was no sign of them, so they had *N amount of*

Martyn's spaghetti bolognaise to share. It was a recipe his Auntie Eve had taught him; one she'd learned from her in-laws from Bardi. Martyn called it 'spag bol', as though it was something he cooked up most days. To Jac it was *exotic*, a taste he'd need to acquire. After 'lunch' (Jac had to get used to calling it that, too) they settled down in the front room to talk – and play.

And thus The Word Association Football Game. Everyone had taken another turn, so the chain had four more links to it, and Martyn was about to give it all another twist.

"Wales Forever Young, Gifted and Black Magic Lantern Show me the way to go Home Run Rabbit Pie in the Sky when you Dai… Llewellyn… the Great… Train Robbery… with Violence… *is Golden.*"

Barely allowable as a kind of pun (the *Jac Morgan Rule*), but droll. Petra's turn. Without missing a beat, she finished with "…Violence is Golden *Breakfast Cereal.*"

Jac was beguiled into adding a twist and a pun of his own: "…Violence is Golden Breakfast *Serial*… Killer."

And that opened the door for Catherine, who to her own delight – she rarely won games like this – triumphantly added a homophone of her own: "Wales Forever Young, Gifted and Black Magic Lantern Show me the way to go Home Run Rabbit Pie in the Sky when you Dai Llewellyn the Great Train Robbery with Violence is Golden Breakfast Serial Killer *Whales… Forever Young Gifted and Black…*"

Whales had taken her back to *Wales*. The circle of phrases was complete. "*Finnegans Wake!*" they all shouted, and collapsed into laughter.

Afterwards, Jac would remember that afternoon, up until the Stranger appeared, as the happiest hours he'd known. Four friends, four companions – witty, thoughtful, bright, hopeful – with no need to prove anything, being as nearly themselves as anyone can be in company, talking and talking, sharing the way they saw the world. A glimpse of some ideal way of being, of living: a grown-up version of summer nights he remembered from boyhood idylls on his relatives' farm in Ceredigion. There

194

had been four of them then too – two boys, two girls, him and his distant cousins allowed to take blankets out to the barn after the dark, telling jokes and stories until they literally hit the hay; young as he was, he'd been more than half in love with one of *them*, too.

Here, with Catherine, Petra and Martyn, it was just as easy, just as natural. Though the chatter was more sophisticated, and insightful, it wasn't that anything astounding was revealed. It just all felt *right*. As though it could go on for ever. They talked about Dylan – Bob Dylan, not the Welsh poet. About Bowie's talent for mime. Jac lightened the mood (taking a risk the others wouldn't have been aware of) by confessing that he had "an older relative who thought that Glam Rock was something to do with the geology of Glamorgan." If his Auntie was offended, she didn't react.

Martyn picked up on the 'glam' reference by going unashamedly camp for once. "Glamour," he cooed, "is when all is *present*, but not all is *given*," emphasising his lisp ("*pwesent*") and channelling his inner Ivor Novello. That got them on to vintage romantic songs (Petra put on one of her father's compilation albums), and so to *Casablanca*, and so to Paris. Jac knew that Martyn had been planning to go there for a long weekend that summer, to brush up his conversational French before Oxford. Now Petra admitted that, daringly – she'd told her parents she was going to stay with Catherine in *her* family's caravan in Porthcawl – she had gone with him. They'd watched the sunrise from Montmartre, toured the galleries, drunk *espressos* and *carafes* of *vin rouge*. Short of cash, they'd wandered late into the night around the Marais. In the end, they found a cave-like café-bar, Le Paradis, with Toulouse-Lautrec posters plastered over the walls and ceilings. Some Breton students paid for their drinks, and they stayed until *everyone* had left, and then they stayed on again and talked to the *patron* after that.

"And then, the next night, we walked every street and alley in that part of town again, but we couldn't find the place at all," lamented Petra.

"*Les vrais paradis sont les paradis qu'on a perdus,*" quoted Martyn, and Catherine and Jac had enough French – just – to follow.

That was the only hint of *tristesse* all afternoon. Because it was indeed like a Paradise Regained, recovering what they'd had during those last, long weeks of rehearsal, the very soul of The Society of Friends. Martyn seemed restored to himself, galvanised by the prospect of university.

"Soon I'll have an Oxford man," boasted Petra. Jac wasn't going to let her get away with that.

"*Oxford man?* Like hell he is! He wears a pink suit."

Martyn didn't; though he *might* have, he'd have looked *swell* in one. And that's how they got on to *The Great Gatsby*. Martyn waxed lyrical about that moment when Gatsby pauses with Daisy in his arms, realising that, once he kisses *this* girl, surrendering his heart to this beautiful but imperfect creature, once he makes his love *contingent*, his innocence will be ended, and he'll never again be truly free.

"He looks up and sees this pathway to the stars. But he knows he can only go there if he goes alone, that he can only experience the divine if he renounces the mortal. And then… he goes ahead and kisses her anyway."

And with that, Martyn got up, walked over to Petra in her armchair, bent and kissed her full on the lips, as though it was just the two of them there; and yet as though, somehow, he meant to include Catherine and Jac in the moment, too.

"*The Great Martsby,*" said Petra, untangling herself. "Isn't that what you call him, Jac? What's he like, eh?" But Jac was thinking of that line that Fitzgerald had written about Jay Gatsby, the line which had come to him when Martyn had greeted Petra just as flamboyantly at the Beach: *if personality is an unbroken series of successful gestures, then there was something gorgeous about him.*

They talked politics, too: worried themselves over the crisis in Ulster and how Ciaran might be affected; speculated about Wilson's government and the prospect of another Election. Catherine told them she'd been thinking over the summer that she should train as a nurse after A levels, rather than go to university. Martyn tried to persuade her that it was her right to go to Uni if she wanted to, that she'd be well capable of making a success of it. Jac was glad she was thinking otherwise, that she had the guts *not* to follow the expected path to higher education. She hadn't put it that way, but it sounded to him like a political choice as much as a vocational one. Though choosing *not* to go to university would also – *wouldn't it?* – be something to do with her step-brother and his death at one.

Jac wanted to ask more, to make sure he'd understood properly – there was often a veil of reticence over her words when she talked about herself – but just then there came a fierce knock at the door.

Petra went to answer it. They heard Penry's voice, someone else's too. Penry appeared, looking like a drowned rat (the rodent, not the skinhead Greaser). Theatrically, he raised his arms and opened his palms to the heavens.

"The Lord has sent another Great Flood to sweep the Iniquitous from face of the Earth."

It wasn't like Penry to joke like this – he lived in fear of torrential rain.

"I think you've got your Bible wrong there, butt'," Jac corrected him, remembering Noah and his Ark from Sunday School. "That was precisely what God vowed *not* to do, not ever again. Remember the rainbow, Penry? It's meant to be a sign of that promise."

But then Jac was startled to see that it wasn't Penry he'd been talking to. A *second* Penry, the real Penry, had come to stand in the doorway behind the first.

"This is my cousin Cadogan," said the real Penry.

"What's his first name?" chorused the two girls in perfect synch. Jac felt a shiver travel down his spine. That moment at the dress rehearsal when he'd mistaken Petra and Catherine for each other. *An apple, cleft in two, is not more twin.* Now there was another pair of lookalikes in the room.

"Cadogan *is* his first name."

"*Cadogan Cadogan?*"

197

"Verily, verily," bellowed Cadogan Cadogan. "Original, isn't it? Like sin."

"He never normally ventures outside the borders of Gelli," said Penry, as though that explained something. They were all of half a mile away from the Cadogans' hometown.

"He's *a Stranger come to Town*, then," acknowledged Jac, prompted by his Auntie.

"We *all* are strangers in this world," boomed Cadogan Cadogan.

Now that Jac studied his face, he saw that Penry's cousin might be a year or two older than them, no more than that; but clearly his attitudes came straight from the Old Testament. He fixed Jac with a zealot's stare. And then it softened, as though he'd recognised something.

"You're not Davy Morgan, are you?"

Peculiar question. Jac gulped. Did he look that old?

"No... no, I'm Davy Morgan's *son*."

"That's what I meant. I saw you together once. Wonderful preacher, your father. Heard him many times. Mighty in the Spirit. He's brought scores, hundreds of souls to the Lord. Where do you stand today...?"

Cadogan was fishing for something. Jac's name. He hadn't even been properly introduced yet. Jac felt guilty, as though it was his own fault.

"I'm *Jac*..." He'd nearly said Jacob, as though he ought to give his full name, as though the roll was being called up yonder.

"...where does your soul stand today, Jac? Is it with your Dad's, safe in the arms of your Heavenly Father? Or, if the Lord should come in Glory this very day, is it *in peril?*"

"I'm... today... I... Glory... If... Peril..."

It sounded like a very bad round of The Word Association Football Game.

"*Peril*... Risk," said Martyn, cutting across Jac's stuttering non-answer. "Let's have a game of Risk."

Jac felt as though he'd been saved. Saved by Martyn and *his* self-sacrificing pun: Martyn *hated* playing Risk. Petra went and found the game at the back of a cupboard somewhere. The others cleared the table. They were *actually* going to risk a game of Risk with this fanatic. Clearly, he shared the Cadogan family trait of untrammelled gregariousness. Coupled with his faith, it was like being trapped in a thicket of nettles to Jac. He was *stung*, stung back to that evening in the Vestry in Bethel, when another evangelical naïf, another fundamentalist with no filter, Ernie the Cripple, had made him pray and surrender his soul to God. Now Jac had made the schoolboy error, albeit inadvertently, of challenging a Bible-basher on the facts of Scripture, on the Flood and the Punishment of Sinners. It didn't matter that he'd been right. *A hard rain* would fall.

And indeed, whipped up by that traumatic childhood memory, a rising tide of emotion began to sweep over Jac's defences. He was suddenly adrift on it, unmoored. In a kind of apocalyptic vision, more real than the game going on around him for all that, he saw that the Great Separation which the evangelicals preached, the separation of the sheep and the goats, the saved and the damned, the separation on which they built their churches, their faith, their whole world – that that separation was *real*. That they were right, about this one thing. That you had to be on one side or the other. Jac felt, keenly, as keenly as a knife parting the tissue of his inner organs, *separated...* separated from his mother and father, from all that had formed him, from all that was deepest within him, so deep that he would surely perish as it was ripped away. *This* was the price he had to pay for his story starting, for growing up, for independence. To be exiled from the bosom of those he knew best, from those he would cling to; exiled from them and all that they stood for... He stood now instead with Martyn and Petra and Catherine, with Gatsby and Bowie and the young Wordsworth, with all of the Fallen, the Unredeemed. Jac stood with them, but stood – in the eyes of Cadogan Cadogan, in the eyes of his own father – cast out from Eden, his Paradise Lost, estranged from the Love of God, in peril of an Eternity in Hell. But no; that was wrong, that was where the evangelicals, the fundamentalists had gone astray.

Because how could a loving God damn His own creatures to never-ending exile? The separation was real, terribly real, but it was not in Eternity, not in some unimaginable after-life; it was here and now, in this world, and it was the more terrible for that. It would last a lifetime, the only lifetime Jac had – a life-sentence, unless he were to surrender and bow the knee to *their* God.

The game progressed. Jac was playing like an automaton. Cadogan Cadogan played like the Devil Incarnate, moving his pieces across the board with a precise destructiveness. He was no innocent abroad, after all. He had no compunction about lying, whispering falsehoods about the other players' intentions, then double-crossing his confidants, playing with no principle other than *victory at all costs*. They were Lambs lying down before his Lion. Being eaten up. And as he played, he hummed under his breath, seemingly unconsciously, wordless snatches of melody. Jac recognised them though. Hymns and choruses he knew only too well: *Onward Christian Soldiers*; *I'm in Lord's Army*; *Stand Up, Stand Up for Jesus...*

The cards and the dice seemed always to fall in Cadogan's favour. His forces – the Armies of the Lord – charged in from the East. *Forward into battle, see His banners go!* They swept the globe, taking every territory, overrunning Martyn, the last man standing. The Society of Friends had been annihilated. Penry's cousin had captured the whole world, a crushing Victory he dedicated to the Lord: a sign that God was exalting the Righteous in preparation for the Last Days. They too would gain the Victory, blessed by riches and bounty in this world, as they surely will be in the next. But he seemed to take little personal pleasure in winning. *For what shall it profit a man* – he actually began to declaim this, as if reciting from the King James Version in a Sunday School Anniversary – *if he shall gain...* But then he expressed an urgent need for the toilet and disappeared. In his absence, Penry, mortified, apologised.

"He turned up at my house like he does every few months demanding to know where I was going today. I made the mistake of telling him. He *interrogated* me about you all: were you chapel-goers, were you believers? I kept him talking for as long as I could, but in the end, I couldn't take it anymore. You can see what he's like. *Mea culpa*. Probably not the right phrase, but you know what I mean. Don't worry, I'll take him home now. He shouldn't be let out of Gelli in all honesty."

And though Petra smiled and began to say that they were welcome to stay, of course they were, the Cadogans left together. Poor Penry. It was still raining, biblically so.

The original quartet were alone again. Catherine reminded them that Nerys hadn't turned up. Neither had Lydia.

"I wonder why?" asked Petra, rhetorically. Lydia would be with her Biker Boy.

"Let's go down to Clydach, anyway, and see what she's up to," suggested Martyn.

"She probably won't be in."

"True. But we could do with a change of scene."

He was right. The house still seemed *possessed*. They got their coats and set off. Catherine sat with Jac on the bus, cajoling a little humour out of him. Jac felt his spirits begin to rise again. The clouds lifted, as though the pathetic fallacy wasn't a fallacy after all. By the time they got off at Pandy Square, evening was coming on, and the rain had almost stopped. A low sun poked through the clouds. For the second time that day, Jac crossed the Square. There would be a third Traverse before the night was out. He set himself for the long climb up to Lydia's house. But then Catherine jogged his elbow.

"Look, Jac, look… over the valley, over Penrhys…"

It's a lasso in the sky, said his Auntie, who'd been quiet since Cadogan Cadogan's arrival.

But it wasn't. It was a rainbow, arched perfectly over the estate, as though in a child's drawing, or one of the storybooks from Jac's Sunday School. A promise. Unworldly, otherworldly.

"Look at that," said Catherine again, unnecessarily now. "Glorious, isn't it?"

26

Tonypandy Square was the best place.

Glorious, it was, Pandy Square. And its Three Traverses.

Already that day, Jac had crossed the Square whilst he'd Invented A World-Conquering Musical Genre (*or his Auntie had*). Now, The Society of Friends were traversing it after they'd Lost The Whole World (*But Regained Their Own Soul*). All that remained was The Glorious Traverse That Was Worth Waiting For (but there were still another couple of hours to wait for that).

Martyn fell in step with Catherine, and they forged ahead up the hill to Lydia's. Petra and Jac were soon twenty yards behind. It was often like this, when Petra and Martyn were in company – they were careful to be open, to share themselves around; or maybe it came naturally to them not to couple up with each other all the time. It was a real gift. A proper, grown-up partnership, facing the world together, not turned in on themselves. One day, Jac often told himself, I'd like a relationship like that. He took the chance now to give Petra some overdue thanks.

"I've been meaning to say… how much it meant to me, that Advice you gave me on the day of dress rehearsal."

It took a moment, but Petra cottoned on to what he was talking about. Maybe Jac's thinking of it as Advice with a capital A clued her in.

"And how's it going, Jac, the *taking yourself seriously* bit?"

"Well… I *have* invented a world-conquering musical genre today…"

Even he could hear how ridiculous he sounded. In his embarrassment, he couldn't even bring to mind what this new thing was called. Or anything about the silly 'song' he'd been making up on the way up to Petra's.

"Oh, Jac, you just can't help yourself, can you?"

She was right to be exasperated. The connection between what was going on in his head and the real world outside was so tenuous sometimes. How did people like Lydia manage it?

Manage to stay so rational all the time. How did Petra, come to that? But there'd been sympathy in her tone, as well as irritation. It gave him the courage to seek her counsel again.

"Actually… there was something *serious* I wanted to ask you…"

"Something *serious*? Ah… Something about Catherine, then?"

Was it that obvious? O dear.

Jac's heart was thumping. So much hung on what Petra might say next. It felt as though she was choosing her words carefully.

"I don't know how much I can help you, Jac. Not even best friends… not even girls who are best friends… share everything with each other. So I don't know, I really don't, what she feels about you. But I do know one thing. You don't know either. And there's only one way you'll find out."

He must have looked so hopeless then, so fearful, that she took his arm.

"Look, you've just played a game and lost. Maybe you have to roll the dice again. That's the only way to win. But there are no guarantees. It's the name of the game. Risk."

They carried on, up the hill. He knew what she was saying was right, he just didn't know if he had the courage to act on it. As though she was reading his thoughts, and had decided to take pity on him, to go one step further than she'd intended, Petra did something only she could do: she *became* Catherine. Catherine in one of her agitated moments. She took on Catherine's gait, her posture, her gestures – the tilt of her head, her wind-milling hands, the nervy energy – and she spoke in those husky, over-emphatic tones…

"That Jac Morgan, I just don't get him. It's like waiting for a bus home to Gilfach. You hang around for ages, and when one finally turns up, you put your hand out, and it just drives straight past. I swear to God, you'd be better off walking."

It was so convincing that, there and then, Jac nearly asked *Petra* to go out with him. But there was no time to consider her performance or ask about the message it conveyed – whether it was something Catherine had actually said, or a guess at what *might* be going through her mind, or just an *ad lib* which Petra thought would spur him into action. Because they'd arrived, breathless, at Lydia's. Lydia's Mam was opening the door. With a brief, warm hello, she turned back down the passage. The four Friends followed, assuming Lydia was inside. It wasn't until they'd begun to take their coats off, that they realised that she *wasn't* there. And her mother, it turned out, had made a false assumption too: that Lydia was arriving home with them, hidden somewhere at the back of the group when she'd answered the door. Confusion all round.

Lydia's mother was an older version of Lydia herself. Even her specs were like her daughter's. A little more weight, and the honey hair was permed, and dyed probably to maintain its original colour, although such things were mysteries to Jac. Lydia, like Jac, was an only child. Her father had died when she was ten or eleven. But though Betty Peake was all by herself, watching TV on a Saturday night, she was dressed smartly, and made-up, lipstick and all.

She was very welcoming, despite the odd circumstance. She already knew Petra. Jac remembered Lydia saying how Petra used to come over on Sunday nights so that the three of them could watch *The Onedin Line* together.

Perhaps they all had a thing about Peter Gilmore. Jac wondered if Catherine did too. Or was it just rock stars she was into? *Catherine, Catherine, Catherine.* Waiting for a bus… *Or a Ferry…*

Mrs Peake was explaining her daughter's absence. Lydia had gone off with "that nice young man of hers" on his motorbike first thing that morning. For a spin over the Rhigos. Then he was going to drop her off at Petra's for dinner ("or did she say *lunch*?"). But at two o'clock, Lydia had phoned home from a kiosk to say the bike had broken down over the other side of the mountain. She was letting her mam know, in case her friends should turn up looking for her ("and now you have!").

Mrs Peake insisted they stay and wait, since they'd come "all that way from Pentre". Lydia would be bound to be back soon.

"Now, then, since it's only between ourselves, I want to hear all the gossip about this Society of Friends that Lydia keeps talking about. But first of all, just give me a minute…"

She disappeared into the kitchen. Jac was surprised to hear a cork being pulled. In no time, she was back, with a tray loaded with crisps in a serving dish, a glass of pop, and four wine glasses sitting next to a bottle of white which wasn't even Liebfraumilch!

The pop was for Jac.

"I gather you haven't quite got onto the strong stuff… yet," she teased him. "Dandelion and Burdock alright? You had a *smashing* time with the last bottle, didn't you?"

Betty Peake made puns! And she seemed to know almost as much about them as they did themselves.

Mrs Peake knew about Clydach and its past too – that their Headmaster really *did* ride up there on the back of a horse to court his wife, for instance; and the whole history of the old Bush Houses where she'd grown up. Lydia's father had been a face-worker at the Cambrian. He'd died two years after the Disaster.

"He was never the same after that," she said. "All those men he knew, his butties. Terrible."

Behind her spectacles, her eyes moistened. But she brightened, and told them a funny story that happened soon after he'd been buried.

She'd been sorting the headstone out, and it was taking some time. Meanwhile, she'd decided to buy a new bed, trading in their old one in part exchange. The monumental masons and the furniture shop involved both went by the name of Edwards. When one of their reps knocked the door announcing he'd come *"from Edwards's"*, she'd rushed him upstairs, thrown herself down on the old bed, patted the mattress, and had got as far as inviting him to try it for himself "to see how firm it was", before – of course – realising that the petrified man was there to sell her a gravestone. It was obvious she relished telling the tale, and had done so many times before.

"Lydia calls it my *Hustling Edwards Bed-wards Story*. I wouldn't have minded, either – he was a nice-looking bloke."

They giggled with her. As *risqué* anecdotes went, it was tame enough; but Jac found himself shocked by the openness with which she told it. So many small things that seemed to be taken for granted here – the lipstick, the wine, the suggestive story (even such an innocent one) – were alien to Jac's home. He realised afresh how old-fashioned, how puritanical, how *prudish* his upbringing had been. And he started to experience again that awful sense of *separation*, the separation from his own flesh-and-blood, which had overwhelmed him when he'd been confronted by Penry's cousin. He fell quiet. The others chatted and laughed and sampled their wine. He wanted so much to be one with them, too. The Society of Friends. And, indeed, here he was. With them. His mood shifted again. He began to think that this was the hour he'd been waiting for: that here, among Friends, in this most homely, safe setting, this *convivial* setting, with this wise and witty woman, *now* was the moment he should overcome his fears at last... and take a drink of alcohol!

He hesitated briefly. What if his father noticed the smell on his breath when he got home? But his mind was made up. Lydia's mother had the bottle in her hand, ready to pour.

"Mrs Peake...?"

"Just a moment, Jac..."

And she quickly emptied the last of the bottle into Catherine's glass before turning back to him.

"... and call me Betty, please. Now what is it – a refill of Dandelion and Burdock, yes?"

"O, yes," joked Martyn, "Jac's always ready for *a drop of pop on top.*"

So the moment passed.

Still no sign of Lydia. There were more stories and a second bottle of wine, but by then Jac had lost his nerve. Catherine took another glass, but she seemed more interested in the novelty of sharing confidences with one of their friends' parents. Petra was drinking, but slow and easy too. Even Martyn was *sipping*.

Late on, always alert for such things, always eager to intuit what was going on with his Friends' feelings, Jac sensed a change in Catherine, as though she'd come to a decision. Lydia's Mam kept up a stream of small talk. If she was worried that Lydia hadn't been in touch since that first call, she gave no sign of it. She was telling them how quickly time goes by, how you never knew what was around the corner, how precious these years were that they had right now, how they should take their chances whilst they had them.

Poor Jac. He'd just missed one chance. Was he going to miss another? Wasn't that what Petra's impersonation had been warning him about? He turned towards Catherine. Their eyes met, not once but twice, and he saw... *What exactly?* He couldn't be certain. He hoped. But then he'd hoped before.

The stories went on. As so often when they were all together, time seemed to stretch, and then collapse in on itself again. Suddenly it was late, almost too late for the last buses. Still no Lydia. The four of them struggled into their coats, rushing their goodbyes to Lydia's mother on the doorstep.

Then they were half-running, half-tumbling down the steep length of Court Street, high on youth and friendship and all that they'd shared together that day, and for the weeks and months before. Martyn and Petra, arms around each other's shoulders, belly-laughing and whooping, keeping each other – just about – from falling. And, seemingly without planning it, Jac and Catherine doing the same, arms linked, close behind.

They careered onto the Square, sweeping down past the Naval Club and the new block of flats that stood sentinel below the final corner.

Petra and Martyn reached the stop as the Blaencwm bus was about to pull away. Jac and Catherine, who'd be heading in the opposite direction, came to a halt twenty yards away, shouting breathless goodnights.

Petra and Martyn boarded, and then it was just Catherine and Jac, alone in the echoing dark of the Square. The last bus to Gilfach due any minute.

Jac hoped – he all but prayed, despite his lack of faith – that it would be a long time coming. A shiver went through him. The cool of the night? Nerves? He shook himself. After all this, what if he was simply mistaken? But Catherine smiled.

They'd ended up in the shadows some distance from their bus stop, close together, yet not so close that he could reach out and put his arm around her. All was quiet. Then, from De Winton Street, they heard a bike approach, a misfiring motorcycle. It turned the corner by the Pandy Inn, lost momentum with a metallic judder, then leapt forward again and sped past them on the other side of the Square, taking the road up to Clydach which they'd just run down.

'*Lydia!*' they shouted together. But the helmeted biker and his pillion passenger were gone.

After a beat, as though sharing some undeniable muscle-memory of the sword-fight they'd rehearsed together so many times, they turned at the same instant towards each other. Still Catherine with that smile on her lips. Still Jac hardly daring to believe it could be happening, happening then, happening… at last. At last.

She simply reached out and slipped her arm around his back, he pulled her closer and she snuggled against his shoulder. Her hair brushed his cheek.

Jac shut his eyes and tried hard, very hard, to focus on nothing and no-one but this, not to let memory or words cut across the wonder of the moment, not to think about Pandy Square or Churchill or 1910, or the voice of his father echoing across this space in Open Air Gospel Meetings, pleading with him and all the passers-by to turn and follow Christ. Tried *not* to bring to the surface of his mind what Martyn had said that afternoon about Gatsby and the mystical passage where he first kisses *his* true love.

But when Jac looked again, looked up to the hills over Catherine's warm head nestling against his neck, he couldn't help realising that the frontages of the flats, storey above storey, really did form a ladder that mounted to some secret place way above the mountain, and that angels might well be ascending and descending there, on the heights of Glyncornel; that he too could climb to the heavens, and glimpse the face of God, if he was willing to surrender himself to that Glory and climb alone. But, standing there on solid ground, on this patch of sweet and bitter earth, he knew that when he kissed this girl, and settled his dreams upon *her* instead, everything would be changed utterly.

And then – when Catherine lifted her head and raised her mouth to his, parting her lips so very gently – Jac, who'd never touched a drop in all his long teenage years, tasted for the very first time the elixir of wine.

More kisses followed, not enough, never enough, but greedily and rapidly accumulated, because Jac knew it would be just his luck that the bus would come on time for once, and then it would be over.

"Slow down, boy," Catherine whispered, but tenderly. "It's taken us a while to get here. Enjoy the moment."

It *was* a moment worth waiting for.

And yet, in truth, none of the kisses was so long or deep that Jac completely surrendered to that moment. He felt exposed there on the bus stop at the side of the Pandy Inn. There was a *cul-de-sac* just behind where they were standing, a narrow alleyway forecourting the Picturedrome. He thought about leading Catherine to the darkness there, but a fear he would somehow lose her, that she would slip from his grasp even in such a simple, short manoeuvre, kept him rooted in the half-light, seemingly shameless in that open public space.

He stood upright and pressed against her, layers of clothing chastely between them, so that he could scarcely feel the shape of her breasts or the heat of her thighs. Between each kiss they stopped, and pulled back a little, opening their eyes and gazing deep into each other, as though for the first time, and – *yes!* – smiling. After a while, Catherine pulled back further, as though trying to get his face into focus.

"Those eyes of yours, Jac – they actually *are* couple-coloured."

"*Brown inside blue, like a round stone down in a deep pool...* Was that really you? Made up on the spot, in the middle of that game Osmond made us play?"

"Well, I'd been thinking about it for ages. And I like to think I'm a keen observer."

He considered *her* eyes. Just the one even colour, but now that he really looked at them, looked *into* them, he saw that they weren't so many gradations lighter than the blue that was in his own. Not the ice of a clear winter sky; a shade closer to a storm cloud.

Something passed between them then, something profound: a challenge issued, a challenge accepted, though who was challenging and who accepting he couldn't say. All this in a matter of a second or two. Some instinct told him not to make too much of it, not there and then anyway.

"Yours," he said, but lightly, though still fixing her eyes with his, "are the sweetest… I've ever seen."

She cocked her head to one side, raised an eyebrow, and then she snorted and cuffed him gently around the ear.

"That's Elton John!"

"Bernie Taupin, if you want to be pedantic."

They laughed again, together. She pretended to be offended, and he had to grab her, squeezing her into his arms again.

"More kisses, please."

But it was that first kiss that Jac knew he would remember, the one that would always count for him. The tender touch of her lips, the shock of the bitter-sweet taste, or after-taste, of the wine on them and on her tongue and her breath. And the way the kiss had resolved the strange, overwhelming irruption of Gatsby and *his* vision into Jac's mind, into Jac's story. The ladder. And the angels. The sense of abandoning a grandiose dream, of tumbling, of falling, yet trusting, knowing he would be caught… would be accepted, after all, for who he was, in all his awkwardness and inadequacy. The dawning confidence – not that he'd date and court and marry this one girl, not even that he would hold her ever again like this, but that this was possible and was really happening, happening now. That was enough, that was far, far more than enough. It made all the difference, now and forever.

Whatever happened next, however fleeting this closeness, this embrace, this affirmation might be, whatever he'd come to think about this intimacy in the unimaginable lengths of time from this one night until such things might cease to matter, Jac would always and forever have these few precious moments when he was at home in the world, body and soul. When he was absolutely in the right place at the right time. It might not be Paris; it might not be Scott Fitzgerald's America; but it was somewhere that was far more romantic, far more real. Romantic and real to him at any rate. Tonypandy Square.

The Third Branch

AUTUMN

27

Tonypandy Square is the cruellest place.

Pandy Square. The beacon of hope. The pit of despair.

The place where Jac had kissed Catherine. Less than twelve hours later, he'd convinced himself it was the only place that he ever would.

He could see it down there. The crossroads. The fulcrum on which the whole world might tilt in one direction. Or the other.

From here, up on the 'Roman Road', high above the Black Tip, it looked insignificant, a node on the spider web of streets. A stranger's eye would struggle to pick it out. Jac could pinpoint it instantly, a tiny detail in an urban sprawl. The whole sweep of mid-Rhondda was laid out beneath him. Clydach Vale and Llwynypia, Trealaw, Dinas and Williamstown, the massed terraces of Penygraig and Tonypandy itself directly below him. And everywhere, covering the valley floor, houses, houses, houses. Hundreds upon hundreds of them. Thousands.

On a map, Jac liked to think, Rhondda presented two fingers to the world. Or indeed to Winston Churchill. Two fingers, one slightly fatter and longer than the other. Little Rhondda and Big Rhondda. Rhondda Fach and Rhondda Fawr. Dearest Rhondda and Rhondda the Great. Two deep river-valleys running north-south, joined in a V, like Churchill's famous Victory sign, with those unspoiled, barren mountains enclosing them. What he was looking at was the knuckle of the fatter finger, mid-Rhondda, the heart of the Rhondda Fawr.

Before coal, this had been a stunning rural paradise. Sublime, Wordsworth would have said. But now it was a Linear City, right enough. And the transformation had been so rapid. How Jac would have loved to have lived through it! His father used to say that in 1850, a squirrel could have travelled the dozen miles from one end of the valley to the other without touching the ground, leaping from tree to tree; by 1900, a household cat might do the same, along the rooftops of the unbroken line of terraced houses. Rhondda's population was increasing at a rate rivalled only by New York and Chicago. Yes, this was American Wales, a melting-pot, a cauldron of commerce and industry.

Jac closed his eyes, and a vision came to him – what he might be seeing down below him if the wealth that Rhondda had generated had *stayed* here, and gone on multiplying, as filthy lucre does. It wouldn't be houses filling that bowl down below him. It would be *skyscrapers*. Scores of them. Towers of concrete and glass thrusting upwards, hundreds of feet into the air, right up to a level-height with his vantage point here on the mountain. Mid-Rhondda would be a European Manhattan, a matrix of urban canyons pulsing with fashion and art, cocktail bars and concert halls, restaurants and galleries. Its streets gridlocked by honking yellow taxis. Banks and corporations scrapping for prestigious addresses in Blaenclydach, Tyntyla or Craig-yr-Eos, as close to downtown Tonypandy as their riches could buy.

It could easily have gone that way. Perhaps it did, in some Alternative Universe. The seeds of it had all been here. In the *Library* off Pandy Square, researching for that essay Dai Toads had set, Jac had come across notices in Rhondda's Edwardian newspapers for theatres and music halls, cafés and pubs, churches, chapels, clubs, libraries and institutes: shared spaces where this new society came together to laugh and pray, eat and drink, think and argue – to argue with itself and the wider world, and to forge a new way of looking at that world. And the shops! Milliners and drapers, chemists, barbers, grocers and greengrocers, flannel merchants, haberdashers, department stores, opticians, dentists, ironmongers, shoe and boot shops, and all the latest fashions. Dunraven Street, built to trade on Tonypandy's affluence in the boom times, was a retail wonderland which, in 1910, became the target for penniless miners locked out from their places of work. This was what they'd turned on, smashing shopfronts, helping themselves to fancy goods and luxury garments, but then parading in their purloined finery in an atmosphere said to be less Riot than Carnival. The Misrule of Twelfth Night choreographed by Syndicalists. *Tonypandemonium* if you insist (*it all comes down...*). Rising up, more like, rising up against the consumer society their labour had created, which was now starving them of the means to consume. Venting their frustration, yes, but expressing their determination, too – their determination to define their lives, their community, *their* Rhondda in their way. Turning the established order of things upside down. And this, only *after* they'd been prevented from picketing their real objective, the owners' citadel, the Power House at the pithead; only after they'd been smashed back by those police baton charges, smashed back as far as...

Tonypandy Square.

Now it had another meaning.

Opening his eyes, Jac fixed his sights on the exact spot where he'd held Catherine, playing the scene over yet again in his mind. Those moments when the alienation went away, when he felt whole, felt recognised and understood. Then, right on time (*typical!*), the bus had arrived. The rumble of its engine, the whoosh as the doors opened, the bright electric light inside dispelling the aura of romance. The other passengers – ignorant of how momentous this night was – paid them no attention: just another courting couple, heading home from a Saturday evening out.

Jac knew he'd be getting off first – soon, at the Naval Colliery – leaving Catherine to continue alone to Gilfach Goch. It was the sensible thing to do. This was the last bus: if he stayed aboard to see her home at the journey's end, he'd be faced with a five-mile hike back to Penygraig well after midnight. But he didn't want to be sensible. He wanted to make a Grand Gesture. To stay with her, to escort her gallantly to her door. He wanted the night never to end. *Never ever, Catherine Evans.* Against that, he worried (and cursed himself for it!) that his parents would be worried if he didn't get home until the early hours. *But they were already in bed, asleep.*

The bus had reached the Lights, the traffic lights by Central Hall.

Red. Red and amber. Green.

Time to choose.

In the end, it was Catherine who decided. Quickly, she suggested they could spend next Saturday together, all day if he liked. They'd go on a 'proper date' to the pictures in the evening, and afterwards take the bus all the way to Gilfach together, and he'd get to see to her home then. She insisted that for tonight she'd be fine on her own, she'd done it hundreds of times before. It seemed like the grown-up choice. And now he had a whole day with her to look forward to, not just the butt end of the night. So, with a squeeze of her hand – he was too shy to kiss her in front of the conductor – he stood up and pressed the bell.

"Promise, mind?"

She nodded and smiled. They were at the stop. He got off. And the bus carried her away.

Next morning, later than usual, Jac surprised his parents by arriving downstairs not in Sunday-best ready for chapel, but in jeans and tee-shirt.

"I've decided… I need a walk," he said, as boldly as he dared. "I've got some thinking to do."

Davy Morgan looked at his son questioningly. Occasionally, now that Jac was in the Sixth Form ('too much homework') it was understood he'd miss the morning service. To absent himself for any other purpose was unprecedented. But his Mam smiled and simply said, "Good idea."

Quickly, he grabbed his Wrangler jacket, and headed out. Up the *gwli*, along Hughes Street, to the bottom of Gilfach Road. The gradient began to burn in the muscles in his legs, but he counted off the side streets as he climbed past them: Penmaesglas, Wyndham, Mikado, Penpisgah, Thomas Street. A steep, twisting unmetalled lane, hemmed in by dry-stone walls, a little bit of pre-Industrial Rhondda, took him out onto the mountain. This was the ridge where Carncelyn Farm once stood. Seventy years before, he'd have seen the boxer Tom Thomas

218

here, training for another bout, sparring with a bull, or so his Auntie said. Now, he passed the paddock where Harry Owen kept an arthritic brown mare. "'Arry Howen 'ad ha 'orse", the boys used to chant if they saw him there, mocking his misplaced aitches, like they were prize-winning elocutionists themselves. "Hand 'e 'ad hit hunder 'is 'horse-pisses'." Jac always held back – it was Harry's daughter, Belinda, who'd stolen his steering wheel and made him cry with a sucker punch. He didn't dare open old wounds.

On he went, skirting the Black Tip on a sheep path, past the Top Feeder. The gloopy, algae-infested colliery pond was said to conceal in its depths sacks and sacks of unwanted puppies, unwelcome kittens. It was used, nevertheless, by boys more daring than him as a summer swimming pool.

On again, up through the ferns, already dying back with the first hints of autumn, towards the summit on this farmer's track – it was indeed as straight as a 'Roman Road', though it must have been made a thousand years after the legions had left Wales. Local legend – passed on with credulous delight by bloodthirsty nippers as Jac well remembered – claimed that an invading Roman legion had marched down this pathway to find the men of the valley below away hunting. The legionaries slaughtered the defenceless women and children. But then the men came home and slaughtered *them*.

In some versions of the tale, the foreign raiders were Saxons, but the result was the same.

So here he was, having conquered the worst of the ascent, catching his breath, looking back down at his valley. This was his *thinking place*; up here alone, only larks and sheep for company. He'd come here whenever there were things on his mind.

There was only one matter now – Catherine.

The more he replayed how the previous night had ended, the more foolish and spineless his decision not to see her home became. He'd have had a ninety-minute walk back, down to Tonyrefail, up again over Barn Hill, all in the pitch black. But so what? It would have showed her how much he cared. Why the hell had he let his worries about his parents come into his thinking? How could he have been so dutiful? He tormented himself with the idea that he'd let her slip through his fingers, that his *gauche* inexperience in how to start a love affair would already have put Catherine off. Grown up? He was just a boy. *Giving it all away.* He made a determined effort to get Roger Daltrey's unhelpful lyrics out of his head, only to find The Who frontman upstaged by a voice even less reassuring: his Auntie.

For Catherine, all it was, was a bit of a drunken snog.

Could that be true? *Just a snog?* He knew Catherine's backstory, knew all about her and Gerwyn Evans. It wouldn't have been the first snog she'd ever had. But that's not how it was last night, he trusted himself enough to know that. He trusted Catherine. Anyway, she'd agreed to go out with him again this coming Saturday, and all day too.

That date will never happen, said the voice in his head, like the bloody Sybil.

Well, that would be unreasonable, Jac told himself calmly. It'd be unreasonable and unkind to finish with me, when we've only just... started, simply because I didn't stay on the bus. She was the one who urged me to save myself that long and dangerous walk home.

So if she's going to finish with you because of that, said his Auntie perversely, *she doesn't deserve to be your girlfriend anyway.*

That wasn't what he meant! What was his Auntie doing to him? What was *Catherine* about to do to him? He resented the implication that he didn't care enough to go out of his way for her. And then he realised he was in danger of blaming her for something she hadn't said or done and had given no sign she was even considering. He'd got himself in a real *penbleth*. His confidence, in himself, in Catherine, in what they'd agreed, was ruinously undermined. The certainties of last night were gone. *What's to come is still unsure.* Everything seemed to be hanging on next Saturday.

He knew he was overthinking it – but now that he'd started, how could he stop? What else was there to think about?

He turned on his heel, and marched up the 'Roman Road', determined to soldier on to the top of the mountain, no matter how foul a mood he – and his Auntie! – had got himself into. Reaching the final crest, he veered away from the track, over the mossy grass, up towards the Triangulation Stone. Now he could see southwards, over the Vale's rich farmlands, to the flats and office blocks of Cardiff, the coast at Barry, Aberthaw, Southerndown and beyond. For once, it was a fine day. Flat Holm and Steep Holm sat ashimmer in the Bristol Channel, the Somerset hills in plain sight on the far side. And below him, the reason he'd made the climb: Gilfach Goch. Somewhere down there, in Evanstown or Garden Village or Gilfach itself – he'd never visited her home, didn't know where exactly it was – Catherine would be… doing what? He tried to guess, but for once his over-active imagination failed. But he felt better simply for being there, for being able to see where she was, even if he couldn't see her.

He didn't linger, fearful he'd think himself into a mood again. Instead, as always, he went right up to the Trig Point itself and touched the tapered concrete pillar. Then he did something that always gave him a thrill. He stretched out both his arms, squarely to each side of his body, so that his open hands were aligned precisely with the cardinal points, East and West. Because this was a special place. Not that it was a challenging climb or any great height, just 1300 feet above sea level, that's all; but there was an extraordinary fact about it. If you went due east from here, on exactly this line of latitude, you'd cross the lower reaches of Gwent, run north of the Cotswolds into the flatlands of southeast England, cross the North Sea into the Netherlands and traverse a vast swathe of the European continent… all before you were ever standing as high as this again. By then, you'd be in the Urals! And strangely, in the same manner, heading due west at this precise latitude, there was no point in Wales, southern Ireland or eastern Canada that was as high as the spot where he stood right now, not until you came to the Rockies, thousands and thousands of miles away. One day, Jac thought, I must check out whether this is actually true. Or maybe I won't. Maybe what's important is that I think it's true. *It all comes down to what you believe in the end.* With his arms outstretched like that, he *believed*. He felt a mystic connection, if not to the whole wide world, then to enough of it to make it seem as if he was reaching out to humanity in all its diversity. Kerouac would have approved, but it wasn't just hippie-dippy nonsense: it was political. Now, though, it was the *struggle* with his love-life which gripped him. He imagined his super-charged line of latitude running through Catherine's house, right through her home down there below him in Gilfach, joining them to each other, to the entire human race.

Re-energised, he danced away from the obelisk, back towards Penygraig, throwing himself down into a small hollow, the Crow's Nest. Another well-honoured tradition. He remembered flopping into the springy turf here the first time he'd ever made the climb, with a gang of older children from Hughes Street. It had seemed like a great adventure – he'd only just started walking to school on his own. It was a hot day. His Mam had filled his toy plastic water-bottle with weak orange-squash so that he wouldn't get thirsty. By the time he reached the Crow's Nest, there was more plastic than orange in the squash. A decade on, he could still taste it coating his tongue.

Resting there, gazing up at the clouds – *why is the sky so high when I lie on my back?* – Jac summoned a massive effort of will and forced himself to relax. Calm, calm, calm. He knew, thanks to Wordsworth, that poetry, great poetry, was emotion recollected *in tranquillity*; and he'd planned to spend time now, up here, above the drama and messiness of his life, perfecting the poem, the *epic* poem, that he'd begun on his holiday in Haworth. The walk he'd taken there, up to the ruins of Top Withens, the farmhouse which inspired *Wuthering Heights*, had been pleasant enough on a summer's day. But he'd always pictured himself arriving after an heroic trek through a darkening snowstorm. In balmy sunshine, he'd failed to *connect* with Catherine Earnshaw, as he'd hoped. That was how his epic would start. But he wanted it to be an imaginative bridge, too, between Emily Brontë's moorland and Carncelyn, this bare mountainside he called his own.

He reached into the top pocket of his denim jacket, pulling out a tiny notepad, barely bigger than a matchbox. At the Brontë Museum, he'd seen the miniscule books in which the sisters wrote their childhood stories and poems. A book of that size might inspire him, he'd reckoned. He'd brought a biro with him. Opening the notepad, he began to set down his title and the opening lines he'd already composed, in the smallest writing he could manage:

On Carncelyn
for Catherine

I walked with you on your moors, I longed to hear your voice;
But at the Withens there was no breath of wind,
No frenzied scrapings at the casement,
Just sunshine and shadow, a plaque upon the wall...

The following lines would express his anguish: the balmy weather was a sign that he was no more than a Linton, the powder-puff *son* of Heathcliff; not the powerful, tempestuous hero-villain of the novel that he aspired to be. Then the scene would shift here, to Carncelyn, in ancient times. Those Romans and Saxons marauding across the mountain. Jac wanted a sense of standing over a millennium and more of history: 'the face of the earth breathes under the dung of a thousand years, Man-pocked mudpack of the ages.'

You're proud of that line, aren't you? said his Auntie. *Just because there's Senghenydd in it.*

Cynghanedd, he corrected her.

That's the one. Chains of chiming rhymes.

He ignored her and tried to focus on the next section of his poem. Set in the Depression of the 1930s, it would link Penygraig and Gilfach Goch (and so Jac and *his* Catherine): the true and tragic story of two miners from the 'Graig, a face-worker and a better-off pit deputy. In tough times, they could find work only over the mountain in Gilfach. Walking home one winter's night, they'd lost their way in a blizzard (like the one Jac imagined at

223

Top Withens), perishing together near the very spot where Jac was resting. By the time, days later, their bodies were found, exposure had altered their features; each was mistaken for the other and each was taken to the other's house for laying out. Before they were properly identified, the poor collier was already in the bespoke oak coffin intended for the deputy, and so he had the decent burial his own family could never have afforded.

There were two problems with this egalitarian parable. First, despite weeks of thinking about it, Jac had barely half-a-dozen lines completed. Second, the title and first four lines had already filled the whole first page of his tiny notepad.

Jac was frustrated. On paper, his poem didn't look much like the Brontës' work. His writing would have to be much, much smaller to fit a decent chunk of verse onto a single sheet, to make it flow for the reader as he'd imagined. He realised he needed practice to achieve the right effect. He remembered his Rough Book, how he'd filled two entire pages with *Catherine, Catherine, Catherine...* He used her name again now, her surname too, experimenting with how many times he could cram the two words 'Catherine Evans' onto a single page. He managed it 37 times at his first attempt, 46 at the second, an impressive 64 on the third page, though by then his writing was scarcely legible. And his fingers hurt. He fell into a kind of reverie, or maybe just a plain old doze (he hadn't had much sleep the previous night).

When he came to, the sun had moved west. The little notebook lay on the grass beside him. He picked it up, tucked it back into his jacket pocket, fastening the denim flap firmly over the metal button. Then he got up and began to tramp back down the mountain towards home. On the flat, marshy field below the Crow's Nest, the moles had been at it. The burrowing mammals, not the spies. Small, black pyramids of earth stood everywhere.

They're making molehills out of mountains, said his Auntie.

Jac realised how much easier life would be if he could master the same trick.

He pressed on. When he reached the paddock, the old nag trotted up to the gate, hoping for a treat. 'Arry Howen's 'orse was no shining stallion, but, petting her, Jac was put in mind of Rhiannon, the *Mabinogion*'s Horse Goddess, riding effortlessly beyond her admirer's reach. Would Catherine be equally elusive? Harry's poor beast, he decided, would be as reliable an oracle as his Auntie. He felt silly, whispering his Big Question into an equine ear, but he did it all the same: "So, will I get this date come Saturday?"

Answer came there none. The mare turned tail, silently cantering away.

At least she didn't say neigh, admitted his Auntie. Though clearly, she remained unconvinced.

28

There was an Election on. The votes were being counted. Within
hours, the results would be declared. Meanwhile, as is traditional,
the hiatus was filled by psephologists and pundits and pointless
speculation.

"Not since 1910 has the electorate been in such a rebellious
mood. The establishment is about to come crashing down. How
the mighty fall! Though, of course, it's pointless to speculate at
this stage."

"Thank you, Bob McKenzie," replied the anchorman.

It was actually Penry who'd delivered this mild parody. And
Jac who was playing the role of studio presenter.

"Now over to Robin Day who has some fascinating guests
with him in the Girls' Cloakroom."

It was the First Day of Term. A new school year. Jac's Upper
Sixth – his final year. And there *was* an Election on. For Head
Boy and Head Girl, and Deputies for each. The Staff and the
Sixth Formers had cast their ballots: the electorate balanced out
fifty-fifty, teachers and pupils. Gathered in the *Li-bury*, the latter
waited for the results with a mixture of tepid interest and outright
apathy. Even a psephologist as sharp as Bob McKenzie would
struggle to predict how it might go. Last year, Lydia had been a
Deputy. Martyn – who'd have been a shoo-in otherwise – had
made it clear he'd no interest in standing. This time, Petra was
thought to be in with a chance. They all hoped that Swotzi *wasn't*.
But, of course, he'd put his name forward, just to impress. And
now, sooner than expected, silence fell as Bull charged in,
bellowing a name: "Catherine Evans!"

Well, that was a surprise. Even Jac hadn't imagined Catherine
topping the poll.

He'd got to school that morning earlier than he'd managed
since Form One, determined to get a word with her before
Assembly. Everyone else turned up in good time (except for
Ciaran: *was he still in Ireland?*). But the bell was ringing before

Catherine arrived. And there'd been no chance of a private conversation since. Now she was a shock Election winner. Or was she?

"Catherine Evans," repeated Bull, dropping the decibel level by a half – she was, if it were possible, *more* intimidating when she lowered her voice. "This is not on!"

So it wasn't the results that had sent Bull stampeding into the Library.

"Tell your correspondent, whoever they are, that this is a scholastic institution, not a *post restante*."

With that, she tossed a package to an embarrassed Catherine, and trotted out, muttering about having better things to do than delivering parcels for pupils: the results of this morning's needlessly democratic exercise would now be delayed.

Jac took his chance, sliding into the seat next to Catherine. What was going on? He recognised the writing on the address label. Still in shock, she tore it open, and read – once, very quickly – the letter inside. She passed it to Jac and started unwrapping the other object in the packet, which by the look of it was a 7-inch single. The disc appeared to be miraculously intact, despite being handled both by the Royal Mail *and* the Deputy Headmistress. The letter, as Jac suspected, came from Ciaran.

"Dear Catherine, Sorry to send this to school, but I haven't got your home address. The teachers won't mind, I'm sure. It's just to let you know some news, and to ask a favour. I've decided A levels aren't for me. Catching up with the Welsh syllabus doesn't seem worth the effort. My mother has found me a job – in Marks and Spencer's in Pontypridd. The pay is rubbish. But they're offering training, so it's not a bad option. It means I won't be coming back to school. Would you let people know? I start work on Monday: a month in Ponty, then they could move me anywhere – Cardiff, Swansea, England even. Of course, I want to say a proper goodbye to everybody before then. So here's the favour... Over the summer in Portrush – there's a big caravan park there too – I was thinking about your family's caravan in Porthcawl. You've told me so much about it, in those heart-to-

227

hearts we've had. This is bold of me, I know, but I was wondering… could we all get together there for a party one weekend? Just a day trip, not staying over or anything. Lots of *craic*. I'd understand of course if it's not on, but it'd be grand to have a Saturday to ourselves (or a Sunday – but then Jac couldn't come, could he?). I enclose a little present, just to show that I *have* been thinking about you. Regards to the others. Love, Ciaran."

By the time Jac had read the letter, twice, Catherine had unwrapped the record. It was that summer's No 1 hit, *When Will I See You Again?*

Just then, Bull marched back in. It hadn't taken long to count the votes after all.

James Taylor, it emerged, had barely a dozen. "All from *teachers*," stage-whispered Jac, prompted by his Auntie. He managed to keep it *just* quiet enough to avoid a telling off. Relieved, his thoughts wandered off elsewhere. He hardly heard Petra being announced as Deputy Head Girl. He failed completely to realise who'd been elected Deputy Head Boy until Penry slapped him on the back in congratulations.

What had preoccupied him, of course, was Ciaran's letter. Why, when he had Jac's address, and Penry's too probably, did he post it to Catherine? What were all the *heart-to-hearts* they'd been having? And what about the record? Was *When Will I See You Again?* intended for all of them or just Catherine? *Were they in love, or just friends?*

"Well, that was pretty unambiguous," said Catherine, ambiguously. Jac's mind was still on Ciaran's gift, but she meant the Election result. "Well done, Jac. I'd no idea my boy was so popular."

My boy. That sounded good. Not as good as *my boyfriend* perhaps, which would have removed this further ambiguity altogether, but much better than plain *you*. For the first time that morning, Jac felt encouraged.

"A 23% swing against the Nasty Nazi Party," said Penry, back in Bob McKenzie mode, taking the chair alongside them.

Catherine ignored this and told him instead about the letter, Ciaran's news and his idea of an outing to Porthcawl. Penry half-sang his response: "Ooh, I do love to be beside the seaside."

"My family won't mind," said Catherine. "Thing is, I know the caravan's booked up for the second half of September, and then Martyn and Lydia will be off to Uni. The season's practically over by then anyway, and everything shuts up. So the only time we could do it, realistically, is this coming Saturday. But we'd have to get our skates on to organise things in time for that."

Saturday. Their date!

"I'm free on Saturday. Sounds ideal," said Penry, unhelpfully. "What about you, Jac?"

"Ah, I've got... *something* on, this Saturday." Jac turned towards Catherine, appealing. "At least, I think I have."

"Let's take a walk, Jac," she replied coolly, "and see if we can sort *something* out."

If Penry thought it was odd, he betrayed no sign of it. Catherine and Jac left without a word, the Three Degrees record still in her hand. If Ciaran meant it for her alone, it was pretty direct (*unsubtle, more like!*); but there was no comparison – surely – with the classic that was *Tapestry* which Jac himself had bought her for Christmas.

They walked on, up to the Top Yard. It was she who broke the silence.

"I know you're disappointed. And I know why. That's quite sweet, Jac: I'm touched, I really am. I did promise about Saturday, I know. But remember all those times you've told me that what you admire about Petra and Martyn is that they're not turned in on each other? That they embrace the rest of us, no matter how strong their feelings are for each other? Are you really saying that you want me and you to begin by doing the exact opposite, when we've a chance to do something... something that'll bring everyone together, for the last time before people head to university? Because I'm not sure that I want to start off like that. And, come on – it's not like you and I will be spending the day apart. It'll be fun."

Jac couldn't remember telling her *all those times* how he respected Martyn and Petra for being open-hearted (although of course he did). There were so many conversations he'd had with Catherine inside his head, but had he actually said that to her? And hard as he tried to think, there was nothing he could say now to counter the way she'd put things. He was skewered. Eliot's Prufrock, pinned and wriggling on the wall.

He turned towards her in one last silent plea. Their eyes, narrowing, didn't lock as they had on Tonypandy Square, but Jac saw as clearly as he did then the challenge in hers. She was tough as well as compassionate. Shrewd yet fair. Thoughtful about others, but sure of her own ground in a way that he hadn't yet learned to be. But there was still something wild there too, something wicked, a lust for life. The Bad Girl, the Sixth Form Scholar *and* the Nurse-To-Be – Catherine past, present and future, all rolled into one.

He realised then why he'd pursued her, why he was pursuing her still. And that he might never catch up with her.

29

He didn't even get to sit next to her on the bus. That was what got to him, he reckoned afterwards.

Saturday morning was unseasonably hot. He was at the bus stop early. Time to think. To worry. *Don't worry,* said his Auntie, unhelpfully. *Put your mind to other things.*

He tried to.

When he was small, Porthcawl was a favourite destination for him and his steering wheel: the summer service operated jointly by Rhondda Transport and Red & White, as he noted carefully every time he updated his version of the timetable. The hourly buses alternated between the companies. His family were such poor timekeepers he could never be sure whose single-decker they'd manage to catch, which only added to the excitement. Jac loved the complexity of the route: from faraway Aberdare over the mountain to Maerdy, down the Rhondda Fach to Tylorstown, up and over Penrhys to mid-Rhondda, before picking him up, not at the Naval Colliery where all Valley buses allowed boarders by request, but only here by Jones the Fruiterer's, down at the bottom of the hill. This journey was special! The terminus, an hour-and-a-half distant (with a circular tour of Gilfach Goch thrown in) would have been the star attraction for any other child: Porthcawl's golden beaches and all the fun of the Fair. For Jac, the real thrill was Bridgend Bus Station. On arrival, he'd steer his vehicle gingerly past the row of buses already parked up, coming to a precise stop nose-in to the stand. Then, after a five-minute break, he had to *reverse* away from the stand, avoiding – oh, my goodness! – pedestrians and other traffic, before turning towards the Station exit for the last leg to the coast. He never failed to execute this delicate manoeuvre perfectly, even on the return journey, however drowsy he was from a day on Coney Beach, however weighed down with a tummyful of toffee apple and doughnuts.

But how would he handle his manoeuvres today?

It was barely 10 o'clock, but the sun was so warm he'd already taken off his Wrangler jacket. Spotting the Red & White single-decker approaching along Dunraven Street, he dangled the jacket over his shoulder, his index finger hooked through the loop of denim inside the collar. He looked cool, he hoped, posing like that, as the bus pulled up: a Valleys Kerouac. *Jac* Kerouac. He didn't feel so cool inside.

"*Poseur*," he heard Martyn say, as he got on.

"Probably thinks he looks like Jack Kerouac," shouted Penry down the aisle.

Was he so transparent? He paid the driver for his day return. Thankfully, apart from the Friends, there was hardly anyone aboard. It was the end of the first week in September: mass Valleys migrations to the seaside were over for another year.

Penry looked unusually resplendent in a harlequin check top, an *homage* to his role as Feste, perhaps. Resplendent or just mad, thought Jac, with uncharacteristic cattiness. Penry's jibe must have got to him. He was on edge.

Ciaran, the instigator of this unexpected outing, was also wearing check: but his shirt was a classic understated navy-and-white with a button-down collar. Ben Sherman, Jac guessed, and then asked himself how come he was so interested in fashion all of sudden? Martyn hadn't bothered with a jacket either, just a tight-fitting mauve top and a pair of Oxford bags. Petra looked blooming in a sleeveless cerise blouse, the very picture of a young woman a month short of her eighteenth birthday. In front of them, on her own, Nerys: Catherine had seen no reason to assume that Nerys wasn't included in Ciaran's plan, and Jac couldn't think of a way to stop her being invited, though he knew it would make Martyn nervous. Lydia had told Catherine that Biker Boy was working a hobble that Saturday morning, so she'd come down with him on the motorcycle and meet them by The Knight's Arms mid-afternoon. That just left Catherine to join them as the bus made its circuit around Gilfach. Jac deliberately took an empty double-seat behind them all so that she could come and join him. He was already seeing it as some kind of test.

Annoyingly, as the bus made its way through Penrhiwfer, Martyn slid out of his seat beside Petra and joined Jac. If he stayed put, Jac's calculations about seating would come to nothing. Martyn wasn't planning to park himself there for long though.

"Slip these into your jacket for me, butt'," he whispered, "I've got nowhere to keep them, except my trouser pocket, and they're a bit obvious there."

Martyn palmed a small, thin box over to Jac. *Cigarettes? Too small.* Jac took a peek. A pack of three. Condoms. Jac wondered if he was blushing. He'd never before held such a palpable manifestation of immorality, as his family would have seen it. Should *he* be embarrassed? He fumbled the packet, nearly dropping it. Then, as he tried to put it safely out of sight, he realised his jacket's top pocket was already crammed with something: his little notebook from Carncelyn. He'd forgotten it was there. By the time he turned the jacket over and opened the other pocket, the bus was swinging round the corner by The Guckoo. Swaying off balance, he grunted. Nerys turned to see what was going on. Jac worried that she must have got a good look at what he was trying to hide.

At least Martyn had gone back to sit with Petra: the seat beside Jac was free again. As they turned off to Gilfach at Hendreforgan, his heart beat faster. It had been a difficult week at school. He'd never got another chance to speak to Catherine alone. He'd thought about asking her to move their date to one of the weekday evenings – *why not?* – but, after the conversation they'd had on the Top Yard, the courage to risk rejection had leaked away. Neither of them, it seemed, had told anyone else about what had happened on Tonypandy Square. So were they going out with each other at all? The Three Degrees' questions kept coming back to haunt him. Was this the beginning or was it the end?

She was on the bus stop, wearing a pair of flared trousers in shocking pink.

A shocking pair of pink trousers, said his Auntie, unkindly.

But Jac thought Catherine looked magnificent. He shuffled over, right against the window, to make sure that she could see that there was plenty of room beside him. Then – disaster! – Nerys practically grabbed hold of her in the aisle, pulling her down into the seat beside herself, telling her how much she *loved* those trousers and Catherine *must* tell her where she'd got them. It wasn't like Nerys to show an interest in clothes, especially not colourful girly clothes, but with no pause, they were nattering away, and Ciaran was ideally placed to join in from the seat opposite. The whole centre of gravity of the group had shifted, isolating Jac at the back. He felt himself falling into a sulk, a right *pwdu*. It shouldn't have mattered who sat where – the whole day was still in front of them – but it *did*. He stared pointedly out of the window. He thought of the journey ahead, a whole hour still, and all the things he'd planned to say to Catherine.

Just as well, said his Auntie. *You'd have bored her rigid with a list of bus stops. And stories about your steering wheel.*

Jac had to smile. His Auntie knew him too well. But it wasn't enough to lift his mood. He'd wound himself up and for what?

He spread his open jacket over himself like a comfort blanket. He felt the shape of the packet inside the top pocket. It had been a shock to him, that Martyn would have such things. Another reminder of how gormless he was. If he'd thought about it at all, he would have realised that, a year into their love affair, Martyn and Petra would be enjoying more than an occasional *cwtsh*. This was 1974, not the nineteenth century. They'd spent a weekend in Paris together, for goodness' sake. But Jac had never considered the practicalities of what that might mean. Why bring the condoms to Porthcawl, though? Were they going to....?

They must have plans *for the evening. Back in the Rhondda. Before they go home.*

Jac couldn't bring himself to wonder about it any further. Gormless he certainly was. Sheltered. Sex was taboo at home, never mentioned. He saw again how different to the others' his upbringing was, how Victorian, how crippling. He stared even more fixedly out of the window. Everything was spoiled. His great romantic plans for the day already thwarted. The sordid reality of lust sitting right there in his jacket pocket.

You've even missed the bus station, Jac.

It was true. They were already heading out of Bridgend.

Soon, they caught their first sight of the sea, and then they'd arrived. Trecco Bay: thousands of caravans set out in a perfect grid on the gravelly sands above the beach, with *tar-mark* access roads between the rows every twenty vans or so.

Just like Manhattan, said his Auntie.

With single-storey holiday homes instead of skyscrapers, obviously.

Catherine's pink trousers led them unerringly through the heart of the grid. Jac saw Ciaran looking with wonder at the scale of it. All they could see was caravans.

"It's the biggest static park in Europe," Jac informed him.

"And that's a good thing?" asked Ciaran, incredulously.

The caravan was baking. They opened the windows, letting the air in, and the sickly smell of Calor Gas out. It was a six-berther, plenty big enough for their gathering, with a fold-away table and a galley kitchen. Photos of Catherine's family stood on a built-in sideboard.

The plan was to refresh themselves here, before walking over to the Esplanade in time to meet Lydia. Petra had brought four flagons, *just to keep them going*. Thirsty after the journey, they poured out the cider. Everyone, Jac apart, toasted Ciaran with a brimming glass. Everyone, Jac apart, was in high spirits.

"Time… for a game!" announced Penry, adopting his TV quizmaster persona.

"The Blank Game," suggested Ciaran, who'd cottoned onto their *penchant* for such things.

Great, thought Jac, Ciaran's back's back. Thankfully, the others vetoed it as being too strongly associated with school. Penry proposed The Word Association Football Game, but by the time they'd got halfway through explaining the rules to Ciaran, the jollity had gone out of the prospect. In the end, they decided just to play trumps with forfeits. Again, Jac's Puritan upbringing put him at a disadvantage. Sets of playing cards, The Devil's Bible, were banned from his house. He was unfamiliar with even the best-known games. And he hated forfeits, always had done since his steering wheel was snatched from him, all those years before.

He lost the first three hands and was forced to dance around the outside of the caravan singing *Puppy Love*; to reveal his most embarrassing childhood incident – the loss of his beloved toy and the fight with Belinda Owen (*why was he always so honest?*); and to put lipstick on himself blindfolded.

"It's a good thing we're not playing Strip Jac Naked," quipped Penry.

Worse was to come.

By some fluke, he avoided losing the fourth round. Martyn had to sing a nursery rhyme in the style of Marilyn Monroe: Jack and Jill went up and down the hill more sensuously than ever before. But Jac's luck ran out again with the next deal. It was Nerys's turn to impose the forfeit. A wicked smile played on her lips.

"Alright, Jac, show us what's in the top pocket of your Wrangler jacket."

Bastard. Jac felt trapped. Pinned and wriggling again. The longer he delayed, the more the others (Martyn aside: he *knew*) sensed that Nerys was onto something.

The jacket sat like a hand-grenade on the seat next him. Nerys picked it up and dropped it into his lap. What was he supposed to do? Hand her his notebook with the poem dedicated to Catherine and her name written 147 times; or reveal Martyn's pack of condoms?

Ciaran thought he recognised the bulging shape in one of the pockets.

"It's a packet of fags."

It was open season on Jac now.

"He's grown up and started smoking."

"Wait till his Mam and Dad find out."

"Wait till Penry's cousin does."

There was no good outcome. In the end, he chickened out of making the choice himself.

"Do you mean the left-hand pocket or the right-hand pocket?" he said weakly, trying one last time to delay the inevitable.

"*This* pocket," shouted Nerys, grabbing the jacket again and pulling out… the condoms.

"Jesus, Mary and Joseph!" That was Ciaran, of course.

"Oooh, Jac Morgan thinks he's going to get lucky tonight." That was Penry.

Jac turned towards Catherine, trying desperately to convey without speaking that this wasn't what it looked like. But her head had dropped, and he couldn't see her face under the curtain of her hair. No doubt, though, it was already pinker than her trousers, and reddening several shades deeper. In fury rather than embarrassment.

Tell them they're not yours, suggested his Auntie, without much conviction.

"They're not mine," said Jac, stupidly adding, "I'm minding them for somebody."

"Oh yeah?" said Nerys. "Who's that then?"

Another silence. Everyone followed Jac's eyes, and the penny dropped. It was Petra's turn to blush.

"Thanks a bunch, *butty boy*," hissed Martyn.

Jac snatched his jacket back, stuffed the packet roughly back inside the pocket, and rushed outside, his face still covered in lipstick.

30

It was Petra who came to find him.

He'd been staring out to sea, for goodness knows how long, on the rocky promontory that divided Trecco from Sandy Bay. He'd managed to rub most of the lipstick off.

In the distance, they could hear the distant rumble of the Water Chute. The weather was brilliant, but there was just a sprinkling of locals strolling along the beach. No Sunday School outings or club trips bound together in a circlet of deckchairs. The donkeys had all left.

"Come on, Jac. The others are walking up to town."

"How's Martyn?"

"Oh, you know. Martyn's Martyn. He'll be fine once he gets a drink into him."

"And you?"

"Don't worry yourself."

"What about Catherine?"

Petra said nothing. She didn't have to. He knew it was over. Over before it had begun.

They walked side-by-side with hardly another word and caught up with the others by the Fair. No-one said a thing. A wagon plunged down the Water Chute, landing with an almighty splash in the tank at the bottom. Two young girls aboard screamed. Jac wanted to join in. Anything to puncture the mood. He *would* shriek with the next lot, he decided, but there were no other thrill-seekers ready to ride.

He stared at up at the wooden scaffolding supporting the track, avoiding eye contact with Catherine. After the long summer, the white paint was blistered and flaky.

They all walked on over to the Harbour. The tide was in, the surging water breaking on the breakwater by the Lighthouse. The *mole*.

On again. Nearly time to meet Lydia. The Sea-Front. An end-of-season vibe. The Grand Pavilion already advertising its

Christmas Panto, *Jack and the Beanstalk*. Penry tried to joke about it. Something sarcastic about everyone being full of beans today. It felt flat. The title reminded Jac of his plans for a band of musical incompetents. That wasn't going to happen either.

The awkwardness between them was too much. Jac knew it was his fault, but it was too late to apologise now. He was carrying his jacket, the cause of all his troubles. The sun had scorched his bare arms. He felt blistered and flaky, all of him, not just his exposed flesh, like that paint on the Water Chute.

He searched for something, anything to say.

There was something about *sunburn* he'd been pondering earlier on the rocks, something important, but it wouldn't come back to him now.

Even his Auntie was out of ideas.

Eventually, eyeing the Pavilion, Jac realised that Ciaran would see only a tatty seafront Variety Hall, wouldn't know its history.

"This is where they hold the Miners' Eisteddfod…"

And before he knew it, he'd embarked on a lecture about class and culture, about Paul Robeson singing down the transatlantic cable, and the international solidarity of the workers, and what it must have been like to be a black artist blacklisted in the 1950s…

"Jac, just shut up, will you?" snarled Martyn finally.

"I just thought Ciaran might appreciate…"

"Your problem, Jac, is that you've got a child's picture-book version of the whole of Welsh history and God knows what else bouncing around inside your head. And you think you've got a grip on class politics. But as for imagining what it's like to be anyone else, any other single human being, what it actually feels like for somebody who's not you to be around you, what it means to *suffer*… well, you haven't got a bloody clue."

Jac was aghast.

It was like Martyn had struck him across the face.

"Hang on, Martyn…" began Petra, but Ciaran was speaking over her.

"That's a bit harsh – but, Jac, seriously, and I mean this in a helpful way… *think* about it, will you?"

Jac's first thought was that it was so *unfair*. If he had a talent for anything, it was for getting alongside others, for sympathy; not for politics or history or anything to do with hard facts. Beyond that, he saw himself as an artist, a would-be artist, not terribly gifted perhaps, but a sort of song-maker, a composer – though how could he say it now, after the way he'd behaved all day? – of a kind of moral music, a poetry that carried the weight of principle. Anyway… it wasn't his fault that Martyn had turned up with a packet of condoms and nowhere to hide them.

Thankfully, he was prevented from voicing any of this.

It was Lydia who came to the rescue, waving to them cheerily from the other side of the road, hurrying along the Front on her own. Biker Boy had got talking to some other motorcyclists outside The Knight's Arms, and he'd headed off for a spin with them down to the Gower.

"How was the ride down, Lydia? Did he give you a *Tonypandy Ton-Up?*"

"None of your business, Penry! Though he did warn me that there's a lot of vibration when you're astride his Gold Flash."

Innuendo was never the 'old' Lydia's style: she really must have loosened up.

The others sniggered too loudly, too long. Desperate for a laugh. Jac merely wondered how someone else knew about *Tonypandy Ton-Ups*. Had he been ruminating aloud again without realising it?

They headed back, in pairs, towards the Lighthouse.

Jac was with Penry. Behind them, though he tried to tune it out, he could hear Petra briefing Lydia about everything that had happened – the forfeits, the Wrangler jacket, Jac's hesitation in revealing what was in his pocket, the spat at the Pavilion… the whole, dreadful saga of what was said, what was done.

They'd arrived at the breakwater. The sun was still scorching. They walked out on the narrow ledge. The ocean pounded the wall beneath them.

"But why didn't he just give her what was in the other pocket?" Lydia was asking. She was so acute, far too acute.

"What was so… *embarrassing* about whatever it was he'd hidden in there?"

Jac lost it. He'd be damned if, after all this, he was going to be forced to reveal the notebook too. The *fucking* jacket was over his shoulder, where it had hung like an albatross all day. His finger was hooked through that loop of material at the neck. He started to twirl the thing, above his head. Round it went. Round and round and round. *Like the boy called David and his Sling.* There was no space on the seawall for the others to get away from it. Penry was short enough – *just* – for it to clear his head. The others flung themselves to the ground. The phrase *whirling dervish* came unbidden to Jac. And then, two flashes of memory: Belinda Owen flinging his sky-blue steering wheel into the stingies over the edge of the tumps; and Penry and Jac's Corona bottle. Channelling all his frustration, all his bitterness into one defiant flick of the wrist, he hurled the jacket away from himself. It flew, high, out over the breaking surf, describing a long, long, beautiful arc. Gulls screeched.

Just as the denim lost its outward momentum, at its furthest point away from them, over the open ocean, a pocket of air must have got trapped inside it. It reared up and billowed out, *athwart* the wind. The sleeves were caught and spread-eagled. It hovered there, as though looking back at them, looking down at them. Like a crucified man. Like a cowboy Jesus. And then it began to fall at last towards the saltwater. Seconds later was sinking, down, down and out of sight below the waves. As it finally disappeared, Jac remembered that it wasn't only his notepad that had gone with it. Martyn's condoms were still inside too. And his own return ticket for the long bus journey home.

241

31

It was Penry's Eighteenth Birthday Party.

The Eighteenth Birthday Party That Wasn't An Eighteenth Birthday Party. The Party where The Society of Friends signed up for an Improbable Rendezvous. The Party that ended in Credible Threats of Incredible Violence.

The Three Unlikely Upshots Of Celebrating A Coming Of Age, said Jac's Auntie afterwards. *You could make a Modern Welsh Triad of it.*

(On *Jac's* Eighteenth, something far more Improbable would happen: he would marry the *girls* of his dreams. But that comes later in the story, and by then his Auntie... well, we'll see.)

The Friends had gathered in the Bracchi's on Station Street, in Porth – Catherine, Petra, Nerys and Jac. Martyn joined them, out of school uniform now: Lydia had already left for university in Canterbury, but he was still a fortnight away from the start of term in Oxford. Even Ciaran had come up on the train from Ponty during his lunch hour.

And the Birthday Boy was there, of course. Penry's birthday, September 18th, fell as the first of theirs during the School Year. There'd been no talk of an evening celebration on the day itself: it was so close to the start of the school year that they'd assumed he was waiting to have a joint party with someone later on. In the aftermath of Porthcawl, no one had been focused on it, so it was left to the last minute: a surprise gathering in the middle of the school day. Then Penry got to hear about it, but they decided to go ahead anyway.

Since the disastrous day out, the others had been wary of Jac. Catherine had hardly looked in his direction. He'd kept his head down, got on with his schoolwork and his new duties as a prefect, trying not to show how miserable he was. One morning, at the school gate, collecting names of latecomers, Petra tried to tease him into a better frame of mind. For a laugh, to see if anyone would notice, she persuaded him to swap the little enamel badges they'd been presented with. He became Deputy Head Girl; she wore the Deputy Head Boy's badge. No one did clock on, and they never swapped them back.

So here they were, the third week of term, their final year ahead of them, and Jac, for one, sure he'd already messed it up beyond repair. But a birthday was something to celebrate, even if it was only in Bacchetta's at Dinner Time.

The Friends loved the café. One of the original Bracchi's, it had had a facelift in the Swinging Sixties: a jukebox, formica-topped tables, bench seating with fake leather cushioning in red. Now it was all going shabby again; but for frothy coffee and steam pies, it was the perfect refuge in the middle of a school day. As always, they commandeered a couple of tables tucked around the back, all cosy and dark. Petra had bought a big silver 'Key of the Door' card in a presentation box. When they gave it to Penry, he managed to look even more embarrassed than your average 18-year-old, which wasn't like him. It wasn't until they'd sung *Penblwydd Hapus* and Nerys had pulled his hair eighteen times (and one for luck) that he finally made his confession.

"The thing is, there's a bit of a misunderstanding…"

"Don't tell us," said Ciaran, "today isn't your birthday."

"No, it *is* my birthday. But not actually my Eighteenth."

Penry, it turned out, was only 17. He'd been such an outstanding pupil at Gelli Juniors ("That's not saying much" – Martyn) and, with his September birthday, so 'old' in his proper School Year, that he'd been put up for the Eleven Plus a twelvemonth early. So he'd started Grammar School at 10, and stayed a year ahead of where he should have been right through. He'd kept this quiet – until now. Everyone was amused by the revelation, but that didn't stop them giving him a hard time.

"Keep growing at this rate, and you'll be four-foot-eleven by the time you're really eighteen."

"Imagine when he reaches twenty-one…"

Talk turned to what they'd all be like, what the world might be like, by the time Penry reached that distant milestone. Four years away: *unimaginable*. The course of their lives would be set by then, but they'd have so much to live through before they got

243

there. Light-hearted stuff, but Jac sensed his mood darkening. The bond, the connection they'd had between them, the closeness that he so valued: Porthcawl had shown him how fragile it was, how fleeting it might be. Already, Lydia had moved on, into the next phase of her life. Very soon, Martyn would do the same.

Jac felt a tug, an ache in his guts: more than anything, he wanted what they had together to be something that *endured*, something that stood the test of time, that would last until they were twenty-one and way, way beyond that. Despite all that had gone wrong, the pain and hurt he'd caused, he *knew* that there was something real in it, something to treasure and to nurture. A still point in the turning world.

Penry was on a roll. Arms spread aloft, he stared down into his teacup, seeing the future there, reading the leaves like a clairvoyant, revealing the terrible misfortunes that would befall his friends by the time he was twenty-five, thirty, thirty-five…

"Jac… he'll be as bald as a coot. And weigh three times what he weighs now. Toby Belch without the hair. He'll be divorced. His wife will cite unreasonable burping. Martyn will have four Oscars. And a liver transplant. He'll be divorced too – *five times*. From the same woman. Not the same woman as Jac, of course. Petra… Petra will be having an affair with the banned captain of the Welsh rugby team… Ninelives Bowen. And Catherine will be nursing *him* back to health. Ciaran will be Tea Shop, or whatever it is they call it over there, of a United Ireland, and he'll announce that they're going to build a bridge to Wales. Like in the *Mabinogion*. Nerys, of course, will be in Parliament. As a cleaner."

"We'll have a Free Wales by then," retorted Nerys.

"We'll have a *Free Gelli* long before! And we'll be taking holidays on Mars. Provided free, by the Free Gelli Government. And when I get to forty…"

Forty! Life would be over by then, despite the *cliché*. They all understood that.

"…on the very day of my fortieth birthday, I …"

But Penry suddenly ran out of inspiration. It was Jac, still pondering seriously, who filled the silence.

"What we should do on your fortieth is come back here, all of us, and see how it's all worked out…"

"That's rather improbable, isn't it…?"

It was Martyn who'd begun to object, but he stopped short, realising that he wasn't attuned to how the others had taken Jac's idea. Something in Jac's tone had stilled them, stopped them from poking fun at his eccentric notions for once, made them realise that there was something important to him in his weird proposal. Or maybe they just wanted to cheer him up.

Anyway, Martyn turned his scepticism into a smile, and let Jac continue…

"…so let's promise each other now, that we'll meet here again, at twelve o'clock, on Penry's fortieth, September 18th…"

"His official fortieth or his real one?"

Everyone laughed, but Jac wasn't to be deterred.

"His *proper* one, what will it be… twenty-three years from today. Come on, let's make a… *vow*, a solemn vow – why not? – as The Society of Friends, that we'll be here to wish him a Happy Fortieth."

Jac remembered that other vow he'd made. On Tonypandy Square. To grow up. To be serious. Well, this *was* serious. And Penry, at least, took it seriously. He went round them, one by one, making them pledge that, whatever happened, they'd be back in Bacchetta's to see him turn forty. And they all seemed to mean it.

"Bet you any money my predictions come true," Penry added. "*'Specially* the ones about you, Jac."

Jac had to laugh at the idea of himself as a fat, wrinkled baldy. But he felt encouraged, *validated*. It might only be a small thing, but they'd taken his notion in earnest when they could have treated it as just daft. And *they* noticed the change in him.

They chatted on, easily now, teasing Penry about his fear of rain, and his cousin, and the time he nearly killed Osmond because *there was a drop of pop on the top.*

They were about to settle up and leave, when Ciaran's eye fell on some graffiti that had been scratched out of the formica tabletop. Four names. MauMau, Parrot, Rat, Dodo.

"Who are these guys?' he asked, clearly not having clocked Rat's presence at the *Thirteenth Night* party. "Rhondda's Fab Four?"

"Yeah," said Jac, "Willy Russell's just written a play about them – *MauMau, Parrot, Rat, Dodo... and Treher-BERT*."

This was far too convoluted and obscure for Ciaran to understand. Only Martyn seemed to get it, and he didn't chuckle.

"They're just some boys from 'Pandy," said Petra, mildly, clearly wanting to change the subject.

"*Just some boys from 'Pandy?*" shouted Jac, in mock outrage. "A gang of motorcycle maniacs more like. Biker bullies. Hooligans with Hondas. Yamaha yobs. Vandals with Vespas – well, maybe not..."

Petra was trying to interrupt him throughout this litany. But Jac was in his *hwyl* now. So was his Auntie. She'd remembered that time Rat had sat in front of Jac on the bus, just as they were making up that rhyming thing about Penrhys. Rat with his head shaved like he'd just been let out of prison.

Actually, I heard something about them the other day...

Now both Catherine and Petra were making faces at Jac. But once the opening for a joke occurred to his Auntie, it was all but impossible for anyone, Jac included, to stop her from using him as her mouthpiece to express it.

"The four of them got taken in for questioning by the police," Jac continued, out loud. "Something about speeding, I suppose. Or drugs. Anyway, they were all released eventually and MauMau said, "Don't worry boys, I didn't grass on you." "O, sorry, MauMau," replied Rat. "I'm afraid I... *ratted*." "Me too," Parrot confessed, "I *squawked*." "Don't feel bad about it," said Dodo, "I *squawked ages ago*.""

It wasn't a bad joke, as his Auntie's jokes went. But the girls didn't seem amused. In fact, they looked appalled. Jac finally realised that they were staring over his shoulder.

246

Don't turn around, but look who's behind you, advised his Auntie.

Too late, Jac felt James Taylor shove him in the back. He'd been at the next table all the time.

"I don't think my friends would appreciate you mouthing off about them like that, Jac. They'd want me to *do* something about it. Now, it'd be a shame to cause a fuss in this tidy little café, wouldn't it? So unless you want your lights punched out right now, I'll see you outside, butt'. *In one minute.*"

Jac blanched.

His *bloody* Auntie! She'd given Swotzi the perfect excuse to get his own back for being suspended last term *and* for Jac's snide comment about the Head Boy vote.

Resigned to his fate, Jac started to haul himself to his feet. His Friends were petrified. Only Ciaran seemed untroubled.

"Hang on, Jac. It was just a joke," said Catherine, but uncertainly. "I don't see why you have to go out there... just because he's threatened you."

Petra got up: "Let me see if I can go and talk some sense into him."

"Sit yourselves down, both of youse," said Ciaran decisively. "Don't be bothering yourselves with that skitter. I'll have a wee word myself. He'll soon wise up."

Before anyone could object, he was on his way. Penry began to suggest that they should follow Ciaran outside to support him. Ciaran had been so definite, though, so resolute.

Jac sat paralysed. Surely, they should do something?

But in no time, Ciaran was back, unscathed. Happy to carry on as though nothing had happened. The circle of questioning faces demanded an explanation though.

"He won't be bothering you again, Jac. Not for a fair while, anyway."

"How come?" asked Catherine. "What did you do to him?"

"I didn't do anything. I'm just after telling him that I have a few friends flying over for the weekend. Lads from the Falls Road with a bit of... *experience.* I asked him if he'd ever heard of kneecapping. I didn't mean anything by it. But I suppose..."

what's that thing youse are always saying about my accent? It can sound a wee bit *aggressive*, sometimes?"

No-one seemed sure whether laughter was an appropriate response.

"Is it true?" Catherine wondered aloud. "About your friends…?"

"It's true I've friends from all over Belfast. I'll not say more than that."

A pause. It took a moment for Jac to take his cue.

"Thanks, Ciaran. I owe you. A favour."

"You owe nothing. That's what friends are for. That's what a Society of Friends is for."

It was masterful. Jac recognised it. And he recognised that the others were impressed too. Catherine no less than any of them.

32

My editor is now telling me breaking up the narrative with 'interstitial reflections' is not such a bad thing after all. The reader needs a rest from all this teenage angst, apparently. Honestly, *there's no pleasing some people.*

Alright, then. Here's a thought about friendship. And its long-term effects. A chapter of 'What Ifs'. A piece of pointless speculation. Something farfetched that might have happened if the world was slightly different. An alternative reality. Like one of those parallel universes that moviemakers are fond of. And novelists.

What If… on a random date, a very Strange Thing were to happen at a random location?

Well, a fairly Strange Thing, but with a very, very Strange Effect.

Be more specific, says the editor. Fair enough.

What If… at 12 noon on September 18th, 1997, on Station Street, Porth, a middle-aged man happened to be waiting outside one of those Italian cafés that you still see up and down the Valleys?

And?

Twenty-three years before that, to the exact day, let's imagine this man had come up with the idea of asking a small group of friends to promise that they'd all meet there at precisely that time. An Improbable Rendezvous. All the same, this man had shown up.

He was just the sort to plan it carefully, to arrive exactly *five minutes before the appointed hour. So he'd have to wait. Time ticked by. As he'd been half-expecting, it looked like none of the others were going to make it. The man wouldn't know, but maybe his old friend who'd turned forty that day had fully intended being there. But What If the friend's wife had woken him that morning with a Big Birthday surprise – tickets to fly to Paris, a long, romantic weekend all booked and paid for?*

In Porth, the wait would go on. It was always odds-on it was going to be fruitless. But the man reckoned he might as well give people a decent chance to turn up. After half-an-hour, still *nobody else had arrived. Perhaps they'd mistaken the time or the date, the man would be thinking. Or got the wrong year – because when they were teenagers there'd been confusion about exactly how old the Birthday Boy was. Maybe they'd just forgotten. Or simply decided not to come. He'd lost touch with a few of them. They might be on the other side of the planet. Sick. Or dead.*

The waiting man – he wasn't stupid, his common sense had told him this would be the outcome all along – would decide it was time to give up. Naturally, he'd feel a sense of disappointment (his friends had dissed the appointment). But What If, as he swivelled his wrist to check his watch for the umpteenth and last time, the Strange Thing were to occur just then?

What If… a bright-red butterfly were to land on the back of his hand?

It might seem to him, on this scruffy street in the middle of a large conurbation – a Linear City – on an autumn day, that it was an extraordinary, almost miraculous event. A big, beautiful red insect sitting there on his skin. And him, gazing at it in wonder. At the intricate patterns on its wings. At its antennae twitching.

So there's the man, studying this creature, rapt in attention to its tiny perfect splendour, with a smile, a beatific *smile, beginning to light up his face.*

Now in all probability, the butterfly would rest there for a very short time. Half-a-minute. Less. Call it ten seconds. Then, it would fly away and be gone forever.

But in those few seconds, five people, say, might pass by on the street. Let's think – a tall, pretty woman with greying red hair and a faded Burberry; a retired bus-conductor; an ancient *pensioner in a scarf struggling to afternoon bingo; two young sweethearts, mitching off from the Sixth Form (the girl might be the daughter of a man who'd been an infamous swot and thug at the same school, back in his day).*

These five passers-by would notice the butterfly and the man and his beatific smile. To them, too, the sight would be extraordinary. A grown man lost in admiration for a beautiful insect. On a street in Porth. It would gladden their hearts. In the next few hours, without reflecting on what they were doing, or why, each of them might pass on that sense of serenity, that notion that the world is a wondrous, delightful place after all – by making a small but significant gesture of kindness to (let's say) half-a-dozen others who happened to cross their paths. So the burdens of those thirty people would, in some small but helpful way, be lightened; and, before evening came, each of the thirty – again, without really being aware of it – might transmit their *sense of having 'a good day' onwards to seven other people.*

250

Five people who each met six people who each met seven. What were the chances? Seventy times seven to one, or something like that, probably. The positive effect – the Butterfly Effect, let's call it that – would by now in each individual case be scarcely measurable as it spread far and wide across the Rhondda. But what if there was one final ripple to come, one final gladdening of hearts in this unlikely wave of causation?

And this is where the fable stretches unbelievability into absurdity, I hear you say. (Frankly, what did you expect? It's an anti-novel. If it was realism you were into, you'd never have read this far.)

We all know that small changes of mood can cause big changes in behaviour. So… What If, thanks to the Butterfly Effect, those 210 (5 x 6 x 7) people each behaved with a sliver more of humanity than usual towards eight *other people they encountered, in shops and pubs, buses and trains, or on the street as darkness fell. They were just a bit more considerate than they might have been, that's all. Now we have five who met six who met seven who meet eight. Well, then, what might happen when all of* those *people, all 1680 of them at the end of this implausible chain, talked about how they were feeling to each of their partners that evening? (Really?* Really?? *Every single one* of them *conveniently had a partner to influence???* "If this were play'd upon a stage now, I could condemn it as an improbable fiction," *as Shakespeare wrote in… um,* Twelfth Night. *But, believe it or not, there's a reputable concept in statistics, the Improbability Principle, which codifies the paradoxical idea that such extremely unlikely events do happen – and frequently).*

As they made their way to their polling stations that Thursday night, September 18th, 1997, they and their partners might discover that something had moved, something had shifted. *That they felt a tad more positive about the place they lived in; half-a-degree warmer about their neighbours; the teeniest bit prouder of how sociable, cooperative and egalitarian this community of theirs had managed to remain, despite all that threatened to make it no different to any other part of southern Britain, or the rest of the hard-hearted world come to that. Put simply, how* friendly *it was. And that that was something worth having, worth protecting.*

So, in primary school halls up and down the Valley, in the privacy of their little wooden booths, with a single piece of paper in front of them, they might, all of them, hesitate with their stubby pencils poised above a box

251

marked 'No'. And maybe, to their own surprise, they'd find that their pencil had moved, had shifted… a few centimetres. Now, it was making a mark to signal assent instead.

When the votes were tallied, there would be 3,360 fewer than might have been in the 'No' column; 3,360 more for 'Yes'.

And What If there was one final switch voter?

At the stroke of 10 o'clock, seconds before the ballot boxes were sealed, a former swot and thug whose daughter had just told him a tall story about a butterfly, might have felt his heart touched in a way that no-one who knew him would ever think possible. He might – possibly, improbably – cast his ballot counter to the way in which he'd been telling everybody he intended. Across Wales, his compatriots, unaware of any of this, would have voted exactly as they'd planned, in a Devolution Referendum which most of the UK and the rest of the world would ignore. But instead of the creation of a Welsh Assembly being rejected by a single vote, there would be a wafer-thin edge for Yes. 50.3% to 49.7%.

My tale is preposterous. Clearly, it never happened like that.

Strangely, though, those are the percentages that were recorded in the real world. That was the precise and tiny margin by which Wales decided. A nation of three million people voted not to vote itself out of history. By 6,721 votes. Who knows why? Who knows what minuscule factors made the difference? The difference between a plebiscite and plebicide, pace Jac's Auntie. Maybe it wasn't a butterfly alighting on a man's hand. But when a result is that tight, how can anyone say what's truly responsible?

We all have an impact on each other, we understand that. A much bigger impact, perhaps, than we ever realise; more profound in ways we never dream of. So, I'm going to assert this, and my editor can tell me that it's ludicrous, but that doesn't matter (it all comes down to what you believe in the end). Once upon a time, there was a group of friends. Each made a solemn promise. Only one of them kept it. But without all of them, without all that they meant to each other, without all that they meant to that one friend, there would never have been a promise to keep. In the end, the bonds forged between them many years before did make a difference. All the difference. Because, if a butterfly can lift a man's mood in ten seconds (and you will at least allow me that), imagine the mountains true friends, true Friends, might move over the course of whole lifetimes. Even if, after their formative years, they *never ever (Trevor Evans) managed to get together again. Who could deny the influence, the unseen sway they must be having, on each other, on the scores, the hundreds, the thousands of others they've encountered across the decades since then, simply (simply?) because they learned from each other, at the beginning of their journeys, what true friendship is? And a lot of other things, besides.*

If a small, unimportant group of teenagers can do that, what might a People's Assembly or Parliament achieve? No matter how weak its powers are. No matter how insignificant the country it represents (google 'Future Generations Act Wales', if you think that such an institution can't have a visionary impact far greater than conventional political wisdom determines is possible). No matter how Improbable it all seems.

This friendship, these Friends did more than influence each other's lives. They changed *each other's lives. So they changed Wales. And that means they changed the world.*

No? Yes! 'Yes' — yes? Yes.

33

When he'd seen off Swotzi at the Bracchi's, Ciaran had been quick to assure Jac that no favours were owed in return. But he wasn't long in asking for one. Not so much asking; taking it for granted. He sent a postcard (another picture of Portrush: perhaps it was difficult to get hold of postcards of the Upper Rhondda). He needed 'Advice', he said, inviting himself to Jac's house for tea. Jac's Mam started fussing about whether the house was in a fit state to receive a guest *from overseas*. Jac tried to assure her that Ciaran lived in Treorchy.

To be fair, the family home had recently been little more than a building site. Now that Jac's grandparents were dead, his Mam and Dad had felt free to 'modernise' it with the help of a government grant. The original Edwardian layout was no more. The covings had been stripped out, the ceilings artexed, smart white radiators replaced the open coal fires. The 'back kitchen' – their cosy sitting room with its free-standing stove – was now a modern kitchenette, with made-to-measure work surfaces and built-in appliances. The lean-to bathroom, scullery and outdoor toilet had been demolished: instead, a flat-roofed extension housed an up-to-the-minute avocado-coloured bathroom suite. The wall between the front parlour and middle room had been knocked through, a pair of full-length sliding glass doors between the two allowing for some privacy. Whilst Jac and his parents were away on holiday in Yorkshire, the builders had fitted the doors with trendy semi-opaque tulip-patterned glass. The tulips on one door were upside down, but it was too late to do anything about that now. Only the *cwtsh*-under-the-stairs remained: a reminder of how old-fashioned it all used to be.

When Ciaran arrived, straight from work the day after they'd got his postcard, Jac's Mam led him through the new archway – the glass doors had been left open for the purpose – to admire the view from the bay window at the front. She did this with every first-time visitor. To her, the vista was scarcely less impressive than the one Jac loved on Carncelyn, though you were looking *up* at the mountains from here. To the right, Graig Park, the new rugby ground, built where Naval Colliery's *in situ* spoil tip once stood, was crowned in the distance by the Nightingale's Peak, Craig-yr-Eos. Opposite, above ranks of terraced houses, the mass of Mynydd Trealaw imposed itself. To the left, below Penrhys, the green flanks of Tyntyla caught the autumn sun. Beneath the unspoiled pasture, long lines of slate roofs led the eye northward, teasing it with a hint of the *cwm* opening up again towards Treorchy. Completing the panorama, black crags topped the sheer slopes of Glyncornel, once stark, but adorned now by Blinginate's upright Scots pines (Jac's Grampa, who'd scarcely been further than Cardiff in his long life, had always delighted in the afforestation: *"Duw, it's just like Switzerland, myn!"*).

Jac's mother *knew* the splendour of it all would impress a visitor from Belfast. She waited in silence. He'd need time to drink it all in. Finally, she decided the time was right to prompt his appreciative response.

"*Beaut-i-ful* view, isn't it?" she sing-songed.

Ciaran was genuinely puzzled.

"It's… *a petrol station*," he replied at last.

He was right, of course. Large as life, just yards away directly across the main road, on what had been the colliery water-feeder, was the Shell Petrol Station. It wasn't that Jac's mother couldn't see the cars and the *tar-mac*, the pumps, prices, Shell logo and all. She simply screened it out in favour of the bigger picture. Perhaps it helped to have a lifelong attachment to that Biblical verse, 'I will lift up mine eyes to the hills'.

Ciaran's confusion – he said later that he really didn't know if she was setting some kind of test for him – made Jac see the whole scene anew. For the first time, he realised how telling it was: this filling station on the site of what had been a working mine. Where they'd dug coal, now they pumped petrol. From this exact spot had come the black diamond that propelled warships, cargo vessels and great ocean liners to the far ends of the earth. Now the fuel was brought here, to fill up cars for shopping trips, journeys to work, sunny-day outings to 'beauty spots': private needs, domestic, local. The world had moved on, the motive force that drove it had changed. What the Rhondda had once been – the engine-house of modernity – other places, faraway places, were now becoming: Texas, the Persian Gulf, the Oil States of the Middle East. Power had shifted. That was what the political and economic crisis had been all about. Oil, and the power of oil. That was why there was galloping inflation, why the pound would have to be devalued, why the Labour Government would have to go cap in hand to the IMF, as Rhondda colliers once had had to go to the mine-owners.

It was all here, right in front of him, but Jac had never realised it in all the time he was growing up. King Coal was dead. Oil now ruled.

Mam fach, there'll be an Almighty struggle over it one day.

"Would you like your tea now in a minute or now just?"

Jac's Mam had posed another teaser for Ciaran. He had no idea what she meant.

"He'll have it straightaway, Mam."

That sounded good to Ciaran, but soon, he was thrown again. All he got instead of a sit-down evening meal after his long day at work, was a mug with a hot drink put into his hand.

"Do you like the work we've had done here, then? Tidy, isn't it?"

"Mam, Ciaran never saw the house before we had it modernised, did he? And I think he'd like something to eat pretty soon."

"O, well, won't be long. Fish and chips, is that alright? I expect you have fish and chips in Ireland, don't you? 'Course you do. Silly me. But while it's cooking... Jac, you tell Ciaran about the attic. The insulation. That'll be an eye-opener for him."

His mother showed no signs of heading to the kitchen. She was determined to ensure Jac told the story.

One Saturday morning before the building work had begun, Jac and his father had gone up through the tiny trapdoor into the attic to measure up, so that they could fill in the form for the

Loft Insulation Grant the government was offering. No-one had been up there for decades. Jac went first, up the stepladder, poking his head warily into the dark space beneath the eaves. Dad handed him a torch. What its beam revealed *was* an eye-opener. Across the floor of the whole attic, lying between each rafter, a full six inches deep, there was already a form of insulation. It was pitch black. It was powdery. It was coal dust.

"This house is fifty yards away from the upcast shaft of the old Naval Colliery," Jac explained to Ciaran. "The dust had been settling there ever since the house was built."

"Imagine putting the washing out... or trying to keep the house clean in an atmosphere clogged with dust like that. Imagine working underground..."

Ciaran considered this.

"So, we never got the insulation after all," concluded Jac's mother, "As Jac said, there wasn't any point – it's perfectly draught-proof as it is. Mind you, I suppose if our house went on fire, you and your mam could be warming your hands up in Treorchy."

She went back to the kitchen. Ciaran *would* be fed – eventually. He turned to the window, looking again, slowly, deliberately; trying, Jac assumed, to screen out the petrol station, to picture the scene in the Naval Colliery's heyday. Or perhaps still wondering if the whole set-up was a send-up.

Just then, Jac's eye fell on a headline in the *Rhondda Leader* which his father had left lying on the sofa: *Police Spot Man Praying In The Rain*. Intrigued, Jac read on: 'The suspicions of two Panda car patrollers were aroused last Sunday in Gelli, when they saw a man in shirtsleeves staring at the sky in the pouring rain, hands clasped as if in prayer. Challenged, the suspect was observed attempting to dispose of a small storage tin he was carrying. On examination, what advertised itself as a food cannister was found to contain a quantity of cannabis resin. Appearing before Porth Magistrates, Cadogan Cadogan, of Ardwyn Terrace, Gelli, admitted possession, but claimed that "the Lord commanded me in a dream to partake of the drug, so that I could better

257

understand lost sinners, and bring them back to Him." Sentence was adjourned for four weeks for psychiatric reports.'

Well, well, thought Jac, how are the mighty fallen!

Jac heard his father coming down from the bedroom where he'd been preparing next Sunday's sermon. Davy Morgan didn't just read the Bible, he studied it, he worked to understand it. But he wasn't the sort of Christian who was so heavenly-minded that he wasn't any earthly good. His was the kind of wisdom that people who'd never darken the door of a church would seek out. Strangers from all walks of life came to the house, burdened with problems. Sometimes by appointment, sometimes not. Quiet conversations in that front parlour. Practical issues. Deep spiritual torment. Whatever it was, they'd leave lighter in their step.

Tea was ready at last – Mrs Morgan was a notoriously *methodical* cook. The trout they ate had been caught by Jac's father himself, back in the summer, at Glyncornel. Ciaran seemed genuinely interested, so Davy Morgan enlarged on the intricacies of tying flies, the pleasure he'd had fishing the Lake over the years. He regretted, he said, that he'd never managed to pass on the skills to his son.

"I didn't inherit your patience, Dad," admitted Jac.

"That's true. But dexterity was more the problem, in this context."

His father wasn't usually so sharp. Ciaran's presence at the table seemed to have unsettled the family equilibrium in a way that all those front-room visitors never did.

"Jac has always been all fingers and thumbs," said his mother, in the kindest of ways, as though it was something to be proud of.

"The Lord gave us dominion over fish: they're part of His Royal bounty," his father pronounced. "But it's far more incumbent upon us to be fishers of men."

Jac squirmed. What would Ciaran make of that? There were plenty of evangelicals in Ulster, but he probably hadn't *broken bread* with one before. Jac considered trying to gloss the Biblical

258

turns of phrase, but instead – maybe he was narked by his parents' blunt admission of *his* failings – he found himself making the kind of clever-clever remark he'd never have made if Ciaran wasn't there.

"I see from the *Rhondda Leader* that one of Gelli's 'fishers of men' has got himself hooked."

It was an awkward matter to raise in front of a visitor. So awkward that Jac had to check himself to make sure it wasn't his Auntie who'd put him up to it.

Davy Morgan knew right well what his son was referring to.

"Sometimes young Christians can be *too* zealous in serving the Lord."

Jac heard the subtext in his father's words. *This is not a subject to discuss with guests in the house. Not a good witness to the Lord.* But, having gone this far, Jac felt obliged to explain the story for Ciaran's benefit.

"I suppose you have a lot of problems with drug dealers in a big city like Belfast," interrupted Jac's Mam, as soon as she could, trying to move the conversation onto less sensitive ground.

"Oh no, Mrs Morgan." Ciaran's rebuttal was very matter of fact. "As I was telling Jac the other day, say what you like about paramilitaries, but kneecappings do wonders to keep the petty crime rate down."

Now it was the hosts' turn to be uncertain how to take what had been said. Ciaran filled the silence by embarking on an amusing story, well told, about his friend Aidan. He'd gone to buy joss-sticks in Belfast's only 'hippie shop'. When he got there, he couldn't remember what they were called, and got so tangled up describing what he wanted that he was sold cannabis instead. Ciaran teased him so much about it, that in revenge at school the next day, Aidan planted in Ciaran's satchel a package which looked for all the world, when opened in class, like dope.

"Well, I suppose you had to forgive him for that," said Jac's Mam, mildly.

"Not at all," retorted Ciaran, with petulant sideways flick of his head. "He's *dead* to me now!"

Jac's Mam jumped in her chair, all but upsetting her plate. As if there actually *had* been an assassination. Ciaran's accent made it sound so vehement, so final. But Jac caught an echo of something else, something he thought he'd heard before in Ciaran's judgements, despite the decisiveness they projected. Something fey, almost coquettish: the hurt of scorned love? Did Ciaran regret leaving Belfast, regret leaving Aidan behind? Jac wondered what their relationship had been like, and whether it *was* all over now.

After dessert – tinned peaches and ice-cream – Jac insisted that he and Ciaran were heading out together. Given the misunderstandings that had already occurred, it was best to discuss whatever it was Ciaran had on his mind *outside* the family home.

"But it's just coming to rain," said his Mam, stating the obvious.

They put their coats on.

"It's been good to welcome a Roman Catholic to our home," said Davy Morgan, in all sincerity, with a firm handshake of farewell. It occurred to Jac that it might be the first time his father had broken bread with a Catholic.

"Yes," said his Mam on the doorstep, "Come along with Jac to one of our *Christian* services sometime."

They walked down past the Lights to the bottom of Dunraven Street. Since cannabis had been discussed (for the first time in the Morgan household), Jac thought it might be amusing to take Ciaran to the Calypso, the only non-Bracchi café in the whole of mid-Rhondda. Dim lighting took the edge off the psychedelic colours on the wall, but couldn't disguise the whiff of wacky baccy that lingered most evenings. The Welsh Joint Education Committee must have been neglecting the place. Or perhaps not.

Flush with his first pay packet, Ciaran made a beeline for the jukebox. Van Morrison was clearly a favourite. They ordered cokes and took seats in a corner. Ciaran seemed reluctant to begin talking. That put Jac back on edge. They fidgeted with the straws in their bottles.

"So…"

"Thanks for taking the time, Jac…"

"Well, as I said, I owe you one. But even if I didn't…"

"It's tricky…"

"You wanted some Advice."

"The thing is… I've got a secret…"

Surely to God, exclaimed Jac's Auntie, *not another one!*

"The way things are in Belfast… the way religion is a *big, big* thing for us… I mean, I can see it is in your family… but it's not the same for *everybody* here, not the way it is at home… in Northern Ireland, that is… Jeez, I'm explaining this *really* well, amn't I?"

Jac was taken aback. Here was a very different Ciaran. Gone the straight-talker who saw things as they were and said things as he saw them. Gone the self-possessed performer who'd breezed through the audition for *Twelfth Night*, the smooth operator who'd sent *When Will I See You Again?* to Catherine. Gone the tough guy who'd defused that whole situation with Swotzi.

"I can see what you're thinking, Jac: you're thinking this is strange, aren't you? Coming from me, who always comes across as so assured."

Was Jac that transparent? He must be. It wasn't the first time a Friend had read his mind.

"See, that's what it's like when you're Irish – you're *expected* to perform, sing and dance, tell stories, to put yourself out there. And being here, in Wales, every day, not just with *Twelfth Night*, it's like I'm putting on a show, just to get people to begin to understand who I am. But when it's *not* a performance, when it's actually me…"

Well, this was making sense at least. Ciaran might have lost the mask of self-assurance, but he hadn't suddenly become stupid.

"The thing is, Jac, when all's said and done, I can trust you. I know whenever I met you that first time, Bull *instructed* you to look after me. But I know you're not doing that because you were told to. You're loyal. To your friends. When you say you'll help

261

them out, you will. So... help me now. Because I've never... never ever..."

Jac managed to stop himself from finishing the phrase with a quick *Trevor Evans*. He sensed that whatever was coming, was coming from a place inside Ciaran that he hadn't shown any of them until now, and it didn't need anyone trampling all over it. Was Ciaran's *secret* a Sorrow, some hurt that he was still recovering from, and feared he never would? Something that made him need to protect himself from being hurt like that ever again. Yes, a *Secret Sorrow*. Or a *Terrible Tragedy* – an infatuation across the sectarian divide that ended, for the object of his devotion, with a kneecapping, or worse. (It never occurred to Jac until months later, when it was far too late to do anything about it, that Ciaran's uncertainty might have been all an act. A ploy, to neutralise Jac, to take him out of the reckoning. That he was being *played*. But even then, Jac couldn't quite bring himself to believe that Ciaran could be so duplicitous, so calculating. He wasn't *that* good an actor. Was he?)

Ciaran poked the straw into his bottle for the nth time and took a different tack. It turned out to be just as incoherent. What he seemed to be saying was that the Troubles had shut down opportunities for Belfast teenagers to meet in what he now understood was the 'normal' way elsewhere. They couldn't get to the pictures, rarely went to dances; sometimes, for weeks on end, they couldn't venture out at all at night. There were bomb scares, roadblocks, riots. The buses (Jac sympathised with this bit) were set alight, or didn't run west, or east, or north to south. And the area where Ciaran lived – a Catholic enclave surrounded by Loyalists – made all of this much worse. Jac wished that he would just get to the point. But what would the point be?

"So... believe it or not... I never... asked anybody out. Not over there. And no-one here, of course, either."

Ah-ha. So that's what it was. Inexperience in asking for a date. How it was done in the Rhondda. As though Jac was an expert! He was the last person Ciaran should have come to. And it was a real puzzle to Jac that he had. But maybe Jac wasn't so odd after all: maybe *all* boys, even ones as outwardly composed as Ciaran, turned to jelly at the thought of asking a girl for a date. Jac searched his memory – he did have some experience in the matter after all. The technique his Auntie had clued him in on with Juliette: pretend, even as you put the question, that the answer's of no account, and that it wasn't your idea anyway.

But what did Ciaran mean by "I've never asked *anybody* out"? Was it *a girl* he had in mind? Jac remembered the night Martyn had confessed *his* secret. This was proving just as tortuous.

"So, Jac, I wanted to ask…"

On the jukebox, Van Morrison was complaining, slowly, circuitously…

"…to ask you, Jac…"

…Van couldn't get the words out, he was tongue-tied, he was trembling…

"… if you would ask Catherine out…"

… he was tortured at the sight of his lady coming back from the Fair.

"…for me, I mean…"

There was another pause, during which Van the Man seemed to complete another whole verse, another whole traverse of *Cyprus Avenue*.

"…if you'd ask Catherine out on my behalf. You understand? I'd like *you* to ask *her* if she'd go out with *me*…"

Someone was caught. But it wasn't Ciaran. And it wasn't only Van.

"Would you ever do that for me, Jac?"

34

Dearest Catherine,

It feels strange to be writing a letter to you - seems overly formal and a bit too grown-up for me, doesn't it?

I'm sure it's strange for you to be reading it. Bet you're thinking, 'What's that nutter Jac up to now?'

Sorry about that.

There's nothing here that I couldn't say to you face-to-face, I suppose, but you know what it's like in school: you can never guarantee you'll get peace and quiet for a proper conversation. When there's something important on your mind, you don't want to rush it because the bell is about to go, or because you're in danger of being overheard, or interrupted, or whatever; and then you end up getting the words wrong or being misunderstood.

The thing is, that I've been thinking about us. I wanted to ask you seriously if you would consider giving me one more chance.

We never did get that proper date we were going to have. That's all my fault for being so stupid and awkward. But my feelings haven't changed. I'm hoping that yours haven't either, not deep down anyway, though I can understand entirely if you feel a bit annoyed with me just now.

We've known each other as friends for such a long time, almost a year, and our friendship is really, really important to me.

I think about all the times you've been kind to me, even when I've been thoughtless or silly or teased you too much. So I certainly don't want anything to come between us, which is why I've hesitated before saying any of this. But I think it's still possible that we could mean even more to each other. We really do care about each other in a special way - we've proved that over time.

And we have so much in common - our backgrounds and 'Twelfth Night' and the laughs we've had and our tastes in music and the friends we both care about.

I've thought about what you said to me that time up on the Yard, about being open to others even if you're a couple, and I'm up for that, if you'll give me the chance to prove it.

Anyway, this is turning into an essay, which is the last thing I intended. So thanks for reading it, and I'll end now with a simple question (before anybody else snaps you up, lovely girl!): would you consider going out with me, properly this time? Please?

x Jac

35

Dear Catherine,

It's strange to be writing a letter to you - seems too formal, doesn't it? And it's probably weird for you to be reading it. Sorry about that, but I've been put in a bit of an awkward position which I'd like to explain properly, and you know what it's like in school: you never get peace and quiet for an uninterrupted conversation.

Ciaran came to see me today, and he begged an unusual favour. The thing is that he'd like to go out with you. I won't go into the long-form explanation he gave me, but to put it simply he feels too shy to approach you himself, so he asked me if I would put the question on his behalf, and I promised him I would. He doesn't seem to know anything about you and me being interested in each other, or he wouldn't have involved me, I suppose; and I didn't tell him anything. But he's a good friend to both of us, so I'm letting you know how he feels in the most straight-forward way I can. And I would understand completely if you wanted to say 'yes' to him.

In fairness to everyone, though, I feel it's only right to tell you something else: that I still think about you, too, and my own feelings haven't changed. I can't help hoping that yours haven't either, not deep down anyway, though I can appreciate that you're probably annoyed, or confused anyway, by the way things have turned out between us. But someone asked me the other day if I'd ever thought about asking you out, and it set me wondering if you'd consider giving me another chance: if you'd be willing to go on that 'proper date' that we never had, after all.

There - that's two boys asking you out in the same letter. Has that ever happened to a Gilfach girl before, I wonder? (Please don't tell me it's a regular occurrence for you!)

One more thing. I trust that you know that being friends with you means the world to me. Above all, I wouldn't want anything to spoil that, so whatever you decide to do, please let's continue our friendship, as close as it's always been, now and into the future.

With love, your Friend,

Jac

36

Dear Catherine,

It's strange to be writing you a letter - but in the circumstances I think it's the simplest thing. Sorry if it feels odd.

Ciaran came to see me today, and unexpectedly asked a favour.

I won't go into the long-form explanation he gave, but to put it simply he'd like to go out with you, and feels too shy to approach you himself.

So he asked me if I'd put the question on his behalf, and I promised him that I would.

He's a good friend (to us both), so I'm glad to be able to do this favour for him.

In case you're wondering (probably not, but just to avoid any doubt), if you're minded to say 'yes' to him, I would be pleased for you both.

I'm sure you know that you mean a great deal to me, and anything that makes you happy is fine by me. So whatever you decide to do, let's go on being Friends, just as close as we've always been, now and into the future.

Your friend,

Jac

37

Dear Jac (or Dear John: may I call you by your real name for once? Though it's odd to be writing a 'Dear John' letter),

Since we've slipped into letter-writing mode, I thought I'd write one of my own. To you. Well, I say 'to you'… It's hardly the same as me sending an email to a friend, is it? Whoever 'you' were half a century ago, 'you' will never get to read this. But, these days, it's fashionable to write letters to our younger selves, letters of advice, letters of comfort. You see them in the Sunday magazines all the time. It's a form of therapy, I suppose: putting to rest the agonies of our formative years, forgiving ourselves for our own naivete, for the callow decisions and schoolboy errors that have distorted our lives, or narrowed our choices later on.

I like to think of them as a modern form of prayer. Seems strange, I know, given that I've never really understood or practised prayer, never quite 'got' what millions of the faithful are doing when they pray. It's one of those things like rhythm or pitch or fly fishing that I seem to have no aptitude for. I just don't have a talent for God. Or maybe it's a lack of patience in listening for Him.

Anyway, as far as I can tell from the outside, the way most people pray, intercessory prayer, is a transactional thing: you ask God to change the way the world is going for your own benefit or someone else's. You pray hard at moments of crisis, pray for God to heal or protect someone you care about, to bend the normal rules of causality for once. You promise to live a better life, or at least to give God the credit for what He's done, if only He'll act in your favour now. And you expect an answer. You might even stop believing in God if he doesn't give you one; and all the more so if He does, and it's not the one you want.

But I understand – because several individuals I care about do it – that there's a more profound, more demanding form of prayer. A sort of confessional prayer, a spiritual discipline that true saints and more thoughtful people of faith practice. It's a deep meditation on past sins/mistakes, and on the way they live now. It may be guided by reflection on the Scriptures. It's not about changing God's mind, it's about changing yourself. It doesn't demand or even expect an 'answer' as such. Supplication, the act of asking seriously for something, some form of grace or forgiveness, doesn't change the Will of God, but it does affect your own heart, bringing you into conformity with His Will, more closely aligned to His Purposes, to a form of acceptance that can *alter the future, or at least make it bearable, although that's not really the point.*

What am I saying? That I think there's some kind of parallel here with writing a letter to our teenage selves (and my editor tells me this whole novel is a letter to my teenage self). *We know, surely, that that self is beyond our reach; that however much we'd like to, we can't change the course of the past; that we can't communicate our wishes and our wisdom to whoever we were back then. But it's a significant act all the same. What's actually happening – if it's done wholeheartedly – is that we're learning to accept who we were, because in accepting who we were, in all our immaturity and ignorance, our arrogance and inexperience, we can also begin to accept ourselves as we really are now.*

So, in that light, what do I have to say to you, dear Jac, dear John? What Advice can I give to you, my younger self? Like most of those newspaper columns I've read, it's all pretty trite; and some of it seems self-contradictory, but I'll come to that.

To state the obvious, your poetry and your 'song-writing' aren't up to much: I wouldn't waste much time on them if I were you (I was you, I know). It only feeds your moodiness and your tendency to feel sorry for yourself. You are *creative and imaginative, but that part of will find a natural way to express itself. Don't force it. You're no Chatterton (thank goodness), and you know it. Look outwards, not in. Look at the world more. Look properly.* Study *it. There's beauty everywhere, and often it's very different to the way it's commonly seen. The light under bridges. Birdsong. Earlobes (did you* really *look at the shape of her ears that time you told 'Catherine' they were beautiful?).*

You can't sing – you're well aware of that, so let it go (it doesn't matter – don't pout about it, or anything else). You're not much of an actor either, but your speaking voice is deep and sonorous when you're not trying too hard, and you could learn to do more with that.

The bouncy, boisterous 'you' can be fun, but needs calming down, or rationing, at least. You're spirited, and lots of your acquaintances will appreciate that, but try to remember that it's not always appropriate: not every moment is the *moment. You go way over the top sometimes, and some people will never be able to cope with others being even moderately loud and jokey (you could tell better jokes, by the way).*

You were on-the-button in that first thought you had outside the Grand Pavilion, when 'Martyn' snapped at you in Porthcawl: your true gift is for listening, for empathising. Because of your background, you have the knack of doing that with people from all walks of life, of all ages and temperaments, and of both genders. You're able to find ways to get on with those who think they're the great and the good, and with 'ordinary', less self-important folk too. It's part of your creed that nobody is too grand or too lowly for you to treat them as equals. You know how to build bridges to others. You like women, and you do a pretty decent job (for a male of the species) of understanding them. All of this is good.

You're quite bright, academically anyway, but you don't intimidate people with your intelligence. So don't let other bright people intimidate you: they're not always as brilliant as the picture they paint of themselves. And whilst everybody deserves to be understood, or at least a chance to explain themselves without prejudice, remember that not everyone is as guileless and well-intentioned as the people who brought you up.

You're naturally modest, and that's alright (though sometimes your self-deprecation slides from charming into grating): it will open doors for you. On the other hand, my goodness, you ought to stand up for yourself more! You let so many opportunities slip by because of fear or anxiety or a sense of having to be fair to everybody else. Send the first of those three letters to 'Catherine', not the third! Put up a fight for what you want, and let others look after their own corner. And take yourself more seriously. 'Petra' was right about that. You don't need to resort to puns to avoid conflict or deeper engagement. You don't need to deflect criticism with zaniness. You should be more serious, but — and here's the bit that sounds contradictory — not so intense. Relax. Yes, relax.

So now we've got to the nub of it, to something that could be the very definition of futility: advising a teenager to be more relaxed about themselves. Jac, John, it's impossible, I know. Until you grow into your skin, until your insecurities aren't so deep and tumultuous, you've no chance. I speak as a sensitive boy who never grew up. So I'll finish this letter to my young self by telling you a story. It's a story with a point to make, but the point is directed at me, now, and at anyone who presumes to offer such counsel, not at you back then. Forgive me. I love you.

Once upon a time, I'd started working in the most high-pressure job I'd ever done. My boss called me in for my first Annual Appraisal. The big, big boss – my boss's boss's boss – was trying to turn it into 'a results-orientated business', as the jargon went. Everything had to be measured and analysed to within a percentage point of its life; and then measured and analysed all over again, and benchmarked against the results of other divisions and of our competitors, before being published for staff and stakeholders to read in a glossy Performance Review document, replete with goals, targets, fancy bar-charts and bullet points. As it happened, the 'metrics' (yuk!) on my initial year in the post were good, and the verbal feedback was all very positive. "So there's just one piece of advice I could give you," said my boss, finally. "It's going well. You can afford to relax more."

Relax? I smiled and told him it was funny he should say that. To be given that as serious professional Advice in such an overly-scrutinised, driven, ultra-competitive environment reminded me of something. Something I'd happened to see on the telly that week. One of those fly-on-the-wall documentaries. A top-flight professional soccer team was struggling down at the foot of their league. Halftime in a crucial relegation battle, and they were losing (again). Their whole season hung in the balance. The producers had secured unprecedented access to the dressing room. The camera zoomed in on the manager as he blasted the team, one by one, for the way they were playing. He deployed the F-word. A lot more than you ever did, Jac. In his Scouse accent, it came out as fook: *"Fook me, get hold of the fookin' ball!"; "Fookin' 'it 'em fookin' 'ard!"; "Fookin' 'ead the fookin' thing!"*

Contrary to my expectations of elite football, there was no subtle tactical analysis, no attempted master-stroke of changing the formation or bringing on a super-sub; he just ranted and raved. Fookin' this and fookin' that: "Don't fookin' fook it up a-fookin'-gain, yer fookin' fooker!" Finally, he got round to the captain. He'd been sitting ashen-faced on the bench all this time, head in hands, listening intently to the 'Advice' his team-mates were getting. The gaffer bent down, pushing his face right up against the player's. Their noses were practically touching. The manager paused for a few seconds. Then his eyes widened, and he bellowed directly at him: "FOOKIN'… RELAX!"

38

Relaxing would have been easy on that brilliant autumn morning.
If you'd been in the mood.

Where was the rain the one time Jac would have preferred it to be teeming down? When he didn't want things standing out in stark relief. When he *ached* for a blanket of cloud, some mist or fog, some ambiguity to hide himself in?

After a troubled night, he had no idea which of his three letters he should give Catherine. He'd come to school with all three tucked into his satchel.

Like unexploded bombs.

Tick... tock... tick... tock...

As long as the ticking went on, so they said, you were safe.

He walked out of Assembly just behind her. He could have done it then. It would only have taken a moment to pass the letter over.

Tick... tock... tick...

But which one? The chance was gone.

...tock.

The morning took a century to pass. No other opportunity to offload his explosive cargo came. Dinner Hour, when it arrived, lasted for a whole geological era. Catherine, like the dinosaurs, had disappeared off the face of the earth.

Tick... tock...

Jac tramped around disconsolately, searching everywhere for her. He couldn't bear how sunny it was. His head was *whomping*, as Penry would have said.

Tick... tock...

Abandoning his quest, he climbed, with enormous effort, the steps to the Top Yard. There was a game on, Third Formers, a background hum of onlookers commentating. He found the corner where he'd talked with Catherine before the Porthcawl trip, and sat on the low wall, turning his face to the burning sun, eyes shut.

A memory came: of the time he'd fled, humiliated, from Catherine's caravan that day. The noises around him had been different, but he'd been surrounded by a pulsing resonance then too, in that space before Petra came to find him: gulls, and the waves beating on the rocks. And he'd closed his eyes against the sun there, lifting his face to absorb its rays. More than that – he'd tried to *face down* the sun, to take in more than it had to give him, more than it had to give the whole earth, to suck the light out of it and envelop it with the darkness he was feeling. *He was stronger than the sun!*

Such a futile boast. When it hit him how arrogant it was, he'd been left empty and beaten. Suffering, like he'd seen Martyn suffer. But then, strangely, a comfort had come to him, a blessing from the universe: *this is necessary, but wait – this too will pass.* As though he was receiving a grace, the very thing he lacked: patience.

There was a connection between patience and suffering, he remembered now, in the derivation of the word. He must look it up sometime.

For those few moments in Porthcawl, he'd felt *ready* to suffer, ready to grow, ready to begin life in earnest. By the time Petra had found him, the epiphany – if that's what it was – had gone. Shrivelled in the sun. Certainly, it had no effect on his behaviour when he'd joined the others again. He'd forgotten it altogether in the indignities of the rest of that day (his *sufferings*, petty and self-inflicted as they were: hadn't Martyn thrown the word back at him in that tirade outside the Pavilion?) But, here on the Yard, something of that sense of timely grace began to seem possible again. He thought back. He remembered – *how could he have forgotten? but he had* – that he'd composed a piece of verse in his head then, there above the beach. He found the words returning now.

The sun's warm womb of light is night to me:
I bathe alone in sun's dark sea and wait.
The moment comes for me not soon or late
But in the sun's appointed course I swoon and burn, am born.

That was it. Not a brilliant poem. Hardly a poem at all. A touch of *cynghanedd*. The beginnings of an idea. A sense of being born again – but as himself, not as someone broken apart and moulded back together in a misshapen image of the Evangelicals' Jehovah. Of having the wisdom to wait until that happened. That was all. It wasn't much. Scarcely enough to build a life on.

Just then, the bell went, ending Dinner Time, fracturing his reverie, leaving him with no sense of what any of it meant.

First thing that afternoon, Double English. *The Canterbury Tales*. Middle English. Just what you needed when you were suffering, when your head was already splitting apart. When you were going barmy with sunstroke. Even *inside* the classroom, the light was too bright. Jac felt it shining right through him, like an X-ray, illuminating, for all to see, the paralysing uncertainty inside. The epiphany was gone again. Evaporated. What was the point of these moments of clarity when they were so evanescent? He hungered for a faith like his father's, something that lasted, something that could anchor you, 'steadfast and sure while the billows roll'.

At least Catherine had turned up in class. He made himself promise that, whatever happened, he *would* pass one of those missives to her as they filed out at the end of the second lesson.

"The story we're looking at today, *The Nun's Priest's Tale*," Osmond began, "is a love story."

Ooh, I love a love story, gushed his Auntie, putting down her Mediterranean beach romance.

"The central character sees himself as a Great Lover. But he's gripped by a sudden dread. He becomes so anxious that the object of his passions falls right out of love with him."

Jac knew he was losing it again. One of his *funny turns*. The sun had been too much for him.

"The set-up is simple: an impoverished widow struggles to keep body and soul together for her family by carefully tending her small assortment of livestock…"

"Oink, oink," snorted Nerys, just quietly enough to avoid being heard by Osmond. She was sitting near the windows, backlit, streaming sunbeams turning her into a strange silhouette, which might just have been that of a pig.

"...but there's a savage beast lurking nearby, a fox, waiting to pounce on this fragile household."

"Mehhhhh," bleated someone from the back row, as though in fright. Unlikely as it seemed, it was Ninelives Bowen.

Get a grip, said Osmond, or maybe it was Jac's Auntie.

"The most impressive of the woman's animals, the hero of the story, is Chanticleer, the cockerel. But he's afflicted by a horrible dream, a premonition of the fox's attack. He can feel the beast's jaws gripping his throat. And the hen he's in love with is put right off by how pathetically he allows this nightmare to undermine him. Let's look at what she says – it's the section I asked you all to paraphrase into modern English... Catherine, if you wouldn't mind..."

Catherine never relished being singled out. But she'd done her homework.

"For shame on you, you spineless thing," she read out from her notes. "Honest to God, you've lost my heart now and all my devotion. I'm telling you, there's just no way I can love a coward. Despite what any of us women say, what we really want in a man is for him to be tough and serious, brave and daring and determined; not to come crying to us like some silly wimp just because he's scared of something and doesn't know what to do..."

She paused and looked across the classroom. Jac was sure she was searching him out.

"So don't come snivelling to me, feeling sorry for yourself. How come you've got a big butch beard but not the heart of a man?"

You have got a beard, said Jac's Auntie.

She was right. He did. It was a souvenir hanging up in his bedroom. The beard he'd worn as Toby Belch. But was he full of manly courage?

He wanted to object that Catherine's denunciation of him – because he *knew* that that's what he'd just heard, not a translation

279

of Chaucer – was so unfair. *Ciaran* was the one who didn't have the guts to ask her out.

"Excellent work, Catherine. You've really entered into the emotions of the character. Clearly, what she's feeling strikes a chord with you."

Something in the very core of Jac's head burst. But Osmond's voice droned on.

"This style that Chaucer's using is called the Mock Heroic. And the whole point about the Mock Heroic is that it simultaneously demeans and ennobles. It belittles its subjects, even as it puffs them up."

Jac heard a sound as though of air being pumped into a tyre. Wales' Smallest English Mistress was being blown up… into a colossal figure, bestriding the narrow classroom. And Jac hadn't even been physically assaulted this time! Perhaps Swotzi had slipped something into his drink at Dinner Time. But then he remembered he hadn't had anything to drink. Or to eat.

Osmond's surreal, inflated head gazed down on Jac from some great height. A large cockerel had come to perch on her shoulder.

"Chaucer writes of hens who quote the great philosophers…"

Osmond was now so enormous that Jac realised that the schoolyard rumours were right: once upon a time she really had been a big figure on the arts scene, engaged to be married to that famous broadcaster, a rising star in her own right.

"…farmyard animals who debate the meaning of dreams with scholarly references to the Classics and the Bible."

From his seat next to Nerys, Penry interrupted her with a loud "Eeyore!"

Osmond shrank, back to her normal, tiny size: a teacher in middle age, trying to interest a menagerie of schoolkids in the literature of the Middle Ages.

"Stop horsing round, Penry," objected Petra, "The poor widow never had any equine stock."

Jac fought to focus on the lesson, on Chaucer. But the author himself had now joined them. He had a little grey goatee, and some sort of black headdress. Otherwise, he was dressed in a smart pinstripe suit.

"By seint Peteres belle," quod Chaucer, "Ye seye right sooth."

"EEYORE!" said Penry, much louder.

Chaucer squinted over towards the sunlit window, probably trying to make out whether Penry was a schoolboy or a donkey.

"The ass is braying in the light," pronounced James Taylor.

"I suspect that what's in your befuddled mind," snapped Jac, revelling in that fact that he didn't have to be afraid of Swotzi anymore, "is *the light is braying like an ass*. But that's Edith Sitwell, not Geoffrey Chaucer…"

The Father of English Literature nodded sagely.

"… and it's an example of synaesthesia, not the Mock Heroic."

Chaucer felt moved to turn and give Jac the thumbs up. "I see you have a fine student of letters here, Miss Osmond. I shall note that in my Inspection Report."

Evidently, the great man was able to speak Modern English too. It was a relief to some of the class who were struggling to keep up. Jac smiled back at him, smugly, his own worries fading for the first time that day. But his self-satisfaction had got under the skin of Nerys the Pig.

"Jac Morgan," she squealed, "do you realise how pedantic you are? And not half as insightful as you suppose."

"Quite right," cackled Catherine, like a hen, but damningly all the same. "He might be hot on critical comprehension, but he never understood me."

Jac began to groan in his throat like a man having a nightmare. Startled, the cockerel flew off from his perch on Osmond's shoulder and settled on Jac's desk. Just as Chaucer had written, Chanticleer's comb was indeed red and coral, indented like a castle wall. His legs and claws were sky-blue, his nails a whiter shade of pale. Now that he could see it all close up, Jac realised the author's description, though heightened by the demands of the Mock Heroic, wasn't much exaggerated. Chanticleer was a striking specimen. And quite unlike anything in real life.

"Oh, Sir Geoffrey, what an enormous... *rooster* you've got," simpered Jac's Auntie, simultaneously being both outrageously suggestive and primly coy; inventing, perhaps, a kind of Mock Erotic.

"By all accounts," said Osmond, "Chanticleer's got a lot to crow about when it comes to satisfying the hens."

"True enough," replied Chaucer. "Though he has a favourite, a number one in his pecking order..."

"*Petralote!*" confirmed the cock, cockily.

Jac knew full well that the hen in question was called *Pertelote*. But Middle English spelling and pronunciation were notoriously inconsistent; objecting would only draw further accusations of pedantry down on his head. Which had begun to throb again.

"*Petralote, Petralote, Petralote!*" screeched the cockerel, all of a flutter.

"Sometimes he has her twenty times before breakfast," noted Chaucer, quite matter-of-fact about it.

"*I lurve having Petralote a lot a lot!*" confirmed the randy beast.

"That's nice," cooed the real Petra, unabashed. Her tongue flicked sensuously over her lips. She was at her most sultry.

"I sometimes wish Martyn would be a bit more..."

Just then, the bell rang for the end of the double lesson. Three times. Like a cock crowing.

'I know about those letters in your satchel,' it seemed to say. 'So which one are you going to give her?'

Jac shook himself to clear his head. To *de-Chanticleer* his head. His Auntie was still clucking inside it, which didn't help...

You won't give her any *of those letters. You'll talk to Petra, and tell her about Ciaran's visit, and ask* her *to pass his message on to Catherine.*

If I did that, thought Jac, I could explain to Petra the way I still feel about Catherine as well. And ask her to tell...

You could, conceded his Auntie. *But you won't. You've been unmanned by Catherine's translation. You're chicken...*

Chicken. Jac's Auntie knew him too well. His *penchant* for puns at critical moments.

The class packed their books away, shouldering their satchels.

Jac closed the straps on his, the three letters still inside.

Tick... tock... tick...

Everyone moved towards the door. Catherine and Petra were first there. Jac pushed his way through and caught up with them. From behind, they looked identical. Twins. Osmond had been so astute in her casting. But, of course, he knew which was which.

Are you sure? queried his Auntie.

Of course I'm not sure, thought Jac. That's what this has been all about.

He reached forward and tapped *one* of the girls lightly on the shoulder.

"Have you got a minute? For a word?"

His voice cracked at the end of the phrase. He felt the fox's jaws close around his throat.

It was Petra who'd turned around. Even then, Jac wasn't certain that that's what he'd intended.

39

There was an Election on. Within hours, the results would be declared. Meanwhile, as is traditional, the hiatus was filled by pundits and pointless speculation.

"It's her mother's idea," ventured Nerys. "Her Mam laying down the law. Quite right. Petra *should* celebrate her birthday on the day itself."

None of them were entirely sure what they were doing there, at short notice, in an Upper Room on Pandy Square, on this Thursday night. Gathered as though for a Last Supper. Was there a Good Friday to come?

Petra had been absent from school that week, four or five other Sixth Formers too. The first coughs and flus of the year. But she'd phoned Penry (*why him?*) to tell him that the upstairs lounge of the Pandy Inn had been booked for Thursday night, and asking him to get the Friends – not the whole Sixth Form – to come along. It was October 10th, Petra's Eighteenth. The obvious inference was that it was a party to mark her coming of age. But the plan had always been for her to have a joint celebration with Catherine in December, when Martyn would be back after his first term in Oxford. No explanation was given for this new arrangement.

Petra hadn't appeared. No-one from her family either. A buffet had been laid out. A morose DJ was playing ELP. But Jac didn't pay much attention to that.

Because just then, at the doorway, quite simply, was Catherine.

Well, not simply Catherine. She was with Ciaran.

Jac had guessed that they'd be coming along together. After the 'Nun's Priest's Tale Lesson', as deranged as he was, he'd managed to talk to Petra. He'd asked her to pass Ciaran's message on to Catherine. He hadn't given her any of the letters or said a word about his own feelings. And Petra hadn't asked. It had all seemed unreal, not just the psychedelically coloured cockerel and Chaucer himself turning up in class, which Jac realised (he wasn't crazy!) was the unfortunate combination of forgetting to have lunch and an overwrought imagination; but the whole situation. Unreal.

All the same, the outcome was real enough. The following week, Catherine had let slip that she'd been on a date with Ciaran. Naturally, Jac had gone into one of his moods. A right *pwdu*. Mentally, he drafted again and again the letter that he *could* have sent Catherine, the one that *would* have won her back. It was an exquisite torture, like some deeply harmful drug he was dependent on. He played over and over in his head the conversation he should have had with *her* instead of the one he'd actually had with Petra. In that imagined showdown, he was articulate, bold, sensitive, persuasive – everything he'd failed to be in reality, everything Pertelote had wanted Chanticleer to be. And Catherine would have looked deep into his eyes and seen him again as he really was, as she'd seen him that night on Tonypandy Square.

He talked to no-one about this. He took walks on Carncelyn. He wrote a poem and tore it up. On his stereo in the front room, he played Don McLean's *Crossroads* and Joni Mitchell's *A Case Of You* so often that the vinyl would surely wear through. Without looking down at the *American Pie* album on the turntable, he could position the needle so that it fell, time and again, into the narrow gap before the final track on side one, a single groove before the doom-laden piano intro and the needless reminders that he was all tied up on the inside, that he'd taken the wrong direction, that only *she* could make him whole. If it wasn't that, the pick-up was descending unerringly on *Blue*, side two, track four. Never having had so much as half a glass, he had to depend on that infamous imagination of his to understand what it might be like for Joni to contemplate drinking a whole case; but he dwelt endlessly on that kiss on Pandy Square, on the aftertaste of wine on Catherine's mouth. There were addicts – he knew this for a fact, and he must be one – who got hooked after just one sip.

His whole world had come to an end.

And then, one morning, to his own great surprise, he woke and he realised that it hadn't. That, somehow, he had the capacity to take an interest in it again.

There *was* an Election on. A General Election.

Jac read the newspapers again, watched the current affairs shows. The outlook was promising and depressing, at one and the same time.

Having gone back to the country, Harold Wilson seemed likely to get the sustainable majority he was seeking. But what would he do with it? Hold down wages to try to control inflation? It was hardly a sounding of the Revolutionary Trumpet. The charged atmosphere of the Miners' Strike and the Three-Day Week had evaporated. Shrivelled. The Labour candidate in the Rhondda, a pleasant, decent man, would be re-elected by a huge margin. But as for any radical new thinking, or even reforming zeal, he might as well be a Tory.

The politics gave Jac *some* perspective, at least, on the immaturities of his love life. Whatever he felt for Catherine, he forced himself to recognise that it hadn't been tested by the realities of a 'proper relationship'. She'd never been his girlfriend, as such. And he could see that there might be more important things – not just the 'big picture' stuff of politics, the Election and Northern Ireland and Chile and Vietnam, but even in his own small world. It would be a denial of everything he professed to value if the whole network of his friendships unravelled, as he could see that it might, just because Catherine was now with someone else, and he couldn't bear to be in their company. If he really did care about her, if it was more than an infatuation, shouldn't he be *glad* if she was happy elsewhere, as he'd suggested in one of those awful letters?

Hallelujah! his Auntie rejoiced at this breakthrough in his thinking. *In the words of the late, great Martin Luther King, that's one small step for a man…*

But if Jac was moving forward at all, it was hardly a neat, linear progression.

286

Amidst this emotional distress, a postcard arrived from Martyn. Jac studied the picture at the breakfast table: the mediaeval quadrangle of Martyn's college, a large pillar at its centre, topped by a stone-carved bird.

What was it? Not a cockerel anyway.

"A pelican," said his father, who seemed better briefed on Oxford iconography than Jac had imagined. "It's an ancient symbol for the Lord Jesus himself. People believed it cut its breast open with its beak to feed its young with its own blood. Just as He gave his body and lifeblood for us."

Despite the way he'd behaved during Ciaran's visit, Jac's father wasn't given to sermonising at home. He'd have noticed the turmoil his son had been going through – Jac had no talent for hiding his moods. Perhaps his Dad thought that this was, at last, the moment he'd prayed for, the moment when Jac's stony heart would be broken, when he'd turn in anguish to the Lord for Salvation.

And maybe that *is* the answer, thought Jac. If he couldn't have Catherine, he could throw himself into the arms of Jesus instead. And that would be the end of pain and doubt.

He turned the card over. On the back, in Martyn's spidery handwriting, just six words: 'to be wise is to suffer'.

"One of Martyn's favourite quotes," explained Jac, seeing his father's puzzlement. "Sophocles. Tiresias says it, I think, in *Oedipus Rex.*"

"Ah, those Greek philosophers: clever and learned men. But, for all their insights, do you know, my son, without the light of the Gospel to guide them, they were blind…"

"I think the point is that it's only after Oedipus suffers and blinds himself that he's able to seek the Truth."

Jac knew less about the Classics than he was pretending. And he felt bad about scoring points off his Dad. Did he sense frailty there, an inkling, for the first time, that the balance of power between them, father and son, might be shifting, as inevitably it must with the passing years? He remembered the fit his father had had. That was at breakfast too. The epilepsy was under control now, the tablets took care of that. Had it taken a toll all the same?

It was a moment when they *might* have talked truthfully, openly. When Jac might have confessed what he really believed – and *didn't* believe. About the similarities he saw between Martyn and his dad, despite their differences. But he'd said it now, his line on Oedipus – and to his own father! Jac sensed his dad pondering whether he should persevere, whether he should remind Jac that Jesus healed the blind man, perhaps – 'one thing I know, that, whereas I was blind, now I see' – or that *He* was the Truth. There were any number of *apposite* verses which Jac would have recognised; but his father hesitated. And just then Jac's Mam came in from the kitchen with a second mug of tea for them both, and that was that.

On the bus to school, Jac's thoughts turned again to the postcard. Martyn would have phoned Petra. She must have told him about Catherine and Ciaran. The bleak message was Martyn's way of saying that he knew what Jac was going through, of telling him that he *understood*. What the card was proof of, what it *redeemed* for Jac, was something he'd lost sight of, in all the misunderstandings between them: Martyn's astounding capacity for empathy. The ability he had to hope and feel for others. Somehow, now, he'd managed to restore all of that – in just six words.

Martyn. But he was in Oxford. And here they all were, in the Pandy Inn, waiting for his girlfriend and not sure why. And here was someone else's girlfriend, Catherine, making her entrance, her debut with Ciaran. If you'd asked Jac the next morning, or even as he walked home alone in the echoing dark of Dunraven Street later that night, what she'd been wearing, he wouldn't have been able to say. All he knew was that she looked different. Serene? Yes, she looked *serene*. More serene than she'd been all year, since before her step-brother died. And *well*. She looked as though she'd spent a week in the sun. It was only when she left Ciaran's side and stood in a pool of light as she greeted Nerys that Jac realised she was wearing make-up. Her pallor had become a tan, like the one she had back at the end August, when... Jac stopped himself.

Ciaran was walking over towards him. It was the first time they'd met since the evening he'd asked Jac to ask Catherine out for him.

You can cope with this, said his Auntie. *A piece of easy peas. Like shooting fish up a drainpipe.*

Yes, I can, thought Jac, just watch me. As long as he doesn't thank me...

"Jac! I need to thank you..."

Ciaran reached out and took him firmly by the hand.

"...for passing on that message I gave you."

For passing on that message. Not *giving Catherine that message*. He must know then – *of course, he must* – that Jac hadn't spoken directly to Catherine. If Ciaran hadn't worked it out for himself, Catherine must certainly have told him by now *why* Jac wouldn't have felt able to do that. Jac felt *exposed*; exposed and stupid. For all the hours he'd spent obsessing over the sequence of events, it hadn't occurred to him that that's the way it would have gone.

The moment passed. The music changed. That distinctive bass opening. Carly Simon. *You're So Vain*.

She's married to James Taylor now... said his Auntie, finding nothing more substantial to distract Jac than another piece of music trivia she'd picked up from goodness knows where. *The American one. Not the boy from Penmaesglas.*

Jac was still staring at Ciaran. "Son of a gun,"whispered Carly, and then she began to sing. Right on cue, as though it had been rehearsed, over Ciaran's shoulder Jac saw Petra make an entrance. And not just Petra, Martyn was with her. Martyn!

There they were, the two of them, he in his pin-stripe suit, she in a posh black frock, walking into the party, like Burton and Taylor, like JFK and Jackie, like Gatsby and Daisy, like Carly Simon and whichever of Hollywood's leading men was she was singing about... like they were walking onto a yacht.

It was a real *coup de theatre*. What was Martyn doing back here? He was in Oxford. Term had only just begun! Yet, despite the enormous surprise, Jac couldn't help noticing, in that first glimpse, as with Catherine, something different about Petra. But perhaps it was him who'd changed, not them?

He looked again, studied Petra's face.

Paler than usual, drawn.

Had she swapped complexions with Catherine? Well, she'd been sick, so it wasn't surprising.

Martyn's hand was clasped over hers, advertising their *coupleness* in a way they seldom did in company. Backed by Carly Simon, they watched themselves *gavotte* to the centre of the room. All that was missing was the hat and the apricot scarf.

"Ladies and gentlemen…" announced Martyn with a flourish; but then he dropped the tone to something lighter, with a nod towards Jac and Penry "… boys and girls…"

He paused like the actor he was, the audience hanging now on his every word.

"Petra and I have some news…"

Another perfect beat.

"We would like to let you know that… we're getting engaged!"

He dragged Petra's hand aloft, revealing the ring for all to see. There were whoops, applause. Penry shouted *hip hip hooray* and they all joined in.

Catherine came over to hug Martyn affectionately, and then – like it was part of some formal ceremony – to examine the diamond on Petra's finger.

Drinks were called for. A toast for the happy couple. Nerys wanted the whole story of the proposal: "Did he go down on one knee?"

"Keep it clean," jested Penry. "There are children present, apparently."

There was laughter and joy, and for Jac just a fleeting shadow of something else. But they all linked arms and danced in a big friendly circle. It felt good, felt right to be with these true Friends, to be *here* and *now*, together at the beginning of something so significant.

Jac decided to step outside, to let his thoughts settle, to fix the moment in his mind. In the corridor, he found Martyn, returning from the gents.

Jac remembered the postcard from Oxford, how grateful he was for it.

"Great news, butt'. Wonderful to have it all settled, with you being away and all. You both know where you stand now. We all do. Congratulations. You caught us by surprise, mind."

"It was a bit of a surprise to me…"

Well, jiw, jiw, said his Auntie. *Petra's in the pickies!*

Jac didn't cotton on. Martyn had to spell it out.

"She's expecting, Jac. Petra. She's pregnant."

"Oh. God. O God, Martyn. I'd no idea… O God… That *is* a surprise. But that's good news, right – a baby?"

Martyn looked straight back at him, grim faced. Jac reached out, put his hand on his Friend's shoulder.

"Sorry, I'm being stupid. You've only just started in college, and Petra… it's her A level year. She won't be able… she might have to postpone… until… even then, I suppose… O, bloody hell, sorry, Martyn, I'm so…"

Jac stopped gabbling. A terrible thought had struck him.

"It wasn't my fault, was it? That day in Porthcawl? When I threw the condoms away? Is that how…"

"Sod off, Jac!"

Jac stepped back, alarmed by the abrupt fury. Something pent-up had exploded in Martyn.

"Only bastard Jac Morgan could be so self-bloody-centred to ask something like that. 'Was it the jolly time we had when Jac hurled his jacket into the sea?' As though it matters if it was then, or any other *fucking* time. Not everything's about you."

Not everything's about you. The postcard. *To be wise is to suffer.*

So that had been about Martyn, then, not Jac. How stupid, how blind he'd been.

Jac gazed at his friend now, imploring him silently for forgiveness. And slowly Martyn found the grace to relent. The anger subsided.

"No, Jac, if you must know, it was the trip to France. Or so it seems…"

They'll always have Paris, then.

That was Jac's Auntie. Sometimes she was *so* inappropriate that Jac couldn't deal with it. He ignored her, and put his arm around Martyn, who looked, suddenly, lost and taut with strain. He wasn't acting now.

"We hadn't realised… We didn't know she was pregnant, the day we went to Porthcawl. We thought we were being careful. But, as it turns out, those condoms wouldn't have been any use anyway."

Jac tried *not* to imagine what might have happened if the Pack of Three hadn't featured at all that day, whether he and Catherine…

His Auntie recognising the danger, cut across this futile, embittering line of thought with one of her 'witty' queries: *So will Martyn be going back to Oxford? To finish learning how to be a master of French letters?*

And then, wisely, she shut up, and left them to it.

The Fourth Branch

WINTER

40

Tonypandy Square
(words and music by Jac Morgan and Don McLean)

The snow lies still and deep on Penrhys mountain,
The rain falls still as hard on Pandy Square,
The wind sweeps down the Valley like a spirit,
Touching everybody everywhere.
But it don't shake me,
No, it can't break me,
No, it won't take me down when it blows,
Bumping into people as it goes.

There was a Crisis. *Something must be done.* Everyone could see that. Lydia could have seen it without her specs on. Even a Fool like Penry could see it.

Jac certainly did.

Two Friends, two of their dearest friends, were in trouble. *In the pickies*, as Jac's Auntie had so indelicately put it. In need of support. Emotionally. Practically too. Big decisions to be made. Just when their relationship with their parents would be raw and strained to breaking point. When their relationship with each other would be tested as never before (*never ever, Trevor Evans*). So much to be sorted. Accommodation. Finance. Employment. Education. Would Petra stay at school? Would Martyn stay at college? If they kept the baby…

If they kept the baby: that might be the first agonising question they were considering.

They'd need their friends now, need the strength of that bond, that mutuality they'd all invested so heavily in. Now it would prove its worth.

Though he didn't admit it to anyone (he could scarcely admit to himself), for Jac, who'd been directionless ever since things went wrong with Catherine, this mishap gave him a goal, some forward momentum. He was motivated. He was back *on song*.

Yes, *something must be done* alright. And Jac knew what it was.

A Rock Opera.

He would write a Rock Opera about it. A *Tommy* for The Society of Friends. A *Jesus Christ Superstar* for the new baby. A Rhondda *Quadrophenia*.

The scenario, the story, the characters – it was all there, just waiting for the words and music. And what a cast list! The Tortured Genius turned Oxford Man; the Pregnant Girlfriend he leaves behind; the A Student who rides off with a Biker; the Stranger who comes to Town to steal love; the Jester who sings for the King and Queen; and the Royal Pair themselves – the Sensitive Boy Who Never Grows Up and the Bad Girl Of The B Form who's reformed, but then lost to him forever. On a bus to Gilfach.

Or is she?

Yes, a Rock Opera. That was the thing. How hard could it be, after all, if Andrew Lloyd Webber could do it? Musical pastiche, overblown angst, light comic relief, deviancy, a sprinkling of mildly memorable tunes, flamboyant choreography, a Big Number with a show-stopping chorus to reprise as an encore... *and Ernie's your wicked Uncle!*

Actually, the more he thought about it, the more Jac had to admit it was a big ask, even for someone who'd not long ago created a whole new genre of music. He'd need help. His pedigree as a composer (his *track-record* ha! ha!) would be attractive to a big-name collaborator. Obviously, he'd be willing to share the song-writing credits.

Yeah, Don McLean is dying to work with you.

Was his Auntie was being sarcastic? Jac didn't care. Because if Don said no, he had other options. Joni. Carole. Elton and Bernie (though they had each other, so that was a long shot). But Carly Simon... or James Taylor (the American one). Or were they hitched musically as well as maritally? What about Bowie? Bowie! Rumour had it he was looking for a new direction, that he needed to reinvent himself again. Sounded like he'd be open to offers.

Of course, Jac wasn't *entirely* serious about signing up a famous name. But even if it was only an *imaginative* collaboration, even if it was only in his own mind that he had a stellar partner alongside him, in the room, as it were, when he was writing, then the results might be very interesting.

Yes, he could see it working. For the West End and Broadway stage show – the major motion picture would be sure to follow – the set would be an idealised version of Tonypandy Square. Huge and imposing. The Hub of the Universe. The Still Point in the Turning World. The action, though, would move back and fore between past, present and future. 1910. 1974. 2010, perhaps, if that wasn't too unimaginably distant for the audience to get their heads around.

Having struggled with the *beginning* of his Anti-Novel, the thing that troubled him now was how to *end* his Opera. Something melodramatic, of course. A birth? A fatality? Suicide? Murder? The Hero and his Heroine back together? Or separated for Eternity at the last, at the death, like Orpheus and Eurydice?

Jac began work. Don McLean turned out to be – Jac had to admit – a pleasure to write with. Jac had worried that the time difference might be problematic, but transatlantic collaboration turned out to be as easy as (American) pie. By the time Jac woke in the morning, there'd be a fresh verse sketched out and ready to polish up.

If I could I'd build a big red sky boat,
Throw out the sand and glide up through the air;
But oxygen in the dizzy heights of heaven
Would be too pure for Rhondda lungs to bear.
And I can't breathe there,
No, I can't see where
I could really soar above the blues:
Bumping into people you get bruised.

Of course, what Jac had really been hoping for was a sprawling multi-verse compendium of a hit, encapsulating the whole history of the Rhondda, with a kaleidoscopic cast of local characters, and a bang-to-rights, singalong chorus: an eight-and-a-half-minute blockbuster that radio stations would refuse to playlist, only to bow to popular pressure as it powered its way to the top of the charts. But it would have been unfair to expect McLean to come up with something like that. He hardly knew the Valley. For now, Jac was content with their big opening number. *Tonypandy Square*: it was no *Crossroads* (*I thought that's precisely what it was*, said his Auntie, predictably), but when it was reprised at the turning point of the plot, the last verse would tellingly echo the first. A Baby would be born, a Saviour, a Son of Destiny, a Wonder Child. But the people, the mass chorus-line, bought off by consumerism, dulled by opiates, wouldn't recognise what had been brought to birth amongst them.

> *The snow lies still as deep on Penrhys mountain,*
> *The rain falls hard as bullets down on the Square,*
> *The drinkers fill the Pandy Inn this evening,*
> *No room around their little tables there.*
> *But I can't condemn*
> *This Bethlehem –*
> *I'm only one of them you sometimes meet*
> *Bumping into people in the street.*

Jac was chuffed. With himself and with Don. *No room* at the *Inn* in this modern Bethlehem: that was clever. *The drinkers* at their *little tables*: a dig at those too apathetic to stand up for their rights, a prophetic warning about the future they were drifting into.

Despite their musical differences, Morgan/McLean laboured away, industriously, fruitfully. Day and night. Even the excitement about the General Election result – Labour squeaking home by three seats, the narrowest majority ever recorded – couldn't deflect Jac from the work in hand...

And, then, he was made to see his folly. His big mistake. *His big mistake.* No point in blaming his song-writing partner. The fault was plain to see, once his eyes were opened to it, in the message he'd intended to preach in the work itself. It wasn't his neighbours who'd turned their backs on the future, the impending birth. It was Jac himself...

He hadn't gone near Petra. Fair enough, she hadn't been back at school. But he hadn't gone to visit, hadn't even sent a letter. How could he have been so selfish, so self-absorbed?

It was Catherine who brought him to his senses. She sought him out in school one day. They took another walk together up to the Top Yard. Catherine had news – disturbing news. Petra had left home. She'd never really seen eye-to-eye with her Mam. Well, that was an exaggeration. There were times when they got on perfectly well. But this wasn't one of them. When Petra confessed her secret, they'd had a blazing row. So angry was Mother, that Mother-to-be had moved out.

There'd been no question of Petra going to Martyn's – it just wouldn't have worked, given the situation with his father – but to Jac's surprise, it was in Lydia's house that Petra was staying. Jac knew that Petra got on well with Lydia's Mam – all those evenings watching *The Onedin Line*. But he instinctively bracketed Petra with Catherine, rather than Lydia, and if he'd thought about it (which he clearly hadn't) he would have expected Petra to turn to *her* in an hour of need. But he supposed it made sense: Mrs Peake had a spare bedroom with her daughter away at university in Kent. It was Lydia who'd phoned Catherine with the news.

So it's a Canterbury Tale, said his Auntie. Another 'helpful' reminder: that traumatic Chaucer lesson.

"We should go and visit Petra. Would you come with me, Jac? It's easier when there are two of you."

Catherine was asking *him* to go with her. Him, not Ciaran. New horizons opened. Despite all that had gone wrong between them, there was a world where he could be her confidant, someone who mattered to her, who she trusted, even if...

Even if her heart belonged elsewhere.

He pulled himself together. This wasn't about him. And it wasn't about the two of them. Catherine phoned Lydia's mother. An arrangement was made.

So that Saturday, Jac found himself dodging puddles the length of Dunraven Street, heading towards the Square to meet Catherine. She'd be on the bus from Gilfach. They'd walk together up Court Street to Lydia's … the exact reverse of the journey they'd made the night they'd kissed. The notion had played on Jac's mind. As he scooted along the rain-soaked pavements, his Auntie lectured him about how much drier he'd have been if he'd waited in the house until Catherine's bus was due and then popped out to board it at the Naval Colliery. But that would have made it a complete mirror-image: it was the very stop where he'd taken the fateful decision to get *off* that night, leaving her to travel home alone.

Saturday morning on Dunraven Street had never been about retail for Jac: it was a social experience. As a young boy, accompanying his mother shopping, he would be bored and frustrated by the sheer number of people she stopped to talk to. Though this was a Linear *City*, the connections between its citizens were so close that there were no strangers. You *knew* your neighbours. Even if you couldn't name every passer-by, you acknowledged their presence. No wonder that phrase *bumping into people* had worked its way into his song-writing. By now, he treasured this gregariousness, this camaraderie that seemed so natural but was so hard-won. One Saturday, after walking solo up to the Square and back, he'd made a list of those who'd stopped to talk to him. Relatives, neighbours, friends of the family, men and women of all ages. Thirty-one of them. Eager to chat, or to give him a message to pass on to his parents. All that lived experience, all that *humanity*. The true wealth of the place. People. Thirty-one souls. Exactly the number, he realised later, as had perished in the Cambrian Disaster.

Absit omen. He walked on, struggling to keep Catherine from his mind, to focus on Petra. He glanced across the road, up at the War Memorial. Another Latin phrase came to him, from a poem they'd been studying together, he and Petra (but, of course, Catherine had been in class too): 'dulce et decorum est pro patria mori'.

Ah, the old lie, whispered his Auntie. *Better to have loved and lost than never to have loved at all.*

She was on form this morning. Tennyson turned in his grave. Wilfred Owen spun twice as fast. Jac mentally curled his lip at her. Well, not just mentally, in fact.

In his anxiety, Jac had left home far too early. There'd be half-an-hour to kill on Pandy Square before the bus got there. *Catherine*'s bus.

He tried to slow his pace, window-shopping at Boots – perfumes he'd never buy for Catherine, cameras they'd never use to take snaps of each other. He crossed the road to the Wishing Well. Cards he'd never send her. Books they'd never read together.

There was a little model Wishing Well in the window pointing up its twee trading name. Jac considered going inside and tossing in a coin or two: he could do with some luck.

Why don't you just use one of those Three Wishes you've got, said his Auntie. *Your wish is my command, and all that.*

It was as unconvincing as the Genie of the Lamp in a local panto. Clearly, his Auntie was still in a huff about his reaction to her translation of that Latin tag.

Jac decided to humour her. He didn't want her getting into a proper strop. Not this morning. Alright, he asked, knowing he was falling for some sort of gag, what Three Wishes?

Did I never tell you? Every special child like you – you know, children with… um, what am I? Not exactly a guardian angel, but you know what I mean?

A manifestly insane interior voice which is proof of your host's manifest insanity?

Don't be rude to your elders, Jac. And take yourself more seriously. But since you asked: special children such as yourself have Three Magic Wishes to call on before their Eighteenth Birthday. Just like in the fairy tales.

Pull the other one.

It's true. On my mother's sister's life.

And his Auntie had never thought to mention this before?

It never came up. What would you have used them for anyway?

Be careful what you wish for, wasn't that what they said? In those fables, sorcery turned out to be more curse than blessing. And now that the subject *had* come up, Jac couldn't think what he would have chosen.

Other than Catherine…

Ah. True enough, the guarantee of a lift back from Gilfach late one night back in August might have changed the world if it could have been sorted out in advance. Was that the kind of wish his Auntie could fulfil?

I could probably have got you a ride home on 'Arry Howen's 'Orse.

Jac wondered about her sometimes, he really did. The closer he got to his Eighteenth, the more childish she was becoming.

He sauntered on, to the bottom of Gilfach Road. The Tonypandy one. *Gilfach* Road. Signs, reminders of Catherine everywhere. He told himself sternly that he was there as a *friend* today. To support Catherine in supporting Petra. He was grateful, at least, that the rain seemed to be clearing up. He stopped outside Spice: 'Ultra-Modern Style On Your Doorstep: Everything for the Smartly Dressed Young Man'. Yes, Dunraven Street still punched its weight as a shopping centre. Mind you, this was nothing compared to its Edwardian heyday. 1910. That great variety of shops. With their windows smashed in. *Tonypandemonium.*

Standing where he was standing, with that history hanging in the air, Jac suddenly felt embarrassed to be gawping at a three-piece suit. Dark brown, pinstripe, wide lapels and big, big flares. A symbol of opulence, of superiority, not solidarity.

Chic, whispered his Auntie. *Martyn would love it. And 25% OFF!*

Still too expensive.

But if you persuaded your parents to buy it as an early Christmas present…

…he could wear it to the Sixth Form Dinner Dance!

He checked himself: that message from his Rock Opera, railing against consumerism – he was as culpable as anyone.

Nothing's too classy for a good worker. And there's always your Three Wishes. You could use one of those.

And so, he did. He just stood there like a big kid and wished that his parents would buy him the suit. Just to get his Auntie to shut up.

With that, the shop door sprang open. A burly customer emerged clutching two plastic bags stuffed full of purchases. Blinginate Jenkins! Come shopping all the way from Blaenllechau – and not for a rugby kit! There was mileage in this for Jac, good gossip for the Sixth Form *Li-bury*. Jenkins must have realised it too, because he hurried away as fast as his hooker's legs would take him. But not before Jac had exclaimed, loud enough for him to hear, "Blinginate people who can afford to shop here!"

Time to move on. But still too early for Catherine's bus. Without thinking, Jac found himself in the Record Shop on the Square. The usual Saturday crowd were browsing the racks. Greasers flicking from album to double album for the umpteenth time, reluctant to commit. Teenyboppers rushing to buy their first single. From behind the counter, Mal greeted him like he was his best customer, which he certainly wasn't. Though if he ever bought a record, it was here. Jac glanced at the LP charts. Bryan Ferry at No 8. *Another Time, Another Place*. If only. And there was the man himself, staring back at Jac from the cover. White tux. Black tie. Cigarette. Almost as cool as Martyn, thought Jac. He turned the sleeve over. Side One, Track One: 'The In Crowd'. Was that what The Society of Friends was?

More like The Out Gang, his Auntie scoffed.

But they *were* a gang, still. A gang against the world.

Bryan Ferry: Jac reminded himself *yet again* to think about Petra, not Catherine. *Petra, Petra, Petra.* It worked. It worked so well that he began to have one of his weird hallucinations about her. It was an odd delusion (*aren't all delusions odd?* asked his Auntie). His vision was unaffected, but his ears were filled with the sound of some middle-aged crooner congratulating Petra for getting pregnant. *You're Having My Baby*, he kept singing. On and on it went, this mawkish ballad full of unpleasant details about seed growing inside her and the like. Ach-y-fi!

But then Jac realised that it *wasn't* a delusion. There actually was such a song, and it was being pumped through the Shop's sound system right now. There was an old punter – nearly thirty – up at the counter: he must have asked to hear it, and was actually going to buy it.

"Paul Anka – excellent choice, sir," lied Mal. "And right there at No 17 amongst this week's top singles."

The customer handed over his cash.

Hope I die 'fore I get old, thought Jac.

I've told you once already, scolded his Auntie. *Don't be rude about your elders.*

The lyrics had moved on to lauding the mother-to-be for deciding *not* to have an abortion. Jac fled the shop and crossed the Square to wait there instead. Even so, the song kept playing in his head. *Having My Baby…*

The Gilfach bus was late.

Having My Baby…

But at long last, here it was.

Having My Baby…

And here was Catherine, looking lovely and carrying a white bouquet for Petra.

Chrysanthemums. Go on, urged his Auntie. *Say it. Tease her. Tell her you love them, but she shouldn't have…*

Catherine got in first.

"I know what you're going to say, Jac, so don't even bother."

"I was just going to comment on the quality of the chrysanths."

They smiled. Together. It was going to be easier than he'd been fearing.

On the way up Court Street, they talked. Like friends. Jac even found it in him to ask about Ciaran. He was doing well, and now knew more about women's clothing sizes and materials than Catherine herself. Good old Marks and Sparks.

Jac relaxed. It was all fine.

Lydia's mother came to the door and took the flowers from Catherine with a smile. But then she stood there without inviting them in.

"Sorry about this, but the doctor's just called to see Petra. Would you mind coming back in half-an-hour or so?"

Her tone was reassuring, neutral at worst. But as she turned to close the door, Jac saw the worry in her eyes.

41

"Bringing a baby into the world. It's not exactly child's play, is it?"

Another classic straight from his Auntie. As Jac repeated it aloud, he realised how idiotic he must sound to Catherine. His voice bounced off the bare walls. The starkness of the place they'd found themselves in only amplified the stupidity.

They hadn't been sure how to fill the 'half-an-hour or so' before they could return to Lydia's. A coffee down in Melardi's? But then they'd have to struggle back up that hill for a second time; and spending more time than necessary together on Pandy Square was best avoided. Walking over to the Bush, where Lydia's Mam had grown up, was his Auntie's suggestion. As soon as Jac had voiced it, and Catherine had acquiesced, he regretted it. Killing time amidst the ruins of a deserted community wouldn't be much of a laugh. But in the absence of any other idea…

They left Clydach's main street to cross the few hundred yards over to the Bush. Piles of freshly deposited horse manure sat on the roadway. Another lovestruck Headmaster, perhaps, riding up here to do his business, as it were. Jac spotted the mess in time to avoid fouling his shoes. He remembered the bitter-sweet passage in *Ash On A Young Man's Sleeve* where Dannie Abse's naïve protagonist takes his first girl, *his* Lydia, Lydia Pike, on what he hopes will be a romantic walk to an allotment overlooking Cardiff. He tries to kiss her and proves inexpert. The pay-off is that on the way back down the path, he treads in a pile of dung which earlier he'd been careful to avoid. Jac made a mental note for his own return journey.

They reached what was left of the two short Bush terraces. They were separated by a triangle of grass; very unlike the Rhondda, almost on the pattern of communal gardens in a fashionable London district, or one of those streets off Cathedral Road in Abse's Cardiff where ships' captains resided in a grand style built on the profits of transporting coal. But this was no lap of luxury. The Bush Houses dated back to the 1860s, early in the Valley's development. They'd known a century of grinding poverty and more than a few false dawns. In the end, after the Cambrian Disaster, when the pit had been shut, they'd been abandoned. By then, as much as those who were left living there loved it – the tight neighbourliness, the sense of belonging to a community within a community, their own little Rhondda – these homes would have been classed as slums. It was a time when thousands were being moved out of such places to new estates, to Penrhys or – like Catherine's family – Gilfach. Or far from the Rhondda altogether.

The people had gone. Empty space was all that remained. Some of the houses had been demolished to the footings. Others were half-standing, roofs holed, walls crumbling, damp window-frames rotting. Four mangy sheep occupied the end house, sheltering against the back wall. Here and there, signs of lives lived, a human past. A scrap of lino, a bashed-in kitchen pot, a child's rag doll. Jac believed in the Rhondda, in its people, believed that *their* Labour government, even with such a tenuous grasp on power, could, would make a difference; but he couldn't help seeing all this as a forewarning, a glimpse of what the whole Valley had coming when London determined that even those mines that were still working were *uneconomic*.

A crazy idea came to him then. A vision. There was just enough of the dwellings left standing to imagine it could actually be realised. The Society of Friends – and one or two others with the practical skills to do it – rebuilding this place house-by-house, moving in, living. Not as a commune, exactly; but *together*. A haven. Bringing up Petra and Martyn's child, all their children. Together and for each other. Standing against what was coming to overwhelm the Rhondda, against all that the Rhondda, despite his belief in it, might give in to.

Ghosts of the past. Fears for the future. A hazy notion of another way. Standing in what was once a family's sitting room, Jac searched for a way to express his milling thoughts. He and

Catherine had so much in common – school, music, drama, friends – but he longed to connect with her on this level too, on the wider notions he had about the Valley that had shaped them. He knew that her values, her plans to go nursing, her commitment to caring for others, were ones he stood by; but they'd seldom discussed them. And it *wasn't* that in focusing on the upbringing they shared that he would have something to offer her that Ciaran couldn't. It was that these things – a sense of history, a thirst for fairness in the society they lived in, a concern for what they'd bequeath to the generations to come – *mattered* to him. He wanted to be sure they mattered to his friends. But Jac knew they had futures more personal, more immediate to talk about. Once again, he couldn't work out where to start.

His eye fell once more on the tattered doll at his feet. That was when his Auntie came up with her corny aphorism about the responsibility of parenthood: *it's not exactly child's play, is it?*

Even as he was repeating her words, Jac experienced a flash of rage – with himself, with this barmy voice inside his head. He considered using one of those Magic Wishes to get her to shut up for good and all, but then he realised that that would be even barmier. And much to his surprise, Catherine seemed to take what he'd said seriously. He was right, she said, pregnancy could be a terrible burden.

Of course. Jac cottoned on to his own stupidity. Her step-brother.

She began to talk about the girl he'd been involved with, down in Swansea. She'd given birth in the summer. There were issues involved, *political* issues – Jac was glad to hear Catherine say the word – failures of the system to respond to the needs of young single mothers, the insincerity of social workers, the loss of dignity, the loss of income, the clawing back of a student grant.

The situation was personal too, distressingly personal. The girl, the new mother had severed all contact with Catherine's family. Catherine's step-mother found it impossible to bear: losing her son, and now 'losing' his child too. Jac felt the passion in Catherine's voice, the hurt, the sting of injustice. It was a chance to open up the very things he wanted to talk to her about. There was so much he wanted to say, but – not for the first time – he missed his cue.

After a beat, she went on, and in a direction he hadn't anticipated.

"I ought to tell you why I asked you to come today, Jac. The thing is, Petra and I had a bit of a falling-out… before all this came to light… the news that she's expecting, I mean. It involves you, in a way. I wasn't going to say anything, but since we've got these few minutes together…"

Another pause. They were standing shoulder to shoulder, staring in the same direction out of a window that was no longer there.

"It happened in school, that afternoon when Petra passed on Ciaran's message to me, asking me out – the one he'd sent via you. You know what I'm talking about?"

Of course he did.

"She told me what you'd said to her. Then she said – and she made it plain that this was just from her, not you – that she knew somebody else was still interested in me, someone who was really genuine. And that if she was me, she'd think carefully about that."

Jac's mind was awhirl. Thoughts, questions, feelings broke onto the surface; he had no sense that he was in control of them. Amazement that Catherine was telling him any of this (she could be very matter-of-fact about things, but still…). Gratitude to Petra for having spoken up for him, even though he hadn't asked her to. Jealousy and – yes – anger that even though he'd been put back in the frame, even though Catherine had been invited to reconsider, she'd chosen Ciaran after all.

Later, thinking back over the conversation, Jac couldn't help wondering *why*. Not so much *why* she'd chosen Ciaran, but *why* she'd chosen to share what Petra had said with the suitor who'd lost out. Surely, she could have conveyed the essence of the spat without rubbing it in.

Was it because she wanted Jac to be crystal clear about the decision she'd made? Out of kindness, to save him from harbouring false hope. Or... could it be there was some part of her that remained unsure, that there was still a glimmer of a chance for him? And that led to another *why*: why had he stayed dumb then, and waited for her to carry on talking? Wasn't it his opportunity, an unlooked-for second chance, to press his claims? The perfect time to try, at least, to win her back? To show the anger he was feeling, to make sure she understood that he *did* care?

But she hadn't finished. And he was too polite, too considerate to interrupt. The moment had gone.

"I'm afraid I didn't react very well, Jac. I told Petra to mind her own business. Well, worse than that... I said things that I shouldn't have..."

Jac remained silent.

"You see, somebody had told me something about Martyn. Just gossip. Hearsay. But not very pleasant. And I *was* narked by what Petra had said to me. The uncalled-for Advice. So I told her she'd be better off watching her own back."

Jac knew what Catherine had heard. And from whom.

"I realise now that it can't have been true. About Martyn. I mean, the way things have shown themselves. The way things already were with Petra. And I'm mad at myself for upsetting her. I would have been anyway, but at this time, of all times... That's why I asked you to come today, Jac. You're good at this. You've a gift for helping people make peace with each other..."

It was how he often thought of himself, but now that Catherine had voiced the notion, it sounded more like his father than him.

"You're a true friend, Jac. You are. You value friendship. I know you do."

So that was how she saw him after all: a friend.

Well, that was what he'd been telling himself to remember all morning long. He'd lost nothing. Even though he'd felt like he'd lost the whole world. All over again.

It was time to head back to Lydia's. As they neared the main road, Jac remembered the young Dannie Abse and made doubly sure to avoid the manure. It felt like he might as well have stepped in it all the same.

It was coming to rain again. In the damp silence, the hook of that awful song from the Record Shop re-colonised his brain. *Having My Baby...* Like a needle on a scratched disc, jumping incessantly back to the same groove. *Having My Baby...* He knew he should be reassuring Catherine about meeting Petra. *Having...*

Summoning all the emotional energy he could, he killed off the music in his head. And then he managed to say some of the right things: about The Society of Friends, about the things that bound them together, about Petra and Catherine being right at the centre of all that, the longest-standing friendship and still the closest, about how alike they were and how much they liked each other, about a silly misunderstanding being nothing measured against everything they'd shared, everything they'd done for each other, everything they still meant to each other. The fact that Catherine had made this arrangement today, that she cared enough to come and see her friend, that counted for more, for far more, than any silly squabble.

Even though Jac's heart wasn't in it, Catherine's gratitude was evident. She was more ready, she said, than she'd been all morning to face Petra.

Lydia's mother answered the door looking as though a weight had been lifted. But she told them straightaway that the doctor had advised Petra to rest, so she'd gone back to bed. There were apologies for the wasted journey and the fruitless wait, thanks for the flowers, and a promise to be in touch as soon as Petra felt up to a visit. There was nothing for it but to turn back towards the Square, to go and wait in the rain for a bus that – once again – would take Catherine back to Gilfach, and Jac only as far as the Naval Colliery. It wasn't entirely clear, despite Mrs Peake's reassurances, whether they should feel comforted or still anxious. Two friends, and no more than that, a little chastened, pondering what might happen to a third.

42

Jac's Auntie was right. It's not exactly child's play, is it? Bringing a baby into the world. Not in real life. Not in a novel, either, as it turns out.

Since I began writing this story, friends, relatives, those whose lives were the inspiration for it, strangers in parties, practically everyone I've been brave enough to mention it to… people *have been asking me the usual questions that people ask novelists (I've done it myself). What's your novel about? Where do your ideas come from? Do you write at set hours every day? Do you suffer from writer's block?*

Curiosity is understandable. It's more than that: it's flattering that people take you seriously enough to be interested. The awkward bit is when they describe, as they almost always do, the moment that they've read about so often in interviews with famous authors, or in features about what makes good writing: that magic moment when the characters themselves come alive and take control.

It must be so thrilling, so moving, they'll say, when creatures you've invented assume a life of their own. Just like your children growing up before your very eyes. When they start feeling things, thinking things, doing things that you had no idea they were capable of and you didn't plan for them to do… At what point did you experience that with this story? *they'll* ask. Has it happened yet?

No.

That's my answer. Clean and simple. I'm that blunt about it. Thanks for asking, but that's not the way it works for me.

Listen: I'm *the bloody author.* I'm *in charge. I've been doing the hard work, sweating my guts out for months and months now; and I'm not doing it so that some ditsy creature who knows nothing about life, who's never slogged their way through school, never done an honest day's work, never had a heartache, never had a headache unless I've given them one, who doesn't even exist outside of* my *writing… so that* they *can suddenly decide that they know best what should happen next. What they should feel and think and say and do. No way. It's difficult enough sustaining the momentum of the story, keeping the narrative moving forward in as much of a linear fashion as I can manage, without fictional entities suddenly deciding they've got the right to head off in random directions that upset the course I've carefully charted, obscuring my artistic vision and the message I'm trying to get across.*

As you can tell, I feel strongly about this. I'm just not having it. It would be like giving in to an imaginary voice inside your head.

Of course, critics (my editor is one) are going to point out that there's only really one character in this novel. That it's all autobiographical. No wonder the author is never surprised by anything that happens, no wonder he feels as totally in control as the Evangelicals' Jehovah. My will be done, in the Fourth Branch as it is in the First. *I'm not going to dispute that. How can I, given what I've just expressed so forcefully? But so what? Arguably, Tolkien did alright with just a single character who has any sort of internal life. Not that I'm comparing 'Jac' to Gollum.*

What I will say is that I find myself, at this point, facing a dilemma. A moral dilemma you might say. I've got Petra pregnant. I know, I know –Martyn is the father in the story; but be in no doubt that it was me, The Novelist, who actually got her in the pickies, *to borrow Jac's Auntie's inelegant Rhondda phrase once more. It was never inevitable that she would conceive, no matter how much* plaisir d'amour *there'd been in Paris, no matter how much* joie de vivre *she and Martyn were sharing, no matter how* laissez faire *they'd been. It was* me *who determined that she'd fall pregnant. Fiction, says my editor, is a lie that tells the truth. But – whilst this* is, *of course, a work of fiction, and names have been changed and incidents invented for dramatic effect etc – I have to confess now that this is the first time in the whole saga that something important has happened to one of the main characters which is completely* counter *to the historical record. It's a fork in the road. In real life, 'Petra' never got pregnant in the Sixth Form. But in this novel, Petra has. Because that's what the plot seems to demand, if it's to say something about the truth of these characters and their search for themselves and for something beyond themselves to live their lives by. But it wasn't something I saw coming. It's an unplanned pregnancy in every sense.*

So what happens now? What does she do? What does Martyn do? I don't know!

She's having my baby. *She could sweep it from her life, as the lyricist of that sickly ballad so (in)delicately puts it (had he been taking song-writing lessons from Jac's Auntie? He certainly wasn't working with Don*

313

McLean!). Or I could arrange a miscarriage. Wouldn't be difficult. I'm God around here, after all. And, clearly, Lydia's Mam is already worried about the possibility.

The truth is, I don't know what to do. You'd think I'd have worked it all out by this stage of proceedings. And I thought I had. One neat twist, and away we go towards a final chapter where the loose ends are tied up. It can't be that far off now.

But it seems it's not so simple after all. Petra may not have sprung to life herself, may not have taken control of her own narrative; but, suddenly, I discover that I'm not free to do exactly what I want with her either. You see, I've come to care about her. She's beautiful and strong and talented and caring and loyal. And sultry sometimes. We've been through so much together. I know that it's her 'twin' that Jac has a thing about, but even he struggles to tell them apart. If Martyn hadn't been on the scene, who knows? Anyway, why can't I have feelings for Catherine and Petra?

The point is, if you care for somebody and they're carrying your child, the last thing you want is to put them through the pain of an abortion or a miscarriage. But, equally, there's no way that I can see Petra being happy-ever-after as a teenage mother. Can you? Of course, she'd be a great Mam. Mother to a Wonder Child. But there's so much more I can see her doing, so much she might achieve without the burdens of parenthood tying her down before she has a chance to take on the world on her own terms. As mature as she appears to Jac, she's scarcely left childhood behind herself.

And what about Martyn? Is he going to stick by her? What about his 'true nature', if that's what it is? Is he ready to be a father? Is he cut out to be a husband? If he goes ahead and gets married, what then? If you're looking for omens, think of those golden couples who sprang so readily to Jac's mind when Martyn and Petra walked into their own engagement party: Burton and Taylor, the Kennedys, Gatsby and Daisy, Carly Simon and her vain beau. Not a happy ending amongst them.

So where does this *end, this Rhondda Romance, this Great Welsh Auntie Novel? Is it a light farce, a black comedy, or a terrible tragedy? Is there a happy resolution, like the one played out in* Twelfth Night*? Because even that, as Osmond said, is Shakespeare's Night Before The Morning After: it finishes with the spectre of puritanism in the air, the puritanism that will crush Toby Belch's carefree japes, the puritanism that* *strangled Jac's young life. In the long run, will there be* no more cakes and ale? *Are we headed in any case, like* The Great Gatsby, *for a more immediate comeuppance, for things falling apart, for the snuffing out of a decadent dream, for a body floating in the swimming pool (as though people had swimming pools in the Rhondda in the 1970s!)?*

There's a myriad of possibilities, of course: any number of ways to finish this. Birth? Death? Marriage? An enigmatic coda, resolving nothing. Or the silly melodrama of Jac's Rock Opera – you remember the alternatives: the Hero and Heroine together again? Or separated at the death for Eternity, like Orpheus and Eurydice?

How about Alternative Universes (they've been mentioned already), a multitude of endings happening simultaneously? Not very satisfactory, perhaps, but it's a way out of the cul-de-sac…

Why am I asking you? Good question. Here's my answer. Because, for the first time, the right path isn't obvious to me. I really don't know myself.

Ah. I don't know myself. *There's the problem. I need to think deeper, more rigorously, to plumb the depths of my own psyche. Isn't that the Advice editors give to aspiring writers? If you want to find what's really at the heart of your story, find what's in your own heart.* To thine own self be true. *It's the kind of thing Jac's Auntie might say, at any rate. If she could ever quote anything accurately.*

For now, let's carry on. Let's push the story forward. Let's get through the next chapter. Maybe, just maybe, things will work out for the best. Or the worst. Or maybe they won't work out at all. A Happy Ending? A Tragic one? There's a clue in the title of this whole final part, perhaps: Winter. Doesn't sound comforting, does it? But then again, if Winter's here, can Spring be far behind? So don't get your hopes up. But don't give up, either. Please. Remember the lesson that St Augustine (or was it Samuel Beckett?) told us we should learn from contemplating the mystery of the Crucifixion.

Do not presume, one thief was damned; do not despair, one thief was saved.

Or was it the other way round?

43

"Now the birth of Jesus Christ was on this wise. When as his mother Mary was espoused to Joseph, before they came together…"

In the pulpit, Jac lifted his eyes from the Bible in front of him to survey the congregation. He'd listened to enough sermons to know the power of a dramatic pause.

"…she was found with child of the Holy Ghost."

Christmas was upon them. They were in Bethlehem. The chapel in Porth. Calvinistic Methodists, just like Gosen in Treorchy, where Martyn had…

Concentrate, Jac!

The chapel was full to bursting. Not a single empty seat. People perched on the steps between the pews in the gallery. An attentive, reverent hush. Every eye focused on him. Every ear waiting on the Gospel he was proclaiming.

This was how it must have been the length and breadth of Glamorgan during the Revival. At Christmas, like this, exactly seventy years before. The chapels full, the pubs empty. Under the ministry of Evan Roberts, hundreds, thousands pleading with the Lord to enter their hearts, to change them utterly. The Holy Spirit, like the rushing of a mighty wind, sweeping down the Valley, touching everybody everywhere. At the coalface, foul-mouthed miners forsaking profanity for fervent hymn-singing. Their ponies recalcitrant, confused, failing to recognise the shouted commands which were free, for the first time ever, of obscenities.

If the prophecies should be fulfilled, if the prayers of Penry's cousin should be answered, Wales would soon witness such scenes again. Revival. Triumphant Revival.

Apart from the pit ponies, obviously.

Jac, an Evan Roberts born again (as it were), had the congregation in the palm of his hand. It might be only for the length of this reading, but he sensed the power that a real hellfire evangelist might have. As Deputy Head Boy (or, as his badge still said, *Girl*), his place in the annual ritual of the School Carol Service was assured. As the Son Of A Preacher Man, and being unfortunately tone-deaf (or rather, *a vocal cripple*), he was nailed on for a speaking part. But gazing down at the rows of upturned faces – his own Dad amongst them – he regretted he'd been given this passage, this particular account of the Nativity. Because Petra was there. She who had been found with child, not of the Holy Ghost, but of Martyn Rees.

The Carol Service was the culmination of a difficult Term. The news of Petra's pregnancy had set the Sixth Form rumour mill spinning. Those who felt entitled to comment, without even having set eyes on her, said that it was a good thing that the pregnancy was slow to 'show'. Wherever they'd got their information, it was accurate. Petra had always been slim, but there was no sign she was carrying a baby. It led to cruel talk that she wasn't expecting at all: it was just a ruse to get Martyn to marry her.

Petra had moved back in with her parents: it was the sensible choice. When Jac finally got to see her, she told him she'd decided to *postpone* her A levels. She wanted to return to school the following autumn. Jac calculated that the baby would be barely three months old by then. Having belatedly come to accept their daughter's situation, the prospective grandparents were now actively pressing their services as child minders. Would Petra be allowed to resume her education? It was anyone's guess if Bull would even consider it.

Catherine and Ciaran paid her a visit too. The two girls made their peace, as Jac knew they would. They did it without his mediation (which didn't please him quite so much). Martyn had been absent from the Rhondda ever since the Engagement Party. That didn't stop people from asserting that they knew what his plans were: to complete his studies at Oxford come what may. How – or even if – he would support his child in those circumstances wasn't clear. Others talked of a Wedding in the New Year, well before the baby was due.

Petra had now officially left school. Nerys was promoted from prefect in her place, getting a badge of her own to match Jac's, so now there were two Deputy Head Girls, as it were. The Rugby Boys suggested viciously that she'd been chosen only because the School was desperate to avoid *another* scandal involving a senior pupil: she was the girl least likely to get pregnant.

Jac and Nerys now shared the finnicky, thankless task of organising the Christmas Dinner Dance – booking the venue, the catering, the buses; pricing, designing, printing and selling tickets; chasing up payments… There'd be well over a hundred going, all told. They had to balance the books and aim for a small surplus to donate to the Sixth Form's chosen charity, a Women's Refuge which was being set up locally. It involved handling more cash than Jac had ever seen; and doing that with someone he didn't feel completely at ease with. Luckily, Nerys insisted she was happy to sort the money out, leaving the practicalities to him. Every time they sat down together, though, it felt like she was trying to pump him for information about Martyn. He played dumb.

As it happened, he knew more than anyone, Petra aside, about Martyn's state of mind. He'd got a long, rambling letter from him, evidently written under the influence. There were some touching passages. He'd found returning to Oxford heart-wrenching. Saying goodbye to Petra, he'd tried not to show it, because it wouldn't have helped her. He'd had a dream about Nerys, a dream he hoped wasn't an omen. He admitted he still had a big decision to make, but it was hard to focus on it 'amidst the Dreaming Spires'.

The second half of the letter – he'd evidently been getting increasingly drunk as he wrote – was taken up with a rambling anecdote about rounding off the previous weekend at a pub near the college. Martyn had been invited there by an older student, not realising that it was a Sunday night haunt for 'camp followers', as he put it. His friend had turned up in a smoking jacket. They'd been accosted ("Hello Honky Tonks!") at the bar

318

by an outrageous character dressed like Dick Emery's Clarence. Shaking his gold bracelets at Martyn, he'd leered, "Do you need warming up, dear?"

The letter claimed Martyn and his mate had abandoned their drinks and fled; but Jac's Auntie wondered if Martyn had really stumbled into the Oxford gay scene *just by chance*.

Martyn ended with a couple of hugely puzzling sentences – the drunken scrawl was hardly legible by then – which seemed to say that Jac shouldn't worry: Martyn wasn't his new friend's type. Mr Smoking Jacket was much more taken with Ciaran's blond locks. And he *loved* Ciaran's confrontational accent.

What?! exclaimed Jac's Auntie. *How has this person encountered Ciaran? Has Ciaran been to see Martyn in Oxford?*

No. Catherine would have mentioned it.

If she knew! There's been a clandestine *visit, mark my words. But for what purpose?*

Jac was determined to clear all this up as soon as Martyn got back to the Rhondda. And now here he was. At the Carol Service, sitting unashamedly with his betrothed. He had a beard! Like a proper student.

But why had they come? Jac's Auntie's suspicions – *Jac's* suspicions – about that letter resurfaced. He struggled against a growing anxiety to focus on the words of Scripture he had to read.

"Then Joseph her husband, being a just man, and not willing to make her a publick example, was minded to put her away privily."

The prophetic parallels in this account of Christ's Nativity would surely be too much for Petra. Mary: unmarried, pregnant. Her man: perplexed, hesitating to go through with his promise to marry her. Jac pictured the scene all too vividly – not the Biblical one, but the one here in *this* Bethlehem. Petra fainting with humiliation, having to be carried out. Or becoming hysterical, interrupting him with a tearing of her hair and a shouted confession: "I have sinned: for I have transgressed the commandment of the Lord."

319

He urged himself to have more faith. Petra was made of sterner stuff. She could scarcely have made this *publick* appearance otherwise.

"But while he thought on these things, behold, the angel of the Lord appeared unto him in a dream, saying, Joseph, thou son of David, fear not to take unto thee Mary thy wife: for that which is conceived in her is of the Holy Ghost."

Jac hesitated again.

That's clever, said his Auntie. *A pregnant pause.*

Jac gripped the lectern firmly. Too late. The anxiety, the neurosis had taken hold of him. It was happening again. One of his weird episodes.

There was nothing he could do about it. This was no longer Bethlehem, Porth in the Year of Our Lord one-thousand-nine-hundred-and-seventy-four. It was Bethlehem in the Holy Land in 4BC. But also, simultaneously, Hendrecafn, Jac's old Junior School, in 1964. A decree had gone out from the Headmaster, that a Nativity Play should be performed. The Play was a Rock Opera which Jac had had a hand in writing. So Martyn had come with Petra, his espoused, being great with child (though not showing it much). There they were, at the back of the chapel, there being no room for them at the inn.

The Magi – Dai Toads, Osmond and Jac's father – were arriving. All three wore towels on their heads. They'd travelled not by camel, but on 'Arry Howen's 'Orse – or two of them had anyway – guided by a Star from the East.

"A cold coming we had of it," annunciated Osmond.

'The East' must mean Little Moscow, explained Jac's Auntie.

"Just the worst year of Time," pronounced Dai Toads, fluffing his line like a five-year-old.

"Yes, Maerdy was frigging freezing," complained Davy Morgan, following the family tradition of uttering a profanity in the House of the Lord. He was driving an imaginary car, holding out in front of himself Jac's lost sky-blue steering wheel, which 'Arry Howen's daughter had somehow recovered. Except that it wasn't Belinda Owen. Jac could see who it really was now: Nerys.

The Magi joined the *tableau*. The cattle were lowing. Apart from Bull. She was *bellowing*. Penry brayed like an ass again, in the light of the Star which was shining down on Petra and Martyn. Jac couldn't spot the shepherds, but the Rugby Boys had turned up – as sheep.

"They're the Baa-Baas," explained Catherine, who looked heavenly.

But, then, so did a host of others.

Swotzi, dressed as a suave Herod (or was it Bryan Ferry?), didn't get her joke. He knew nothing about rugby. But he presented two fat fingers to the world. No matter: Ciaran, the Angel of the Lord, would *smite* him. And there were *flights* of angels, not just Ciaran and Catherine, ascending and descending, from the floor of the chapel to the gallery.

Somehow, Jac finished his reading. Cherubim and seraphim bore him back to his place in the body of the chapel. 'Arry Howen announced the final congregational item, *Ho Little Town Hof Bethle'em*.

Ow silently, Ow silently the Hwondrous gift his given;
Ow God himparts to uman earts the hwonders hof Is Eaven.

Jac sang with exaggerated gusto and perfectly misplaced 'H's, just to spite 'Arry's daughter, Belinda or Nerys or whatever her name was.

No hear may ear Is coming, but gathered hall habove,
Hwhile umans sleep the Hangels keep their hwatch hof hwondering love.

And slowly, as the carol drew to a close, the chapel resumed its familiar appearance, animals became people again, angels crossed their wings to veil themselves in realms of glory beyond the compass of mortal sight, and Jac was standing next to Penry, who raised an eyebrow at his over-enthusiastic singing. But he always did that. There was no indication that anything untoward had happened.

The service was over. Jac was congratulated on the reading. The memory of what he'd experienced was already fading; but enough remained with him for him to know that it wasn't right. How had he managed to carry on with such absurdities going on

321

in his mind? The human brain was a mysterious, delicate instrument, fair enough. But still. Was it the stress of performing? The heat and humidity of a full chapel? Was he going mad? Had he always been mad? Wasn't it the definition of madness to believe someone else's voice was inside your head?

No-one seemed to have noticed, but his imagination was becoming radically unstable.

Unstable? queried his Auntie. *I thought it* was *a stable you'd imagined.*

Something in her execrable word-play gave the game away, clued Jac in on something he should have realised long, long before. It was her pun about the *pregnant pause* that had set him off. *She* was doing this to him. These delusions, these visions. *She* was responsible, triggering the hallucinations that kept afflicting him. Miners' leaders from decades ago appearing on Pandy Square. Welsh heroes taking over his history lesson (well, that might have been partly Swotzi's fault). The mirror image of Lydia and her Biker Boy in Glyncornel Lake which *wasn't* a mirror image. Chaucer and his Psychedelic Cockerel. And now *this*: this Neurotic Nativity. His Auntie had conjured them all up.

But how was that possible? It was troubling beyond. He needed to know the truth. He would know. Was it her who was doing this to him? Was it?

Think of it as a novel…

Jac nearly exploded.

…a novel form of education.

It was abuse, that's what it was, mental torture.

You have to suffer to grow.

He told her in no uncertain terms that he couldn't stand it anymore. And he really, really wished she would stop doing it.

Fair enough, my boy, if that's what you want.

She sounded disappointed – in him.

Your Wish is my command. Mind you, that's the second of your Three used up now. Just the one left.

She could be utterly maddening sometimes. Literally, it seemed.

322

Looking round, Jac saw Petra and Martyn talking to his Dad. Seriously. What was that all about? Was that why they'd turned up, to speak to his father? Why? Jac didn't have the energy to work it out. He was exhausted. Shaky. He felt like he needed a drink. Or, at least, needed to be somewhere where other people were getting drunk. Fortunately, that was the plan.

44

They set off together for the pub by the Bus Depot, Catherine on Ciaran's arm, Petra on Martyn's, Penry and Jac at the rear.

"Lovely reading, Jac," said Petra, with no hint of embarrassment about the subject matter. "You really got the pathos of the Nativity."

"Yes, you read like a dream," said Catherine, seemingly without any hidden meaning.

"I fell asleep anyway," joked Penry.

"They've news, Jac!" Catherine nodded towards Petra and Martyn. "They've set a date."

"Second Saturday in the New Year," confirmed Petra. "Jac's father is going to marry us – to *officiate*, I should say."

So that's what they'd been talking to his Dad about.

Petra looked back over her shoulder at Penry and Jac.

"I hope you're free, you two. We'd like you to be ushers."

It took Jac a moment to understand the implication. If he and Penry were ushers, someone else would be Martyn's Best Man.

Ciaran was beaming broadly.

Ciaran. Of course.

Martyn stopped to light a fag.

The others walked on, but Jac stayed with him. The match-flame highlighted Martyn's new hirsute profile.

He's got a butch beard, observed Jac's Auntie, *but does he have the heart of a man?*

If she thought referring back to that Chaucer lesson again would restore her to Jac's good books, she clearly was losing it. He ignored her. Instead, he found himself asking Martyn, idly enough, what Oxford was really like.

Martyn took his time with the cigarette before answering.

"What's it like? *What's it 'like'?* It's not 'like' anything, Jac. It is what it is. Unique in its own nature. You won't impress anyone when you get to university if you look for comparators for everything."

It was just a jokey piece of Oxbridge undergraduate logic-chopping, but sharp enough to remind Jac of the time that Martyn had snapped at him in Porthcawl. He was hurt, put on his guard.

"It's just that you seemed to be having doubts, in Oxford… judging by that letter you wrote…"

Martyn took a long drag and turned away from Jac in what looked like a deliberate fashion. Finally, he looked back and spoke. The nub of the matter was this: Petra was desperate to marry; Martyn still wasn't sure whether he could go through with it.

"I love Petra. I do. And people see us as some kind of glittering couple, don't they? I get that. And if she's having my baby…"

Jac noted the 'if'.

"…well, then I've got responsibilities. But… Look, she's the one I love, the only girl I've ever loved. But she's the only girl I've ever been attracted to. Every other time I've fancied someone…"

They exchanged a glance. That night at the Archery Club. Awkward.

Slowly, the end of the burning cigarette fell away onto Martyn's coat. *Ash on a young man's sleeve.* He brushed it off, irritably.

"Jac, I'm gay. That's what I am. You know that. Being in college, being out of the Rhondda, I've seen myself for what I am. I'm a different man up there: an Oxford man…"

Jac raised an eyebrow. It was enough.

"I don't mean I'm like Gatsby, I'm not saying that. I just mean I'm becoming someone else now that I'm there… and I'm not sure I'd fit in back here again."

They walked on. Jac tried to see things through Martyn's eyes. But he was rattled all the same. Martyn had only been away a Term, a short Oxford Term at that. How could a few weeks make such a difference? How could anyone from the Rhondda change so quickly?

Jac thought of the conversation he'd had with Petra and Lydia, on the bus, way back in February: about wanting his 'story' to start before he left home – not amongst strangers at university who wouldn't understand where he was coming from. If Oxford could change someone as uncompromising, as much his own man as Martyn, and so swiftly, maybe it *was* a special case, not 'like' anywhere else. But perhaps Jac had been wise to worry that *any* university would cut you off from your roots. That's what universities did. Catherine's step-brother, he remembered, had gone only as far as Swansea.

The pregnancy, Petra's pregnancy, must have been a huge shock. Martyn had suffered, was suffering, fair enough. And *you have to suffer to grow*. So now Martyn was growing, growing in a different direction, growing apart…

It made sense, Jac could see that. But something didn't ring true.

The reference to Gatsby, perhaps. It sounded – almost – rehearsed.

Martyn was a consummate actor. Was that what Jac was picking up on? Was there an element of performance in this whole conversation?

Jac still hadn't got round to asking how Ciaran fitted in to all of this. *Had* he been in Oxford?

But they were already joining the press around the pub door. There *was* room at the inn. But only just. The Rugby Boys had got there first, of course. Blindside Pugh was blind drunk already. As captain, he had to set an example. He'd skipped the Carol Service and started early.

In the *mêlée*, Jac got separated from Martyn and found himself next to Petra. It was strange to see her sipping a soft drink.

"It's brave of you to come tonight."

"Brave? Not really, Jac. Expecting gives you… strengths you never *expected*. After those first few weeks, I've been feeling *full of life*."

Jac had to laugh. He was the one who did the puns. Him or his Auntie.

"Still, it's not exactly…" He nearly said *child's play*. "… what you'd planned."

She smiled.

"No, it's not, Jac. And who knows, really, where we go from here?"

Her candour surprised him, her calm humour too. But before he could ask more, he was pushed aside. More under-age, barely-of-age drinkers arriving, fresh from the Carol Service. The pub was infamous: the age limit of 18, it was said, was a maximum here not a minimum.

Jac got squashed into a corner with some Fourth Formers – and Nerys. His funny turn in the chapel was already hazy in his memory, but… he'd a notion he'd conflated her with someone else.

Belinda. Yes, *Nerys was a bully*, that's what he'd seen. A Friend, but a bully. Not as blatant as Swotzi, but just as hurtful to her victims. And there was something else he needed to tackle her about. The Dinner Dance tickets. The balances didn't add up.

The Rugby Boys kicked off the singing. *If I Was The Marrying Kind*. Not very Chrismassy. It was hard to hear himself speak, but Jac was determined to put her on the spot about the money all the same.

"Don't worry, Jac, it's all sorted."

He wasn't going to let it go. Her hand rose involuntarily up to her cheek, touching her mole. Guiltily, he thought. But she matched his look with a steely one of her own.

"It's hardly the time and the place, is it?" she said, reasonably enough.

The Rugby Boys had started another verse. This time it was the fly-half's daughter they'd have married if only they'd been the types to commit. If they were making a point about Martyn and his nuptials, he was taking it in good part. In fact, he'd joined in with them. Nerys clocked Jac's interest.

"I'm surprised lover boy over there has come back. He's more at home in Oxford by now, I should think. Able to be more himself."

Jac didn't like where this was going. Now it was him thinking it wasn't the time or place. Nerys had a way of turning the tables like that. He tried to shift away from her, but the crush was too great. She carried on.

"I just don't get it. It can't last – with Petra. You know that, don't you? It's not in his nature. I know what he is. I should do. And you know too, Jac. I know you do. *Marrying kind*, my posterior! If he's the marrying kind, I'm a prop forward."

Jac looked at her. Actually... But she wasn't finished.

"It's not fair. Not fair to either of them. Or to the baby. If there is to be one. It'll never work. And if you don't tell him that, Jac, before it's too late, I've a good mind to tell him myself. I know... what he's like."

Jac surprised himself with the ferocity of his response. Maybe he was still angry about not being Martyn's Best Man. Maybe it was her half-echo of his naïve question to Martyn – *what's it like?* Or maybe he'd just had enough of bullies. The Rugby Song had finished. But he didn't care anymore who might overhear him.

"Just mind your own business for once, would you, Nerys? Whatever Martyn is, he's one of a kind. Unique in his own nature. He's not *like* anything or anyone. There are no *comparators*..."

Nerys pulled a face. It was an odd word. But Jac didn't care how it struck her. Her or anyone else. He must have sounded peculiar singing in chapel, if not in his reading. He sounded peculiar right now. So what? From the corner of his eye, he saw Penry fighting his way across the room towards them. But he was set on finishing what he had to say.

"Whatever Martyn is, anyone can see he really loves Petra. He loves her. Get that? It doesn't have to fit into your idea of what love is. Forcing someone to behave the way other people think they should – I wouldn't have thought you'd approve of that. So just keep your big fat mouth shut for once and let them get on with it. It's hard enough for them as it is."

Penry arrived. With a request. The Rugby Boys had surprised him by asking for the duet he'd sung with Nerys in last year's Carol Service. Everyone was shushed. The two of them began.

Ar Gyfer Heddiw'r Bore. Nerys and Penry. Voices made for each other, and for the *plygain*. Exquisite harmonies. Something magical made itself manifest, the very spirit of Christmas. When they came to *yn faban bach, faban bach*, the repeated line about the darling baby, the Wonder Child, Jac couldn't bear to look at Petra. Even Blinginate Jenkins seemed affected. The applause was long. Penry was clapped on the back so vigorously he was still sore on Christmas Day, he claimed afterwards.

Nerys paid for no more drinks that night. She raised the first glass that was put in her hand towards Jac, mouthing a toast – 'iechyd da!' – and blowing him the campest of kisses. She might have the voice of an angel, but, as Martyn had told him once, there was no correlation between virtuosity and virtue. Meanwhile, Loosehead Jones and Tighthead Jones started singing about what Tom and Mary had got up to in the dairy *All Through The Night*.

Later, much later, when Jac got home, he found his father waiting up. He'd taken his bedtime tablets – the little pill bottles were on the table in front of him – but he was tying flies as an excuse for keeping late hours.

Jac knew the truth was that he'd been unable to turn in until he was sure his son was home safe. Jac was relieved that, although he'd gone to the pub feeling like he could use a stiff drink, he'd stayed with Petra on the soft stuff, long as the evening had been – and despite his *contretemps* with Martyn and with Nerys. It crossed his mind that his Dad might mention his reading, even if he hadn't noticed anything strange. Just as a pretext to question Jac about his (lack of) belief in the Virgin Birth. But that wasn't how his father operated. He never tried to corner Jac at home.

"Petra and Martyn asked me to be an usher. I gather you've agreed to marry them."

"A thoughtful young couple. Talented. Petra – now, she would make a good teacher one day. And you've told me a great deal about them. I'm glad they've asked."

"You do know…"

"Yes, Jac, I understand the circumstances. It's not the ideal start to married life. And it's not the Lord's way…"

What about Mary and Joseph? *Wasn't that precisely…* But Jac let it go, let his father go on.

"They want to get married in chapel, that's the most important thing. I take it as a good sign for their future together. I'll talk to them again, to make sure they know what it means – the commitment they're making before God. A solemn vow: not something to undertake unless you're doing it wholeheartedly. But if they're as certain in their minds as they were tonight, I don't foresee a problem. Do you?"

Jac simply didn't know how to answer. His father quietly packed up his fly-tying bits and pieces, and – with his usual "keep faith, there's a good son" – climbed the stairs, whistling 'O Little Town of Bethlehem'.

45

He loved hymns, my father. He'd whistle the tunes incessantly. I found it endearing, but it drove some people in the family mad. He and Mam sang together, too, at home and in places of worship; the classic Welsh hymns usually. But, strangely, what comes to mind now is a Scottish hymn Dad was fond of, O Love That Wilt Not Let Me Go. *The words are cloying, Victorian, composed in a hurry by a blind minister who'd been overcome, on the night of his sister's wedding, by the memory of a broken engagement of his own. It talks about weary souls and ocean depths and tracing rainbows through the rain (although the original had him climbing rainbows, which is a bit more interesting, not to say psychedelic). It ends with the gothic, almost vampiric 'I lay in dust, life's glory dead, and from the ground there blossoms red, Life that shall endless be.'*

Why was my father drawn to it? The tune, just as cloying and Victorian, is 'St. Margaret'. Margaret was my mother's name. But Dad wasn't sentimentally romantic, and it was the words *that counted for him. He didn't need a particular reason, I suppose: the hymn's message is conventional enough to appeal to many Christians, Evangelicals especially, as a cursory search on the internet will show.*

The reason I connect it to him is that first line: O Love That Wilt Not Let Me Go. I understand what it's trying to express – the utterly dependable nature of God's concern for His children. He'll come to their rescue and hold onto them however rough life's seas become. Will Your Anchor Hold? *and* Blessed Assurance *(another of Dad's whistling favourites) claim the same. But a love that refuses to release the beloved sounds to me not very much like love at all; certainly not the most admirable, selfless form of love that even fallen mortals, imperfect as we are, are capable of at our best.*

My father loved me. I always knew that. Remarkably, given the cast-iron convictions of his theology, and the centrality of his religion to his whole life, it was a love that was *willing to let me go. He never did corner me, and at home he never used pressure – psychological or any other kind – to get me to bow the knee to his God. He was man of real authority and deep faith, but – unlike others who shared his creed, I would have to say – the way he practised that faith wasn't coercive, constrictive, condemnatory or glib. He was unshakeable in his belief, sure of his place in the Grand Plan of Salvation, but always willing to set aside his own plans to serve the needs and wishes of others, cherishing every small human contact that came his way, open to the humanity in every person he met. And I knew he loved me for* myself, *not because I did what he wanted. What child can say more?*

If it's the measure of a man that what he says and what he does hang together, my Dad stood tall. To me, he was (to use one of his 'Illustrations', based as I now understand on false etymology) sincere – *sine cera, 'without wax'. He was no flawed sculpture with its faults covered up with a false cheap overlay. He was the genuine article, through and through. And it's not too much of an exaggeration to say that I idolised him (though he would often preach against idolatry). His love seemed complete, unconditional. His wisdom without fault. His patience rivalled Job's. His strength, moral and physical, far surpassed mine – perhaps that's why I was blind to his infirmities. Though I dreaded his judgement and tried to hide my shortcomings from him, he was always ready to forgive. Yes, I idolised him. Maybe that's why I didn't need God. I had a* gracious, loving father *of my own, not in heaven but here in flesh and blood. (When I was a small, small boy, that phrase by which he and others addressed the Father in their extempore prayers always brought to my mind not some bearded, divine patriarch up in the sky, but* him, *my real life Dad, and always with the same flash of mundane infant memory: I'm looking down the hill at him as he crosses the street near the traffic signals – the Lights – at the bottom of Trinity Road. Had I absorbed the concept of the* Trinity *somehow, and regarded him as part of it? Improbable.)*

When he died, I was – naturally – bereft. But I found that I had the self-composure to speak at his funeral. I did it from the pulpit. It gave me a perspective not unlike the one 'Jac' had in reading at the School Carol Service (hallucinations aside).

The chapel was packed with hundreds of mourners. The singing echoed the hwyl *of the Revival. What I said – in essence, a version of what I've just written about the way he practised his faith, fleshed out with a short biography and a few anecdotes – was intended as a counterblast to the evangelical certainties I knew would follow in the minister's 'official' eulogy. I wonder how many (or how few) of the fundamentalists present understood it as such; but that doesn't matter. I was glad I did it, and I still am.*

However, it failed to convey — how could it, in those circumstances? — all the ambiguities of our relationship. Because, yes, my father did love me, as I loved him, in a way that transcended my lack of faith. But that's not to say that my unbelief wasn't important in our relationship. It was hugely *important. It was the main thing. Yet we never spoke of it, not really, not without caveats, get-outs, sufficient vagueness to allow each of us to believe that there was still room to find an accommodation. We never bottomed it out. Because as well as love, there was fear between us. Fear that if we were led into exposing what was actually in my heart, the strength of my resistance to his credo, if we opened that up with no ambiguity, no equivocation, just plain speaking, then the gap, the chasm between us could never be bridged again. How could he live with the thought that his beloved son, in whom he seemed well pleased in almost every other respect, had rejected decisively what he revered as life's central truth? And, in doing so, had condemned himself to Eternity in Hell? How could I have lived with the knowledge that, as deeply as I loved my father, I didn't love him enough to bring myself to do the one thing he most desired, by accepting the Salvation his God was freely offering me?*

So we went on, tip-toeing around the issue, skirting it, speaking in riddles, codes, half-truths, until it was too late.

There were absurdities about the way we dealt with it: the pretence, for example, to his dying day, that I never touched a drop of alcohol, the puritanical shibboleth which I had *observed faithfully for his sake for so long, for much, much longer than anyone of my age I knew (though there was fear in that too,* my *fear of losing control of myself), until eventually I succumbed.*

Teetotalism was — in those days — a common after-effect of evangelical conversion, but it was never a precondition for it. Yet for my father, my (supposed) repudiation of intoxicating liquor became a cipher for the hope that I wouldn't go on forever and a day repudiating the Truth of the Gospel. That my stony heart was not completely impervious, that I hadn't put my soul irredeemably beyond God's reach. The symbol became almost more important than what it stood for: certainly, it was easier for us to acknowledge. Admitting that I did take a drink might extinguish this best, last hope he clung to for my Salvation, might be the straw that broke the camel's back. In that sense, abstinence was as salient as acceptance.

333

Yet to the very end, the love remained, the respect, the deep, deep regard we had for each other; the forbearance, the delicacy, the self-denying instinct that, above all else, we must not cause the kind of hurt from which our relationship could never recover.

But the courage to speak the whole, plain truth – that, we never found.

46

PORTH COUNTY COMPREHENSIVE SCHOOL

presents

THE ANNUAL SIXTH FORM

CHRISTMAS DINNER DANCE

Friday 13th December 1974

8 till late

THE SHOWBOAT, PORTHCAWL

Ticket includes Food and Coach

Fights arranged by 'Ninelives' Bowen

Mr Jenkins' Wardrobe by Times Furnishing, Pandy Square

The Society of Friends were back in Trecco Bay. Petra and Martyn. Catherine and Ciaran. Penry, Nerys and Jac. Even Lydia, a returning guest, and her Biker Boy too. They looked gorgeous. All of them. The whole Sixth Form did, Jac included. He'd *shaved*. He had his pinstripe suit on. But so did Blinginate. Embarrassing. *He*'d bought exactly the same one as Jac had got from Spice (yes, Jac had got his Wish!). There seemed little danger, though, of them being mistaken for each other. They didn't look like twins.

The date was far from auspicious; Porthcawl held awkward memories; Jac's worries about Martyn and Petra, his doubts about Martyn and Ciaran, hadn't gone away; and, whether or not it was his Auntie's doing, Jac was wearing the same outfit as a hooker. But, somehow, he managed to put all of that to one side. There was a crazy rumour, probably started by Swotzi, that MauMau, Parrot, Rat and Dodo and their gang of Hell's Angels planned to ride down from 'Pandy for a confrontation with the

Rugby Boys outside the Showboat at midnight. But even that couldn't dant Jac's spirits.

Five buses headed down from the Rhondda, picking up ticket-holders in both Valleys. Jac had engineered the routes and timetables so that the Friends could travel together. Arriving at the club, Ciaran and Catherine, Martyn and Petra posed for a photograph together: the Famous *Five*, as Penry had wickedly taken to calling them. Ciaran in an expensive navy-blue suit (it *wasn't* from Marks'). Catherine in a tight sleeveless gown in chocolate brown that suited her colouring, all made up as she was, her hair cut slightly shorter. Martyn, still bearded, in a dark pinstripe three-piece, black shirt, white tie. Petra, *still* not 'showing', in a black Japanese-print dress. It was mid-winter on the Severn Estuary, but they'd have graced one of Jay Gatsby's sumptuous summer parties in his waterfront West Egg mansion. Jac tried to recall a line from the novel, something about whisperings and champagne and stars. And beyond Sandy Bay, towards the Lighthouse, below the rising moon, wasn't that *the green light on the dock* that symbolised all of Gatsby's hopes and dreams?

As at West Egg, there was a surfeit of food. Jac and Nerys had over-catered: even after the Rugby Boys had got stuck in, there was a mountain of leftovers. But eating wasn't the point. Martyn and Ciaran sat necking their drinks, with plenty to say to each other, while Petra and Catherine danced away together. Catherine looked stunning – they both did, but Jac couldn't stop himself from looking at the girl he'd *necked* once, the girl who'd chosen Ciaran when she could have had him. He tried to settle himself, to find some equilibrium in his swinging moods, to define where he was in all of this now: him and Catherine, Ciaran and Catherine. Was there a time in their story when, rather than Ciaran's, it might have gone Jac's way? If so, he wondered when it was, that pivotal moment. If he was a god, or a Time Lord, if he could go back and make her his instead…

His brooding – or maybe it was that crude pun about necking – had woken his Auntie up.

Well, my boy, she cooed wickedly, *you've still got one of those Wishes left.*

For a whole song – it had to be Carole King's *It's Too Late*, didn't it? – Jac gazed at Catherine as she danced, wondering. But he couldn't do it. It was ridiculous anyway, this Three Wishes thing, fairy story stuff, a child's fantasy. Even if he played along, pretending there was something in it, that it wasn't just his stupid Auntie teasing him, he simply couldn't 'wish' that Catherine would walk over to him now and tell him that she'd made a mistake, that it was him she'd wanted all along. Because if he did that, and it happened that way – not that there was the slightest chance that it would – then he could never ever (*Trevor Evans*) be sure that it was because that's what she truly desired, if she'd made a free choice of her own; that there wasn't something else, some Improbable magic that no-one knew about, which had drawn her to him, rather any virtue he might possess.

Are you sure about that? his Auntie asked. *It's tempting, isn't it?*

Was there a seed of doubt? He dismissed the thought. He just wished with all his heart that life wasn't so complicated.

Ooh, that's a difficult one, said his Auntie, quick as a flash, before he'd even realised the way he'd formulated his frustrations in his own mind. *Not very specific, is it? Removing complications is complicated. But it* is *your Third and Final Wish... so, since it's what you* really *want, I'll see what I can do.*

And with that piece of patent nonsense, she absented herself, and Jac found himself face-to-face with a burly bloke in his forties who was wandering around asking for Nerys. The Club Steward.

Jac introduced himself as the other organiser of the event.

"Ah, it's *you*. Someone told me Nerys's assistant was wearing a poncey suit with ridiculously flared trousers," said the Steward bluntly. "I thought it must be that herbert over there." He pointed at Blinginate. "I can see now, there's two of you."

With that, he presented Jac with what he'd been intending to give Nerys: a receipt for the payment she'd made in advance. Just a folded slip of paper, no envelope, all very casual. Jac was about to put it in his jacket pocket for safekeeping, but something – not his Auntie, she'd gone very quiet, but some instinct of his own – told him to take a quick look. He swallowed hard.

The cost of the buffet and hiring the club was *hundreds* of pounds less than Nerys had shown in her accounts.

Jac double, triple checked his memory of the figures, wanting to believe he was wrong. But he knew that he wasn't. All of a sudden, the anomalies he'd wanted to talk to her about made sense. This was serious. There was a word for it. *Embezzlement.*

What to do?

Jac looked for someone to talk to about it. It wouldn't be fair to burden Petra. Everyone else was drunk or getting there. Even Lydia looked tipsy.

He walked over to the lobby, out through the doors, into the night. It was cold outside, but he wanted to clear his head.

Seconds later, he sensed that someone had followed him. Nerys. She had that determined look in her eyes.

"Everything alright, Jac? Only I saw you talking to that steward. Everything *hunky dory* is it?"

"Seems fine. A great night everyone's having. Getting their money's worth, I suppose. Anything… bothering you?"

"Well, actually, there is. I came to tell you that tonight's the night, Jac. I appreciate what you said after the Carol Service, but I haven't changed my mind, and it can't wait any longer. If you won't tell Martyn, I'm going to tell Petra. I know what you think about it, but I'm her *friend*, and that's what friends do: they tell each other the truth. I can't let her go through with this… *sham* marriage. And I can't see how you could either, if I'm being honest."

It was almost plausible. But if it was *that* simple, why didn't she just go ahead and tell Petra herself? Why did she need to involve him, to *implicate* him?

He squinted up at the moon, high now over Coney Beach, way above the green light on the dock. It suddenly looked false to him, a lamp on a stage set, an illusion for anyone gullible enough to buy into it. He turned back to Nerys. She'd softened her looks for the Dinner Dance, all dolled up for once like the other girls. Jac was surprised to see a certain prettiness there.

"I've realised something tonight," he said quietly, as much to himself as to her. "I was just talking to... somebody... about what I'd wish for, if I could wish for anything and it would come true. All this time I've been wanting everything to be alright, wanting all of us to stick together no matter what. The Society of Friends. Like it was when *Twelfth Night* was on. When we *lived* for each other. When we would have died for each other, at least that's what it felt like sometimes. My dearest wish was for it to go on like that. Unchanged and unchanging, loyal and faithful to each other. Forever."

He looked again at Nerys, as though for the first time. He'd almost forgotten she was there. But he wasn't finished.

"Remember how we promised we'd meet up for Penry's fortieth? I thought we all meant it, I thought we were serious. *I* was serious. I believed it was possible, that what we had between us could last that far into the future, that was it was... everlasting, in effect. That it would always be like this. That the bond we had... and I'll still stand by it, that bond, it was for real, I'm not mistaken about that... that that bond was unbreakable. And if anything did threaten it, if the cracks started to appear, that I could make it *whole* again, simply by wanting it to be whole, if I wanted it be whole with all my heart. Or if I was shrewd enough, if I was clever enough to put it back together. If I was good enough. If I made *us* be good enough, if I made us all stick to it as our true purpose, above everything else we cared about. If we made it our ... I almost said 'our God', but I suppose it would have been our fetish, our way of accessing the divine, our way of finding our way to Paradise..."

The words, overwrought, over-fanciful, kept pouring out of him. He hadn't planned to say any of it, he didn't know where it was coming from or how much of it was *true*. He hardly knew what some of it meant; but it felt right somehow, right for him to be saying this, and saying it out loud. It was the most confessional 'speech' he could ever remember making. A soliloquy, that's what it was, but it was a soliloquy he was speaking in the presence of Nerys, Nerys of all people, and *that* seemed wrong. So wrong. But she'd said nothing, and even now she had nothing to say. Something in his passion, his sudden flow of words, had stilled her tongue. So he went on again.

"I can see now… that I was mistaken. Naïve, at least. There are some things that don't last, some things you can't fix, no matter how much you wish it, no matter how kind or well-intentioned or clever you are. This… this *mess*: this mess that's happened to Petra, the mess that's happening to Martyn, who it is that he really loves, what really he is… it can't be fixed. Not in the way that I thought it could anyway, not by being nice to everyone, not by sweeping the difficulties under the carpet, not by holding fast to fantasies, impossibilities. The world isn't like that. It doesn't mean that what we had wasn't real, or that I was wrong to put my faith in it. It's just that it's not something that's forever, that's all."

Nerys was still standing there, looking at him. Did she understand any of it? Did she believe him? Did she think this… revelation he'd come to was genuine? If she did, it was because he'd spoken as though she hadn't been there. But now he recovered himself and remembered who he'd been talking to all this time.

"You're right, Nerys. Tonight's the night. And do you know what? I'm going back in there and I'm going to do it. I'm going to tell the truth. Even if it breaks everything apart. Because the truth will set us free. And that's what you've always wanted, isn't it? A Free Wales!"

With that he pushed past her, quickly, too quickly, pushed on through two sets of doors and across the dancefloor. On he went, straight on, and up onto the stage.

47

Jac drew his hand sharply across his throat in a slitting motion. It terrified the DJ. He was playing the Festive number one, *Lonely This Christmas*. It was a golden rule not to stop a song once you'd put it on. He hesitated to obey Jac's crude signal to cut the music instantly. The singer was wailing about the cold. About emptiness. Jac spotted Catherine in Ciaran's arms down on the dancefloor. Still the DJ wavered. But Jac wouldn't be denied. The music died. Groans of disapproval from the dancing couples. The whole room turned to see what was going on. Silence.

Jac stood above them, holding the DJ's mic in his hand now, like… *like a sword.*

Yes, just like that swordfight with Catherine. Though he hadn't planned or rehearsed it, he experienced that *grace* he'd known with her back then, that poise and assurance and connection. He felt time itself flow through his body, at his command. There was a flash of will there too, of bending events his way, a flash of that arrogance which had made him imagine he could face down the sun, that time he'd stormed out of Catherine's caravan – that had been here in Trecco Bay, too – and those lines about being born again had come to him.

"I've got an announcement. It won't take a moment, then you all can get back to your smooching …"

Nerys had followed him in. Horrified, she was mouthing silently at him: *No, No, No!* Too late.

"I'm delighted to tell you officially, on behalf of Nerys and myself as organisers of tonight's celebrations, that the proceeds are well in excess of what we'd budgeted for. We've made a big profit, which will benefit this year's Sixth Form Charity Appeal massively. In fact, we've made so much, that Nerys has kindly agreed with my suggestion that, for the next ten minutes, all your drinks will be absolutely *free*…"

A huge cheer. A stampede for the bar. The dancefloor emptied, apart from Nerys. She stood, hands on hips, impotent to prevent the rush for free booze. *Free! Booze!* The DJ sized up the situation, put on The Kinks' *Alcohol* and let them all get on with it.

Jac rushed back down the steps, tripped over his flares, and fell flat on his face...

No. He was careful *not* to let that happen. He walked slowly over to Nerys and made a big show of hugging her, even though everyone was too busy pushing into the queue at the bar to pay the slightest attention. In the clinch, her whispered into her ear: "If you say anything to Petra, anything at all, I'll make damn sure that *everybody* knows exactly what your little scheme was. All that cash you thought you had your hands on – it's *forfeit* now."

Jac had no idea if she understood why he'd used that word. But he'd got through to her anyway. She was puce with rage. Still, she managed to keep her voice low enough so no-one else could hear.

"You *ass-head*, Jac! The plan was always to give *all* that money to the Refuge. Every penny. Now there'll be a pittance left. A pittance for women who need it a hell of a lot more than these drunks and tossers, I can tell you. And you – you pretend you're some big socialist and a teetotaller as well – you're the one who's made sure it'll all get *pissed away*."

There was a time when he would have fallen for it. But Jac just smiled and told her to sort out payment with the Club Steward who was already striding across the empty dancefloor, coming to find out what the hell was going on. Jac turned on his heel. His mouth felt dry. The crush at the bar was six deep, but Ninelives was already getting served. Jac shouted his order to him over the bobbing heads of the crowd.

"Just a *coke*, butty?" came the reply, "You deserve some *coal* ... a whole pyramid of it!"

The rest of the evening was as uncomplicated as Jac could have wished it to be. As uncomplicated as he *had* wished it to be. Midnight came and midnight went. No sign of Hell's Angels. Lydia hinted that her Biker Boy might have had something to do with defusing all of that. Good on him. If he could stand up to

MauMau's gang *and* feel at home amongst The Society of Friends, he must have something about him.

It might have turned into another of those nights when Jac went as crazy as the rest of them, where his body manufacturing its own alcohol really did seem the only plausible explanation for his exuberance. But he couldn't quite stop himself wondering about Nerys and the money. Had she actually intended to give that bumper bonus to charity? Either way, he didn't feel inclined to harbour regrets, if even the *free* bar was a notion that had occurred to him because of a pun. If Nerys's intentions were good and proper, she should have told him about them, not cooked the books in secret. But then *he*'d acted unilaterally, and let that surplus get frittered away. Life was still complicated, after all. Perhaps there were things even Magic Wishes couldn't fix.

It was smooch time again. Elton John's *Don't Let The Sun Go Down On Me*. There was a line in the song about being frozen on the ladder of his life that Jac always heard as "the ladder on my tights". He chuckled childishly. But then he remembered his vow *to grow up*, the vow he'd made so long ago on Tonypandy Square. So he thought instead about his namesake from the Bible, about Jacob's dream at Bethel of a ladder reaching to heaven, the angels of God ascending and descending on it. And about Gatsby's ladder, the ladder that would have led him to Paradise if only he'd climbed by himself. Jac's Paradise, the one he'd always imagined, the one he'd just told Nerys about, was only reachable if he climbed with others, with his Friends, if they were with him and he with them. But a ladder, it occurred to him now, was something you could only really climb alone.

Well, he was alone. Ciaran and Catherine, and Martyn and Petra had coupled up again on the dancefloor. Jac was surprised to find that his only emotion was to hope that that was the happy ending for them all, out there right now. *His* dream, *his* Paradise, whatever it was, was elsewhere. *Something had moved, something had shifted.*

The DJ played *Lonely This Christmas* again, all the way through this time. Penry was smooching with a girl from the Lower Sixth.

343

Baby snatcher, thought Jac, instinctively. But then he remembered that Penry was a year younger than he purported to be, and properly belonged in the same school year as his partner. She was at least a foot taller than him. He'd have to get a ladder of his own.

Too soon, it was time to board the buses again. Jac was still the hero of the night, clapped as he took his seat. He'd never been so popular, not since his Auntie intervened in the Tom Jones incident back in Hendrecafn School. And all it cost was a couple of drinks. Each.

Despite the free alcohol, there was just one unscheduled comfort stop before they were back in the Rhondda. Jac could have got off at the Naval Colliery, but he stayed on until the final stop on Pandy Square, ostensibly to thank the driver. He needed the walk back along Dunraven Street to come down properly.

It was three in the morning. He left the bus stop. The street echoed to his solitary footsteps. What a night! He'd faced Nerys down. About the money. And about Petra and Martyn. But he was sober enough to realise that his intervention had changed little. It bought some time, that was all. The fundamental issues remained. Petra would still have her baby. Martyn would have to decide whether to go ahead and marry her. And if he did, what that meant. Whatever was going on between Martyn and Ciaran still needed resolving. And Ciaran and Catherine? If Jac was a novelist, he'd have some way of sorting it all out, some plot device or twist that could make everything fine again. But even his Three Wishes were spent now.

If it *had* been a novel, that pretty Redhead would surely come tottering under the railway bridge towards him now, like on the night of the February Election, and as she passed, she would say something *significant*. His journey would have come full circle. But the road was deserted. When he reached the corner of the Empire hill, though, he did come across an Improbable circumstance. Outside Woolworth's, a formally dressed couple stood in a ballroom hold, as though waiting for a tango to start, with eyes only for each other. Juliette Llewellyn and the rising

344

star of the Penygraig First XV, Meurig Montague. They must have been at the Rugby Club Christmas Dinner. But what were they doing there, posed in the middle of 'Pandy, at that time?

Passing them, Jac voiced a casual "alright?", as though it was three o'clock in the afternoon. The subtle humour was lost on them. They were wrapped up in themselves. Young love, eh? Jac remembered how he used to picture it: Martyn and Petra's relationship as the Great Affair, Burton and Taylor all over again, a grand obsession fuelled by alcohol. It didn't feel so glamorous now. All the same, he was glad Juliette had moved on from Swotzi. If this new relationship of hers was to stick, one of their two religions – evangelicalism or rugby – would have to win out. Jac's money was on Juliette. Athleticism was transient; faith endured. He half-expected his Auntie to add *nothing lasts except permanence*, or at least to point out the charged synchronicity of Juliette's new *beau*'s surname, but she stayed mum.

His thoughts circled back to Porthcawl. Had he, after all, been too hurried in acting on his suspicions? Nerys might be a bully, but how likely was it that she was a thief? Not very. But he stood by his intentions – she should have declared the bonanza, not fiddled the figures to cover it up. However good the cause. Siphoning off funds without consultation was all of a piece with her assumption that she held the right to determine the course of someone else's love-life. Jac had responded impetuously, but being impetuous, or at least instinctive for once, was good: he was always thinking things out too much. He was glad he'd stood up to Nerys, even if it made no difference in the end – she might still try to come between Martyn and Petra.

There was something else that his big bold move hadn't changed: his dream about The Society of Friends was over. Everything that he'd said in his 'soliloquy' was true, and it remained true. Try as he might, he wouldn't be able to keep the Friends together. The bond between them – even if it didn't snap under the pressure that was on it right now – would loosen with time. People would move on. He would have to let go, to give up his most cherished desire.

Walking there, on Dunraven Street, desolate as it was now, but still alive with its own history, where the past still counted for something, he tried to figure out where that bond had come from. Out of the closeness of rehearsing and performing together? Spontaneously, out of all they said and did and shared in those moments? To picture it like that ignored what each of them had brought to it, the experiences that had formed them. It *hadn't* come from nowhere; it had come out of somewhere concrete, out of the street where he was walking now, and streets like it.

Jac heard another voice in his head then. Martyn's. Martyn telling him that for so long, he – Jac – had been wanting two contradictory things: to move forward with his life; and to stay forever in this Sixth Form idyll. Not just wanting those things, *aching* for them. But to try to preserve their Society as some kind of closed system, to draw a circle around his Friends, however special, and to shut out everything else, that would be... *self-defeating*. Self-defeating, because no new, hard-won experience could be brought to sustain it. It would be like those courting couples he'd told Catherine he despised because they were turned in on themselves, like Juliette and her man Meurig outside Woolworth's just now, too bound up with each other to pay attention to anything else.

But that didn't mean there was no value in The Society of Friends. It would always be part of his story. A huge part. Where it began. It was the steel against which all his relationships, his alliances from now on could be tested. But it wasn't the cocoon, the retreat, the haven he'd dreamt of. It was more precious than that, and more resilient. It had been forged out here, out here in the streets where everyone shared a common history but not everyone was a special friend. And it owed a debt to this place, a debt it could repay.

He'd reached the Lights at the bottom of Trinity Hill.

Red. Red and amber. Green.

He readied himself to enter the darkened house where his parents would be asleep. Suddenly – but irreversibly – he felt

346

properly grown up for the first time. The realisation came like a blessing, fully formed, not simply for *now*, or the next day; but that this is how it would be from this moment on, wherever he was, whoever he was with, whatever he did. He'd been… *anointed*, that was the word, anointed with autonomy, with *agency*, that word that Lydia had found for him once. No longer was he a child struggling to make sense of an adult world. He was ready to explore that world on his own terms. He had so, so much still to learn, so much growing to do; but now he had weight, he had stature in his own right, had the capacity to criticise and not just accept, to make his own statement, not just to mimic. To stand up to the world, to face down its bullies, to partake of its pleasures without guilt or shame. To take himself seriously. *His story had begun*, properly this time.

It was an extraordinary moment – he walked taller, his back suddenly straighter. He could feel the blood surging through it, almost as though he'd sprouted a pair of wings there, or become aware of wings he'd always possessed which were now – at last! – fully fledged. He could, if he wished, soar into the skies and look down on this place, his place, in all its tortuous history, and claim it as of right as his.

There was no going back. There did not need to be. He was himself, and he was glad. He smiled, and despite all the challenges he knew lay ahead, a delight rose from deep within him.

And right then, he became aware of something else…

Without a struggle, without regret, but just as irrevocably, his Auntie was taking her leave of him.

Jac experienced it not as an emptiness or a lack or a void. Whoever *he* was simply flowed into that part of his mind which she was vacating, where she'd presided for so long. Like the inrushing tide covering a rock pool, making it one with the rest of the ocean. But now that she was no longer there, it was also like a kind of reverse conversion experience. Not the Holy Ghost irrupting into his innermost being; but something departing, leaving him healed and whole.

347

She *had* gone. There was a sharp pain in his forehead, like an exit wound. Being the Son of a Preacher Man, the phrase *the veil of the Temple was rent in twain* came to mind. If his Auntie had still been there, she'd have said something silly about the Temple of his temples. But she wasn't. And he knew for certain that she never would be again. The pain lasted a few seconds, no more. Then, everything was normal. The veil was intact again, and his; his alone. She'd left him to his own devices, to deal with whatever it was he'd have to deal with from now on. By himself, or with those he chose to ally with. By his own lights.

48

Jac had come of age. He was an adult. A grown up.

The date – January 10th, 1975 – had been fixed in his mind for as long as he could remember. But now that it was here, it was overshadowed by something happening the following day: Petra and Martyn's Wedding.

Naturally, the wedding took precedence in everybody's mind. Turning eighteen is a significant milestone, but once passed, it's merely something to look back on fondly: it has no enduring effect on how we live our lives. A marriage has to be negotiated every day and lasts a lifetime. Sometimes, anyway.

Jac's Eighteenth fell on a Friday. The wedding – as was traditional – was to be on the Saturday. But a rehearsal, a walk-through of the ceremony for the principals, was arranged for Jac's birthday itself. So for his Friends, the day was dominated by other matters. Flowers to arrange, cards to write, presents to wrap; but these were for the 'happy couple', not for Jac.

Jac scarcely minded: he was preoccupied with what yet might happen to prevent the marriage from going ahead. Nerys seemed to have learnt her lesson: she'd backed off from interfering. But Jac was still unsure of Martyn. He'd seen little of him over Christmas and the New Year. Did he actually have the guts to go through with it? Jac still hadn't found the moment to confront him about Ciaran and Oxford. Was he fearful of asking?

At the appointed hour, they gathered at the chapel for the rehearsal. Jac's birthday wasn't even mentioned as they greeted each other, which *did* hurt, just a little. Penry was there, Jac's fellow usher. Lydia as Chief Bridesmaid had charge of the two flower girls, infant cousins of Petra's. Best Man Ciaran couldn't get the time off work, so Catherine was standing in for him: it was becoming a tradition for her to act as a man.

Jac's father, the officiating 'licenced person', welcomed them all. Well, not quite all. The groom hadn't turned up. He was late. Five minutes. Ten. Petra kept saying she was sure he'd be there any moment. In the circumstances, she exuded calm, coaching the flower girls in processing down the aisle. But Jac sensed her unease below the surface. Tiny footsteps echoed around the sanctuary.

Another ten minutes passed. Still Petra held her nerve. Jac less so. He *knew* something was up. Now that it had come to it, the moment of truth, Martyn hadn't been able to face up to his responsibilities. Yes, he loved Petra, Jac knew that, loved her deeply, but something even deeper in Martyn's nature had reasserted itself.

Time ticked on. The certainty grew in Jac's mind. Martyn wouldn't be showing up.

Poor bride. Poor baby. But what could be done?

Petra was strong. Family, Friends would rally round. Catherine and Lydia would be there for her. Jac began to worry more about Martyn and his moods, his *depression*s. Petra hadn't seen him since he'd left her the previous evening to go back to his parents'. He might have stopped for a drink on the way. A few drinks. Then what?

If he'd realised he couldn't face the Wedding...

What if he'd come to that lonely conclusion, but couldn't handle the humiliation of not being man enough to stand by Petra? What if he'd found himself caught in an impossible bind? What if he'd decided to do something stupid?

But surely, if that had transpired, they'd have heard by now. Martyn's Mam would have been in touch. Unless he'd never reached home, and she'd assumed that he was staying in Petra's. Or what if it had happened this morning?

Jac told himself that he was letting his imagination run away with itself again.

And yet... wasn't it a circumstance very like this that led to the suicide of Catherine's step-brother, Daniel? And Martyn knew about that, would have thought about it...

The young cousins were getting bored. Everyone was unsettled. Jac's father's patience was legendary, but even he seemed irked. He looked tired, suddenly. He suggested – told them – that if Martyn hadn't arrived in another five minutes, they go should ahead and walk through the ceremony without him.

Jac got more and more jumpy. Worries that had become certainties now became horrors. Martyn's body was lying undiscovered somewhere. Or he was in a speeding ambulance, its sirens blazing, the crew desperately pumping his stomach. Or…

Of course, there was another explanation. A much more likely one. Martyn wasn't the only principal absent. Ciaran wasn't there either. The two of them…

The word 'absconded' came to Jac's mind. All those little things, those clues he'd been trying to ignore. Ciaran – *fey*, *coquettish*, as well as cocksure. Ciaran and Martyn huddled together, talking secrets. Ciaran staying over at the College, camping it up with Martyn's camp friend. Ciaran: Martyn's Best Man. An image presented itself: the pair of them, blond and dark-haired, leaving the valley, a suitcase between them, heading for Oxford, or London perhaps. It was the cowards' way out, leaving Petra in the lurch, leaving Catherine too.

But what if it was love? What if it was true love that had driven them to it? Wouldn't it be better, despite everything, despite the heartbreak it would cause, if they were faithful to that, rather than living a lie? Perhaps Nerys had been right all along.

The five minutes were up. Jac's father took his place in the Big Seat.

"We'll just run through the words, and the exchange of rings, so that at least everyone who's here knows what they'll be doing tomorrow. We need someone to step in for the groom. Jac, would you do the honours, please?"

And that was how Jac found himself, on the day of his Eighteenth Birthday, going through a form of marriage with a pregnant woman, accompanied by his 'Best Man', the girl who would always be his first true love.

Petra, Jac, Catherine. They stood together in the sight of God, calling upon those persons there present as witnesses – Jac and the two of them, the girls he cared madly about and always had, the girls he sometimes found it impossible to tell apart, his twins, his sisters, his soulmates. They spoke their sacred vows. Reader, he married them.

Or, at least, for a few moments, he let go of everything else, his anxieties about Martyn, his new-found maturity, all that he'd grasped about The Society of Friends, and he gave himself to the moment. Until a clatter at the back of the chapel jolted him back to reality: this was a 'till death us do part' that could never be. And he understood too something about that *never*. It would last a lifetime. *Never ever, Trevor Evans.*

The noise was the doors opening and banging shut again. It was Martyn. Clean shaven. And someone else. Ciaran! They walked down the aisle together. The blond and the dark-haired. A handsome couple.

Ciaran apologised for their lateness to Jac's Dad.

"There was a hold up. At the solicitor's...."

The solicitor's? Martyn and Ciaran? Jac's head was reeling.

The story emerged bit-by-bit; some of it before, some of it after they went through the rehearsal again, this time with everyone taking their proper parts.

Since late November, Martyn and Ciaran had been in cahoots: they'd worked out a scheme to secure a place for the newlyweds to live. The property was Ciaran's mother's house in Treorchy. She and Ciaran were going back to Belfast – for the time being anyway. Ciaran's father had been released unexpectedly, and his mother wanted to see if they could make a fresh start with him over there. Catherine, it seemed, had been characteristically big-hearted enough to accept that the McGuires' intentions were for the best, even though she must be calculating that a long-distance romance with Ciaran would be unlikely to survive for long. It was he who'd suggested that rather than sell up in a hurry, and burn their bridges here, they could rent the house to Martyn and Petra. It would be ideal for them to set up home together, at least initially. The difficulty was the mortgage. The bank was unhappy about the property being sublet to a couple with no income and a child on the way. Eventually, it was Martyn's aunt, Eve – *his* great Welsh auntie – who'd solved the problem by agreeing to stand as guarantor. But the paperwork hadn't been finalised and signed until half-an-hour ago.

"It's been a long haul," sighed Martyn. "Life is never without its complications, is it? Last term, Ciaran was having to phone me in Oxford virtually every day. Sorting out legalities on a pay-phone isn't something I'd recommend. But it was the only way to do it. The funny part was that there's this… *camp* student who lives in the room next to the college's public telephone. He got fed up with Ciaran ringing all the time, demanding that he come and fetch me to the phone. It wasn't till I happened to show him a photo of Ciaran that he calmed down. I think he quite fancied him. He loved his accent anyway!"

"Catch yourself on!" muttered Ciaran, embarrassed.

"But you are quite handsome," said Catherine, loyally, "even if you do sound *a wee bit* aggressive sometimes."

She put her hand on Ciaran's shoulder. Jac turned away, feeling more than foolish.

His father was up in the pulpit, tidying his notes for the next day. Higher still, in gold and blood-red lettering above the organ pipes, the bold text proclaimed *Believe on the Lord Jesus Christ, and Thou shalt be Saved.*

Jac heard voices raised in song. He turned back towards his Friends. They were singing *Happy Birthday.* In chapel! But they'd remembered after all. There were cards and presents too. Everyone had been waiting until the rehearsal was over to give them to him.

They began to gather their things together to leave. Jac found himself in a far corner with Petra.

"You're a dark horse, Petra Griffiths: you knew about this house plan all along then…"

"You'll have to get used to calling me Petra Rees after tomorrow, you know that don't you? And yes, *Jacob Morgan*, I knew. Of course I did. I could see you were worried earlier, but I knew where Martyn was – though I didn't want to jinx things at the last minute by saying anything. Sorry."

"There was me imagining…"

"And there's another thing I know, Jac…The other evening, Martyn sat me down and told me what he told you – that night after the party in the Beach."

Jac didn't know what to say. A sense of relief came to him, a burden lifted – relief that Martyn had been open with her before she entered into this commitment. He started apologising for not having shared Martyn's confidence with her.

"Not at all. It wasn't your place to do that, Jac. Don't worry. I understand."

She looked over to where Martyn was still chatting to Ciaran.

"Anyway, thanks to the McGuires, it looks like we have a decent shot at making this thing work."

"He loves you, Petra, whatever else…"

"Yes, Jac, I know that too."

And then she did her impersonation act, mimicking the man she was about to marry: "Life is *newuh* without its complications, is it? *Newuh ewuh Twewuh Ewans.*"

49

This absurd attempt to turn some of my experiences into an absurd novel, this Magical Rhondda-ist fable, is drawing to a close. One final chapter to wrap up events in the 1970s and we'll be onto the preacher's – sorry The Novelist's *concluding remarks. My editor says it's 'extremely rough', even as a first draft: she rates its chances of being published as Improbable. But then…*

Anyway, if you've found this in the back of a drawer after I'm gone, you're probably wondering what happened to these 'characters' in later life. It's none of your business, really; but since you've done me the courtesy of reading this far, I suppose there are some things I can say to satisfy your curiosity. It's a tricky thing to do, and my editor strongly advises against it. She reckons you'll feel cheated: I've changed so many details of my friends' lives, and invented things that simply didn't happen, or not in that way *anyway, and she says revealing it all will be a downer. But I couldn't have been clearer from the start that this is a work of fiction and that I'm an unreliable narrator. So…*

Let's begin with the less contentious stuff. About Swotzi, I know nothing and I can find nothing. Google 'James Taylor' and what comes up, of course, is stuff about the American folk-rocker. He is *still alive, still* compos mentis *(amazingly, after all the drugs) and has a new album out. In a promotional interview, he described his time in Laurel Canyon, which coincided with our Sixth Form years, as a Golden Age which actually was one, a time and place where the young and the politically aware and the creative found a true haven. Makes it sound like a hipster version of Jac's dream for the Bush Houses. Or maybe not. But good for him, and good riddance to Swotzi (even if he voted for Devolution, which I doubt).*

I hear of the Rugby Boys from time to time. Occasionally, I come across them in person, usually on a match day in Cardiff (confession: I'm a bit of a Rugby Boy myself these days). The truth is that they don't deserve the lampooning I've given them, and never did. Most are newly retired from lucrative and/or worthwhile and/or distinguished careers in medicine, chemical engineering or accountancy, or software or hardware, or other some discipline that actually makes the world go round. They may be running to fat, their knees may be shot, they may live in mortal dread of a catastrophic cardiac episode, and the more successful amongst them may never ever (Trevor Evans) go near the Rhondda anymore, unless it's to a family funeral; but they're the salt of the earth.

Of course, when I first hear or read their names, and bring their faces to mind, they're frozen as they were all those years ago, in the Sixth Form Library or on that night in the pub when they got sentimental about a Welsh carol that few of them understood, and none of them could sing. Still taut, tough, determined; still with all their hair. Still with the girlfriends they had back then. That, at least, is not far off the mark: many of them did turn out to be the Marrying Kind. Off the top of my head, right now, I could name a dozen of them who're still hitched, happily, half a century later, to girls they 'courted' in school, or women they met soon after. Dismiss this as sentimental or anecdotal if you like – but there's something about the Rhondda, something that marks its sons (its daughters too, I'm sure) not just with our accents and memories, but with a streak of decency, of faithfulness. Of seeing the value of seeing it through, of seeing it out. Stickability, as my father used to put it. And I'd say – but then I would, wouldn't I? – with something more than that too.

You see, the more pertinent question is this: what do they make of me, those Rugby Boys? What would they think, if they were ever to read this? That my sense of humour is still infantile, my sense of the world still skewed, that I never had a clue what life was all about, and I still haven't. That I'm still The WelshMadWordMadManiac. That I was a swot, good at exams and mildly amusing, but never as funny or as clever as I seemed to think I was. And this only goes to prove it. That (and here's the point I'm getting at) I've got it all wrong, that my Rhondda is nothing like the Rhondda they knew. The history, the politics, the radicalism – it was all dead and gone, long before we were born.

Ah, well, tell me your truth, and I'll tell you mine, as Nye Bevan may or may not have said. It all comes down to what you believe in the end. And I believe that there was something handed down to us, gifted to us, something that was still vital and tangible, a glimpse – how did I put it? – for one brief season when we were in the right place at the right time, if not of a way of living, nor a set of values that humanity has always been searching for, then at least of the ghost of an idea that it wasn't futile to hope for such a thing, and that the pattern for it had been laid down in the very place where our young lives were being played out. That's what The Society of Friends experienced anyway.

And they *are the characters you really want to hear about, I guess, The Society of Friends. I'll use the names I've given them in my story, though you'll understand they're not their real ones.*

'Lydia' has been married to her Biker Boy for more than 40 years now. He was, of course, a brilliant choice, even though it surprised us at the time. And even though he is *from Trealaw. We should have known that someone as bright and level-headed as her could never have chosen badly. He turned out to have a heart of gold as well as a Gold Flash.*

'Nerys' has a wife now, and – despite my lifelong one-man boycott of the gigs and gatherings she organises – a stellar career in event management. By now, only she knows if she actually threatened to expose 'Martyn', or whether that was just his self-dramatisation and (understandable) paranoia: the arguments between her and 'Jac' about it… they're what novelists do. There was never any question of her being involved in financial impropriety.

'Penry' is a conflation of two of my schoolfriends. Sadly, one of them is dead now. I've lost touch with the other; in fact, my whole network of friends seems to have lost contact with him. All we know is that he married a girl he met at university who was nicknamed 'Stan' (as in 'Stanley'; her surname was Matthews). She was taller than him, though probably not by a foot. If – and it's a seventy times seven to one chance – this book does get a wider readership and you happen to know the couple, please do contact the publishers and pass their details on. I'd love to hear that voice raised in song again. Penry's dream of a Free Gelli remains unfulfilled for now. (His cousin, by the way, is a complete invention of mine, though the arrest of a cannabis-user praying in the rain, by officers on patrol in a Panda car, was reported in the Rhondda Leader *in 1974, so it must be true.)*

'Ciaran' wasn't actually from Belfast, though he did have an Irish background. He was handsome, stylish and confident, and he didn't need any help in asking 'Catherine' out. Their relationship went on for much, much longer in real life than I've imagined it would here, and was significant for them both; but for reasons I've never understood (it's none of my business, really), though he always behaved honourably, something kept him from committing, from making it permanent. He lives away from the Rhondda

now, and aside from the recent death of his mother, I hear little news of him. 'Catherine' herself… well, we'll come to that.

And so to 'Petra'. As I've tried to make plain, her circumstances weren't anything like the ones I've described in these final chapters. Knowing her, she'll have the generosity to forgive me my alternative fictional version. In real life – and here's where I need to beg your pardon as a reader – she never married 'Martyn'. There was a pregnancy, but it came later, and 'Martyn' wasn't the father. "Life is never without its complications," as they said themselves, and these things are never black-and-white, but it happened at a time when friends felt she was still on the 'rebound' (as the ugly phrase goes) from the end of her relationship with him. Little about the situation was perfect, except for the baby and the way that 'Petra' mothered her. Fast forward all these decades, and she's found a balance in life that's graceful and rock-solid. She's remained the lynchpin of her own family and she returned to Porth County educating new generations of Rhondda children (thereby fulfilling the prophecy 'Jac's father' made about her potential as a teacher). She has fun and political convictions. She belongs to a radical nonconformist chapel and is no stranger to licensed premises. Her second husband, a character and a real gent, suits her down to the ground. Her friendship has been a constant in my life. 'Petra': as precious as the sister I never had.

Tragically, when I come to 'Martyn', his is not the ending I wish I could have written. Though he struggled and suffered, he couldn't reconcile his genuine love for 'Petra' with his underlying nature. He wasn't long an undergraduate before he brought their relationship to an end, breaking their engagement. But living his sexuality openly was no panacea. He remained an angry passionate soul crying out against tortuous mediocrity. He moved far beyond my reach, but I felt he was always searching, in a dissolute 'year abroad' in Paris, in the rest of his student days at Oxford and afterwards. Searching in art, in music, in drama; in alcohol and drugs, and in sex, I suppose. Searching for something that was as complete and intelligent as the love that 'Petra' gave him; and maybe, just maybe, for a haven that was as secure and stimulating as The Society of Friends. But how could he find what he'd already left behind? After Oxford, for a brief period, his star shone brightly. His name may have been known to you, if you followed the 'scene' at the time. But then his partner died, as so many gay men did in those years.

358

'Martyn' sank into drink and depression. I saw him from time to time; but he didn't want to be helped, I suspect. And now, like Shelley's Keats, he's gone where 'envy and calumny and hate and pain, And that unrest which men miscall delight, Can touch him not and torture not again.' It was far from a serene, edifying end. But in those last days, I trust that, if only fleetingly, he was able to look back and realise how thrilling his talent was, how life-enhancing his company, how miraculous the happiness he found for a while with 'Petra'. Les vrais paradis sont les paradis qu'on a perdus.

So, I'm having it both ways with 'Petra' and 'Martyn' after all. A happy ending, a tragic one. A Night Before and A Morning After. The sweethearts marry. The sweethearts part. The girl who's left behind finds fulfilment. The boy who moves on perishes in his vain quest to regain elsewhere what he'd felt impelled to relinquish. Life is never without its complications.

O dear, that's such a pat way of putting it. On reflection, my editor was right. It's a mistake to try to bring the story up-to-date, even in such a sketchy form. Neater to say nothing, to tie things up in 1975, to leave it there. Certainly, these 'characters' would have approved. They knew that the choices they were making when they were 17, 18, 19 were choices for life. That everything depended on what they decided right then. And that once those decisions were made – who to settle down with, what line of work to pursue, where to live – one's life-story was basically over. It would be like that ever after.

But… how could they know, at that age, that things don't end at that age? That there's no such thing as an ending while life goes on. How could they imagine that desire and doubt are as troublesome in your sixties as they are in your teens? That life isn't a linear progress: it hurls us round and round, back to the same questions over and over again, at a higher or deeper level perhaps, all depending on whether we're spiralling up or down. That things go on happening, things that simply weren't in the plan. That most of us still haven't found what we're looking for, and we're running out of time. That we haven't grown up yet.

And that we might even wish we had a strange guiding voice in our heads to tell us what to do about that.

50

The Three Great Mid-Winter Meteorological Omens of Mid-Rhondda.

Thirdly, *Snow*, dressing the Black Tip in white, signifying a Marriage.

Secondly, *Rain*, baptising the slopes of Penrhys, signifying a Birth.

Above All, *Icicles*, hanging *inside* the windows at home, signifying a Death.

It was a Sunday night, the last in January. Jac sat in his usual pew in Bethel, distracting himself, shutting out the sermon by codifying in his head this new Triad, taking stock of the portents in hatches, matches and dispatches.

Already that winter, there'd been Snow on the Black Tip. And a Marriage.

As for Rain, *it raineth every day*, or not far off, in Gelli and other parts of the Rhondda. A Birth was expected imminently, a Wonder Child, a perfect cross of the talents and beauty of the young parents.

But Icicles dangling, like swords of Damocles, inside the window frames: they were a thing of the past in Tylacelyn Road, now that the house was modernised and there were radiators everywhere. Death would surely pass them by that winter.

Jac gave no credence to auguries, but something was spooking him all the same. He felt isolated in those dark January days. The newly-weds, Petra and Martyn were in Oxford. The College had provided married quarters, and they were treating it as an extended honeymoon before returning, in time for the birth, to their new home in Treorchy. How they'd manage from then on wasn't entirely clear. Ciaran had left for Belfast with his mother. Lydia was back at University. Penry was spending all his free time with his new girl from the Lower Sixth (*it must be love*: she wasn't even from Gelli). Nerys wouldn't speak to Jac.

Even Catherine kept a wary distance. He gathered that she was writing regularly to Ciaran, but she was nothing if not a realist: she'd told both Petra and Lydia that she couldn't see how the relationship could last. Jac didn't allow himself to regard it as an opportunity. That ship had sailed, had gone beyond the harbour wall. He was convinced about that, though he'd been wrong about so much else – wrong about Martyn and Ciaran, about Martyn and the Wedding, about Nerys and the Money (probably). The only thing he'd got right was Lydia courting a biker, and he'd thought that one up as a joke. No, not a joke – wasn't it a piece of overwrought bitterness from that time he'd messed things up with Catherine at the Beach?

She had colonised his thoughts, his dreams for so long. He'd allowed himself to build whole futures with her; but they were imaginary futures, idle daydreams.

Now that they'd evaporated, he realised how little substance they'd had.

It felt like the end of an era, *the death of the old gang* (was that the Deadly Portent he was fearing?). But what came next? Here he was, still faithfully, faithlessly in chapel – he couldn't face the conversation he'd have to have with his father if he refused to go. He hardly heard the reading (Ephesians 6, tonight - 'My brethren, be strong in the Lord… Put on the whole armour of God… And take the sword of the Spirit…'), but he knew he needed something to fight for, a cause, something to save that would save him…

He thought of that hospital closure protest years ago, the first time he'd set eyes on Catherine. All those nurses and miners, doctors and housewives, together, united. All singing that clever parody of *Tipperary*. He wanted, he needed to belong like that, still. To stand alongside others, to stand up for what was right with them. But how could that be, if he didn't believe in any orthodoxy, if he couldn't bow the knee to God or toe the party line; and when he'd come to see that his own crusade to reach the Promised Land with a band of special brothers and sisters was illusory?

He wanted someone to share these notions with. He missed Martyn. Could it be he was missing his Auntie too? He thought about talking to Catherine, but there was still too much that was delicate between them. Then it occurred to him, sitting there in Bethel, that there *was* somebody he could talk to. A Wise Woman.

He rushed home after chapel to fetch the book he needed. It was bitterly cold, but he set off again straightaway.

The climb up Court Street was as steep as ever, steeper climbing it alone. He arrived at Lydia's house, his breath in clouds in front of him.

Her mother showed no surprise in finding him on the doorstep, but he felt suddenly foolish, despite the flimsy pretext he'd brought with him.

"Lydia lent me this, ages ago. Dannie Abse. *Ash On A Young Man's Sleeve*. I realised I ought to bring it back…"

"Come on in, Jac. We'll catch our death talking out here. I'll put the kettle on."

He warmed himself by the roaring fire. 'Compo' coal, he realised: a miner's widow's benefit. The body of a winter fly lay upturned on the mantelpiece. Next to it, a framed photograph of a small child, with her father. Jac hadn't noticed it on his last visit. He was still staring when Mrs Peake brought the tea in.

"That's the only one I've got of them together."

"It must have been…"

"Terrible. Yes… it was. I was on my own, and Lydia so young. No family close by. The neighbours rallied round. And the Union sorted out the legal stuff, the pension and so on. But do you know what really helped? The kindness of strangers. People I didn't know, in the street, when I went shopping…"

"That's what the Rhondda's like, though. They *weren't* strangers…"

"You're very attached to the Rhondda, aren't you, Jac? That's what Lydia always says about you. You're loyal to this place. And to your friends. And there's nothing wrong with loyalty, of course …"

Jac realised that without him even asking, she'd intuited why he'd come.

"You're young, Jac. A little bit lost still, though you think you've grown up. Sorry, I don't mean to be harsh, but if you're looking for Advice, I haven't got any great wisdom to pass on…"

His brow furrowed. He'd come on a fruitless journey. But then…

"…other than to say this. Things change. You're only just beginning to see that. It's hard for you to imagine that that never stops. That things just go on changing. For us. And for the place we live in." She looked at the photo again. "Sometimes it's horribly sudden. Sometimes it takes years. But everything comes to an end sooner or later. And the only thing that lasts… is what we make of what's happened."

Not permanence, then.

"Letting go of the past, without letting go of what it means – that's the trick, Jac. The trick we're all trying to master. How to build our lives on something we can never have again. Without making them captive to the longing for what we had."

It was enough. Enough, or too much for Jac to take in. They chatted on for a while – the latest about Lydia and the others – and then he took his leave there in the living room.

"I'll see myself out. As you said, it's too cold to be hanging around on the doorstep."

"Wait till you get to my age. 'Specially if you've got rheumatism. There were icicles inside the window frames when I woke up this morning. And you know what that means."

He shivered. He dared not risk an answer.

"It means I can't afford central heating, Jac!"

Back home, he found his father on the sofa watching the News. Since Jac's grandparents had died, television had been allowed on Sundays, last thing, a relaxation of Puritanical strictures to catch-up on the day's events before turning in.

Tonight, it was grim viewing. In Belfast, the IRA had killed a teenage cadet with a booby trap bomb. Jac thought of Ciaran in the middle of it all. And Catherine at home here. And the cadet, no older than them. Had he gone to Heaven or Hell? Or just ceased to exist?

After the shots of carnage, Richard Baker wished viewers a good night.

"Was Miss Osmond actually engaged to him?" Jac wondered aloud, distracting himself again from the deeper questions. Richard Baker and Donna Osmond. That was the rumour. Years ago. At university. But now she…

"So they say," said his Dad, who never gossiped. "Though if she was, it can't have been meant to last."

Nothing lasts except…

Jac thought about Osmond: all that she'd put into *Twelfth Night*, and what little of it remained now. His father seemed to discern his line of thinking.

"Have you ever considered why people teach?"

"Well… it must be satisfying, to see young people mature, to help them come alive to something you care about."

"True. But… you won't have realised it yet, Jac. Teachers have a secret: how much more they learn from their pupils."

The News was to be followed by a documentary, a portrait of Bowie. Jac expected his father to switch it off without ceremony. His parents saw no value in rock music. They just couldn't 'hear' it. And its implicit message – let's overthrow authority, respect, temperance, and make love instead – struck at the heart of all they lived by.

"Martyn is a fan of this man, isn't he?"

His father's question intrigued Jac.

"Yes, he is. How did you know that?"

"We had a conversation. When I met him before the Wedding."

They kept watching. Jac tried to see Bowie through his father's eyes. Articulate, thoughtful – and ambiguously bisexual. Like Martyn. Like Miss Osmond. But his father wouldn't see that, surely?

Footage showed Bowie's final gig as Ziggy Stardust, the act of killing him off. "I got lost at one point," Bowie was saying. "I couldn't decide whether I was writing characters, or whether the characters were writing me. Or whether we were all one and the same."

Unexpectedly, Jac saw his father get drawn in. The mime clinched it. Bowie was locked inside an unseen cage, or the body of a lift perhaps. His outstretched palms explored the solid, invisible walls imprisoning him. Desperately seeking an opening, or a way of prising the doors apart.

"I'm beginning to understand more about what you and your friends see in this."

"Really, Dad? You've always given the impression you thought it was rubbish."

"Well, the music isn't what I'm used to… but the idea he's talking about, acting out – being trapped, in a character, in a way of life: I understand that. He's searching for escape, longing to be free…"

"But his freedom's not yours. His fight's not the one we heard preached about tonight."

Jac must have taken in more of the sermon than he'd realised.

"We don't always get the right emphasis, Jac – in Bethel or wherever we proclaim the Word. When I spoke to Martyn, he asked me whether I thought God could really countenance sending people like himself to Hell for all Eternity."

Jac was astounded to sense a doubt in his father. Could Salvation be for everybody, after all?

The documentary was ending. The credits rolled. They turned the television off. Time for bed. School in the morning. For them both.

"Why did you agree to marry them, Dad? Martyn and Petra. To let them marry in chapel, I mean. Given what you knew. About her being pregnant. And that he's not a Christian."

Davy Morgan was switching off the lights. Jac's Mam was already in bed.

"We're not Omniscient, Jac. We can't judge what's in another person's heart. Whatever they might say. Only God can do that. But I could tell that Martyn loves Petra. Really loves her. And that's what counts, in the end: love. That's what God is, and what He wants for us."

He reached out to Jac's shoulder. A gesture as eloquent as Bowie's mime, as powerful as Isaac laying his blessing on Jacob. So much said in silence, in reticence and restraint. They were people of the Word, both of them, in their different ways, Jac and his father – but the most important things they'd said to each other, they'd said by not saying, by holding back.

In the small hours, Jac was woken by the commotion. His mother's voice. The panic in it. Like that other time, back in his boyhood. *Look at the clock, Jac! Look at the clock!* she'd said then. Now, it was seven minutes past three. The ambulance crew were with her at the front door. Too late. A seizure, an epileptic fit, one too many, one that didn't stop. Until it was, indeed, too late.

51

"Letting go of the past, without letting go of what it means..."

So, finally, what of 'Catherine', the girl I'd convinced myself meant the world to me, the woman it seems I let go without a proper fight?

In this age of all-pervasive multi-media connectivity, it's hard to fall out of touch with anyone. But even before we were all linked-in, *it seems incredible that I could have lost track of someone who'd meant that much, someone I obsessed over, someone who remained a touchstone in my imagination at every stage of life. But that's what happened. The years went by. We drifted apart. Me accepting the reality of the situation, both of us getting on with busy lives, I suppose, in an era when people weren't as instantly re-discoverable as they are today.*

I'm guessing, from what I know now, that we were seldom more than a dozen miles apart in all that time, though our paths never crossed. But she was always there, *at the back of my mind, brought to the forefront often – by a photograph discovered at the back of a drawer, a Christmas card from one of the old gang, a song on the radio. Bowie would do it. Elton John too. Don McLean or Carole King.*

And sometimes memories just came unbidden.

Every morning one summer – I was in my mid-forties – for no reason I could fathom, I found myself surfacing in the dawn light from a recurring dream, a sweet and frankly erotic dream, of 'Catherine', my Catherine, just as she was when we were young. The experience moved me profoundly. And troubled me. But I never went as far as trying to get in touch with her. It didn't seem appropriate.

Then, a short while ago, after so many years of silence, I heard from the person that this novel has been calling Catherine Evans. Not the girl of my dreams, but the real-life flesh-and-blood woman.

Recently, I've stepped back from full-time work. I'm spending time catching up with myself and – more to the point – idly browsing the internet. I came across her profile on a well-known social network and managed to send her a greeting. Somewhat to my surprise, she responded.

We've exchanged a few messages, privately, since then. Bringing each other up to date. I knew, of course, that she and 'Ciaran' hadn't stayed together. The last I'd heard, she was about to marry someone else, someone she'd met when she was nursing. I was sorry to gather that she'd been widowed as a young woman, and indeed had suffered a number of tragedies in life. But her outlook seemed positive: she's in a good place just now.

So I've caught the bus to Ponty. Free pass, these days: the Welsh Government looks after the older generation, as well as the Future ones. At four o'clock precisely, on this crisp spring afternoon, the First of March, at her invitation – postponed for almost five decades, I can't help thinking – I find myself walking as briskly as is reasonable along the street where she lives now. Strictly speaking, it's Treforest, that part of Pontypridd (not Neath, of course!) where Tom Jones grew up. It's St. David's Day. I have a posy of patriotic daffodils in my hand. And a song in my heart. Not 'Green, Green Grass of Home', but Bowie's 'Changes'. Ch-ch-ch… *Since she last saw me, my head has lost virtually all its hair and my waist has gained four inches (at least, that's as much as I'm prepared to admit). But, as I keep saying, I'm not sure that I ever really grew up, despite what I've claimed about 'Jac'.* Changes. *Growing up? Staying forever young? Can you do both?*

Here's the bungalow. Her neat front garden is filled with a golden host. Daffodils. O dear. Naturally, Wordsworth comes to mind. And the evident fact that I've got it wrong again. Should I turn tail and dump my present before she sees it? I search for omens in the flower beds below the bay windows. Are her daffs already past their best? I decide to carry on up the path.

And now, she opens the door. I fumble with my redundant gift. She smiles her smile. Her pale skin is stretched, almost translucent, whited-out by the slanting sun. Her forehead lightly lined. But she remains recognisably herself. Trim, dressed in mauve and welcoming. She has energy. A presence.

It's been such a long time, I say to myself, or out loud, I'm not sure which. I lean in, just to brush her cheek, that's all, that's all that's to be decently expected.

But before I can catch my breath, quite without warning, and with a shock that I'm sure is as forceful to her as it is to me, she's overcome with emotion. A look rises on her face which I swear I've not seen since that night on Pandy Square. It's so, so familiar all the same. It's been with me all along. And her eyes, the blue in them undimmed. The lust for life, that wild call in them: it's still there.

"Yes," she says, "Yes."

Suddenly, her lips are on mine, and although I've closed my eyes, I can see it, her mouth, its colours as well as its textures, filling my senses, the tip of her tongue, and then bursting over everything, from half a century back, the ghost memory of savouring, for that first time ever, the taste of wine.

'Catherine' and me. Together. At last.

We press against each other, both taken by this enormous surprise. I feel myself stiffen, and we begin to finish what we started all those years ago, on Tonypandy Square.

THE END

52

You'd think I would have learnt by now.

To rein in my fantasies.

My pipedreams.

My 'What Ifs'.

Because, of course, all that really did happen when 'Catherine' actually opened the door was that her lips briefly touched my cheek in the cheeriest of greetings.

Then, she stepped back, smiled, took my ill-chosen flowers and coat, and we edged nervously into the lounge and sat down opposite each other.

"You look well," she says.

"You mean I've put on weight."

But we're not ill at ease for long. How could we be?

Like old friends do, we chat for an hour, over a mug of tea and a shop-bought Welsh cake. Shared memories. The fate of classmates. More recent news, domestic: what our relatives are up to; places we've holidayed. Then back to Sixth Form days – and an explanation from her of sorts, one that hurts, even after all these years.

"You were so bright, so clever. I could see that. But you still had to grow into your skin..."

Well, I've certainly done that, I think, involuntarily patting my stomach. But she's not finished.

"You were too intense for me. And unsure of yourself. You were quite… awkward."

Awkward?

Back then, there was a time when the whole would tilt one way or the other, depending on the smallest signal I perceived as coming from her. No wonder I came across as awkward. (And that's to say nothing about a bloody weird interior voice!)

I seek her eyes, searching for some consolation, for that old connection. They've still the same blue.

Mine too must have retained the couple-colours they had back then, hazel inside blue – the best form of beauty, never fading with age, as she once told me. But no – it was 'Martyn' who said that, not her.

The talk moves on, to safer ground. I'm thinking that my focus is squarely on her, but I must be stealing glances at a photo on the sideboard. Astride a fine white horse, a young girl, sixteen or seventeen, looks boldly at the camera from under her riding cap.

She's slim, very pretty. A china-white complexion. The family resemblance is striking.

Eventually, 'Catherine' can't ignore the way I'm getting distracted by the mystery of who this is.

"Daniel, my brother..." she begins. She registers my confusion. "You remember, my step-brother who died when we were in the Sixth Form? At university in Swansea?"

I remember, of course. The suicide. But I'm at a loss to make the connection, all the same.

"Daniel was involved with someone...? There was a pregnancy?" I venture, struggling to disentangle this old, old story: what was hearsay, gleaned from other Friends; and what I knew directly from 'Catherine' about something we'd never talked about, one brief conversation apart.

She hesitates, but then seems to decide she can trust me with this.

"It was all so difficult. Tragic. He was a lovely young man... There was *a pregnancy. The girl was studying in Swansea too. A year or so older than him. After Daniel... passed away, a baby was born, a boy, David. He's nearly fifty now. And this young lady in the picture – this is David's daughter. So, there she is: Daniel's granddaughter... if you're following me."*

I was – just about.

"And her grandmother? Daniel's student girlfriend? Didn't she cut off contact with your family after... what happened?"

"She did. Understandable, I suppose, though tough on us. But, years later, she died, and David tracked us down, said he needed to know about his father, to hear his side of the story, needed... closure, that's what they call it now, isn't it? So they've become part of the family. David... and his daughter here, Rhiannon."

That name.

For a charmed moment, I'm transported back to the Mabinogion, to the First Branch: the princess, the Horse Goddess, riding by, a wonder of unreachable beauty. And to my teenage yearning for something beyond myself, somewhere I could find myself.

371

But, quickly, 'Catherine' goes on. "They named her after the song. Fleetwood Mac? David was really into them. The family live in Esher, very horsey, as you can see, very Home Counties. But once you get to know them... I've grown quite close to her, even at this remove. Even across the generations. People say she looks like me, though of course I'm not a proper blood relative at all. But – you'll laugh at this – she calls me her great-aunt: her great Welsh auntie."

Her great Welsh auntie. There's a smile on her lips as she says this, a half-laugh of her own. So she remembers, after all; remembers the title she glimpsed in a Rough Book in a Rhondda school all those years ago. And under it, her name, written over and over again. 'Catherine, Catherine, Catherine...'.

Yes, she remembers, alright. It stirs my heart to know it, and it brings a little peace there too. Some closure, to steal the phrase she's just used. So we carry on, talking about things we thought important way back then, but mainly about what's going on nowadays. Nothing world-changing. Then we embrace, perfectly chastely, and say it would be lovely to see each other again, and smile together one last time, as I take my leave. Because all of that was then. And this is now. There are other dreams to dream, other wonders to pursue. And many new fights to fight.

But then, as I reach the garden gate, she shouts down the path, over the daffs, one final goodbye.

"Why don't you write it all down? Everything that happened to us. The whole gang. The Society of Friends. You could do that. You always had a way with words. Make a story of it. A Rhondda romance... no, a proper novel."

Me? Write a novel? A proper novel? I realise what's put it in her mind, of course. But it's the last thing I imagine her suggesting. I mean, she saw my last attempt. I got no further than that awful title. And I've never written anything since. A novel? It would be absurd. Improbable. A novice wouldn't have the resourcefulness, the patience, the stickability to do it. Even if I got going, I'd get bogged down in the middle, I'd never ever...

...get anywhere near The End.

And where on earth would I begin?

ACKNOWLEDGEMENTS

I owe a big debt of gratitude to two far more experienced and brilliant writers, Penelope Middelboe and Prof Dai Smith, who read an early version of this novel (when it was even longer!) and gave me kind, insightful and challenging feedback. No-one seeking to imagine or to understand the real history of 'Tonypandy', the Rhondda and the wider Coalfield can do so without turning to Dai Smith's magisterial work (in fiction as well as non-fiction), which uncovers and explains what that history meant, and why it matters.

Thanks are due to Louise Walters for her professional critique of the draft opening chapters; and especially to Jon Gower without whose expertise, sage advice and enthusiasm I would have had neither the knowledge nor the courage to find the right publisher. Chris Jones at Cambria has been unfailingly supportive: *diolch iddo*.

This is a work of fiction. Its faults are mine, but I would be *twp* not to recognise that it owes everything else to my family and the people of the Rhondda amongst whom I grew up (to the extent that I did), to the staff and classmates I knew at Porth County, and in particular, and most warmly, to those whose friendships have endured well beyond our schooldays.

My children, Róisín, Anwen and Seán, have taught me much of what I've managed to learn since leaving school. They have, of course, heard all the 'jokes' before. Repeatedly.

The final credit, as always, goes to a woman who was a proper grown-up before she ever set foot in Tonypandy, who still delights in the Rhondda as intriguing and complex, who's always allowed me to be who I really am, and without whom I would never have made it this far: *la miglior fabbra*, Angela Graham.

www.ingramcontent.com/pod-product-compliance
Lightning Source LLC
Chambersburg PA
CBHW060814030726
47503CB00002B/489